Cottonlandia

Watt Key

COTTONLANDIA

Penfish Press

www.wattkey.com

CONTENTS

Part I

COTTONLANDIA

1 THE ANNOUNCEMENT

I usually got what I wanted if I argued enough, but not this time. My Christmas vacation had just started, and Dad announced he was sending me down to visit my grandmother in Mississippi.

"I barely remember her," I said. "I don't even know what to call her."

"That's all the more reason for you to visit," Dad replied. "She says she's dying."

"It seems like she's been dying my whole life."

"She's eighty-five years old. She could pass any day."

I looked across the breakfast table at Mom, who was staring at her plate.

"Come on, Mom. Seriously? During Christmas?"

"You'll be back before Christmas, sweetheart. It's just for four days."

Lately she'd spent a lot of time staring at things, avoiding eye contact with us. Deep down I knew whatever worried her was the real reason I had to go. Something was wrong with my parents.

"What about hockey practice?"

"It won't hurt to miss a little, Win," he said.

"But this is right in the middle of everything. This is my vacation. Who leaves New York for Christmas?"

He looked at me like he wasn't hearing anything.

"Why aren't you going? It's your mom."

"It will be good for you to spend time with her alone," he said.

Arguing was useless. I got up, went to my room, and closed the door. I fell on my bed and stared at the ceiling. Mississippi is going to be bad, I thought. *An old lady I barely know, a run-down farm, and my friends left a thousand miles behind. How can it be worse than that?*

I'd soon find out. I was about to face four days that would change my life forever.

2 JULES

I don't remember meeting my grandmother until I was six years old. Now, nine years later, the memory of her was vague and blurry. Mostly I recalled pieces of that visit—a big, gray Cadillac, a driver, bright red lipstick. The sight of my grandfather in an open casket.

Something happened between Dad and his parents. Something before I was born.

"Why doesn't she ever come to visit us?" I asked him once.

"We don't see eye to eye on things," he'd said.

That was it. He didn't give any specifics. He didn't want to talk about it.

I didn't think of my grandmother in a resentful or angry way. I didn't think about her at all. She simply meant nothing to me. And I wasn't really upset about going to Mississippi. Besides hockey practice, there wasn't a lot happening. Except for Christmas itself, which never amounted to much around our apartment anyway.

I got up after a while and started to pack. It wasn't long before my best friend, Jules Brevard, came by. He was sweaty and had his hockey gear hanging off him. We'd first met the year before, in our eighth-grade advanced studies class at Columbia Prep. Jules had the highest GPA in our cohort, though I'd never seen him study or even talk about it. Everything came naturally to him. The girls liked him, he was good at any sport that interested him, and he was even funny. Jules seemed to have everything in life except worries.

On Saturdays I usually met him on the corner and we would walk to the rink together, but I hadn't shown that morning and he'd gone without me.

"Where have you been?" he asked.

"Packing. I've got to go visit my grandmother tomorrow."

"Where?"

"Some town called Walnut Bend in Mississippi."

"It takes you all day to get ready?"

I frowned. "I just didn't feel like playing hockey."

Jules studied me. He didn't get it. He never got anything heavy. "Well, whatever," he finally said. "I've never heard you talk about a grandmother in Mississippi."

"Dad's mother. I've only seen her once."

"Really?"

I threw some socks in my bag. I nodded. "Yeah, it's weird."

Jules dropped his stuff on the floor and sat on my bed. "That sucks. What are you going to do there?"

With Jules there always had to be "something to do." A reason for everything.

"I don't know. Sit around on a cotton farm and be bored, I guess."

"Cotton farm?"

"Yes. It's called Cottonlandia."

"Sounds like an amusement park."

"Yeah, where all the rides suck."

"How much land is it?"

"About three thousand acres, I think."

"Man, that's huge, Win! Are there woods?"

"I don't know."

"You could shoot animals."

"I don't know anything about that either."

"Remember the big deer I killed with Dad in Montana last year?"

Jules's dad was president of the largest bank in Manhattan. He took Jules and his older brother on two adventure trips per year. The trips made me sick with envy. The only ones I took with Dad were when all of us went to the Hamptons for my spring break and Aspen once a year for his board meetings. In the Hamptons he sat around reading financial journals while Mother and our housekeeper, Frances, shopped. Meanwhile, I watched television, bored out of my mind. The condo in Aspen was owned by my father's investment company. At least there I got to ski, but since it was really a business trip, I wasn't allowed to take any friends.

"Yeah," I said. "I remember the deer."

"Forget Granny. You could hunt something."

To Jules, anything was possible. Everything was potential entertainment. "Maybe," I said. "I suppose I need a gun to do that?"

"That would be cool to have your own hunting land."

Whether the idea was a possibility or not, it always lifted my spirits to know Jules envied something of mine.

"So how long are you going to be gone?" he asked.

"Four days."

"You've got to be back for the New Year's Eve party."

Jules's dad always had a big New Year's Eve party at their apartment. This year it was supposed to be bigger than ever, closing out 1999. The food was good, and it was fun watching the adults get drunk, but I think Jules was mostly concerned about being the only kid there.

"I'll be back by then," I said.

"Frances going with you?"

"No, Grandmother has her own help."

Jules got up. "I don't understand what you're so pissy about. Four days of hunting. I'd be stoked."

"We'll see."

"Stop acting like such a loser. Let's go drop my stuff off at my place and head over to the Aston Club for a steam bath."

The Aston Club was one of the oldest and most elite men's clubs in Manhattan. The members were voted in by secret ballot, and even some of the most prominent men of New York society didn't make the roster for reasons that were never known. Dad was on the board, and Jules's father had lunch there almost every day he was in town. Except for the upstairs dining room, it was strictly members only, and you had to be at least twenty-one years old to enter.

"That place makes me nervous," I said.

"Come on. It's not like we haven't gotten away with it before."

A few weeks back Jules had convinced me that because our fathers were who they were, the rules of the Aston Club didn't apply to us. Since then we'd picked several Saturdays when we knew there wouldn't be many people there and lavished ourselves on their charge accounts.

Sneaking into the Aston Club was a typical Jules idea. To him life was a personal cruise ship of adventure. It was impossible to stay in a sour mood around him.

"Yeah," I said. "OK. Let me get my coat and boots."

3 LIFE AS I KNEW IT

It was twenty degrees outside and snowing lightly. The city was alive with the lights and sounds and energy of the Christmas spirit, something I'd never caught. To me it was just more traffic and more confusion, like somebody had kicked open an ant bed.

I followed Jules down Fifth Avenue to the Staples-Pake building, weaving through the masses of people on the sidewalk. It was like walking through a flock of geese going in the other direction. I stayed focused on Jules's back pockets and let the pedestrians blur past.

Jackson, Jules's doorman, let us through the tall, brass doors into the marble-floored lobby, and we took the elevator up to the twenty-seventh floor, where his parents owned a penthouse suite. They were gone a lot, this time on a two-day business trip to Switzerland where the bank had a corporate office and Jules's family also owned a vacation lodge in the Alps. We brushed past Nancy, their housekeeper, who watched us pass suspiciously. We crossed through a cavernous living room with twelve-foot ceilings and back to Jules's room. He dumped his hockey gear into a corner and grabbed a bag with a change of clothes. On our way out, Nancy did her best to get in front of us.

"What are you boys up to, Jules?"

We stepped around her and kept walking.

"Aston Club," Jules said over his shoulder. "Steam room."

"You know you're not allowed in there."

"I'll be back in a couple of hours."

"Jules," she called. "You know what your father said."

7

But we were already out the door.

We entered the club through the back alley off Madison Avenue, took the service elevator, and walked through the kitchen like we were supposed to be there. The staff as always was surprised to see us but went back to their work without a word. Obviously we weren't homeless vagrants off the street.

We bypassed the clubroom and entered the lobby of the fitness center. On Saturdays there wasn't an attendant, so we grabbed two towels from a stack on the counter and made our way down the hall to the locker room. There was only one old man sitting on a bench, exhausted from his workout, struggling to pull on his socks. He sat up and eyed us suspiciously.

"Afternoon, boys," he said.

"Good afternoon, sir," Jules answered confidently.

He studied us for a moment more, then bent to his socks again.

We undressed, wrapped the towels around our waists, and headed for the steam room. In a moment we were soaking in the hot mist, relaxed against the back wall, feeling the chill from outside pulled from our bodies.

"I'll bet the mayor sits in here," I said.

"I'll bet Bill Clinton sits in here," Jules replied.

"Robert DeNiro."

"Jack Nicholson."

"He's from Los Angeles," I said.

"Oh yeah."

"But I'll bet he's been in here before," I said.

Jules closed his eyes. "Bet not," he said. "Members only. Even Jack Nicholson."

I smiled, thinking about the fact I had something on Jack Nicholson.

"I can't believe that old man didn't run us off," I said.

"He probably knows who we are," Jules replied.

"He might rat us out."

"He won't rat us out," Jules said. "He looked so tired he could barely talk."

I didn't respond.

"I can't wait until we own a big company one day, Win. Hang out in here every day."

"Have a secretary," I said.

"Yeah," he said. "Like your dad's."

"Right. A good-looking one."

"We're going to have the life," he said.

"I know."

The steam was so hot my scalp was burning. I didn't know how much more I could take, but I didn't want to be the first to give up. I saw Jules slide down the wall a little, and I did the same. We stayed that way for a few more minutes, our eyes closed, not saying anything.

"You want to go upstairs?" Jules finally asked.

"Seriously?" I mumbled.

"Why not? I'll bet there's nobody there."

I gladly stood up to go. "Sure, if you think we can get away with it?"

"No problem," he replied.

We staggered out of the steam room, red and hot as a couple of lobsters fresh out of the pot. We took cold showers and returned to our clothes to find the old man gone. We dressed and combed our hair in the mirror above a long, marble counter of sinks and complimentary toiletries. Jules even dabbed on a bit of cologne.

My confidence had built, and I led the way to the main elevator and pressed the button for the fourth floor. After a moment, the car arrived and opened to a surprised attendant.

He cleared his throat. "Going up, gentlemen?" he asked.

We stepped inside.

"Yes, please," I said. "We'll be going to the executive library."

The executive library was a large, mahogany-paneled room full of leather club chairs and tall bookshelves with rolling ladders. From the looks of them, some of the books could have been hundreds of years old. All of the current reading material was displayed on a large, antique table in the center of the room. Several copies of the *Wall Street Journal, Christian Science Monitor, USA Today*, and the *New York Times* lay side by side with the latest issues of the major entertainment magazines. I got a copy of *National Geographic*, and Jules picked up *Time*. We sank into two of the soft armchairs and began thumbing through the pages. Within moments, a waiter appeared before us as if he'd been alerted of our arrival.

"May I help you gentlemen?" he asked.

"I'll have a ginger ale on the rocks," Jules said, without even looking up.

"The same," I said.

"May I ask what party you are with?"

"No party," Jules replied casually. "Just by ourselves today."

"You can charge it to the Canterbury account," I said.

"I'm going to have to ask you gentlemen to leave if you don't have an approved escort."

Jules looked up. "His dad's on the board. We've been in here before."

"You realize you must be of age to order from the bar?"

"We just ordered ginger ale," Jules argued.

The waiter hesitated. He twisted his lips a bit. "Very well, gentlemen. Just this once. But I must ask you check in with the front desk next time."

Jules looked at his magazine again. "Thank you. And we'll have a bowl of wasabi nuts with that, please."

The waiter started to say something, and I figured Jules might have pushed our luck too far, but he stopped himself and regained his composure. "As you wish, gentlemen."

The waiter turned and left us. "That was close," I said.

Jules looked at me and grinned with victory. "Man, we could own this place and he knows it!"

After treating ourselves to five ginger ales each and three bowls of wasabi nuts, Jules and I slipped out through the kitchen again and down the service elevator to the ground floor. We exited the alley and slipped back into the crowd, buoyed by a new sense of aloofness. Back in the lobby of his building, I told him I'd see him in a few days.

"Cool. Try to kill something while you're there."

"Yeah, OK. I'll be ready for hockey practice when I get back."

"Maybe we'll go up to the card room next time," he said. "Play some poker."

"Sure. See you soon."

4 GOODBYE, MANHATTAN

Frances woke me at four thirty the next morning to leave for the airport. I got dressed and went into the kitchen, where she had toast and a boiled egg waiting for me. As I sat at the counter eating, I looked out the kitchen door and saw Dad was up and reading the *Wall Street Journal* in the study.

At five o'clock the doorman arrived, got my bag, and left to put it in the car. Mom hugged me goodbye in her nightgown. The hug seemed too long and sincere for just a four-day trip, but I wrote if off to more of her recent strangeness. A few minutes later Dad and I took the elevator down to the garage and waited until the valet parked the Mercedes in front of us. I got into the passenger side, swallowed up by the big, plush leather seats. When we exited the garage, the morning was still dark, and the air swirled with dirty rain and sleet. The inside of the sedan was warm and soft, and it seemed like another world out there.

He rarely spoke to me when we were alone in the car. When he wasn't on his cell phone, which was unusual, it seemed his mind was preoccupied by other things. Usually I didn't mind and watched the city pass outside the window, but that morning it was too early for his cell phone to be ringing, and the silence was uncomfortable.

"Why don't you go to work in the morning anymore?" I asked him.

He stared ahead and didn't answer me.

"Dad?"

The wipers scraped the windshield clean. He glanced in the

rearview mirror, then at me. "What?" he suddenly said. "Did you ask me something?"

"Yes. Why haven't you been going to work as much?"

"What are you talking about?"

"You just don't seem to be going into the office as much."

"Well, I'm taking my *son* to the airport," he said, like it was something special he was doing for me.

"You didn't leave the apartment at all yesterday."

He hesitated. "It's December, Win. Nobody works much in December."

I'd never known him to take much time off in December. I'd rarely known him not to be at the office an hour before the stock market opened, but I could see he didn't want to talk about it. He turned back to the road and I looked out the window again.

"What's wrong with Mom?" I said to the window.

"She hasn't felt well."

"What's wrong with her?"

"She's got some grown-up issues she's working on right now . . . She'll be OK."

I turned to him. "Are you going to get divorced?"

"What? Why—what makes you say that?"

"I don't know. You and Mom don't seem to like each other anymore."

"Win, your mother and I have never discussed divorce."

"Lots of people get divorced."

"Well, that's no reason to assume such things about your mother and me."

"I didn't assume it; I just asked."

"Win, we've got a lot on our minds right now . . . Everything'll be fine."

I wasn't completely convinced, but it was good to hear him say it.

"So is Cottonlandia just a lot of cotton fields?"

"For now. But cotton's risky, so I leased the land to a neighbor to farm catfish next year."

"Catfish?"

"People are making a good return on catfish. And the land there is very suitable."

"Never heard of a catfish farm."

Dad turned to me. "Listen, don't mention anything about that to your grandmother yet. She won't take it well."

"She doesn't know?"

"No. I got a power of attorney over her and arranged it."

"Why would she care?"

"It's just always been a cotton farm since our ancestors started it. Old people get set in their ways. They get sentimental and impractical."

"Does she care if I hunt there?"

"Hunt? What makes you interested in that?"

"Jules said maybe I could. Did you used to hunt there?"

It seemed I could see his mind reaching back. "Yes, you can hunt there. Besides the fields, there's about a thousand acres in forestland. Mostly swamp. When I was your age, I hunted deer."

"Did you kill any?"

"I *did*," he said, like it was something he hadn't thought about for a long time.

"Where can I get a gun?"

"Now *that* I don't know. I used to have a rifle. I suppose it's still there."

"I'm just trying to look forward to something. Maybe I could at least hunt there."

Dad frowned. "Win, most people outgrow deer hunting at some point. Shooting animals for entertainment lacks maturity."

"Jules's dad hunts deer."

Dad hesitated. "Well, I don't know about Jules's dad."

We veered off the interstate toward LaGuardia Airport. Daylight was just starting to turn the black, stormy sky to gray. I heard the whine of a passenger jet overhead and felt very much alone.

5 THE FARMER

After we checked my bag, we met the flight attendant who would make sure I got to my gate. Then Dad's cell phone rang.

"Hold on a moment," he told us. He took a few steps away, turned his back, and answered it.

The flight attendant put her hand on my shoulder. "Sir?" she said to Dad.

Dad held his hand up for her to wait.

"Sir," she continued. "We have to be going."

"Hold on a moment, Bob," I heard him say. He pulled the phone from his ear and turned back to us. "John Case should be at the airport to pick you up. He's the farmer. I'll see you in a few days."

"OK," I said.

Dad started to take a step toward me, then frowned. He jerked his hand up in a small wave and tilted his chin goodbye.

The flight took me from New York to Atlanta. From there the attendant escorted me to another flight to Jackson, Mississippi. The final flight into Greenwood was in a twin-engine plane with twelve seats, seven of them empty. Even though I was more than a thousand miles from home, it seemed I was in the same weather I'd left. The small plane rocked and dipped its way through the sleet and rain, out over the flats of the Mississippi Delta.

When I got off the plane in Greenwood, the wind across the tarmac was wet and cold, carrying bits of ice into my face. I hurried with the other passengers into the terminal, a building made of corrugated steel at the edge of a field. Inside there was a big man wearing boots, overalls, a thick wool jacket, and a greasy ball cap. He appeared older than Dad, but not as old as Grandmother. His face was lined and weathered and looked like it had never formed a smile. From the way he watched me, I knew he was there to pick me up.

"Are you the farmer?" I asked.

He held out a giant hand to shake. I took it, and it was rough and warm. "John Case," he said. "You look just like your granddaddy."

I didn't know how to respond. There was something impatient about the farmer standing inside the building.

"You ready?" he said.

"I'm waiting for my bag."

"Does your bag have legs?"

"Excuse me?"

"Your bag won't get over here by itself. I'll be outside in the truck."

I found my suitcase in a pile of luggage just inside the door. When I pulled it out the main entrance, I saw the farmer in a beat-up, blue, flare-side GMC pickup. Exhaust poured white out of the muffler and into the icy, wet air.

I shoved my suitcase into the middle of the bench seat, slid in, and pulled the door shut. The truck smelled of coffee and tobacco and wet dirt. It seemed just by sitting there I was going to get stains on my clothes. The dashboard was dusty, and the inside of my door was caked with mud. I made sure to keep my leather oxfords in the center of the floor mat. As for the vinyl seat, it seemed clean enough, but I felt the cold of it through my pants. And my toes felt like chunks of ice. It didn't make sense it would be colder in this place, so much farther south, but it was. A wet, penetrating cold—like an icy tongue licking your bones.

"About a twenty-minute ride to Walnut Bend," he said.

"OK," I mumbled. The farmer made me nervous. Like riding with a grizzly bear.

As we pulled away, I positioned my toes so the heater blew over them. We left the airport behind, crossed a levee, and entered the broad expanse of the Mississippi Delta. It was flat and gray and dismal as far as one could see—fields of wet, black earth with the cut stems of cotton plants and bits of cotton pasted to them like wet toilet paper. Distant walls of dark, brittle, leafless hardwood bottoms.

The wind howled across the fields and shook our truck.

As we drove along in silence, the sleet turned to drizzling rain. We passed shantytowns full of people staring from porches and wandering the edges of the road with stocking caps pulled over their ears and their breath streaming. It reminded me of pictures I'd seen of third-world countries. The farmer didn't seem to notice any of it. At some point he had slipped some tobacco into his cheek. Occasionally he spit quietly into a coffee cup.

"I didn't think it was this cold in the South," I said.

He didn't look at me. "Delta winters can be cold. Nothing to block the north wind for two hundred miles."

I frowned.

"Unusual weather right now," he added. "It'll move out soon."

I checked my watch when the truck slowed and saw it had been almost thirty minutes. The rain had stopped, but the sky hung over us like a soggy, gray blanket. I saw a black iron sign on the roadside that read COTTONLANDIA PLANTATION. Then I felt a current of damp air flow through the farmer's window as he rolled it down. He turned onto the dirt road, and I heard it popping beneath his tires. It smelled of wet gravel and clay.

The road was nearly a mile long, nothing more than a raised dike between the fields. On either side were large ditches full of muddy water that could swallow the farm truck if it slipped. Eventually we came to a stand of hardwoods rising from the fields like an island. We continued between an avenue of pecan trees, finally passing through a white rail fence and starting around a circular driveway. The house in my memory stood at the back of the drive, a white, two-story home with Greek columns supporting an upper porch and the roof. Only now it didn't seem so large and impressive. It was a mansion on a miniature scale, the paint faded and flaking. Overall, it appeared weathered, soggy, and lifeless.

The farmer pulled up before the front steps and shut off the truck. He got out and discreetly let the wad of tobacco fall from his mouth to the ground. He didn't offer to help with my suitcase, so I pulled it across the front seat and lugged it around the back of the truck. As I followed him to the steps, I heard the front door open. A wispy, Black woman who appeared to be a hundred years old stood there in an apron so starched it seemed to support her. In her ears, where earrings would normally be, were two pine needles.

"That must be Win," she said.

The farmer reached back and ushered me forward. "Go say hello to Gert."

6 GERT

I went up the three brick steps, and the black lady came close and hugged me. I felt her bones through her skin, and she smelled of bacon grease and wood smoke. She pulled away and studied me and her eyes were wet.

"My Lord," she said. "Look at you."

I did my best to smile.

"Come on inside," she said. "Get you two out of the cold."

The farmer followed me through the door. Once inside, the house was even smaller than it looked. It was only one room deep and three wide, if you counted the foyer and staircase in the middle. On the left was the living room and on the right was the dining room, with a small kitchen directly behind it. The living space was compact, but it was warm. Gas heaters stood against the walls and hissed and popped against the cold. The place smelled of butane and turpentine.

Gert shut the door behind us and hurried toward the kitchen. "Your grandmomma's gonna be so happy to see you," she said over her shoulder. "Put your things down, Win."

For some reason I looked back to the farmer, and he motioned at the base of the stairs with his chin. I walked across the room and put my suitcase on the bottom step. He passed me and said, "Come into the kitchen."

It annoyed me the way the farmer assumed he could boss me around. It annoyed me more when I reasoned he actually worked for my family—my family's employee treating me like he was my father. But he was still big and intimidating. I hadn't built the courage to stand up to him.

When we walked into the kitchen, Gert was busy at the counter. The appliances were all white and rounded and heavy, like they hadn't been replaced since Dad was a boy. The refrigerator hummed and rattled, dominating the small, low-ceilinged room.

The farmer motioned to a breakfast table with two chairs. "Have a seat," he said. Then he continued across the room and grabbed a coffee pot from near Gert, got a cup off a hook over the window, and poured it black. I sat down as he carried his coffee back to the table and sat across from me. He took a newspaper off a shelf beside him and flipped it open and began browsing through it like he'd performed this same routine for years.

"Cold front's supposed to be out of here tomorrow, Gert," he mumbled.

"I hope so, Mr. Case."

She set a mug of hot chocolate before me.

"That ought to warm you up," she said.

"I don't like hot chocolate."

Startled, she hesitated, then reached down for the cup. "I'm sorry, Win." She took it back to the counter and set it down. "Is there something else I can get for you?"

"I'm fine."

I just wanted a room to myself where I could lie down and be alone. I felt the farmer watching me, but I didn't want to look at him.

"Gert knew your father," he said. "Helped raise him."

She turned back to us and smiled, but she was really looking somewhere between us and the smile was a bit forced. "I certainly did," she replied. "Knew him from the time he was born."

"I wouldn't know. He never talks about being a kid."

She faced the sink again, poured out the hot chocolate, and began rinsing the cup. "Well, believe me, he *was* one," she said, implying she knew more than she was saying.

"You know how long this place has been in your family?" the farmer asked.

"No."

"Your great-great-great-grandfather cleared this land."

"That's old," I said flatly.

"Yes, it is."

I felt his eyes on me a moment longer. Finally, he turned away and let his breath out with a whistle. He stood and folded the paper and set it on the table. "Gert, I'd better head home and check on Diane."

"How is she?"

"She's just fine, and thanks for asking. How's Mrs. Canterbury?"

"She's OK. Taking her nap right now."

"Tell her I said hello. And you stay warm."

"You, too, Mr. Case. Take care."

He turned to me. He studied me in a way that made me uncomfortable.

"Stand up," he said.

It made me angry to do it, but I did anyway. He held out his hand to shake, and I took it.

"At least act like you've got some manners."

I felt heat rush to my cheeks. I started to say something but didn't. I was scared of him and angry that I was scared.

After the farmer left, I sat back down. Gert was busy at the sink, her back to me.

"I'm tired," I said.

She quickly wiped her hands on a dish towel and hurried my way. "Let me show you to your room," she said.

I followed her up the stairs with my suitcase. At the top we faced a short hall that ended in a window looking over the backyard. I saw the closed door to what I guessed must be my grandmother's room on the left. Beyond it was the washroom. On the right side was another bedroom where I'd learn my father used to sleep. Gert led me to the door.

"Do you have cable TV?" I asked her.

"No, there's not even a television in the house. I'm sorry about that."

"Serious?"

"They haven't run the lines this far. We barely get telephone service out here."

"How do you make phone calls?"

"We've got a telephone downstairs in the living room."

"Like a cordless handset?"

"No, but it works most of the time," she said.

We entered my father's old bedroom, and the way it was arranged, which seemed like he'd just left the day before, was strange and haunting. The odor of mothballs drifted over me, a smell I didn't recall from when I was there nine years earlier. The room was neat and sparse and had the same old-fashioned look as the kitchen, but in a different way. I stood on a dark carpet beneath an iron ceiling fan. A small gas heater moaned and ticked to my left. In the center of the room was a double bed covered with a white chenille bedspread. Behind the headboard was a window with an air conditioner mounted in it.

Gert approached the heater, kneeled, and turned a knob so the blue-and-orange flame leaped higher.

"Little chilly in here," she said.

I set my suitcase down.

"When will Grandmother wake up?"

"She'll be up for supper in about an hour. She sure will be glad to see you."

"Where's the bathroom?"

"At the end of the hall. I put some fresh towels in there for you."

"I share one with Grandmother?"

"Well, she doesn't leave her bed anymore, so you don't have to worry about that."

I didn't want to ask more questions. I didn't want to know any more about just how miserable I was going to be. Gert walked to a cedar chest at the foot of the bed and opened it. The mothball smell intensified. She pulled out a gray wool blanket and placed it on the bed.

"There's more in there if you need them," she said. "Now, I'll just leave you alone. I'm sure you must be wore out."

I didn't answer her. She hurried past me but stopped at the door. "You want me to close this for you, Win?"

"Sure."

She closed it and I was left alone, standing in the middle of the floor, breathing mothballs, listening to the wind howling outside and tree branches tapping the windowpanes and the heater hissing and popping. I had never felt so out of place in my life. How could I have gotten this far into the middle of miserable nowhere in a one day?

7 GRANDMOTHER

I lay on my back on my father's old bed as the gray afternoon faded to darkness. I was paralyzed with dread, feeling my heartbeat, hands crossed over my chest, thinking nothing.

I reached over the bedside table and picked up an old alarm clock. It was a wind-up, black antique with two rusty silver bells on top. It was stopped at 4:43. Probably from just a day or two after my father last slept in this room. I turned it over and found the knob to wind it and cranked until the spring was tight and it was ticking with new life. Then I looked at the time on my watch and set the clock hands to match. I replaced it and lay down again and closed my eyes.

Sometime later I woke to a knock on my door.

"She'd like to see you now, Win."

I remembered where I was. A wave of nausea passed through me.

I followed Gert across the hall. Before I entered my grandmother's room, the smell of urine and baby powder pressed into me and reminded me of a nursing home I'd visited once. Inside the room was dimly lit. Most of the personal items had been pushed against the walls. The predominant feature was a chrome-railed hospital bed. An oxygen machine purred beside it. She lay there watching me, nothing but beady eyes and thin skin on bones, nearly bald except for a few strands of dead-looking, gray hair. She looked like a skeleton with bright red, wet lipstick.

"Hey, darling," she croaked.

I wasn't comfortable around old people. I approached, and she followed me with her eyes, lifting her bony hands from the bed. I leaned over and she pulled me close and the smell of her makeup was instantly familiar and brought visions of the Cadillac, of her bending over to press her face to my cheek nine years ago.

"How are you?" she whispered.

"Fine."

I pulled away and she fumbled on the bed until she found my hand and squeezed it.

"Been so long," she said.

It was a struggle for me to think of anything to say. I just wanted to get out of there.

"I think it's been nine years," I said.

She smiled and her eyes seemed to plead for something. I waited, but she didn't respond.

"Thanks for having me down," I said. Of course, I didn't mean it, but it was all I could think of.

"You get enough to eat?" she asked.

Gert interrupted. "We haven't had supper yet, Mrs. Canterbury. But I'm about to bring yours up in just a moment."

She cocked her eyes at Gert. "Make sure . . . he gets enough to eat," she said.

Gert came to my side of the bed and put her hand on my shoulder. "I will, Mrs. Canterbury. Don't you worry about it. Now, we're gonna step out and I'll bring your supper shortly."

Grandmother squeezed my hand once more before letting loose of it as I backed away.

"We'll have plenty of time to visit," Gert assured her.

There was nothing I wanted more than to leave that room, but an unexpected wave of guilt coursed through me.

"Bye," I said.

She smiled and didn't answer. Gert nudged me, and we turned and left.

It took me ten minutes to figure out how to plug in and use the rotary phone. It took me another five to discover it didn't have long-distance service. I finally reached the operator and had her place a collect call for me. Dad accepted.

"You make it down there OK, Win?"

"What are you doing home again?"

"It's almost eight o'clock here."

"Oh yeah," I said.

"How is it going?" he asked me.

"Dad, she's almost dead. I mean *really* almost dead. She's like a skeleton with lipstick."

"She claims she's deathly sick."

"She's not deathly sick; she's deathly old. I mean, I don't even think her brain is working. I don't even think she knows my name."

"Of course she does."

"She hasn't *said* it. She can barely talk. How is she supposed to spend any time with me when she can't even get out of bed?"

"Just make the best of it."

"I've got to sleep across the hall from her, Dad. What if she dies while I'm here?"

"Come on, Win. Be reasonable."

"Seriously, if she dies and turns into a ghost while I'm here, I'm going to be pissed."

"That's enough of that talk."

The fact he didn't seem to appreciate the situation made me even angrier. "I want to leave, Dad. It sucks here!"

"Give it some time, Win."

I didn't respond.

"Call Jules if it will make you feel better."

"Dad, this phone is the biggest Davy Crockett piece of crap I've ever seen! It took me fifteen minutes just to figure out how to make a collect call to you!"

"Calm down."

"It's all crap!"

"Take it easy, Win. Your mother is standing here and wants to talk to you."

I took a deep breath. "Fine," I said.

"Hi, sweetheart," she said.

I didn't usually like it when she called me that, but for some reason it felt good this time.

"Hi, Mom."

"It's going to be OK," she said. She sounded tired.

"I just don't see the point in it all," I said. "Mom, it's like me and this old housekeeper and a dying lady upstairs. In some falling-down house that's probably haunted. The only other person I've seen is an asshole farmer. Maybe I could at least go out and kill something if the weather didn't suck so bad."

"Kill something? Win, what are you talking about?"

"Like a deer or something."

"Where did you get that idea?"

"Jules. They kill deer."

"Good Lord, son. Don't get yourself hurt. You know I don't like guns."

"Well, I don't like dead ladies across the hall either, so bring me home."

She didn't answer me right away. "Give it a chance," she finally said.

"I gave it a chance. I want to come home."

"Please, Win. Just hang in there."

I sighed. "How long?"

"Call us back in two days."

"I'll call you back tomorrow."

Another moment of silence. "I love you, sweetheart," she finally said.

"You too," I said. "'Bye."

I hung up the phone and examined it. "Piece of crap," I said to it. As if in answer, the wind gusted and howled around the sides of the house. A magnolia limb scratched its big, frozen leaves across the windowpane, trying to get at me.

"Got your supper ready, Win," Gert said.

I turned and saw her standing in the doorway to the kitchen. I realized she might have heard my phone conversation, but I didn't care. "OK," I said.

"Don't forget to unplug the phone," she said.

"I might need it again," I argued.

"Save electricity," she said.

"Save electricity?"

She whisked away into the kitchen. "Mrs. Canterbury's real big on saving electricity," she said over her shoulder.

I started to respond but caught myself when I realized the uselessness of it. "Oh my God," I said. I bent over, unplugged the phone, and started for the kitchen. "This is total crap!"

8 FIRST NIGHT

I sat alone at the kitchen table while Gert made a plate of food for me. It began to sleet outside again, and tiny ice pebbles sprayed the windowpanes. The gas heater moaned and ticked and fought against the cold slipping through the walls of the old house.

"What is it?" I asked.

"Creamed chipped beef and cabbage," she said. "Your daddy's favorite."

"Never heard of it," I said.

She set the steaming plate before me and I studied it. What looked like runny Elmer's glue smothered shavings of canned meat. Cabbage boiled with ham hock was sprinkled with bits of bacon. She watched me. I looked up at her.

"I can't eat this," I said.

I expected that same hurt look to come over her, but it was almost as if she expected it this time.

"I bet you never tried it before," she challenged me.

"You're right," I said. "And there won't be a first time. What else is there to eat around here?"

"How are you gonna learn anything if you don't try things?"

"Look," I said. "I didn't want to come here. I don't want to be here. I certainly don't want to try new things while I'm here."

She took the plate away. She covered it with plastic wrap and put it into the old refrigerator.

"What kinds of things do you like?" she asked me over her shoulder.

"Hamburgers. Chicken fingers. Pizza. The normal stuff."

She opened the freezer.

"You eat vegetables?"

"Fries."

"That's no vegetable, Win."

"Yes, it is."

"Not in my book, it ain't."

"Well, whoever wrote your book is wrong. Potatoes are vegetables."

She pulled a brick of something wrapped in butcher paper from the freezer and set it on the counter.

"I've got a corned beef, but it won't be thawed until tomorrow. How about ravioli?"

"Sure. That's normal."

She opened the door to the cupboard, stood on her tiptoes, and fingered a can from the top shelf. It was the oldest-looking can of ravioli I'd ever seen, rusty with the label peeling off and yellowed like mice had been peeing on it for years.

"Dad must have forgotten to eat that one," I said.

She didn't answer me.

"Do those things expire?"

She got a can opener from a drawer and started opening it. "I think it'll be fine, Win. If it's not, we'll look for something else."

"Yeah, like in the car. In town. At McDonald's."

She got a pot and started filling it with water. "Got no way to get into town," she said. "Mrs. Canterbury and me, we don't drive."

"Serious? How do you get groceries?"

She lit the stove and placed the pot on the burner. Then she set the can in the pot with the water. "Mr. Case brings us what we need," she said.

I felt the lump of doom in my stomach grow a size larger. "It just keeps getting better and better around here."

She didn't answer me.

"How do you get home?"

"I live in the house out back."

"Like a rental?"

"It's the house I grew up in. There used to be a lot of us here. Everybody's moved away now or passed on."

I looked out the window, but it was too dark to see anything. I looked back at the pot on the stove. "I guess you're boiling that because you don't have a microwave?"

She turned and smiled at me with new resolve. "It won't take long," she said.

After supper the sleet turned to rain again, but the wind kept on like it wanted to tear the house apart. Back in Dad's old bedroom I wished I had video games or at least a book. I wandered over to the old bookcase and opened the dusty glass doors and ran my eyes over the book covers. Rudyard Kipling, Sir Arthur Conan Doyle, Jules Verne, and Daniel Defoe, ancient authors I'd heard of but never actually read. Authors from another age, from the time warp I found myself in. I saw some of Dad's old schoolbooks and pulled out one on English literature. It probably hadn't been moved since the last time Dad put it there when he was my age.

I climbed into bed with the textbook. Inside the cover was his name, Winchester Canterbury Jr., written in the same slashing style he used to this day. Handwriting much like my own. On the opposite page someone had drawn a heart, and beneath, in a girl's curvy handwriting, it said, "Love, Margaret." I'd never heard him talk about anyone named Margaret, but then he never told me much of anything about his childhood. Certainly not about life at Cottonlandia, the place he'd fled and left to rot.

I pulled the bedspread down and stripped to my underwear, leaving my clothes puddled on the floor. When I slid into bed, the sheets were so cold it felt like they were wet. As the bed warmed, I read a Civil War story called "An Occurrence at Owl Creek Bridge," which was very good and somehow appropriate to my situation. Then I turned off the bedside lamp and stared at the ceiling. The flames of the old Dearborn space heater flickered blue and orange and cast shadows across the walls. I tried not to think of Grandmother, the skeleton with the lipstick just across the hall.

"You better not die," I mumbled to myself.

9 STICKERS

What I thought was a nightmare turned out to be the old black alarm clock going off beside me like someone drumming a trashcan. I reached out and hit for it in the darkness, knocking the lamp off the bedside table and finally connecting and beating it silent.

Just after daylight I drifted out of sleep to the smell of bacon cooking. There was something soothing about the gas heat and the pile of heavy blankets over me. I no longer heard the sound of wind and rain. Birds chirped outside, and sunbeams angled across the floor through the window over my head. I remembered the alarm clock and looked at it, lying on its side, still ticking defiantly.

I gathered my clothes and toiletries and headed for the washroom. As I opened the door, I felt cold air press into me. It smelled of rot and mouse pee. There was no shower. Before me was an ancient, iron clawfoot tub with a two-foot-long, brown icicle hanging from the faucet. It was literally freezing in there. I looked about for a heater but didn't see one. I did see water stains streaking the once-white walls and a commode with a gallon jug of antifreeze next to it.

"You've got to be kidding me," I said.

I approached the tub and kicked at the icicle until it broke off and shattered. I turned one of the faucet handles and leaped back as it began to cough and spit and hack rust-colored water. Pipes began rattling overhead and some small animal scurried away through the attic.

"Gert!" I called, staring at it.

There was no answer.

Eventually the pipes purged themselves and the water turned a milky color and then went clear. I approached the tub again and put my hand under the stream. Ice cold. I turned the other handle and waited until the hot water made its way upstairs. Finally, it was warm enough to stopper the drain and wait for it to fill. Meanwhile I opened the door and tried to fan enough warm air into the place to make it tolerable.

After my bath I walked downstairs to the kitchen where I found Gert and the farmer.

"Good morning," Gert said cheerfully.

I sat across from the farmer. He was wiping up the run of a fried egg with a biscuit.

"I don't suppose you have a shower in this place," I said.

"I'm sorry, Win," she said. "It's been a while since we've done much to the house."

"I thought most houses *came* with one."

The farmer didn't give her time to respond. "Your grandmomma wants me to take you riding around the farm," he said.

"Fine," I said. "Whatever."

We walked out to the truck after breakfast. The air was crisp and cold under a blue sky. Birds chirped and flitted about the yard, and squirrels leaped playfully through the trees like they hadn't been out in days. The farmer moved slowly, his breath steaming before him, like he was tired and didn't want to be there. I saw he had a slight limp. He looked up and squinted at the sky.

"Dad says I can hunt here," I said.

He looked back at the truck and didn't answer me.

"My friend, Jules, he went to Montana last year and killed an eight-point whitetail. I heard there's whitetail here."

"You did, did you?" he said.

The farmer stepped into his truck. I walked around and got into the passenger side. "Cottonlandia used to be about fifteen thousand acres," he said. "This was always the homesite, though several houses have burned over the years. Your great-great-great-grandfather planted five oak trees along the driveway. One for each of his children. The oak trees are gone now, tornadoes and such. I climbed on a couple of them when I was a kid. The last one fell about ten years ago."

He shifted the truck into gear and we began to pull away. "They call this Headquarters," he said. "Middle of the farm. About ten acres. They kept the trees to block the wind and dust."

We lumbered across the lawn toward an avenue in the pecan grove. The farmer pointed to a clearing on our left. "The farm office used to be right over there. Your great-grandfather was the last of your family to really farm the place. It's been leased out since the fifties."

I studied the clearing. Nothing more than some tall, brown grass.

"It all goes back to the dirt if you don't have anybody to keep it up," he said. "But at the end of the day, it's the dirt that matters most."

I looked at him. "The dirt?"

"That's right. Mississippi Delta dirt is some of the most fertile in the world. Millions of years of flooding over this plain left as much as twelve feet of topsoil in some places. It's valuable. Real valuable."

I looked ahead at the opening in the trees and the field beyond.

"Why isn't it still fifteen thousand acres?"

"Each of the children got their piece. Your great-great-grandmother got this one. She's the only that held on to hers."

I frowned. "Dad said we might still have some rifles in the house. He said I could borrow one and hunt if I wanted."

"Ever used a rifle?"

"I've shot them at camp."

"Yeah?"

"Yeah. Twenty-two caliber."

The farmer nodded thoughtfully.

"I don't remember any of this," I said. "I came for my grandfather's funeral, except we didn't come out here. We went to a cemetery in Greenwood."

"You've got a lot of kin in Greenwood."

"Dad says they're mostly dead now."

The farmer didn't reply. We passed through the break in the trees, and the fields lay before us like pans of chocolate ice cream, frosted and stabbed with sticks.

"He says you used to work for my grandfather. Dad says he used to go hunting with you when he was my age."

"Your daddy and my son were good friends . . . Your granddaddy was a fine man. He knew a lot about cotton."

COTTONLANDIA

"But he wasn't a farmer?"

"He was what you call a gentleman farmer. A businessman."

I didn't completely understand, but I wasn't interested in the subject. "Have you seen many deer on the place?"

"I see deer most every day."

"Have you seen any big ones—big whitetails?"

The farmer pulled a pressed foil of tobacco from his shirt pocket and set it on the seat between us. I watched as his big hands unfolded and brought out the plug. He bit a piece and worked it into his cheek. "There's one over on the south side of the place. I figure it's about the biggest we got. We call him Stickers. Saw him two days ago. But he doesn't usually show himself."

"Can you show me where it was?"

The farmer spit. "I suppose I can."

"I want to kill it."

He stared ahead. After a moment he nodded to himself.

10 TOURING THE FARM

We drove on in silence, passing abandoned tenant houses. I wondered if he was really planning to show me where Stickers lived. We crossed a creosote bridge, caked over with years of dried mud and wedged with high-water debris. We moved so slowly I hardly noticed when the truck pulled off the road and stopped.

"Over there," he said. He was aiming his chin at a thin finger of trees.

"That's where you saw him?"

"I figure he moves around some, but I last saw him run into those trees."

"Did you see him in the morning or in the afternoon?"

He spit out the window and wiped his chin. "In the morning. It was raining. I don't expect he'll come out in the daylight unless the weather's acting up."

"How many points?"

The farmer put the truck into gear again and pulled back onto the gravel road. "Eight or ten," he said. "I'd guess."

I knew enough to know that was impressive. I smiled at the thought of telling Jules I'd killed a ten-point.

We approached another grove of trees. Before it was a large, metal building, and beside it were five large, green John Deere tractors beneath a metal roof.

"Tractor shed and the shop," he said. "This is pretty much our base of operations for the cotton farming."

I saw a skinny man with a baseball cap walk around one of the tractors.

"That's Hoyt Jones," the farmer said. "He's the foreman. He's putting some new hydraulic hoses on that picker."

"How many people work here?"

The farmer glanced at me and didn't answer right away. "Depends on the time of year. Can have as many as five during the growing season. Right now it's just Hoyt and Luther."

"So what do they do now?"

"They're repairing equipment and getting it ready for the new season. Fixing engines, cleaning, oiling."

We pulled up next to the tractor shed, and the farmer rolled down his window. Hoyt set a wrench down and hurried over to us.

"Morning, Hoyt," the farmer said out the window.

Hoyt stopped just short of the truck and studied me.

"What's up, boss?" Hoyt said. "Who you got in there with you?"

"Meet Win Canterbury, Hoyt."

He jerked his gloves off and shot a hand though the window and across the farmer's lap. "The landlord! Man, we better straighten up!"

I studied his hand, inspecting it for grease or other stains, then shook it lightly when I saw it looked clean.

Hoyt withdrew and pulled his gloves back on. He faced the farmer. "Have we passed inspection so far?"

The farmer ignored the question. "I'm just showing him around the place. We're gonna ride around the west end and circle back to Headquarters. I'll be back in about thirty minutes and help you and Luther clean those tanks."

Hoyt nodded and looked at me again. "Good to meet you, Win. Don't stay around here too long or he'll put you to work."

"I won't be here long," I said.

He tipped his cap at me, spun around, and hurried off. The farmer drove past the shop and took a left on a dirt road that cut through one of the large fields and seemed to intersect with the main driveway nearly a half mile away. He started telling me something about the drainage system and the big ditches, but I wasn't paying attention. I was thinking about Stickers. Eventually he realized I wasn't listening and stopped talking. When we got to the driveway, he took another left that would take us back to Headquarters. When I finished imagining killing the big buck, I looked over at him. "So what's there to do around here besides shoot deer?" I asked.

"You interested in learning about working on farm equipment?"

"Like engines?"

"Yeah," he said. "Some of that."

"No."

He worked the tobacco like a cow chewing cud, no expression. "Not much else to do, then."

"I'm only going to be here for two more days," I said.

"I could find a lot to do in two days. Sometimes I'd give anything for two more days."

I frowned at his useless comment as we pulled up before the house.

"I'll be over at the shop with Hoyt and Luther if you need me," he said. "Or if you decide you might be interested in learning something."

I looked back at him. "How would I even get there?"

"Walk, I suppose. It's only about a mile. Or there's an old four-wheeler in the garden shed you can take if you can get it running."

"What's a four-wheeler?"

"An ATV. Like a motorcycle, but with four wheels."

Excitement leaped through me. "Oh yeah," I said. "I've seen one of those. What's wrong with it?"

"Engine needs a little work."

I realized his trap. Suddenly I was fed up with the farmer. I was through being nice. "I'd like you to send Hoyt over to start it for me," I demanded.

He turned and spit out the window and looked over at me again. "Sorry," he said. "Hoyt's busy."

I felt anger creep into my cheeks. "I could call my father and have him tell Hoyt to help me," I threatened.

The farmer shook his head, leaned across me, and opened my door. "Get out, kid."

"I'll call him," I said again. "I will."

"What you do for entertainment's not my concern. Now go on. I've got work to do."

I got out and closed the truck door a little harder than necessary, not quite slamming it. The farmer drove off and left me standing there. I kicked the gravel. *Redneck old man*, I thought. *I could have you fired.*

11 THE RIFLE

What the farmer called the garden shed was a fallen-in, board-and-batten-wood barn behind the house. I wrested the door open and saw a dusty room full of empty flowerpots, feed sacks, a pair of rubber boots, a few garden tools, and some old tires. What I assumed was the ATV was under a plastic tarpaulin against the wall. I maneuvered my way to it through all the junk and pulled back the plastic sheet. There it was, old and worn, the seat cushion split, and all the decals rubbed away. It was covered with oil and dirt dauber nests. I didn't even want to sit on it because of how dirty it would make the seat of my pants.

"This piece of crap won't ever run," I said to myself.

I slung the tarpaulin back over it. "Smart-ass old man," I grumbled.

I got the door shut again and backed away from the shed. I studied the rest of the backyard for the first time. To my far left was a white frame building surrounded by old tractor tires with plastic flowers planted in the middle of them. I reasoned I was looking at Gert's house. It was a tidy, tin-roofed, one-room structure with a screened porch, built on stone piers with cement steps leading to the screen door. A thin curl of smoke rose from the chimney.

I went back inside and found Gert sweeping the floor of the foyer.

"Your grandmomma's up," she said. "She'd sure like to see you again. She's a little more talkative in the mornings."

"OK," I said. "I need to make a phone call first."

I crawled under the table and plugged up the phone. Then I started the tedious process of making a collect call. After a few minutes I was able to get through. I wasn't surprised Dad was home again.

"What is it, Win? I'm about to walk out the door."

"I said I'd call back today. It's today. I'm ready to come home."

"Two more days won't kill you."

"Dad, there is nothing to do here but talk to the lipstick skeleton."

"The what?"

"Grandmother."

"Win, don't call her that."

"I'm about to have to go up there and see her again."

"Well, that *is* the whole point of the visit. I need—I mean, you need to spend some time with her."

"I don't like the farmer, Dad."

"What did he do to you?"

"He won't help me. There's an ATV here I could be riding if he'd just fix it for me. But he won't do it."

"He's probably got farmwork to do."

I frowned. "If you can just get him to send someone over to fix the ATV, then *I'll* have something to do."

"He doesn't work for me, Win."

"I thought he did."

"He leases the farming rights. That doesn't make me his boss."

I felt my face grow hot.

"Win," he said, "I've got to go."

"Dad, this place sucks."

"Hang in there. I'll be down day after tomorrow."

"'Bye," I said.

"Go spend some time with your grandmother."

"Jesus," I said. "I will."

I hung up the phone. Then started to pick it up again. What did he mean "I'll be down"? Why was he coming down?

Gert ushered me upstairs to see the skeleton. When I entered Grandmother's room, I sensed something had changed. For one, the curtains were open and sunbeams fell across the floor and alleviated the dismal air of the place. She was still in her nightgown but sitting up in bed. Her head was trembling, and her eyes were wet and alert.

In addition to the bright red lipstick, her hair was full and fluffy. She had on a wig.

"Hey, love," she croaked, holding out open arms.

Gert stood by while I approached and leaned stiffly into the skeleton's bony arms. "Hi, Grandmother," I said into her shoulder.

She was stronger than I expected and pulled me to her until the thin skin of her cold shoulder touched my chin. I smelled the musty wig and the faint odor of urine and sour sweat.

She held me there. "How are you?" she asked.

"Fine," I said to the headboard.

After a moment I felt her arms relax, and I backed away. I was frightened to look at her closely, so I looked at the bedspread.

"Did John show you around this morning?"

"He took me out in his truck."

"That's good . . . It's a big place, isn't it?"

"I was thinking about deer hunting."

"Your grandfather used to deer hunt, you know?"

"I know."

She didn't say anything for a moment. I desperately hoped for Gert's hand on my shoulder, signaling it was time to go.

"You look like him, you know?" she said.

"That's what people tell me."

"You're a good young man," she said. "I can see that."

I took a step back and looked at her. The head shook and trembled. "Do you know my name?" I asked her. I didn't say it in a mean way. I just wanted to know.

Her smile didn't change, but it became a little more forced.

"You're a good young man," she said again.

I felt Gert's hand on my shoulder. "Time for us to let you get some rest, Mrs. Canterbury."

"See you later," I said.

"'Bye, 'bye, love," she said.

Gert made me some corned beef for lunch. My only complaint was she cooked it with cabbage, and I hated cabbage. I took it plain with mustard and a slice of bread.

While I ate at the breakfast table, she cleaned the dishes from Grandmother's lunch.

"She doesn't know my name, does she?"

Gert kept her back to me. "Her mind's not as sharp as it used to be."

"She hasn't remembered me since I was born."

She kept scrubbing on something in the sink. "I know it must hurt to not have known your grandmother and grandfather."

"No. It didn't hurt at all. I guess you have to know somebody at least a little before it matters that you *don't* know them."

She took off her apron and hung it on a nail. Then she turned to me. "You need anything else, Win?"

The way she asked wasn't as generous as before.

"I don't think so," I said.

"OK, then. I'm going home for a little while."

Good, I thought. *I've got a rifle to find.*

I found the old gun cabinet in the den. The glass doors were dusty, as though they hadn't been opened in thirty years. I saw only one rifle inside. I opened it and removed a lever action like the one I'd used at the camp in Wisconsin. But this model was antique and heavy, like something from an old Western. Reading the barrel, I made it out to be a Marlin 30–30. More searching led to a box of ammunition in a bottom drawer.

I took the rifle outside and walked past the garden shed to where I found a footpath through the trees. I emerged on the outside of the island, a bare field stretching in dizzying rows for nearly a half mile to the next line of trees beyond. My oxfords were heavy and caked with mud. I sat on the ground, laid the rifle across my legs, and shoved two of the cartridges into the magazine. Then I levered one into the chamber and stood. Holding the rifle at my hip, I cocked the hammer and held it before me like someone offering a shovel load of dirt. I cocked my head to the side so one of my ears was stoppered by the top of my shoulder. I closed my eyes.

KA-BOOOM!

The rifle leaped back, wrenching me in a half circle. I dropped it on the dirt and quickly looked around, surprised at the violence of this gun compared to the .22. After a moment, I regained my nerve and picked the rifle off the ground and studied it. I smiled.

"Wait until you see this, Jules," I said to myself.

On my way back I stopped by the garden shed and retrieved the old gum boots. I stopped on the front porch, took off my shoes, and beat them against the column until most of the mud fell off in big clumps.

Before I went to sleep, I picked up the alarm clock and looked it over. "All right, you evil, black bastard," I said. "What is it you want?"

I found the dial to set the hand for Evil's alarm and moved it from 2:00 a.m. to 5:00. Then I shut off the lamp and lay there in the orange-and-blue light of the gas heater flickering and dancing on the walls. Now that the storm was gone, the night was still. I heard the house creaking and feet scurrying across the attic floor. I thought of the skeleton across the hall, her breath misting above the lipstick. Then I had a brief image of her slipping through the house at night. I shuttered the thought and rolled over and visualized Stickers lying out there, waiting for me.

12 DEER HUNT

At 5:00 a.m., I reached out and beat on Evil until he was quiet again. I lay there for a moment, trying to remember why it was so important I wake before daylight. I couldn't get my mind to spin up all the reasons. Then I slowly remembered the rifle and Stickers.

I dressed before the gas heater, pulling the gum boots on. Then I crept downstairs and got the rifle out of the cabinet. Outside I found the morning cold and still and dark. I set out on the gravel road, following the path I'd driven with the farmer. The rocks crunched and squeaked beneath my feet. The gum boots fit perfectly and, along with the rifle cradled in my arms, made me feel like a real outdoorsman.

When I emerged from the island, the field lay before me under the sky glow. A light breeze swept across my face, and I stopped to pull my hood over my stocking cap and cram my hands deeper into my jacket pockets. I scanned the horizon until I located the distant finger of trees the farmer had pointed out. A turnrow intersected the gravel just ahead and seemed to angle off in the right direction. I stepped onto it and started across the field.

I plodded along, turtled inside my jacket, listening to my breathing against my collar, the rest of the world mute and shut away. I had never felt so alone and so free in such wide-open space. It was exhilarating and frightening at the same time. I would have turned back if it weren't for my goal. I wanted to reach those trees nearly a mile away. I wanted to kill that deer and tell Jules about it.

When I came to the end of the field, the horizon at my back was aglow with the bleed of sunrise. The hardwoods rose before me like a dark, towering wall. The wind was blocked, and I swept back my hood and lifted the bottom of my stocking cap over my ears. I heard the swamp alive before me. Birds cheeped and stirred in its depths. Squirrels whined and fussed from the canopy. It seemed like a jungle in there. As I stood contemplating it, I felt my toes growing cold. I imagined the buck, big as a cow, lying in the thicket watching me. I was suddenly frightened and considered turning back. Then I thought of Jules again. I hugged the rifle tight and stepped into the swamp.

At first the walking was easier than I'd imagined. Large oak and gum trees towered over a floor of matted leaves. But as I moved into the interior, the ground became soggy, and I found myself parting small groves of cane and wading through raspy palmetto fronds. Ahead, it seemed to grow only thicker. I pressed on.

I'd been staring at the cane thicket for several minutes, trying to decide if I should continue, when the pattern of a deer's face appeared between the shoots. My heart was thrown against my chest, and I felt a wave of panic shoot up my spine. I realized in that instant I had not expected to see a deer at all. I froze in position and examined the face staring back at me. In seconds I began to make out the form of the antlers, rising above the head, the same yellowed bone color as the cane shoots. I began to move my hand from the stock of the rifle to the hammer.

I cocked it with a click.

The face didn't move. I wondered if the deer was dead. *Weren't they supposed to run?*

My confidence built, and I took a step forward. The deer rose slowly, heavily, and began to move away, not at a run, but more of a slow lumber. I jerked the rifle to my shoulder, found the iron sights, and focused on the thicket.

The deer was no longer there.

"No!" I yelled. I ran toward the thicket. I crashed through the cane where I had last seen him. A root caught my foot and slammed me to the ground, a loud explosion coming from the rifle. I let go of the gun and rolled over. The rifle lay discharged, with a cavern of black mud and thin, yellow roots blown into the ground.

I picked it up and levered another shell into the chamber. I plowed through the thicket again, desperate. Suddenly I broke from the tangle and faced the field. I saw the buck walking along the edge of the trees, slowly, not looking back.

"Hey!" I yelled.

I was surprised when he turned sideways, but I was quick to take aim and fire.

He didn't flinch.

I levered another shell and fired again. His back snapped downward like a stick broken between fingers. He stood there for a moment on trembling, colt knees, not looking at me even after this, but staring at the ground in concentration. Then he kneeled on his front legs and put his chin to the soil. The back legs still held for several more seconds, the front part of the buck strangely flat against the ground and the hindquarters straight up. When the rear legs collapsed, the entire body rolled over, twisting his chin from the ground. And he lay there, watching me.

I'd only been standing over the buck for a few minutes when I saw the farmer's pickup coming toward me at the edge of the field, rocking slowly over the rows. The deer wasn't moving, but his eyes seemed to watch me, dark and unblinking.

The farmer was soon out of the truck and standing beside me. I pointed to the deer's back where a U-shaped chunk of meat was missing. The deer's shattered backbone showed like cauliflower through the dirt- and grass-pasted hole. I was breathing hard and my hands were shaking.

I pointed. "I think I shot him right there," I gasped.

The farmer looked at me, then at the deer.

"Cut his throat," he said.

I caught my breath. "Is he still alive?"

The farmer reached into his pocket and pulled out a knife. He flipped it open and kneeled beside the deer. His hand went under the animal's chin and lifted it as if he were going to pet it and allow it to gaze across the field. The deer straightened its legs as the farmer drew the blade across its neck with his other hand. I looked away. In my peripheral vision I saw the deer kicking its back legs. When I looked back, it was still.

"He's a nine-pointer, right? I counted nine."

The farmer didn't answer me.

"Is that Stickers? It's him, isn't it?"

"Yeah, it's him," the farmer said. He pulled a handheld radio from his pocket and clicked the transmit button. "Luther," he said.

A second later a voice came over the radio. "Yes, sir."

"We got a deer down on the west end of the stone break. You think you can come out here and help me load it?"

There was a pause. "Deer down?"

"Yeah. The boy shot a deer. It's got some weight to it."

Another pause. "I'm on my way," he said.

A few moments later I saw another blue truck coming at us from across the field. It ambled slowly down the turnrow and finally pulled up before us. The truck door read "Cottonlandia Plantation" in faded, white letters. A giant black man stepped out and ran his eyes over the buck. He let out a slow whistle.

"Who got that big buck deer?" he said, grinning and looking at me.

"I did," I said proudly.

Luther had that same cheerful look in his eyes as Hoyt, but with a little less energy and a slow, lumbering body to carry it.

"That's that big one we always see. That's Stickers, ain't it?"

"It's him," I said. "I killed Stickers."

"Luther, I don't think you've met Win, have you?"

Luther held out his big hand to me. "No, sir, I haven't."

I shook his hand, and it was rough and callous and dusty, but I was too excited about the deer to care. He walked to the animal and grabbed one of its back legs while the farmer dropped the tailgate to his truck. Luther dragged the deer over, got up in the bed, and pulled the animal over the tailgate. He straightened and took a deep breath. "That thing's every bit of two fifty," he said. "You need some help getting it out, Mr. Case?"

"No," the farmer said. "Go on back to what you were doing. I can handle it from here."

Luther dropped to the ground again. He turned to me. "Good to meet you, Win."

"Thanks," I said.

"If I don't see you again, you have a good trip back to New York City."

"OK," I said. "I will."

Luther pulled away and I was left with the farmer and the deer I'd killed. Stickers, the biggest buck at Cottonlandia. I wished more than anything Jules were there to see me.

"What now?" I asked.

"Now you get to finish this," he said.

13 ROBBED

I rode with my face pressed against the rear window, watching the dead deer in the truck bed. We traveled into the island, and the farmer pulled off the gravel and stopped beside one of the large pecan trees.

"We'll pull him up one of these tree limbs," he said.

I watched while he threw a rope over a large limb about ten feet from the ground. He tied one end to the deer's feet and the other to the trailer ball of the truck. Then I stood back as he drove the truck forward. The rope drew tight, and the deer was pulled from the bed, flopped to the ground, and hoisted up until it was swinging with its antlers just scraping the leaves.

The farmer set the parking brake and returned to stand before it. He steadied the animal.

"How old do you think he his?" I asked.

The farmer took a step back and stared at its head. "I'm not sure."

"What would you guess?"

"If they live to ten, I'd say he's that."

"Should I get a picture?"

"You got a camera?"

"No."

The farmer kneeled and used his forefinger to lift the deer's lip. He began to study the teeth.

"How can I show him to people?"

"To what people?"

"My friends back home."

He let the lip fall back into place. "You can keep his horns."

"You think I could mount him?"

The farmer looked at me. "You could."

"Would you mount him?"

The farmer turned to spit. He wiped his mouth and looked at me again. "I guess I would, if I were you."

He pulled the knife from his pocket. I winced as he circumscribed the deer's rear legs. Then he slipped the blade inside the skin and pulled cleanly down to the groin, like slicing an envelope with a letter opener.

"How much do you think he weighs?" I asked.

"I don't know."

"What would you guess?"

The farmer stabbed the knife into the deer's ribs and left it there. Then he removed his jacket and put it in the truck. As he was walking back, I asked him again.

"How much would you guess he weighs?"

He stopped beside me, but his eyes were judging the deer. "Luther's right. Two fifty, maybe."

He rolled up his sleeves and retrieved the knife. He pinched the exposed muscle of the stomach lining between the deer's legs, puncturing it with the tip of his knife and slicing down carefully. I took a step back as the intestines and other internal organs began to press outward through the opening and steam in the cold air. By the time he'd worked the knife to the chest, it seemed every bit of the deer's stomach cavity was about to spill onto the ground. The musky smell of game meat fell over me. Then the farmer stood and put his weight into the knife, popping through the cartilage of the sternum. Black gushes of blood spurted forth and stained the leaves. I felt myself growing weak and queasy. I looked away.

"Pull his guts out," the farmer said over his shoulder.

I shook my head.

The farmer backed away, holding his hands out to keep blood from dripping on his clothes. He looked back at me.

"Pull his guts out," he said again.

"I'm not pulling his guts out."

"Yes, you are. You killed him. You help clean him. Then you eat him."

"All I want is the head."

"I'm not asking you what you want."

I started trembling. I felt offended from all sides—the smell, the gore, the farmer, this place.

"I'm not touching him," I said.

"Then get out of here. This isn't your deer."

I looked him in the eyes. "You can't take it from me. This is my deer! I shot it on my family's property!"

"Go on. Get out of here."

"I'm not leaving my deer!"

"Suit yourself."

The farmer turned and grabbed a handful of the organs and pulled them out. Then he plunged his arm into the stomach cavity and began to slice away at something deep inside. His arm was in up to the elbow, and every time it jerked, more of the guts spilled out toward me. Before I knew it, a giant, steaming gut mass spilled out and hung swinging from the deer. I turned away, leaned over, and puked.

The farmer made two more quick slices, and the load plopped to the ground. He backed away and turned to me.

"Drag that out into the woods."

I stared at the ground, dry heaving, trying to get the sickness out. I saw his feet move away again and heard the soft, swishing sounds of the knife on the hide.

I coughed and wiped my mouth with the back of my hand.

"I hate this place," I mumbled.

"We don't," he said.

"I'm never coming back here again," I said.

"That's too bad."

I stood up and felt the sickness puddled inside me. I didn't want to look at the deer again.

"I want to go back to the house," I said.

The swishing of the knife blade continued. "So you're ready to leave now?"

"Yes. I want to go back now."

"Start walking. Nobody's stopping you."

"I need you to take me. I don't feel good."

"I'll bet you feel better than this deer."

My head grew hot with anger. "Go to hell, old man! And this crappy, redneck farm! And Gert and her pine straw earrings and—

and my grandmother who never gave a crap about me in her whole life! Hell with all of you! You can all just stay around here and die and rot away like the rest of the place!"

He didn't say anything. He didn't even stop cutting on the deer. I turned and started for the house. I'd have run, but my boots were too heavy with mud.

I barged into the house, my boots slinging mud and slippery on the pine floor. As I started up the stairs, Gert called to me from the kitchen.

"I've got breakfast ready, Wi—"

"I don't want your crappy breakfast!" I yelled back at her.

I stomped the rest of the way upstairs, went into the bedroom, and slammed the door. Then I stood in the middle of the floor, my teeth clenched, breathing deeply through my nose, my head racing with hate.

After a moment, the warmth of the room encouraged me to take off my cap and jacket. Then I looked at the red carpet and saw the mud I'd tracked all over it. I looked at my bed with the white chenille bedspread. Gert had already made it up. I approached it and threw myself onto it, boots and all. I kicked them back and forth, rubbing the dirt in. Finally, I relaxed my legs and lay there staring at the ceiling, breathing. My eyes grew heavy. *One more night*, I told myself. *I'm going home tomorrow.* I closed my eyes. I opened them. *I can just stay in this room until Dad gets here. Hell with them.*

14 WARNING SIGNS

I woke to Gert knocking on my door. I looked at the clock and saw it was almost noon.

"Go away!" I yelled.

"Your grandmother—"

"I don't care! Leave me alone."

She didn't say anything else. I heard Grandmother's door open and shut a few times and the creaking of the floor and the stairs. There was some rustling and light clanking in the kitchen below me. Then I sensed Gert was gone. It was almost one o'clock, and my stomach was growling.

I got out of bed and saw all the mud I'd rubbed into the bedspread. It looked like someone had dragged it down a wet dirt road. Then I remembered the farmer and the deer he stole from me, and I took off my boots and tossed them against the wall.

I went downstairs in my socks to get something to eat. Gert had already cleaned the mud from the stair treads and the landing below. Before going into the kitchen, I looked into the living room and saw the rifle back in the gun cabinet. Everything seemed in place again, ready to keep dying just like it had been before I got there.

On the kitchen counter was a plate with a hamburger and fries. A napkin was folded beside the plate with a knife and fork holding it down. I grabbed some ketchup and mustard from the refrigerator and took it all to the breakfast table.

I spent the rest of the day reading some of Dad's old books. It might have been the most boring day of my life. At one point I thought about going outside, but then I heard Gert rustling around downstairs, and I didn't want to face her. I didn't want to face any of them.

Darkness fell over the farm. I bathed and got into my pajamas. When I was sure Gert had gone home for the night, I crept downstairs again and found my supper on the kitchen counter. Same thing, hamburger and fries. I ate it quickly and returned to my room. The sooner I fell asleep, the sooner tomorrow would come.

I lay in bed the next morning, listening to the birds chirping outside and watching the dust hang in the sunbeams coming through the window. The smell of bacon had come and gone. I'd heard the front door open and close several times. Even though I was hungry, I didn't want to go down there. I didn't want to see anyone except Dad.

Evil said eight thirty when I heard Gert creak up the stairs and enter the skeleton's room. Fifteen minutes later I heard her go down the stairs again, the chinaware clinking on her tray. I got out of bed and began packing.

It didn't take me long to get what few things I'd brought into my suitcase and close it up. I waited a while longer until the house was quiet and I knew Gert had left until lunchtime. Then I grabbed my suitcase and took it downstairs and set it before the door. Finally, I plugged in the phone and went to work placing a collect call.

No one answered at our apartment, so I tried Amy, Dad's secretary. She always knew where he was, even on the weekends. She was young and pretty, and I'd always had a crush on her. Just talking to her made me nervous.

"Hello," she answered suspiciously. It seemed she was surprised anyone would be calling. It was Saturday, but that had never been a problem before.

"Hey, Amy. It's Win."

"Oh . . . hi, Win," she said.

"When is Dad getting here?"

"I think his flight arrives at one o'clock."

"One o'clock! That means he won't be here until almost two!"

"It's only four hours from now, Win."

"Is James driving him out after they land?"

"No, he's flying commercial. I think the farmer is picking him up."

"Can I make a collect call to his cell phone?"

"I don't think that will work."

I sighed. "OK. This crappy thing won't make anything but local and collect calls. Can you reach him and tell him to bring me something to eat?"

For some reason she hesitated. "OK," she said. "I'll call. What would you like?"

"McDonald's Big Mac. And a Coke. I haven't had anything to drink but water in four days."

"OK. I'll do it, Win."

"I can't wait to get home. I think I'll go crazy if I have to stay here another day."

She didn't respond.

"Amy?" I said.

"Yes, Win?"

"Nothing. I thought the phone disconnected."

"I can hear you fine, Win."

"OK. I better go."

"Win?"

"Yes?"

I waited for her to reply, but she didn't finish whatever it was she wanted to say.

"What?" I finally said.

"Nothing. It was nothing."

She was acting strange. "OK," I said. "Then I'll talk to you later."

I hung up the phone and stared at it. An uneasy feeling crawled over me. The same feeling I'd been getting at the dinner table with Mom and Dad. Something was definitely going on. Whatever it was, she knew all about it.

15 DOOMSDAY

It was quarter to two when a knock sounded on the front door. I jumped up, went out into the hall, and stood at the head of the stairs. Gert was already opening the door, and the farmer appeared.

"Got a stranger here to see you, Gert," he said.

Dad stepped into the doorway, and they hugged. Gert clung to him like she'd found her long-lost son. Dad stooped over to embrace her, and I saw him put his chin on her shoulder and close his eyes. It was the first time I'd ever seen him hug someone and mean it.

"Hey, Dad," I said.

He let go of Gert, and she took a step back, wiping her eyes. He lifted his chin and looked at me. In the few days since I'd seen him, I would have sworn he'd lost weight, especially in his face. And his skin had that colorless look of someone just getting over the flu.

"Hey, Win," he said.

I came down the stairs. Before I reached the floor, I saw the farmer standing in the background. I felt him watching me, and I made sure not to make eye contact.

I stood before Dad and motioned to my suitcase. "My stuff's all packed."

"I see," he said.

"What's time's our flight, Dad? I hear you flew commercial."

"It's nice to see you, too, Win." He smirked. "You think maybe you could give me some time to visit with my mother and the rest of these folks?"

I frowned.

"I made you some lunch," Gert said. "All your favorites."

"That sounds great," Dad replied. "Let's go sit down."

"I'll be back to get you in a little bit, Winchester," the farmer said.

Dad turned and nodded to him. "Thanks, John."

I watched the farmer as he turned his back, got into his truck, and pulled out. Gert started for the kitchen, and Dad followed like I wasn't even there.

"Uhhh," I moaned. I took a deep breath, sat on the bottom step, and put my chin in my hands.

After sitting on the stairs for fifteen minutes, I went into the kitchen. Dad was at the breakfast table with Gert sitting across from him. He was talking, and Gert was listening patiently. His plate had traces of what looked like creamed chipped beef.

"Dad," I said, "let's go."

"I'll be out in a minute, Win."

"I'm bored."

"Go outside and get some air."

"How much longer?"

Dad looked at Gert. "I better go talk to her," he said.

Gert got up from the table and took his plate to the sink. Dad turned back to me and stood up. "Go outside and wait for me, Win. I'm going to have a quick visit with Mother, and then I'll meet you outside."

"How long?"

"Ten minutes. Not long."

"OK," I said. "Ten minutes. Do you need to call Mr. Case to come get us?"

He didn't answer. He walked around me and headed upstairs.

I waited on Dad in the driveway, my suitcase beside me. I kept checking my watch as it approached and passed the ten-minute mark. I thought about going back inside to complain, but I didn't want to see the lipstick skeleton again, so I paced in the gravel and kicked at magnolia cones. Finally, after almost twenty minutes, Dad stepped out the front door and looked at me thoughtfully.

"It's about time," I said. "Where's Mr. Case?"

"Win, I need to talk to you about something important."

I sighed. "*What*, Dad?"

"Let's take a walk."

"I don't want to take a walk. I want to leave. Now."

But he passed me and started slowly across the lawn. I sighed and followed. "What?" I said.

I'll never forget the feel, the smell, the sounds of that afternoon. It was quiet except for the cawing of a few crows in the pecan trees and the fluttering of small birds in the hedges. The sky was clear, and a light breeze coming across the fields swayed and shuddered the very tops of the water oaks. The air was pungent with rich soil and tree sap. I walked behind my father until he stopped and turned back and faced me.

"Things in life don't always turn out like you want," he said.

I knew it, I thought. *They're getting a divorce.*

"All of our lives are about to change."

It's not like they did anything together anyway. I don't see how it will affect me much.

"I might be going to prison, Win."

"What?"

"I'm in trouble for tax evasion."

"What does that mean?"

"It means I didn't pay my taxes on a lot of money."

"You go to jail for that?"

"It was a lot of money. More than I can ever pay back."

My head was ringing with overload.

"How long?"

"Couple of years, probably. If I get convicted."

"What? How?"

"Just about all my assets are frozen right now, Win. And your mother's sick."

"Sick? With what?"

"She's had a sort of nervous breakdown."

"What's that mean?"

"It's when things just get too much for you to handle."

"She's gone crazy?"

"No, no. She hasn't gone crazy. She just needs a break."

"Where is she?"

"She's in a home."

"But not our home?"

"No. A nursing home."

"Like where old people go to die?"

"It's not just for old people. It's a place to recover."

"For how long?"

"Until she gets better. The doctor says maybe a few weeks."

My head was racing. It was too much to process at once. "Well . . . if she's gone crazy and you're in jail—"

"She's not crazy, son."

"Well, where do *I* go?"

He didn't answer me right away. I could tell despite the horrors of what I'd already learned, there was a final piece of all this that was even worse.

"You're going to live here," he said.

16 THE RUNAWAY

I stared at Dad, horrified. "What do you mean, I'm going to live here? I can't live here!"

He just stood there, staring at me.

"I wanted to come tell you in person," he said.

"Are you kidding me? That doesn't change anything. What about my friends? What about school? They don't even have internet here!"

"Win, we can't afford to live in Manhattan any longer. We certainly can't afford the tuition at your school."

"What about Frances?"

"We had to let her go."

I shook my head. The anger was melting away, and a sickening realization took its place. "No. I can't do this, Dad. I won't live here."

"Cottonlandia is paid for, and it's still in my mother's name. They can't get to it."

I saw the farmer's truck turn into the driveway and start toward us. I watched it approaching like a hearse.

"It's just the way it is right now," he said. "I'm sorry. I have to fly back today and start trying to sort things out."

The farmer pulled up and looked at us across the seat. "Ready when you are, Winchester?"

"Give me a minute, John."

Dad stepped forward and tried to put his arms around me. I spun suddenly and ran to my suitcase. I jerked it up, ran back to the truck, and threw it into the truck bed. Then I grabbed the door handle and started pulling on it. For some reason I couldn't make my mind remember how to open it, and I stood there jerking on it. Dad came up behind me and began pulling me back.

"I won't stay!" I yelled.

"Win!" he said.

I struggled against him. I hadn't even noticed the farmer had gotten out and come around the truck. He grabbed my hand and pulled it away from the door handle. Then both of them dragged me backward.

"I'll hate you forever if you leave me here!" I yelled.

I felt his hand rest gently on my head.

"I'm sorry, Win. I don't know what else to say."

I pulled free and started running. I didn't know where. Somewhere. Anywhere but that horrible place. I crossed the lawn and crashed into the trees. I fought my way through vines and tangle until I broke from the edge of the island. My feet plunged into the soft mud of the field rows, and I fell on my face. I got up again and ran and slipped and tripped my way farther into the field—on toward the far trees, my thoughts smothered by a panic that hung over everything as a high, ringing sound.

When I came to the forest, I kept moving forward into the dark, cavernous cool of tall cypress and gum trees. The vastness of the swamp rising on all sides shocked me back to my senses. The ringing in my head settled, and I finally began to question what I was doing, where I was going. And I thought, *It doesn't matter. I can't live here.*

As I pressed deeper into the cypress I came to a brake of black water. I stopped for a moment and looked up into the treetops. I felt dizzy and turned and made my way along the edge, dodging cypress knees and fallen trees. A flight of startled wood ducks rose before me, splashing and whirring and quacking up through the brittle branches of the gray canopy. I felt my heart beating fast in my chest, fear rising inside. I tried to keep from panicking and kept on running.

I skirted the outside of the brake for what seemed like hours, slogging through the leafy mud, sometimes plunging up to my knees in the cold, black wet of it. Then the water ended, and a depression of damp leaves and cypress knees and dead grass took its place. I tried crossing but sank to my thighs in mud and had to fall onto my stomach and pull my way out again.

Eventually I came to the end of the brake and trudged into

another hardwood bottom. My shoes were caked with mud that clung to them like cookie dough. They were so heavy it was all I could do to put one foot in front of the other. I gradually realized the swamp was getting dark, and I stopped and looked up. The sky was gray with clouds. I didn't know how long I'd been gone or how close it was to nightfall. I felt fear rising inside me again. I tried to shut it away, but it remained, hot and searing.

I pressed on.

I didn't get far before the hardwoods ended at another brake. I stopped and caught my breath. I looked back from where I'd come, and everything looked the same. Even for someone who had never been in the forest at nightfall, I knew I was in the midst of twilight, in the quiet gloom of the swamp. The temperature had dropped, and I felt the chill pass through my light jacket. I was no longer angry. I no longer cared about anything that had happened before. I was scared in a way I'd never been before.

I turned back and tried to retrace my steps as the swamp grew darker. It wasn't long before my shoes slapped into water. I backed away and waded through palmetto in another direction. I soon came to a wall of vines and briars as big around as my thumb. I tried to pick my way through, holding them aside and stepping sideways, but they grabbed me and pulled at my clothes and tore at my face and ears. I didn't care about the pain, and I ducked and held my hands close to my chest and charged on, digging my feet into the mud. I felt the briars tearing deep into my face and ears, and I cried out and kept on. I twisted and kicked and crawled until I broke free of the tangle and lay in a bed of wet gum leaves, sobbing. By then the swamp was so dark I couldn't see to move. My face and hands and ears were slick with blood and burning from the briar poison. I pulled my legs up and hugged them close. I wanted to cry out for help, but even the rustling of leaves frightened me. I imagined every sort of night creature, creeping through the swamp, looking and listening for prey.

It seemed like hours passed before I heard raindrops tapping on the leaves and felt them on my face. Then I heard them hitting the swamp canopy high overhead and rolling off the broad leaves, falling big and cold. I lay still and blinked against them. Soon my teeth were chattering, and my clothes were soaked. I thought about dying there, a skeleton some hunter would find one day.

I didn't think my situation could possibly get worse. Then I heard something howl like a wolf.

Jules had told me about his father hunting wolves in Canada. I imagined a pack of them loping through the night, traveling the edge of the cypress brake, sniffing and searching for a meal with their heartless, yellow eyes. Then the rain slowed, and I heard the howling clearly and fear ran hot up my back and my teeth quit chattering. A minute passed before I heard it again. With horror I realized that whatever it was, it was coming toward me.

17 THE WOLF

I didn't know what to do but lie still as the howling creature drew closer. It seemed to be a mile away, then a half mile. A lone wolf, on the trail of something, coming my way fast. Even were I not frozen with terror, I was lost and trapped in a dark prison of vines and briars and black water.

The howls grew closer, and I was certain the creature was on my trail. I imagined him clamping his jaws on my throat, shaking me, and squeezing the life from me. Then he'd eat me without leaving a trace. A wolf would eat everything, even cracking my bones and eating the marrow inside.

I wanted more time to think. *This is happening too fast*, I thought. *I don't want it to happen this fast.*

The howling grew louder and more excited. Then I heard the beast walking, stepping through the leaves, weaving, crisscrossing my scent, howling like something from a nightmare. I threw my hands over my face, and then it was there before me, its hot breath falling over my fingers, its foul stench pressing into me.

"ARRRUUU!"

I didn't want to see the yellow eyes. I waited for the powerful jaws to snap down on my neck and wrists, crunching all of it at once.

"ARRRUUU, ARRRUUU!" It howled, circling me, torturing me with anticipation.

Through the noise in my head I thought, *It's waiting for the others. It's calling the others.*

It kept howling and circling and darting in and out at me.

Just get it over with, I pleaded.

But the nightmare played on.

"Stop it," I begged aloud. "Stop it."

The beast howled inches from my face.

"Stop it!" I screamed.

Then there was a flash of light, and I thought it had something to do with my death.

"Warrior!" someone shouted.

I pulled my hands away and found a blinding light in my face.

"Back up, Warrior! Settle down!"

The dog shuffled backward a few steps and howled again.

"You picked a bad night to camp out," the voice said.

The nightmare washed away, and relief flooded me.

A radio crackled. "I got him, Mr. Case," the voice said.

The dog howled again. I came out of my fetal position on the ground and backed stiffly against a tree.

"Hush, Warrior!"

"Is he all right?" I heard the farmer's calm voice over the radio.

"He's pretty wet and cold and scratched up, but he'll live. I told you Warrior'd tree him, didn't I? She's got a nose for people."

Warrior howled again.

"Bring him back, Hoyt. I'll see you at the farm."

"Ten-four," Hoyt said.

He pulled the light away from my face and put it on the dog. It was a large hound the colors of Oreo ice cream. Hoyt approached us through the leaves. "Warrior! Come here you crazy hound dog."

He took Warrior by the collar and dragged her to me. "You OK, Win?"

I didn't respond. He put the flashlight in his mouth and reached down and pulled me up by the forearm.

"You stand up OK?"

I stood, my muscles feeling like tight leather. I realized my teeth were chattering again.

"You got the wrong kind of shoes for this, kid. What are those things, Hush Puppies?"

He had his light on my shoes. I looked at them. Now they were just black, dried lumps of mud.

"Cole Haan," I muttered.

"You're clear onto the Rhodes's place," he continued. "You was set to make it *somewhere,* weren't you?"

"I'm cold," I said.

"I bet you are. And you'd be colder if Warrior hadn't tracked you down. There's sleet coming in tonight."

He helped me walk for a few steps until I felt stable enough to make it on my own. Then he let loose of Warrior's leash. "Get on back," he said.

Warrior woofed and trotted away into the brush. I felt him shove something at my hand. "Take this little flashlight," he said. "I'd give you mine, but I got to figure out how the heck to get out of this place."

I took the light and flipped it on, relieved to have freedom from the darkness.

"Stay behind me," he said. "We'll get you back and warmed up."

We trudged through the dark swamp, the treetops swishing overhead before the oncoming storm. Leaves fell steadily before my face. Hoyt led, stopping and shining his light on all sides and up into the canopy, searching for landmarks, talking to me or himself the entire time.

"I've seen you before," he said to a crooked tree limb. Then he swung the light to our left, and I saw the reflection of dark water. "And you," he said.

We started again.

"Staying away from *you,*" he mumbled.

I held a briar out from my face and ducked under it. I hurried to catch up.

"Now, Warrior," he was saying, "she'll tree anything *but* a coon. Possum. Squirrel. Cat. Duck . . . Man, you get a wood duck up in a tree she won't quit. Like to stand there and do flips she's so mad. But a coon—like if a nose has got a part for every animal smell, hers is missing the coon part."

I stumbled over a cypress knee and fell. Hoyt stopped and waited for me to get to my feet again.

"Yep, I lost my money on that dog," he continued. "But I got another one that'll spank a coon's ass. Prize money dog, you hear me? I'm talking big money. *Big* money."

The radio crackled again.

"You still out there?" came the farmer's voice.

"Yeah, we're still out here. Just working our way around the west end of the brake."

There was a pause. "That's a pretty good trip," the farmer said.

"You're telling *me*. I just hope we get back before this storm catches us."

"You got some time."

"Yeah, maybe."

"You gonna take him to Headquarters?"

"He looks like something you'd pull out of the mud. I figure I'll take him to my place and get him warm and cleaned up."

"Fine. Call me if you get in any trouble."

"10-4."

Hoyt clipped the radio back onto his pocket and started out again.

"You think we're lost?" I asked.

"Naw, we ain't lost," he replied.

Suddenly something was walking in the leaves beside me. I was startled to find Warrior appearing from nowhere.

"Warrior's back here," I said.

Hoyt kept walking and didn't turn back. "Yeah," he said over his shoulder, "she acts it, but she don't like being out here by herself any more than we do. She knows we better get back before that storm moves over us."

The wind shook the canopy overhead, and a wet fleck of ice hit my cheek.

"I think it's over us," I said.

18 THE STORM

A mean wind howled through the trees, spitting bits of ice and slipping through my clothes and licking my bones. My feet and hands were numb, and my jaw was sore from clenching against my chattering teeth. I followed Hoyt, dragging my heavy, mud-coated shoes, staring at the ground. Warrior stayed beside me, slinking along like she didn't want to get wet. Sometimes Hoyt turned and waited for us to catch up. He'd stopped talking so much.

"Come on," he'd say. "We're getting close."

And he'd set out again with more urgency.

My mind had gone numb by now to all the pain of the cold and the weariness of my muscles. I plodded ahead, thinking nothing, feeling nothing, somehow following the faint glimpses of Hoyt's light.

At some point I walked into Hoyt's back and was snapped out of my trance. I stepped back, looked up, and heard and felt the wind louder and stronger against my face. The ice stung, and I ducked into my jacket collar. I saw smooth, black dirt in my flashlight beam.

"Rhodes's field," Hoyt shouted.

I felt the shivers pass through me again. *Just go*, I thought. But he stood there like he wasn't sure. Warrior waited with me, the short hair on her back and neck standing in the wind.

"I figure we head down this turnrow and we should hit something."

I realized it was just as much a question as a statement.

"Dang, it's dark," he said.

Just go, I thought again.

"You all right?"

I nodded. "Let's go," I chattered out.

He took a step closer. "What?"

I lifted my chin. "Go!" I shouted.

"Yeah!" he said. "Let's get out of this stuff!"

He turned and started up the tree line. I ducked back into my collar and forced myself ahead. I felt the slippery, sticky mud caking onto my shoes again.

Sometimes I thought I would just have to fall and die, but I kept on. When I stopped, Warrior stopped beside me. When I started up again, Hoyt would be waiting, and we'd all press on.

I didn't know we had come to the end of the field until my shoes hit grass. By then they were like wet clubs of mud. My face was coated in a sheet of ice, and the joints of my bones felt like they were frozen. I took another step forward, and Hoyt was suddenly there reaching out to me.

"Watch out!" he yelled over the wind. "There's a ditch in front of you!"

Warrior passed me and disappeared. By this point I wasn't even shining my light. I stumbled forward and would have pitched face-first into the hole had Hoyt not caught and steadied me.

"Hang on!" he shouted.

He guided me down the embankment and onto a thin strip of ice. Then he scrambled up the other side, pulling me along until I felt hard asphalt underfoot.

"Come on!" he said. "This way! It's not far!"

That was the last thing I remembered about that night. Everything faded to black.

I woke up in the most comfortable bed I'd ever felt. The mattress and pillow were just the right mix of firm and soft. Piled over me was a sheet covered with a stack of wool blankets. An electric heater hummed and glowed orange against a wall not far from my face. I heard the storm pelting the wall behind my head, sleet spraying the windowpanes. Each time the wind gusted, I thought I felt the bed shake. Then I heard a sigh next to me. I turned over and found myself nose to nose with a big hound. The dog blinked. I was too comfortable to care. I rolled over again and went back to sleep.

Some time later I opened my eyes and the hound was still in my line of sight. This time she was standing on the floor between me and the heater. She was solid brown with black ears.

"Come on, Warrior," I heard Hoyt say. "Leave him alone."

I leaned out and saw Hoyt in the doorway. "It's not Warrior," I said groggily. "It's some other dog. She's been in my bed."

The hound trotted away, her toenails clicking against the linoleum floor.

"How you feel?"

"I just want to go back to sleep."

"It's already two o'clock in the afternoon. You gonna start losing weight if you don't get up and eat."

Please just leave me alone, I thought. "Where am I?"

Hoyt stepped into the room and approached me, seeming to grow more excited with each step, like he might talk me into getting up and doing something with him.

"You're at my place," he said. "Tammy's gone to a church meeting. We got the whole place to ourselves."

"Does that mean I can sleep some more?" But I knew I was already too awake to slip into a deep slumber again. Then the nightmare of my predicament came flooding over me.

Hoyt held out his hands, palm up. "Hey," he said, "you're the boss. Whatever you want."

I moaned and rolled over on my back. Yellow and brown water marks spotted the ceiling. Another gust of wind came, and I was certain I felt the bed shake. Hoyt remained standing where the dog had been earlier.

"Pretty comfy, ain't it?" he said.

I didn't answer him. My thoughts were replaying the scene with Dad in the driveway, telling me about going to jail and losing everything.

"Used to be Bubba's room," he continued. He pointed. "Still got his baseball trophies over there."

I tried to block away the terrible memories. I took a deep breath. "Who's Bubba?" I asked.

"My *son*, Bubba," he said, like I should know.

"Where's he sleep?"

"Oh, he's got his own place now. Shoot, he's about to have a kid."

I looked at him. "How old are you?"

"Thirty-eight next month," he said proudly. "You want me to fix you some food?"

"Sure," I said.

"What you want?" he asked eagerly.

"Whatever you've got," I said. "I don't care."

19 HOYT

After Hoyt and the hound left the room, I crawled from under the blankets and stepped onto the cold floor before the heater. I found myself naked except for a giant pair of men's briefs that hung on me like a loincloth, the spandex held together at the waist by a safety pin. I looked around the room and saw it was mostly bare except for the cheap, particleboard dresser with some baseball trophies on it.

I walked out into a hallway and felt the cold press into me as I left the warmth of the heater. Then I was confused to find there were no rooms on the other side of the house. I heard the storm pelting the wall beside me like the place was only as wide as what I'd walked. I shivered and looked down the passageway and saw the brown hound standing and staring at me. I heard pots clanking.

I followed the noises, passing two closed doors on my left and finally walking into a living room with a scraggly, fake Christmas tree against one wall. Beyond was an open kitchen. Hoyt stood before the stove, placing bacon strips into a skillet. The hound stepped aside to let me pass, keeping her eyes on me the whole while.

"Got some bacon and eggs coming up," Hoyt said over his shoulder. "Figured we'd have breakfast for lunch. Get what's left of your day started off right."

"Who put me in this underwear?" I asked.

He turned and looked back at me, one hand dangling a fork over the skillet.

"Dang!" he said, smiling. "Tammy must have suited you up in some of Uncle Carl's grippies."

"Who's Tammy?"

"She's my *wife*," he exclaimed, like I should have known.

"Your wife dressed me?"

The bacon started popping, and its smell flowed over me. Hoyt turned back to the skillet. "Man, you were passed out," he said. "Like a floppy noodle."

"I'd like to give Uncle Carl back his underwear and put mine on."

"Don't worry about it. Uncle Carl's been dead for two years." He turned back to me again. "But you need to wrap a blanket around your shoulders or something. Aren't you cold?"

I nodded. "I'm *really* cold."

"Go get you a blanket. We'll get your clothes washed after breakfast. Get out of the way, Warrior!"

"That's not Warrior," I said.

"Yeah it is. I got two dogs named Warrior."

I started to question him but wanted the blanket more. I returned to my room and threw one over my shoulder and returned.

"Tammy put some iodine on your sticker cuts too," Hoyt said. "That's the orange stuff all over your face."

I frowned. "Great."

Hoyt smiled and turned back to his cooking.

"Why did you name both of your dogs the same?" I asked.

"Because people like coon dogs named Warrior. They pay more money for them that way."

"So you name all your coon dogs Warrior?"

"That's right."

"Both female?"

"Yeah. For puppies."

"How do they know who you're talking to?"

"It's only the one ain't doing right I'm talking to. She knows who she is."

I didn't have an argument, but something about the idea didn't sit right with me.

"Have a seat," he said. "I'm about to put the eggs on."

I sat at the four-person kitchen table and pulled the blanket tighter around my shoulders. "What is this place?"

"It's my house."

"Why's it so skinny?"

"It's a *single*-wide," he said like I'd asked an obvious question.

"What's that?"

"A *trailer* home. A *mobile* home. You know, it's got wheels."

"It moves?"

"Nawww, it don't move. Well, it did when they brought it. Then you don't use the wheels anymore, but they're still under it."

"Feels like it's going to blow away."

Hoyt began cracking eggs in a bowl and tossing the shells into a five-gallon antifreeze bucket lined with a trash bag.

"That wind'll rock her sometimes," he said. "If it's blowing hard like today. You got to scram if you hear a tornado. It'll roll her like a tin can."

I looked at the window. It was gray and streaked with rain.

"Have you ever rolled in it like a tin can?"

He began beating the eggs with a fork.

"Shoot, no! Man, you don't live through something like that," he said like it was a stupid question.

"If a tornado came, where would you go?"

"I'd run outside and crawl up in the drainage pipe is what *I'd* do. It can't get you in there."

I made a point to remember about the drainage pipe.

"Where's the other Warrior?"

"She's outside in the pen. Got a doghouse out there."

He stopped beating the eggs and tapped the fork on the sink. Then he turned to me and leaned against the counter. "Soon as me and Tammy save up enough, we're gonna add on to this place. They can haul in the other half and make it a double-wide. Couple more years, maybe. It's hard to get ahead around here. We go up to the casinos on the weekends sometime. Try to win a little bit, you know. Man, I'd like to win me the lottery. I could solve a bunch of problems with lottery money."

Even through Hoyt's chatter, I couldn't keep my thoughts from wandering over my predicament. It seemed impossible. There had to be a mistake.

"Do you have a phone?"

"Got a *cell* phone," he said. "Company phone."

"I'd like to make some calls."

Hoyt came away from the counter and fished eagerly into his pocket. He pulled out the phone and brought it to me.

"I got *rollover* minutes," he said. "And *free* long distance."

I didn't respond. I got up from the table and took the phone back to Bubba's room. I had to talk to someone. All of this was impossible. There had to be a solution.

20 ABANDONMENT

I called our apartment. There was no answer. I called both Mom's and Dad's cell phones. No answer there either. Then I called Dad's office and got the familiar automated attendant, punched his extension, and waited. After five rings Amy answered.

Typically, she would have said, "Mr. Canterbury's office." This time she just said, "Hello."

"Hey, Amy," I said. "It's Win again."

"Hi, Win," she said sorrowfully, like she knew about everything. "How are you?"

I stared at the underwear hanging between my legs. "Not good," I said.

"Are you still at your grandmother's?"

"No. I'm in a little trailer house with wheels on it with some farmer's helper and his dogs."

"I see . . . Is there anything I can do to help?"

"Yeah. You can get my life back."

She hesitated. "I'm so sorry about everything that happened, Win. I truly wish there was something I could do. We're all in shock. I wanted to tell you yesterday, but . . . you understand."

"No, I don't understand. Are people still coming to work?"

"There's nobody here except me. I just came to get the last of my things. I'm surprised the phones are still connected."

"I tried his cell phone and he doesn't answer. Do you know where he is?"

"Win, your father hasn't been in the office in six weeks."

"How did you know I was still in Mississippi?"

"Oh, I've talked to him. It's just, well, he's had a lot to think about. Work's been the least of his worries."

"You think he'll go to jail?"

I heard her start sniffling. After a moment she said, "I don't know."

"How can I get reach Mom?" I asked. "I have to talk to somebody. They just left me here. I can't stay here. Dad didn't even bring me more clothes. I barely have *anything*."

She hesitated. "I don't know what to tell you, Win."

"So you don't know how I can get in touch with anybody?"

She sniffled again and didn't answer. I imagined her sitting in her cushioned swivel chair by the big window overlooking Manhattan, her long legs crossed and the phone pressed to her pretty face and her shoulder-length brunette hair falling over it.

"I wish I could help you, Win. I really do."

"Then get me home. I don't care how you do it."

I heard her shift in her chair. "You have to understand, Win," she said with resolve. "There's nothing to come home to. We're all moving on. You need to do the same."

"I can't," I said. "Not here. Not like this."

"You have to," she replied. "Now, I've got to go. You take care, OK?"

I didn't answer.

"Bye, Win."

"Bye," I said.

I walked back into the living room, numb with hopelessness. The storm had subsided, and I saw the usual view of a long, black field out the window on my right, beside the front door. Out the window by the Christmas tree I saw a gray stand of hardwoods.

Hoyt came away from the sink and approached the kitchen table with two steaming paper plates of bacon, scrambled eggs, and toasted white bread. I sensed he was proud of his effort. "Eat it while it's hot," he said.

I sat down and stared at my food. Hoyt sat across from me, and I heard his fork scraping eagerly.

"Come on, man," he said, like we were in a race. "I got some red pepper on those eggs."

"I'm not hungry," I said.

His fork stopped. "Not hungry?"

I shook my head.

"I can make some without red pepper."

"I don't want any of it. None of it."

Hoyt hesitated. "Hey, man," he eventually said. "No problem. I been there too. Warrior!"

I looked up at him. "You haven't been here. You have no idea."

He shrugged his shoulders apologetically. "You're right," he said. "They always say walk a mile in another man's shoes, but you can't really do that, can you?"

I didn't answer him. Warrior appeared at the table, and Hoyt reached out and took my plate and set it on the floor. I listened to the hound lap it up.

"No problem," he said again. "Not a bit wasted."

"Can you wash my clothes now?" I asked.

He shoveled the last of his eggs into his mouth and got out of his chair. "No problem," he said. "I already ate my lunch anyway."

He folded the toast around the bacon and threw the paper plate into the trash bucket.

"You wanna stay here or go?" he asked me.

"Go where?"

"Coin laundry," he said. "Up at Denton's store."

"I can't go in this underwear."

"Naw, man, we'll put something over you. I got some coveralls you can slip into until your clothes are done."

"Don't they have a way to wash clothes at Headquarters?"

"Probably. You want me to drop you off? It's whatever you want."

I thought about it. Cottonlandia sounded even more depressing. And the thought of a store where I could finally buy some decent food was a miracle.

"No," I said. "I want to go to the store."

Hoyt slapped his pocket and started toward the back rooms. "Lemme get my wallet and some coveralls. We'll go hang out at Denton's for a while. Nothing else to do on a day like this."

I frowned and stood reluctantly. I couldn't imagine there being anything to do here on even the best day of the year.

21 THE ROCK

I stepped out of Hoyt's trailer in a much-too-large set of camouflage coveralls and a fake leather jacket that advertised Camel cigarettes. For my feet he'd loaned me tube socks and flip-flops made from used tire treads, also too large. Uncomfortable as this footwear was, as long as the old, yellow underwear was hidden, my appearance was the least of my worries.

The wind had died, but the air was wet and cold on my face. The sky looked gray and evil. Hoyt's front yard was nothing more than a square of bare dirt and yellow grass edged up to a worn asphalt road. Beyond was the field I'd seen out the window. A little, white pickup was nosed up to the trailer on my left. Hoyt had disappeared carrying my dirty clothes in a black garbage sack.

"Hey," I heard him call out.

I looked to my right and saw him craning his head around the corner.

"Come check out my place."

I started to object, but he disappeared again, and I realized we weren't leaving until I found him and whatever it was he wanted to show me. I clopped down the cement steps in the flip-flops and started around to the backyard.

Between the trailer and the hardwoods was a small, metal storage building. Hoyt stood beside it.

"My shop," he said. "Got just about every kind of tool you'd need."

"How far is Cottonlandia from here?"

"Not far. Few miles." He turned and started toward the trees. He was always moving, always walking fast. "Come check out the coon dog kennel," he said.

A slapped-together doghouse stood in the middle of bare dirt inside a hog-wire enclosure set back into the trees. Laying about were rain-splattered chew toys and wet dishrags and three old tires. The other Warrior emerged from the doghouse and watched us.

"Check this out," Hoyt said.

He grabbed a long, bamboo pole propped against the fence. Tied to the end of it was what looked like a wet, brown rag.

"Got a coon skin tied to it," he said. He tilted the pole over the fence so the rancid skin hung in Warrior's face. He jiggled it before the dog. Warrior didn't even look at it.

"See," he said. "Nothing. That'd make a *real* coon dog so mad she'd wet her britches."

"Can we go now?" I asked.

Hoyt set the pole down. He looked disappointed in my disinterest, but I didn't care.

"Yeah, man," he said. "No problem."

His truck was small and cramped compared to the farmer's. Hoyt cranked it and turned the heater knobs. Then he quickly worked the gear shifter into reverse and backed onto the blacktop. I felt like I was riding in a toy.

"It'll be warm in about two minutes," he said, shifting into first. I could tell he liked working the gears. The more action, the better.

I stared over the fields. I was still amazed at the expanse of it all, at how far you could look across a space without seeing people or houses. I wondered how much Hoyt knew about my situation. I reasoned the farmer had told him something. Surely he'd asked why I'd run off into the woods. Then I thought about Mom and how sick she must be that she would let Dad leave me here. Let it happen without even calling. And I wondered about Dad and why he hadn't at least called and apologized with more sincerity for leaving me. And what was everybody thinking about him being in trouble for tax evasion? How was it possible he could go to jail? What would Jules think when he found out? I took a deep breath and distracted myself from my thoughts with a giant V of snowy, white geese against the horizon.

We didn't go far before Hoyt made a left turn on a dirt road. The truck fishtailed on the mud and wavered and straightened. The tires made a sticky, slick sound on the greasy clay.

"Shortcut," he said.

I saw him look at me when I didn't respond, but I kept watching the fields. He shifted again and revved the engine and spun the tires a little before they caught, and we raced on.

"You think we're gonna get stuck, don't you?" he said.

"No," I said. "I haven't thought about it."

The heat started pouring over me, and I shifted my feet to warm my toes.

"Got this thing last year. It's used, but you can't beat a Toyota."

I nodded, wishing we could just ride along in silence.

"I call it the Rock," he said.

I could think of nothing the little lightweight truck reminded me of less than a rock.

"Got four-wheel drive," he continued. It seemed he was talking to both of us now. "AC. CD player. Warn winch."

I looked at him. His eyes jerked to me. "That's right," he said, "twenty-five hundred pounds of pulling power. Came with it stocked."

"How much farther?" I said.

He deflated a bit and turned back to the road. "It's right up ahead. We're almost on your place now."

The dirt road intersected the main highway from Greenwood that I hadn't seen since Mr. Case had delivered me to Cottonlandia five days before.

"You got a big place, you know?"

I nodded.

We waited for two cars to pass before Hoyt swung onto the smooth asphalt. Seeing those cars gave me comfort there were still other people in the world.

"Cottonlandia starts right up there where you see the dirt change," he said. "You'll see the church in a minute. Denton's store's that white speck way up there. Mr. Denton, now, he's a rascal."

"I can't believe there's a store right there and I've been eating creamed chip beef."

"Man, that stuff's good!"

I didn't answer him.

"How can you not like creamed chip beef? In the wintertime?"

Suddenly I remembered my wallet. I looked at him. "Did you bring my wallet? It was in my pants."

"*Yeah*, I got it," he said. "It's all in the laundry bag."

"Good," I said.

"Man, don't you worry about nothing. I got you covered."

I looked at the clothes I was wearing again. "Just get me to the store," I said.

22 MR. DENTON

We passed Cottonlandia's driveway and in another quarter mile pulled up to Denton's store. It was a run-down house with old gas pumps out front. Hoyt came to a stop and yanked up the emergency brake.

"This is the crappiest store I've ever seen," I said.

"Man, that place is about a hundred years old," Hoyt said. "Probably one of the tenant houses your ancestors built."

"What's a tenant house?"

"Like where the workers lived."

"Like slaves?"

"Naw, you never had slaves. Your people came right after the Civil War. Had Indians, though. In the old days they helped worked this place."

"Indians?"

"Yeah! They been here for a thousand years. You can still find arrowheads in the fields."

"I thought they all left on the Trail of Tears."

"Not all of them. Some hid out in these swamps. They never left."

I frowned. "Whatever. I hope this store sells Cokes."

He shut off the engine. "What do you mean? They got everything. Come on."

The door had a bell that jingled. It was warm inside and smelled of grease and cedar and cigarette smoke. To my left was a sales counter connected to a glass-front meat cooler. In the center of the store, beneath a low, plywood ceiling, were three aisles boot-worn into the boards. Against the back wall, I saw a small collection of hardware items. On my right were two drink coolers, one for dairy and another with soft drinks. I saw a Coke logo and headed for it.

"Everybody's got *Cokes*," Hoyt said to himself as he approached the counter. "How you, Mr. Denton?"

The old man was probably in his midseventies, but it was hard to tell. His eyes were bright like a younger person, but his face was as wrinkled and dry as elephant hide. He gummed a soggy cigar.

"Afternoon, Hoyt. Who you got with you?"

"That's Win Canterbury. He's Mrs. Canterbury's grandson."

I tried to get my fingers around four plastic bottles of Coke while they talked about me.

"They dress like that in New York, son?" Mr. Denton said.

I ignored him.

"He wants a Coke," Hoyt said.

"I see that. Wants more than one."

I dropped three of them and bent down to try again.

"Wants them bad," the old man continued. "You need a bag, son?"

"Gimme a bag," Hoyt said.

In a moment he was helping me put the Cokes in the bag and then he held it while I put two more in. I started down the aisle. I found ravioli and put five cans in the bag.

"Good stuff," Hoyt said.

"I ate some at Headquarters that probably gave me tetanus," I said.

I dropped in pecan twirls, two boxes of honey buns, three tubes of Pringles, a loaf of white bread, a jar of mayonnaise, a jar of peanut butter, and a jar of jelly. When I got to the meat counter Mr. Denton was standing there waiting on me.

"You have steak?" I asked.

"Got rib eyes. New York strip if you're homesick."

"Man," Hoyt said to me, "you're going all out."

"Give me three rib eye," I challenged. "Cut them thick."

"Yes, sir," he said condescendingly, the cigar wagging in his mouth. I even thought I saw a slight grin.

"Rib eyes," Hoyt said. "Dang."

"And some ham," I said. "For sandwiches."

While I waited for him to cut the meat, Hoyt fished my wallet out of the garbage sack and handed it to me.

"I'll go next door and start this stuff in the coin laundry," he said.

He left me watching Mr. Denton pull a giant side of beef from the cooler and place it on the counter before him. He took his time unwrapping it and then sharpening a knife. He moved so slowly and deliberately as if he wanted to annoy me.

"Heard we had a missing person last night," he said to the meat.

They've been talking to him about me, I thought. *They're all against me.*

He glanced up. "Don't look like you're from New York City."

"He's washing my clothes," I said.

Mr. Denton grunted and went back to his work.

Screw all these people.

I heard a rumbling out front and looked to my left to see a red ATV pull up to the gas pumps. A girl in Bean boots, jeans, a sweatshirt, and a camouflage baseball cap got off and started to unscrew the gas cap. I couldn't see her face well enough to tell how old she was. Mr. Denton stopped what he was doing, walked to the register, and pressed a flashing button. Then he knocked on the window glass and the girl lifted the nozzle from the gas pump and waved at him. She looked to be about my age, and had a pretty, roundish face with shoulder-length blonde hair dropping back from the sides of the ball cap. Suddenly I had a mental image of myself with orange spots all over my face, dressed in the awful flip-flops and overalls and Camel jacket. I felt like the most conspicuous person in the state of Mississippi.

Mr. Denton took his time getting back to me. I tapped my foot. He positioned himself behind the meat counter again, glanced at me, and began wrapping the beef.

The door jingled and I felt my nerves jump. I was relieved when I saw it was just Hoyt. He hurried over and stood beside me and jammed his hands in his pockets like it was the only way to keep them still. Mr. Denton pulled out the ham loaf and set it on the meat slicer.

"You see her out there?" Hoyt asked me.

I didn't look at him. "See who?" I said.

"He saw her," Mr. Denton said, flipping on the meat slicer. The machine hummed smoothly.

"Sikes Rhodes," he said. "That's your neighbor."

"I haven't seen any other houses," I said.

"Well, neighbor around here might mean you live two miles away. Her family's place borders up to yours."

The cigar wagged in Mr. Denton's mouth, and he started pushing the ham back and forth on the slicer, clean shavings falling onto a square of wax paper.

"Now if I was your age," Hoyt continued, "I think I'd get to know my neighbors."

I felt heat rush to my face. Then I heard the doorbell jingle, and a small panic coursed through me.

"Hi, Mr. Denton," she said.

I couldn't look at her.

"Afternoon, Sikes," he said. "Be with you in a second."

She went to the dairy cooler, grabbed a half gallon of milk, and brought it to the counter. Mr. Denton was finished cutting the ham and folded up the sides of the wax paper, taping it with masking tape. He seemed to move a little faster now, his fun with me over. He took the packages of meat and started with them toward the register.

Hoyt nudged me forward. "Come on, man. I'll introduce you."

"That's OK," I said, resisting.

He nudged me again. "Don't worry about it. She's cool."

"Time to settle up, son," Mr. Denton called to me. He was standing near the register, across the counter from Sikes, both of them watching me. I took a deep breath and started toward them.

23 SIKES

"Sikes," Hoyt said. "This is Win Canterbury, your new neighbor."

"Hey, Win." She smiled.

I glanced at her. "Hey," I said.

Her eyes were on my face, but I felt them all over me, taking in how ridiculous I looked. I turned away to Mr. Denton. He was going through my bag of groceries and tapping on the register keys. It seemed he was moving slowly again.

"I heard you were moving here," she said.

"We'll see," I said.

"Heard you shot a buck a few days ago."

"Yeah," I said.

"Nine-point," Hoyt said.

"That's a big buck," Sikes said.

I nodded. Mr. Denton stopped his pecking. "Let's see, young man. Looks like the total comes to seventy-two dollars and eighty-five cents."

"You got mine?" Sikes asked him.

"You're good, young lady. I'll put that and the gas on your account. Tell your parents I said hello."

"OK. See y'all later."

I glanced at her just as she was turning away. Then she was out the door and gone.

"Got to teach you how to work the ladies," Hoyt said.

I got out my wallet and pulled out two hundred-dollar bills by mistake. I separated them and stuffed one back.

"Dang, boy!" Hoyt said. "How much money you got?"

"I've still got my allowance from last week."

Mr. Denton gave me change, but in my confusion I'd already put my wallet away. I just took it all in my fist and shoved the bills and coins into my front pocket. Mr. Denton slowly wagged his cigar with a smile at the corner of his mouth.

I grabbed the grocery bags off the counter. "Let's get out of here," I said.

"What about the laundry?"

"Just take me back to Headquarters."

Hoyt dropped me off at the house and told me he'd bring my laundry when it was done.

"Just call me if you need anything else," he said. "Gert's got my number."

I went inside with my groceries, closed the door behind me, and breathed in the dreadful smells and silence of the place. I walked my bags into the kitchen, feeling like Gert was waiting somewhere in ambush to laugh at me, but the kitchen was empty. I put the Cokes and steaks into the refrigerator and left the rest of the items on the counter. Then I took a Coke and a tin of Pringles upstairs and shut myself away in my room. It felt like a jail cell, but at least I didn't have to deal with anybody.

Gert had already cleaned the mud from the carpet and changed my bedding. I kicked away the flip-flops, yanked off the Camel jacket, and stepped out of the overalls. I unclipped the clothespin from dead Uncle Carl's grippies, let them fall to the floor, and flipped them under the dresser with my foot. Then I inspected myself for any strange rashes. Satisfied I hadn't caught anything, I put on my own clothes and lay on my bed, listening to Evil tick away my prison sentence.

When I heard heavy footsteps coming upstairs, daylight was fading. In a moment there was a knock at my door.

"What?" I said.

The doorknob turned, and the farmer stood there holding my cleaned and folded clothes. "Mind if I come in?" he said.

"No," I said.

He came across the floor, set the clothes on my bed, and sat in the chair against the wall. He studied me for a moment. "I'm sorry about what's happened," he said.

I didn't respond.

"I don't know what I can tell you that'll make you feel better except that you're gonna be OK. But you've got a lot of getting used to in front of you."

"I don't see how it's possible they can just leave me here," I said.

"They've got no choice."

"Do you know how I can talk to him?"

"Yes."

"What about Mom?"

"I'll give you her number when you're ready for it."

"I'm ready now."

"I'll decide when you're ready. You're not gonna call up there and fuss and get her all worked up. As far as she knows, you love it here."

"She knows better."

"Not from you, she doesn't."

I frowned and faced the ceiling.

"Your dad has a new cell phone," the farmer continued. "I'll give you that number."

"Why isn't he here with me?"

"He's going to be working with lawyers until the trial. It's better for everybody that he's up there doing what he can for himself."

I sat and swung my legs over the edge of the bed and faced the farmer. "What about school? Where will I go? How will I even get there?"

"There's a school bus that comes by every morning at six thirty. It'll take you to Greenwood High. I'll enroll you tomorrow."

"School bus?"

"That's right."

"It's a public school?"

"Yes."

I took a deep breath. "What about my allowance? Who's going to give me my allowance?"

"Allowance for what?"

"For whatever. For what I want."

"How much do you need?"

"I usually get three hundred dollars a week."

"Kid, you got to put the pieces together here. There's no more money where that came from. Three hundred dollars a week is more than a lot of the field hands make. If you want that kind of money, you're going to have to get out there and earn it."

"I don't know how to earn money. I'm just a kid."

"Well, you're about to meet plenty of kids your age in Greenwood that can advise you on working weekends and summers. I think you'll pick it up fine."

"You like it that this happened to me, don't you? All of you think it's funny."

"Let me tell you something," he said. "I have never in my life enjoyed seeing anything suffer. We're all here to help and support you. It's up to you how many laughs you give people along the way."

I frowned and looked at the floor and didn't answer.

"So," he continued. "For the last part of this conversation I'm going to give you some advice. You've got a new program. You'll be miserable until you get on it."

I didn't respond.

"So we're gonna get started right now. Gert's not paid extra to clean up after you all the time. Pick those clothes off the floor and put them away. And next time you muddy this place up, I'll make sure you clean it yourself."

I didn't move.

"Get up," he said again.

I wanted to resist, but his powerful voice scared me. I slid to the floor and walked over and began picking up the clothes Hoyt loaned me. I gathered them and put them on the bed.

"They're Hoyt's," I said.

"Fine. Fold them and I'll return them to him."

I began to fold them.

The farmer stood and walked across the room to the door. "You'll be expected to make your bed every morning and keep your room straight."

It seemed ridiculous to be folding Hoyt's clothes. I doubted they'd ever been anywhere but thrown in a corner.

"And there's something under that dresser. Get that too."

I didn't answer.

"Did you hear me?"

"Yeah."

"Yes, sir," he corrected.

"Yes, sir," I said.

"When you're done, come downstairs. I brought some burgers for Gert to cook."

"I've got steak."

"Not tonight, you don't."

24 PRISON

Prison. Complete with a stern warden, a lipstick skeleton, and a wispy, Black ghost. I passed Gert at the top of the stairs, retrieving Grandmother's supper dishes. I hadn't even heard her bring them.

"Welcome back, Win," she said.

I didn't answer her.

I found the farmer in the kitchen writing on a small tablet. He tore out the page, put the tablet in his top shirt pocket, and gave me the slip of paper. "That's your dad's number," he said.

"Can I call it collect?"

"I suppose."

"The phone here—"

"I know," he said, as though he too had wrestled with the issue. "Let me know if you can't make it work."

Gert returned with a tray of dishes and the farmer took them from her and set them on the counter. Then he turned and got a package of meat out of the refrigerator and began unwrapping it.

"Set it down," Gert said. "I got it."

The farmer smiled and put it on the counter.

"I don't like men in my kitchen while I'm working," she said. "Getting in my way."

"Sorry about that, Gert. I'm gonna go sit down."

"That's right," she said. "Go sit down with Win. I don't *mind* you keeping me company."

The farmer sat across from me while Gert started on the hamburgers.

"I'll run you into town tomorrow."

"What about a television?"

"Not gonna do you much good without a cable hookup."

"So no internet and no cable?"

The farmer raised his eyebrows and shrugged. "Not my house, son."

"I got rabbit ears on mine," Gert said. I looked over at her. The hamburgers were popping in grease, and she was moving them around in the skillet with a fork. They smelled good, and suddenly I was hungry. "You can come see mine some time, if you want."

I rolled my eyes.

"Hoyt's invited you to spend Christmas Eve with them," the farmer said. "He'll have the kids over. Might be a little more lively than here."

I realized I didn't even know what day it was. "When's that?"

"Tomorrow. We'll go into town and buy some clothes for you in the morning. Then I can come back and get you for the party that evening."

"I guess," I said. Christmas had never been much of a celebration around our penthouse in Manhattan. A small tree and a few presents. Sometimes Dad even worked Christmas Day. I mostly remembered hanging out with my friends in the afternoon, showing off our expensive toys.

"You can go with Gert to church the next morning."

"Church?"

"That's right," he said.

I frowned.

"And every Sunday morning after that," he continued.

We'd never been regular churchgoers. Dad was an Episcopalian, and Mom had converted from Methodism. On a good year we'd make service on Easter and Christmas morning, mostly because Mom insisted, but I didn't have the strength to fight the flood of unpleasantries washing over me.

"Cheese on yours?" Gert asked.

"Sure," I said.

"Yes, ma'am," the farmer corrected me.

I took a deep breath. "Yes, ma'am," I said. "Ketchup, too, please."

In moment she set a plate before each of us with a burger and a small pile of green beans. I picked up my burger and took a bite. As I chewed, I noticed a strange taste to the meat. It wasn't bad, but sort of like the first time you try a lamb chop.

I looked at the farmer. He was watching me.

"You like it?" he asked.

I lowered the burger to my plate. "What is it?"

"It's what you killed a couple of days ago. Eat up. There's about a year's supply where that came from."

25 THE PLAN

After supper the farmer left and I went back to my room. I waited until I heard Gert leave the kitchen for her house, and then I went downstairs, plugged in the phone, and pulled up a chair. It took me fifteen frustrating minutes of working with the operator before I was able to successfully place a collect call to Dad's new cell phone.

"Win?" I heard him finally say.

"Hey, Dad."

"How are you?"

I started to go into all the things I wanted to say to him, all the angry complaints I'd rehearsed and mumbled to myself over the past hour. But suddenly I couldn't remember them and he was so far away and it was all so useless. I felt a lump building in my throat.

I began to plead with him, tears rolling down my face. "I can't do this, Dad. I can't live here. Please send someone to come get me."

"Win, I don't feel qualified to give you advice about anything. I certainly don't expect you to *take* it from me at this point. But for what it's worth, you need to accept what's happened. It's the only way for any of us to get through this."

I sniffled and wiped my face with the back of my hand. "What's so wrong with Mom that she can't talk to me?"

"She's not herself. She needs some time alone, and you shouldn't take it personally. She knows you're OK."

"But I'm *not* OK."

"Win, I'm facing a prison sentence. Your mother's in a nursing home. All things considered, you're doing pretty well."

I wiped my face again. There was a long silence.

"Where are you?" I asked.

"I'm at home right now."

"By yourself?"

"Yes."

I couldn't think of anything else to say.

"John said he'd include you in their Christmas celebration," he said.

"Yeah, well, he didn't. He's sending me over to one of their farmhands that lives in a trailer."

"That must be Hoyt."

"Yeah," I said.

"Well, you need to start making friends."

I frowned at the floor.

"Win?"

"What?" I said.

"There's something else. It's complicated, and I was going to write you a letter about it once I had time to think about all the angles. About how it needs to happen."

"What?" I said.

"It's the farm. We've got to hold on to it."

"I thought you said they couldn't get it."

"If your grandmother dies, it all goes to me. Then they'll get it along with any money she might have saved up."

"So we have to sell it. Real quick."

"No, then I'll still inherit the cash and they'll get that. She's going to have to leave it to you in trust. Bypass me."

"What does that mean?"

"It means you'll own it, but someone else will be in charge of it for you."

"Like who?"

"I haven't thought about that. Usually a lawyer or an accountant. A third party."

"I can't sell it?"

"Not until you're eighteen."

"Then I can sell it?"

"Yes. And we'll get the income off the leases until then."

Suddenly I felt like he was on my side again. He'd been thinking about me after all. "Dad, she looks like she could die any day."

"She's been trying her best, but I doubt she's as close as she thinks. She's mostly just lying up there feeling sorry for herself."

"You've seen her!"

"Tell her to get up and walk around some."

"She's got tubes hooked up to her!"

"Listen to me, Win. Things aren't always what they seem."

"What do you mean?"

"Just believe me. Now, you've got to convince her to change her will."

"Why wouldn't she? I mean, if she knows we could lose it all."

"Believe me, she'll want to. If there's one thing that really could kill her, it'd be the thought of losing her family's cotton farm. That's why you don't ever want to talk about catfish farming or selling it around her."

"What about all this? Does she know you might go to jail?"

Dad hesitated. "Not yet. No."

"Why didn't you tell her yesterday?"

"I thought it might be better coming from you. I was hoping the two of you might be getting along."

Then it all hit me at once. "So that's the whole reason I'm here?" I said. "You knew this was going to happen? That the feds were going to come after you? That I would have to convince her to leave it all to me?"

"I didn't know for sure until the indictment."

"Why didn't you just tell me? I would have tried harder with her."

"Well, there was still a chance I could make it all go away. That I wouldn't get indicted. Then nobody except your mother would know anything."

"What if *that* kills her?"

"It won't kill her. It might embarrass her, but she cares more about the farm than she ever cared about me."

"So I'll just tell her. I'll tell her tomorrow. Then we'll still have money, Dad. How much is this place worth?"

"Enough. Three or four million, probably."

"I'll go wake her up right now!"

"Calm down, Win. It's not that easy. First of all, you've got to have the papers for her to sign and a lawyer to witness it. But here's the hard part. She's been lying up there telling people she was dying and couldn't do anything for herself for years. You—"

"Dad, she really looks like she is."

"Do dying people put on lipstick?"

I thought about it. I couldn't argue with him.

"That's right," Dad continued. "But she's got just about everybody else fooled. And a will changed by the hand of a dying person doesn't stand much of a chance in court. Especially when you're up against the feds. They'll argue it was coerced."

"So I have to get people to believe she's OK?"

"Yes. She's got to get up and get out and be seen."

"How do I even start, Dad? Do I just go in there and jerk the covers off her?"

"I think once you explain things to her, she'll be on board."

"But nothing about selling it or catfish farming?"

"Absolutely not. She's likely to give it all to charity just to spite us."

"OK," I said, feeling much better about everything.

"Hang in there, Win. We'll make it through."

"I'll talk to her tomorrow. I'll see if I can get her out of bed."

"Good. I'll be in touch."

"How?"

"Keep the phone plugged in."

I stopped outside Grandmother's door on the way back to my bedroom and stared at it. I imagined her in there with the reading lamp on, sitting up in bed, her bright, alert eyes browsing through *Southern Living* magazine. *How can she be OK? How can anyone that looks that close to being dead be OK?* And suddenly I wasn't feeling so good about things anymore. Maybe Dad was desperate? Maybe *he* was crazy? Maybe they're *all* crazy.

I lay in the darkness thinking about four million dollars. *Four million dollars.* I did the math. That was enough to get my allowance more than thirteen thousand times. *Thirteen thousand times! And how much was the lease money? Maybe I wouldn't have to work with the field hands after all?* It didn't matter how crazy Dad's plan sounded, it was the only option I knew of. And if it actually worked . . . we'd have plenty of money again.

"Get up, Granny," I mumbled at the darkness. "It's time to dance."

26 GRANDMOTHER'S RAGE

The next morning, I rose early, bathed, dressed, and went downstairs for breakfast; all the household inconveniences suddenly trivial and temporary. I found Gert in the kitchen stirring eggs.

"Well, aren't you chipper today, Win?"

I sat down at the table and leaned back in my chair. "So what's for breakfast?" I asked.

"Eggs, toast. I'll cook some bacon if you like."

"Sounds good. What's Grandmother having?"

Gert glanced at me with a funny look. "Eggs and toast," she said.

"I guess that's about all she can get down, sick as she is?"

She looked back at the skillet and kept stirring. "Ummm-huh," she said.

I watched her.

"I think I'll go see her this morning," I said.

"I'm sure she'd like that."

"I'll even take her breakfast to her."

"That's mighty kind of you, Win."

I kept watching her.

"You left the phone plugged in last night," she said.

"I know. Maybe we'll get a phone call."

"I unplugged it. You know, Mrs. Canterbury doesn't like to waste electricity."

"Seriously, Gert. How much electricity could a phone use? Maybe like a penny a day?"

"It all adds up."

"Look, if I'm going to live here, the phone's staying plugged in . . . I don't see how Grandmother's going to know anyway, sick as she is."

Gert frowned and shook her head.

"I mean, I'll bet it wouldn't even do any good for me to tell her that her son could be going to jail, and the feds are going to take this farm as soon as she dies."

Gert stopped stirring and turned to me. "What are you talking about, Win?"

"That's right. They're going to take this whole place over and sell it. Then we'll all be out of here. But I don't guess I should tell her about that, seeing as how she's about to die and it wouldn't matter anyway."

She kept staring at me, at a loss for words.

"Unless she's not really about to die," I continued. "Unless she's in good enough shape to change her will and everybody believes she knows what she's doing when she does it."

I smelled eggs burning, but Gert just kept watching me with her spatula in the air.

"But she's too sick, isn't she? Everybody knows she's lost her mind and on her deathbed."

Gert reached behind herself and turned off the stovetop, the smell of the eggs hanging in the air like burned skin. "You got something you need to tell me, Win?"

"I sure do," I said. "Have a seat."

I told Gert everything. Then I told her the plan. There was really nothing she could do except go along with it all. She knew it and I knew it. If Grandmother didn't change her will, we were both in trouble.

"It sure would be a shame if we didn't at least try, wouldn't it, Win?"

"It sure would, Gert."

"We ought to at least try," she said again.

"We should," I said. "And I'm going to. Let me take her breakfast up."

"I need to recook the eggs."

"Don't worry about it." I looked at the stove. "We've got to upset her a little bit."

Gert's eyes grew wide.

"A few bites of burned eggs can't hurt anybody."

"I can't do that, Win."

"It's OK," I said. "I'll take it to her. Go ahead and get the tray ready."

I started upstairs, carrying a tray with coffee, toast, and the burned eggs. Gert remained below, watching me from behind, wiping her hands on her apron, the first time I'd ever seen her nervous.

"I'll be up in a minute," she said.

I kept walking.

"She likes the napkin under her chin," she said.

"No problem," I said over my shoulder.

"I don't know about this, Win."

"Does she like the coffee poured in her mouth?"

"She uses the straw under the napkin."

"All right," I said.

"Make sure it's not too hot."

"OK."

I left Gert to her worries and crossed the floor to Grandmother's closed door. I set the tray down and knocked.

"Grandmother?" I said.

No answer.

"I'm coming in."

No answer. I turned the knob and cracked the door. Then I picked the tray up and pushed the door the rest of the way with my foot.

"Here's your breakfast," I announced.

She was lying there in the same position I had seen her last, like the bed was notched out for her. Her bright red lipstick was as fresh as wet paint. The oxygen machine hummed and clicked in the silence of the room. Her eyes followed me as I brought the tray around the side of the bed and set it on her lap. Then the eyes jerked over the tray and back at me again.

"You're such a sweet boy," she croaked.

"Yes, ma'am," I said. "I'm sorry it's been so long since I've visited. I've just had a lot going on."

She smiled weakly. I turned and got the chair from against the wall and pulled it up next to the bed. Before I had a chance to sit, I smelled the burnt eggs drifting over us. When I looked at her again, she was studying the tray, and I thought I detected a slight twitching in her eyes. I sat and reached for the napkin.

"Let's eat this before it gets cold," I said.

The eyes flipped to me again. I arranged the napkin under her chin and tucked it into her nightgown.

"Or would you like to start with coffee?"

She nodded slowly. "Yes, please," she said.

I stuck my finger into the steaming mug, twirled it a bit, then pulled it out and licked it. "Might still be a little too hot," I said. "Let's let it cool off a bit."

She watched my wet finger as it dropped back to the tray.

"You sure you don't want to start with the eggs? I'd hate for them to get cold."

She shook her head. "Coffee," she said.

I sat back in my chair and locked eyes with her. She knew I was up to something. And I was no longer scared of her. She was a pathetic, tricky old nightgown full of bones.

"Dad's been indicted for tax evasion," I said.

The eyes shimmered with questions.

"Mom's had a nervous breakdown, so it looks like I'm going to be here for a while."

"Tax evasion," she said.

"That's right. And he says he's guilty. As soon as he gets this place, the feds will take it too."

Her lips began to tremble.

"Unless you leave it to me."

I heard the spoon rattling on the tray.

"He says you can change your will, but it won't be legit as long as people think you're sick. The feds will say it was coerced."

The rattling of the spoon grew more intense, and I reached out and took the coffee off the tray and put it on her bedside table.

"How did he let this happen?" she said.

"It hasn't happened yet. But if you don't get out of bed and stop acting like you're dying, it *will* happen."

The eyes grew wet with anger. "He's ruined us," she spat. "How can he do this to me!"

"He says you're just lying up here feeling sorry for yourself. Get up and we can fix it all."

"I'm dying!" she screamed at my face. And it was the most awful scream I'd ever heard. It felt like tiny insects were chewing at the roots of every hair on the top of my head and back of my neck. Suddenly I was frightened of her again. I doubted she was trying to fool us at all. How could someone, something so awful looking really be faking it?

"Get out of here!" she screamed.

Out of the corner of my eye, I saw Gert rush into the room. Then the skeleton's knee popped up and the tray with everything on it came flying at me. The burned eggs hit my face and chest. The plate fell and shattered on the floor, and the rest clattered on top of it. I leaped from my chair and backed away, the eggs falling from me in clumps.

"You're all evil!" she screamed.

"Mrs. Canterbury!" Gert wailed.

"Get out! All of you!"

I stumbled over the breakfast tray and bolted from the room.

"What have you people done!" she screamed.

27 WALMART MAKEOVER

I was standing in the driveway, walking in circles, when the farmer arrived. He rolled up next to me and looked at me out the driver's-side window.

"Feeling OK?" he asked.

I nodded.

"You look like you've seen a ghost."

"I might have," I said.

He studied me for a moment, expressionless. "You ready to go into town?"

"Yes, sir."

"Well, get in."

We drove along in silence for a while, the farmer always looking over the fields, inspecting the dirt, smelling the weather. It was the nicest day we'd had since I'd arrived. I didn't think it was possible to have a completely blue sky in the delta, but there wasn't a cloud in sight. The temperature was in the upper sixties, and the air was still and dry.

"You think my grandmother's really about to die?" I asked him.

The farmer seemed to think about it for a moment. "That's hard to say."

"Dad says she's just up there feeling sorry for herself."

"I can't think of much she'd be excited about."

"But is she really about to *die?* What if it's just all in her head?"

"Sometimes being sick *is* all in your head. That doesn't make it any less real."

"Dad says we're going to lose the farm to the feds if she dies," I said.

"I'm sorry to hear that," he replied, but I could tell he wasn't sorry.

"If we lose the farm," I continued, "none of us will have anything."

He got out his tobacco and bit off a piece. He took his time replying. "Look, son," he finally said. "It doesn't much matter to me whether it's the feds or catfish farms or what have you. It's all the same to me. I've got one more season left on my lease, and I plan to farm it out just like I've done every year for forty years. We'll figure out what to do after that."

"You knew about the catfish?"

"Of course, I did."

"Well, dad's got an idea," I said. "An idea that might fix everything for us."

The farmer got the coffee cup and put it to his lips and returned it. I began to tell him about Dad's plan. When I was finished, he brought the cup to his lips again and replaced it again.

"You think it might work?" I asked.

"Anything *might* work."

"But I'm not sure Grandmother's not really as sick as she looks."

"I guess you'll just have to have that talk with her."

"I did. This morning."

The farmer looked at me for the first time in miles.

"She went crazy," I continued. "I've never heard anybody scream and yell like that. I thought she was about to jump out of bed at me."

The farmer smiled.

"I'm scared to go back in there," I said.

"Sounds like you've had quite a morning."

"I hope I didn't kill her."

"Well, at least you got her moving," he said.

"Dad says I've got to get her out of bed and walking around."

The farmer chuckled to himself. "This I've got to see."

"You want to help me?"

"Nope. But I'll be happy to watch."

I hoped he was kidding, but I could see he wasn't. During our conversation I hadn't been watching where we were going. We stopped at a red light, the first one in fifteen miles. There were actually cars waiting on the other side of the light and traffic moving through the intersection. To my left I saw the outskirts of Greenwood. Then we pulled through the light and the farmer took a left into a crowded Walmart parking lot.

"What are we doing here?" I asked.

"Getting your clothes."

"At Walmart?"

"You have another suggestion?"

I thought about it. I'd never shopped for my own clothes before. I knew most of them came from Brooks Brothers and Macy's and were mail-ordered from other places out of town.

"What else is there?" I asked.

"Nothing else. Not on Christmas Eve, anyway."

I'd never been to a Walmart. It was swarming with people, a complete shock after coming from the isolation of Cottonlandia. After trying several lanes of parking spaces, the farmer pulled the truck into a slot and turned off the ignition. Shopping carts rattled past and family herds shuffled on all sides of us.

"Where did all these people come from?" I asked.

"This place stays pretty busy," the farmer said, opening his door. "Let's go."

I was comfortable in crowds. It was actually the first thing I'd seen around here that reminded me of Manhattan. I wanted to duck and weave and push my way into the store, but the farmer kept stopping and letting people pass in front of us, waving cars by, greeting strangers, and excusing us. By the time we got to the front door, I was about to bust.

"Grab a cart," he said.

I saw the metal shopping carts in a corral to my left, yanked one free, and pushed it ahead of us.

"Let's ask this young lady here where the men's clothes are," he said.

"We'll find them," I said. "Come on."

The farmer hesitated, then fell in behind me. It didn't take me long to find the men's clothes under a giant poster of a cowboy leaning against a fence in his blue jeans. I left the cart and began walking the aisles, studying the clothing lines.

"I've never heard of any of this," I said.

"I imagine they have different fashions down here," he said.

I looked at him. He almost smiled. "Funny," I said.

"Make sure you get some blue jeans," he said. "And some practical work pants."

"What are practical work pants?"

"I like the Dickies, myself."

"Dickies?"

The farmer looked at the clothes racks like he might see some. Then a Walmart worker in a wheelchair pulled up beside us. "Can I help you?" she asked.

"Yes, ma'am," the farmer said. "This boy here needs to get outfitted. Needs some school clothes and some farm clothes. Something to wear to church. Maybe something to hunt in."

She was an overweight and cross-eyed redhead. Her ankles were thick and flaky dry, with feet stuffed into what appeared to be bedroom slippers. It didn't look like she'd walked in years, if ever. She certainly wasn't my idea of a fashion consultant.

"Certainly," she said eagerly. "The hunting clothes are in the sporting goods section, but I can help you with what all the cool kids are wearing these days."

I couldn't imagine her knowing anything about being cool.

"I've got church clothes already," I said.

"OK, then," she said, wheeling over to the next aisle. "Here's a popular line by Boys Town. All the kids like it for school."

A group of kids blocked our way, holding their pants up with one hand and picking through the racks with the other.

"Do you just have some normal jeans I don't have to hold up?"

"Sure," she said, leading us to another section. "Everybody loves the Hot Saddle brand."

She took us to a shelf of jeans and pulled off a pair and held it out to me. It had a saddle with an orange flame on the back pocket. I didn't know enough about jeans to determine quality. Anything except Levi's was all the same.

I frowned doubtfully. "Fine," I said. "Let me try some on."

"They're on sale. Nine ninety-nine."

"Fine."

They were a bit tight in the rear, but I found the size that fit me best, came out of the dressing room, and told her to put six pairs in my cart. Then we went to the shirts. I didn't see anything like what my friends in New York wore, and I was growing impatient. I realized being picky was hopeless. In addition, I had no desire to make friends or impress anyone. I settled on a few button-down, solid-color shirts by Gentlemen's Club. Then I threw in some socks and underwear and several pair of Dickies work pants at the farmer's suggestion.

"Shoes?" she asked.

"I guess," I said. My Cole Haans were stained and briar-torn.

We went to the shoe section, and she helped me pick out some new oxfords.

"Is this leather?" I asked.

"I think so," she said.

It felt like plastic, but I tossed them in the cart anyway. Then I found a pair of Super Foot tennis shoes that fit and threw them in as well. "I've never heard of any of this," I said.

"Oh, all the kids wear Super Foot," she said. "It's the latest thing."

We left her in the shoe section and headed for sporting goods. I got a hunting hat and some overalls like Hoyt loaned me, except my own size. Then I found some hunting boots that looked a little more comfortable than the rubber gum boots and tossed them in the cart.

"Hard to beat a good pair of gum boots," the farmer warned.

"It's not hard to beat any of this," I said.

"Suit yourself," he said.

We made it back to the checkout line and waited ten minutes just to reach the cashier. I piled it all on the belt and after she ran it through and bagged it, the total price tag came to $178.

I looked at the farmer.

"Get out your wallet," he said.

"Serious! You want me to pay for all this stuff?"

"Why shouldn't you?"

"That's almost all the money I have left," I said.

"Why should I pay for your clothes?"

"Because it's the last of my allowance money."

"It'll spend the same."

I stood there with my mouth open in disbelief. The farmer was as moveable as a boulder. I shook my head and got out my wallet and gave her my last hundred dollar bills. She gave back my meager change, and I put it away weakly. Now, on top of everything else, I was nearly broke.

28 GERT'S HOUSE

We rode back from Walmart in silence, the tires humming on the flat, straight, two-lane blacktop through the farmland. I didn't want to look at the farmer. I stared out the window at dark fields and giant, silver grain bins and far tree lines. But I didn't really see any of it. My head was overloaded with injustices I felt no defense against.

As we drew closer to Cottonlandia, all my smoldering anger was extinguished by images of my awful, screaming grandmother and an overwhelming sense that it would be impossible for me to get her out of bed. I doubted I even had the courage to try again. A pall of lonely hopelessness fell over me. As much as I disliked the farmer, he was all I had to talk to.

"You think the idea about getting Grandmother out of bed is stupid?"

"I wouldn't call it stupid," he said. "I can see the reasoning behind it."

"What would make her happy?"

The farmer looked at me. "Now that's an interesting thought, Win."

"What do you mean?"

"Why, if you stopped thinking about yourself so much and thought about how *she* might feel, maybe you'd have an easier time with this."

"I'm the one that's getting screwed here," I said. "Everybody else is just doing what they've always done."

The farmer didn't answer me.

"What can *I* do to make her happy?" I asked.

The farmer slowed and turned off the highway onto the Cottonlandia road.

"Maybe nothing," he said. "Maybe it's just too late."

"Well, what do you think she wants?"

"I think she'd like to see the place appreciated. I think she'd like to be assured her family's not going to sell over a hundred years of blood and sweat and heritage."

"But nobody wants to live here anymore."

The farmer spit into his cup. "So maybe what she wants is impossible," he said. "But if you want to know what might make her happy, that's what she'd like to hear."

I frowned and looked out the window at the old church as we passed it on the right.

"Take that place, for instance," the farmer said. "The siding is rotten. Got parts of the roof missing shingles. Nobody's painted it in decades. I predict it'll be beyond repair in three more years. Headed back to the mud like most everything else."

"Why don't the people that use it fix it up?"

"These people don't have much money. And what they do have they'd rather put into a church they knew wasn't going to get sold and bulldozed."

I didn't respond.

"Your great-great-grandfather built it. Every Sunday it was the center of activity for all the field hands and their families. These people had a hard life during the week. Sundays at that church were happiness for them. That's why it sits out here in plain sight. It gave them hope. Hope for happiness."

Now it was the most depressing church I'd ever seen.

"Well, this place *will* get bulldozed if she doesn't stop acting like she's dying. That should be enough for her."

The farmer let out a sigh of exasperation. "I don't know, Win. Sometimes people just don't have the energy for it all anymore."

"I've got no choice," I said. "I've got to try to get her to give me this place."

"Yeah," he said. "I suppose you do."

After the farmer dropped me off, I stood before the house, dangling my Walmart bags, staring at the front door. After a moment I took a deep breath and stepped inside.

It was quieter than usual. It took me a moment to figure out the heaters were off for the first time since I'd been there. Now there was absolutely no sound to the place. I looked up the stairs and imagined Grandmother waiting for me, ready to pounce and claw at me with her bony talons. I set my bags against the wall and went into the kitchen to get something for lunch.

After a quick sandwich, I went out the kitchen door and crossed the yard to Gert's house. Along the way I passed the old storm cellar and made a note to explore it later. Then I looked at the shed to my right and remembered the ATV the farmer had promised me, and a small spark of hope flicked deep in the recesses of my despair.

I went up Gert's cinderblock steps and through a flimsy screen door and under the low, whitewashed eave of wide, cypress planks. Brown, canvaslike drapes were pulled across the windows, and it was impossible for me to imagine what I was about to find inside. I knocked.

Gert opened the front door. Her hair was no longer tied tightly in a bun, but sprung loose in thin, stiff, gray hairs. It was the first time I'd ever seen her without her apron on, but the pine straw was still in her ears.

"Come inside," she said wearily.

The room smelled of bacon grease and wood smoke. Shag carpet covered the floor. The ceiling was made of the same wide, painted cypress planks. I imagined the walls were, too, but they were covered with flowery wallpaper. The structure was not just one room as I'd suspected, but two. Where I stood served as the bedroom, kitchen, and living room. Beyond was a smaller bathroom. A pot of something boiled on the stovetop, and Gert went to tend it.

"Have a seat," she said over her shoulder.

In the corner was a single armchair facing a wall and an ancient-looking television. I turned the chair around to face Gert and sat in it.

"You shouldn't have done that this morning, Win," she said.

"You did it too," I said.

"We're lucky she didn't kill herself."

"Can I go back up there?"

Gert took a deep breath and shook her head. "I suppose. I hope she's asleep."

"Me too. Did she say anything about losing the farm? You think she even understands it?"

"She understands."

"Can we get her to start acting normal?"

"You can't make Mrs. Canterbury do anything. She's been stubborn her whole life. Most stubborn person I've ever known."

"Is there anything *really* wrong with her? I mean, does she have Alzheimer's or anything?"

"She ain't seen a doctor in years."

"But *you* know."

"I can't go through that again, Win. In all my years I've never seen her act like that. Next time you want to make mischief, make sure I'm not in the house. You're on your own."

I frowned.

"Took me an hour to get her settled down and cleaned up. All that time she's hitting at me and calling me names."

"She went crazy. I didn't think she'd do that."

Gert shook her head and continued to stir the pot. "Unh, unh, unh," she said to herself.

I stood up again. "I've got to think of something," I said.

"Fine," she replied. "But I ain't got nothing to do with it. *Whatever* it is."

I turned and looked at the television again. "You say this works?"

"I get a few channels. Black-and-white."

"I haven't seen a TV in almost a week."

"My husband, Wesley, bought that for me on our fiftieth anniversary." She chuckled. "He watched it more than me. I think he bought it for himself."

I turned back to her. "What happened to him?"

"Cancer. Ten years ago. He was a good man."

"What did he do?"

"Farmed. He helped Mr. Case. And your great-great-grandaddy before that."

Gert tapped the stirring spoon against the pot. I could tell she was still running through memories of Wesley.

"Did you have kids?"

She shook her head. "No kids. We had a happy life, just the two of us."

"Well," I said. "I guess it's OK to go up to my room, then. I've got a bunch of new clothes I need to put away."

She faced me, wiping her hands on a dishrag. "I don't suppose you'll be needing supper tonight."

"No. I'm headed over to Hoyt's house for the Christmas party."

"I know," she said. "Good Lord."

"What?"

"Talk about mischief."

"I can't imagine Hoyt causing any trouble."

"Not on purpose, he don't."

I waited for her to explain, but she didn't. She turned back to the stovetop.

"Well," I said. "I'll be all right. See you later."

"See you later, Win."

29 HOYT'S CHRISTMAS EVE PARTY

The farmer returned to pick me up at five o'clock to take me to the Christmas party. I wore Hot Saddle jeans, one of the Gentlemen's Club shirts, Super Foot tennis shoes, and my light jacket. His eyes looked me over through the truck window, but he remained expressionless.

"You just gonna show up like that?"

I held my hands out, palm up. "Like what? You saw what I bought today. She said it's what everybody wears around here."

"Somebody's having you over for a dinner party and you don't bring anything?"

"What? What am I supposed to bring?"

"Well, seeing as how you don't cook and you're too young to take a bottle of wine, maybe they'd appreciate those rib eye steaks."

"Why should I give him my steaks?"

"Maybe because he spent all night in the freezing rain looking for you and putting you up at his house."

I looked at the ground, starting to feel boxed in by the farmer again. Feeling the frustration of it burn in my cheeks.

"You've got plenty of deer meat left," he continued. "I've cut some of it into steaks for you."

I frowned.

"Go on," he said. "It's the right thing to do. And you oughta know it."

We took the back road out of the farm, past the tractor sheds, and onto one of the old blacktop roads I'd become used to seeing, the asphalt worn away from the gravel and the edges broken off and lying in the yellow grass. There was no center line, and the farmer drove in the middle with one wrist flopped over the steering wheel, the truck tires humming smoothly.

"Whatever you paid for those steaks," he said, "you'll get back tenfold from Hoyt."

It was hard to imagine Hoyt having anything to offer me. I looked out the window at the sun setting over a field of corn stubble. A flock of what must have been three hundred blackbirds rose and fell as one connected system, heading for the trees to roost.

"This party might not be the kind you're used to, but they're good people. People you need to know if you're gonna be living here."

I sat up straight and looked at him. "I'm still trying to work that out," I said.

"And I wish you luck, son. But I don't see any immediate relief headed your way."

I stared ahead. "We'll see," I said.

When we pulled in front of the trailer, a crowd was gathered in the small yard. They were backed up to the blacktop, watching Hoyt on the roof, attaching a rack of four floodlights to the television antenna. A cord of Christmas lights was already strung around the mobile home like a saggy belt of beads on a fat lady.

I counted two women, a man, and three kids between six and ten years old standing on the dirt. Despite clear skies, all three kids were strangely dressed in rain gear. In addition to Hoyt's truck, a red Dodge Neon and another small, black Chevy pickup had dropped off the blacktop and parked in the yard at no particular angle.

The farmer stopped in the road and put his truck in park. Hoyt turned, waved, and bent to his work again. The farmer studied him on the roof.

"What's he doing?" I asked.

"Lord knows," the farmer said. He shook his head and turned to me. "Hoyt says they'll drop you off later."

"OK," I said.

I got out with my bag of steaks and stood on the asphalt as the farmer pulled away.

"Come on, Win!" Hoyt yelled out to me.

The rest of the people looked at me for the first time, then turned back to the show. I stepped down into the yard and approached them.

"Get the cord, Bubba!" Hoyt yelled.

Bubba was about eighteen or nineteen, short and thin, looking much like a younger Hoyt. He stepped out of the crowd and slung a coil of extension cord up to his father. Hoyt caught it, kneeled, and plugged up the lights. They came on, but they were shining behind the trailer.

"Go check it out!" he said, but the three younger children were already squealing with delight, running around to the backyard.

"Now, you come down from there," the older of the two women demanded. I assumed this was Tammy, even though she probably weighed three times as much as Hoyt and it was hard to imagine them as a couple. Then I remembered she was the one who stripped me naked when I was like a floppy noodle and then put me into dead Uncle Carl's grippies. I didn't want to meet her.

"I'm coming," Hoyt said as he scrambled to the edge of the roof.

"Bubba, go hold the ladder for him," Tammy said.

Bubba looked like Hoyt, but he didn't move as quickly. He moved at the speed of a normal person. By the time he was able to grab the extension ladder, Hoyt was already banging down it and halfway to the ground.

The other woman turned to me. She was probably in her midtwenties and had her hands resting on her pregnant belly like she was holding the baby in. "Hoyt's gonna die one of these days," she said to me.

Tammy turned and looked at me, her lips pursed in disapproval.

"He's been keeled like four times already," she said.

"He has?"

"Electrocuted and drowned and throwed through the windshield."

I didn't know what to say to that.

Hoyt rushed up and turned to admire his work. "We get all fixed up for Christmas," he said.

"I see," I said.

"I better go watch the kids," Bubba said, walking away.

Hoyt turned to me. His eyes shot down to the sack. "Man, you didn't have to bring nothing," he said.

"I got those rib eyes," I said. "You can cook them if you want."

"You got to be kidding me! Tammy, you oughta see them rib eyes! Like two inches thick!"

She reached out for them, and I turned them over to her, seeing the last of anything I had to look forward to eating ending up with Hoyt. "I'll put them inside," she said.

I heard an engine crank in the backyard. "Come on," Hoyt said. "We're going for a sleigh ride."

"What?" I asked.

"You don't wanna know," the pregnant girl warned. "Something he came up with for the kids."

"Came up with for hisself," Tammy grumbled.

But Hoyt was already fast-stepping away. "Come on, everybody," he said.

30 DIRT SLED

Hoyt's floodlights had the yellow-grass backyard lit up clear to the trees, where the eyes of the barking coon dogs bounced and glowed at us from the dark wall. An ATV was idling; it looked a lot like the one at Headquarters. About fifty feet behind it, all the kids were piled onto a queen-size mattress. Then I noticed the mattress was harnessed and tied to the back of the ATV.

"They're ready for you, Dad," Bubba said.

"Come on, Poppy!" one of them yelled.

"I'm coming, kids!" Hoyt shouted.

"No running them up in the ditch or the woods," Tammy said.

Hoyt was already throwing a leg over the ATV and didn't seem to hear her. Suddenly he turned back to me. "Go get on there," he said, eyes dancing with mischief.

"I'm OK," I said.

"It's pretty fun," Bubba said casually.

"I'll just watch," I said.

"GO, POPPY!" the kids yelled.

"You'll see," Hoyt warned. "You'll be raring to go when we get back."

He popped the machine into gear and tore out across the yard. There was a little slack in the rope, and once it snapped tight, the ATV came up on its back wheels, roared at the night, and Hoyt rode it down like a bronco.

"*Yeee-hahhh!*" he yelled.

The mattress would have been jerked out from under the kids had they not been prepared. Each of their little hands were white-knuckled on the harness ropes. They'd obviously done this before.

"Is he drunk?" I asked Bubba.

Bubba stared after them, unmoved. "Naw," he said, "he don't drink. They do this all the time. He calls it something different depending on what time of year it is. Waterskiin', Magic Carpet, Sleigh Ride, Summer Sled, Dirt Boat."

"At night?"

Bubba thought about it. "Naw, not usually at night."

Somewhere out in the dark field, we heard Hoyt make a wide, engine-racing circle. After a couple of minutes, the ATV appeared out of the darkness and passed in front of us going at what must have been twenty miles per hour. He stared straight ahead like we weren't there, like he had some place in mind he had to get fast, a certain cockiness about his skills. Then he was gone into the darkness, and out of the night came the squealing mattress of kids, slipping and sliding and jerking, not as gentle a ride as you would expect. Then they, too, were gone, and it was just engine noise and screaming kids out in the fields somewhere.

"He gets pretty crazy on that thing," Bubba continued.

"But them kids love it," the pregnant woman added.

"Makes me need to take a dump," Tammy said.

"How?" Bubba said.

"All that shaking and bumping."

"You ain't never been on it," he argued.

"Who you think he tested it on?"

Bubba frowned.

"That's right," she said. "Took me on the circle of death or whatever hell it is he likes to do."

Bubba cracked a smile for the first time. "I'd like to have seen that, Momma."

Tammy turned and started toward the back door. "I bet you would have," she said over her shoulder. "I'm gonna get dinner going."

The ATV whined and groaned in the distance, overlaid by the sound of screaming kids.

"I'd get on there if I weren't pregnant," the woman said. "It looks like fun."

I assumed she was Bubba's wife. It suddenly struck me it was impossible for the kids to belong to him, or he would have been a father when he was less than ten years old.

"Whose kids are those?" I asked.

"They're mine and Tonya's," Bubba said.

"From my first husband," Tonya added.

"They're good kids," Bubba said. "Even if I do have whip they daddy's ass ever now and then."

"Bubba," Tonya warned.

"All right, all right," he said.

The sound of the ATV grew steadily louder, and I realized the kids were no longer screaming with delight. Then out of the night it came, tugging the mattress, shredded, soggy, and covered in mud. I realized now why the kids wore rain gear. Hoyt came to a stop and craned his head around.

"Wooo-wee!" he yelled. "Santa ain't got nothing on Poppy! What you say, kids?"

The kids came slowly to their knees and wiped uselessly at the mud on their jackets. Then they rolled off the mattress, crawled a few feet, and stood up dizzily, dripping.

"That was fun, Poppy," the youngest girl said.

"I don't like the circle of death," the boy said.

"Let's go again," the oldest girl said.

"We got to let the company go," Hoyt said. "Come on, Win!" he called out.

"I don't have a rain jacket," I argued.

"Bubba, go get him your rain jacket."

"I don't think I want to—"

"You'll be all right," Bubba said, turning to go. "He won't leave you alone until you do it."

It seemed my ride on the crazy mattress was inevitable. Bubba left to get the rain gear while I watched the kids shucking out of their own and flinging them before the back steps.

"It's already wet, too," Tonya said. "It won't go as fast."

The back door opened, and Tammy inspected the scene. "Come help me clean these kids up, Tonya," she said. "They ain't about to track mud all through this house."

Bubba reappeared with a yellow, rubber jumpsuit that looked like something you'd wear to clean a toxic waste dump.

"I don't know about this," I said to him.

He unzipped it and held a leg out for me to step into. "You'll live," he said. "Just one of those things you've got to do."

I began stepping into the suit, like my body was convinced to go but my head wasn't.

"I've never heard of *anybody* having to do anything like this," I said.

But there were no gray areas in life for Bubba. It was all black and white. All facts. "Just got to do it," he said again. He helped me into the arms, zipped it up, and rolled up the cuffs and sleeves. "Don't forget about the hood."

Hoyt raced the ATV engine a couple of times. "Come on!" he called out. "I invented it."

I walked to the mattress and kneeled on the wet, muddy thing.

"Grab the rope!" he said.

I walked on my knees to the harness ropes. What he'd done was shove a piece of rebar through the mattress about a foot from the front. About six inches of the steel rod poked out of each side, and he'd bent it into loops. The rope was tied to the loops and joined about five feet out to form a harness. Another rope was tied across the top of the mattress. This was what I was supposed to hold on to.

As soon as I grabbed the handles, it was like an electric signal had been sent up the rope to Hoyt. The ATV leaped forward and yanked me flat on my stomach. I saw Hoyt, up on two wheels, stand on the foot pegs and lean forward; the machine wound out, straining against what held it. Then I felt slow, steady movement, the grass folding before my face. The front of the ATV muscled its front wheels to the ground, and we began to pick up speed. In a moment I was out of the floodlights and riding in complete darkness somewhere behind the ATV noise ahead of me.

"This is so stupid," I muttered.

At first the ride was gentle. A soft bump every now and then, the grass making a swishing sound beneath me. Two or three times a stick broke against the edge. It wasn't until I heard Hoyt yell, "Hang on!" that things started to get serious. I didn't know if we were about to hit a ramp, slam into something, speed up; the only indicator I had was the increase or decrease in the grass swishing. Then I saw the ATV lights swing back toward me and heard its engine wound out with everything it had, chewing and throwing mud. I sensed a strange pull on the mattress and noticed I was hanging on tighter with my right hand. Once the centrifugal force hit me, I realized I was going sideways.

"Circle of death!" Hoyt yelled out.

I put my cheek to the cloth and hung on as the ATV twirled me in a circle. Mud began hitting me like a giant hail of soft turds. As soon as I felt a big clot smack into my mouth, I used one hand to quickly swipe the hood over my head and hide my face in the mattress.

For a moment I was convinced holding on and getting covered with mud were the only challenges I was up against. I was convinced it was possible I could make it through. Then the mattress slammed up against a berm and jounced me over a giant washboard of field rows, flapping my entire body against the cloth. Then there was a crashing of sticks and debris, and it felt like the biggest, stiffest broom in the world was brushing and tearing the clothes from my back. I thought of riding on top of a car through a car wash. When I hit the field rows again, I clenched my teeth against it all and prayed for the circle of death.

I just wanted it to stop. The only thought in my head that wasn't shaken to pieces was the word STOP! It seemed the ride would never stop. The grass kept swishing and the mud kept piling on.

Eventually I was yanked up a small incline and heard a crunching, gravely, then humming, sanding sound. We were on the blacktop. I pulled my face from the mattress and looked, taking deep breaths of relief. Just ahead I saw the lights of Hoyt's trailer. It was the first opportunity I had to form any kind of sentence in my head.

Please let it be over, I thought.

And it almost was. I saw the ATV lights dive off the road into the front yard. I came after it, down the embankment and past the windows of the trailer. Suddenly I heard a tearing sound and the mattress was instantly gone from under me. I hit the ground and started rolling. When I came to rest, I lay staring up at the stars, a ringing in my ears, my body numb. I had time to connect the dots on a constellation before I heard someone talking to me.

"You OK, man?" I heard someone say.

Hoyt came into focus, standing over me.

"What'd you think?" he persisted.

I couldn't form any words.

"Awesome, ain't it?"

He grabbed my hand and pulled me up. I felt queasy. Everything slowly came into focus. In the distance I saw Bubba coiling the rope. The mattress lay behind him, now nothing but cotton and springs.

"Man," Hoyt continued, "you rode it like a pro! We jerked the britches off that sum-bitch!"

31 CHRISTMAS DAY

We ate my rib eyes for their Christmas Eve party. There wasn't enough for everyone, so we combined the steaks with hamburgers. A side of macaroni and cheese and something that looked like spinach completed the meal. It was all served on paper plates with plastic utensils. The adults, including Bubba, ate at the kitchen table while I ate sitting cross-legged on the floor with the kids. Fortunately, there was a television in front of us. I picked at my steak piece and watched a cartoon I'd never heard of. It wouldn't have mattered what was on. Even though I'd craved television for a week, I could barely pay attention. A weariness crept over me, spreading from my legs up into my arms and into my face to the point that it was hard to even chew. I put my fork down and leaned against the sofa behind me.

"You don't like those collard greens?" I heard Hoyt say.

I looked at him. "What?"

"You didn't hardly eat nothing."

"I ate some steak. I'm not really hungry."

"I grew those collards," he said proudly.

I looked at the boiled, spinachlike leaves on my plate. I felt too tired to have a conversation, but I forced a little more. "I've never seen it before," I said. "I don't know anything about them."

Hoyt said something else but everyone's voices seemed to be fading into the background. I stared at the television again, trying to keep my eyes open. In a moment Tonya bent before me and took my plate away. I heard the back door open, and all the kids were suddenly stampeding toward it. Then Tammy sat on the sofa behind me and swung her legs up and sighed.

"You watching this?" she asked.

I shook my head.

She held out the remote control and changed channels until she came to some sitcom I'd never seen before. It didn't matter. I heard the sink running and pots tinking and clattering.

"Come sit down, Tonya," she said. "You don't need to be doing that."

"I ain't doing nothing," she said. "Hoyt's got it. I'm about to go outside with Bubba and the kids."

The back door opened, and I heard the kids screaming until it closed. In a moment the sink stopped, and Hoyt came over and sat on the sofa with Tammy. I saw a chair cushion one of the kids had left on the floor and scooted over to it and lay on my back, using it for a pillow.

"One of these days, baby," I heard Hoyt say.

I looked over at them. He was stretched out on her with his eyes closed, the back of his head resting on her chest, and she was stroking his hair.

"Don't you worry about it," she said. "We got everything we need."

"Gonna sell some coon dogs," he mumbled. "Get ahead . . . Double-wide this place."

"We're doing just fine, hon," she said. "You go on to sleep."

He muttered something else I didn't understand. Tammy looked over at me. "He gets up at a hundred miles an hour, stays wound up all day, and drops back to zero in about five seconds."

Hoyt began to snore as she stroked his hair. I closed my eyes.

I woke up on Christmas morning in Bubba's bed with the sunlight coming yellow and bland through the cheap, plastic window shades. Someone moved around in the kitchen for a while; then I heard them pass by my closed door. A television came on at the far end of the trailer, where I assumed Hoyt and Tammy had their bedroom. I wasn't tired, but I was sore, and I could think of no reason to get up.

The next thing I heard was the front door opening and Hoyt yelling, "Merry Christmas!"

I didn't move.

In a moment I heard his feet coming down the hall, then a knock on my door.

"What?" I said.

He opened the door and stood there twitching like he'd had five Cokes to drink. "Merry Christmas!" he said again. "Come on, I got a present for you!"

I groaned.

"Let him sleep, Hoyt," came Tammy's voice.

Hoyt backed into the hall. "Mr. Case is on his way to get him for church," Hoyt said. "I got to start him moving."

She didn't answer.

"Come on!" he begged. "It's out in the truck."

Hoyt had the old ATV from Headquarters sitting on his truck bed. It looked much cleaner than I remembered.

"Does it work?"

"Shoot yeah, it works! All I had to do was clean out the carburetor, change the plugs, and put some new gas in it. Got a new battery. It'll paw all fours."

I approached the truck and peered in at it.

"I ran it through the car wash, got the wax and everything. Man, you're all set!"

I felt a pilot light of excitement against my foul mood. "How do you work it?"

"Nothing to it. Turn the key and push the button. It'll fire right up."

I kept looking it over. "Thanks," I said.

He stuck his hands in his pockets and rocked back and forth, watching me, beaming with pride. "Well, you know," he said. "It's Christmas and everything. Got to have something."

I heard the hum of tires on the blacktop and turned to see the farmer pulling off the road. He stopped before us and studied the ATV out the window.

"You get that thing going?" he asked Hoyt.

"There's nothing wrong with it," Hoyt exclaimed. "I bet old man Canterbury didn't have more than twenty hours on it."

The farmer looked at me. "You tell him thank you?"

"I told him," I said.

"Climb in. We've gotta get you back and dressed for church."

"Hey," Hoyt said, "I'll bring it over to the shed this afternoon. It'll be there, ready to go."

Going from the world of Hoyt to the farmer's truck was like stepping out of a rock concert into a school classroom. The freedom and noise and chaos were suddenly replaced by rules and silence and tension.

We traveled nearly a mile down the road before he finally spoke. "How was the party?" he asked.

But I didn't want to talk to him about the party. "I want to call my mother," I said.

"You're not ready to call your mother," he replied. "And she's not in a condition to talk to you."

We passed a small, brick church with a dirt parking lot full of cars. "Why do I have to go to church?" I asked him.

"Because one day you'll realize life's not all about you. And you'll want to know what to do about it."

"That doesn't make sense."

"One day it will."

I frowned and watched a mangy-looking dog slink along the roadside ditch, the hair on its back standing to the breeze.

"When does my school start?"

"You've got off until after New Year's. That'll be Wednesday after this."

I started to think about my first day of school, and it made me queasy. I felt the farmer looking at me.

"What?" I said.

He turned back to the road. "Nothing," he said.

The farmer followed me inside the house and said he'd wait in the kitchen until I cleaned up and changed.

"You're coming?"

"That's right," he said. "Then we're going to have Christmas lunch together. Then I'm headed back to my house to eat again with Diane."

I went upstairs and found myself creeping past Grandmother's room. Even though I knew it was impossible, I couldn't stop thinking about her coming after me like a giant bird. I dreaded the thought of having to talk to her again, but I knew I would have to eventually.

I slipped into my room, got my New York clothes, and went

down the hall to the bathroom. For a place with nothing to do, it sure seemed like I stayed busy.

32 DEACON LEON

When I came downstairs, I found Gert standing in the kitchen with the farmer. She wore a flower-print dress, a wide-brim, baby-blue plastic hat, and real loop earrings. The farmer was studying a water stain on the ceiling.

"I'll get Hoyt to check it out next week," he said to her. "Doesn't look like much."

"Not for this old place," she said.

The farmer turned to me. "Did you wish a merry Christmas to your grandmother?"

"Yes, sir," I lied. I'd actually thought about it, but I wasn't about to go in there again for a while.

"Good," the farmer said. "Let's load up."

He opened the passenger side door and ushered me onto the middle of the bench seat. Then Gert got in and he closed the door. On the drive out to the church, she rode straight-backed and proper like she was on a date. We exited the pecan grove and started the long drive through the fields. Nearly a mile ahead I saw the church on the left and the glint of cars around it like a mirage in the desert. As we drew closer, I estimated twenty-five vehicles in the parking lot. I wondered where all these people could have come from. Even the farmer seemed impressed.

"Must be the busiest day of the year for this place," he said.

"And I always say it's gonna be the last," Gert replied, stiff and dignified.

"Still got Deacon Leon?"

"He's still coming. We're lucky to have him."

"How many churches does he go to now?"

"Lord, I don't know, Mr. Case. He's pretty popular."

"He's got more than one church?" I asked.

"Some of these country churches don't have a large enough congregation to support a full-time preacher," the farmer said. "Deacon Leon makes the rounds to several on the weekends."

When we arrived, I noted most of the cars were older-model sedans. People chatted in the yard or made their way slowly into the building using canes and the support of their companions and even a couple of aluminum walkers. I saw no children. Almost everyone was at least the farmer's age, and most were women as old as Gert. All of them were Black. It was obvious who Deacon Leon was. He stood just outside the front door, looking to be in his late fifties, neat and tight and shiny in a crisp, white suit and gold chain hanging a cross on his chest the size of an Olympic medal. He greeted everyone with enthusiasm, clasping their frail hands between his own and leaning into their faces with appreciation. Behind him, parked right next to the church, was the only new-looking car in the lot, a long, white Cadillac with a license plate reading JESUS3. Besides me, the youngest member of the congregation that day was the woman who stood next to it. She didn't look much older than Bubba, waiting with a pasted-on smile like she'd already watched the same scene five times that morning. She had a fur coat pulled tightly around her shoulders and could have been mistaken for a movie star if it wasn't for her makeup and hair being overdone.

We parked and followed the last of the slow-moving bunch up the front steps. I looked over at the woman next to the Cadillac, and her smile quickly stretched and sprang back on itself. Deacon Leon seemed especially excited to see us and even skipped the older couple ahead of us in his eagerness to greet the farmer.

"How you doing, sir?" he said. "Been a long time, been a long time."

The farmer held out his hand to shake, nodded, and smiled.

The deacon pressed the hand between his own. "Praise the Lord," he said.

"How you doing, Deacon Leon?" the farmer said.

"Couldn't be more blessed, sir. I certainly couldn't be more blessed on this fine Christmas Day."

The farmer looked away and stepped into the dark recesses of the church. The deacon seemed hesitant to release his hand but turned back to Gert and me.

"How you, Mrs. Gertrude?"

"Good as I can be, Deacon Leon. So nice to see you again."

"Merry Christmas! And who's this young man you've got with you?"

"This is Mr. Canterbury's grandson, Win. He's come to live with us."

"Yes, ma'am, it certainly must be. I can tell just by looking at him. Praise God."

We made our way into the church. It smelled damp and rotten like the dirt of the fields, empty enough of the time so that human scent was missing. What light made it into the small room came filtered through orange and yellow windowpanes, a substitute for stained glass. It seemed colder inside the building than out. I saw four small, portable electric heaters along each wall, glowing and rattling. It seemed as if they'd just been put there that morning. They were about as effective as if they'd been outside.

If there had ever been real church pews, they were gone. Folding metal chairs were set in two columns, five chairs to a row. In all, there was seating for fifty people. We sat in the back row, and I counted about forty people.

Shortly after we seated ourselves, Deacon Leon came up the center aisle, his head bowed solemnly, mumbling a conversation between himself and God. The congregation ceased its whispers, and every eye in the church tracked him. Then his assistant closed the door and followed him. Every man in the room, even the farmer, shifted their gaze from Deacon Leon to the assistant. The way she moved was fluid and catlike. She made her way to the front of the room and sat in a chair against the wall, the only chair that faced back on the congregation.

Deacon Leon began talking about Jesus in the manger and that people came from all over to see him and bring him gifts. He reminded us Christmas was a time of giving in the same spirit the poor people gave to Jesus. They had little, but they gave what they could. The congregation began muttering some "amens."

"It was a time to fight the desire for material possessions!" the deacon shouted.

"Amen," Gert said.

"The devil put that desire in us! Time to fight the devil!"

"Amen!" they said.

Our eyes had gotten so acquainted to the assistant that we noticed instantly when she stood from her chair with a wicker basket and began slinking down the rows, holding the basket out. High on Deacon Leon's encouragement, people began to fish into their purses and pockets, pulling out bills and change. The farmer nudged me, and I reluctantly dug into my pocket and pulled out the last of my money. Seven dollars and fifty-three cents. When the assistant leaned over me, I found my face nearly in her bosoms and my hand dropping money in the basket. She started to lean into the farmer, but he was quick to drop some folded bills in and she withdrew. She kept on to the back of the church and disappeared out the door.

The deacon was calmer for the rest of the service. He went into a brief sermon about the weak overcoming the strong through faith, using David and Goliath as an example. Then suddenly he announced the service was over and blessed us all and started down the aisle. By the time I made it outside, his white Cadillac was nearly at the highway with a trail of dust settling behind it.

After church Gert made Christmas lunch for the three of us. Gert served us in the dining room on old china from a top shelf in the kitchen. It consisted of the same spinachlike leaves Hoyt had called collard greens, a small baked ham, and cornbread. The farmer said a blessing, and we all began to eat quietly. It wasn't long before I saw Hoyt's truck pull around the house with the ATV.

"Looks like you've got something to do this afternoon," the farmer said.

It suddenly occurred to me just how much freedom the ATV would afford.

"Where all can I go?"

"Anywhere you want except on paved roads."

I didn't want them to see me smile, but I was about to burst with excitement.

"After lunch," Gert said.

33 FOUR-WHEELING

Hoyt gave me driving lessons out by the garden shed. He showed me how to operate the foot gears and watched me make some slow loops on the driveway. I'd never operated any type of motor vehicle before, and the freedom I felt was exhilarating. On my third pass I built up my confidence and felt the wind in my face a little. Then Hoyt waved me to a stop.

"You think you got it?" he asked.

"Yeah," I said, grinning uncontrollably. "I think so."

"Then get out of here," he smiled. "You got a full tank."

Although there was no speedometer, Hoyt said the ATV probably went as fast as forty-five miles per hour. To me it felt like a hundred. It felt like the world had opened up.

I burst from the trees with blue sky overhead, the engine wound out and the wind streaming tears across my face. For the first time, I forgot all my troubles.

"Waaahooo!" I yelled.

The field rows clipped past, arrow straight to the far line of trees. In the distance was the church, the parking lot empty now and nothing but the two oak trees to scratch its roof and keep it company. Beyond was the highway and two cars moving small and slow. I came to an intersecting dirt road, slowed and swung onto it, and accelerated again. I raced for the trees nearly a half mile away to the north. In less than a minute I was looking up at the wall of hardwoods, their brittle, gray, leafless branches striking across the cool blue. I slowed and eased south on the turn row, searching the damp, leafy-floored recesses of the swamp. Whatever it held was hidden in the green of palmetto and cane.

I traveled the north end of the fields until I saw my tracks from the week before, coming from the island, punched sloppily and frantically into the soft field rows. I stopped and studied where the tracks entered the trees and tried to replay the nightmare of that night, tried to orient myself now that I could see everything in the daylight. Somewhere beyond was a pond of dark water and a tree where I'd spent much of the worst night of my life. All of it seemed so harmless, looking at it now from the seat of the ATV. I shifted into gear and kept on.

As I traveled the north line, I saw two does, a yearling, and an eight-point buck standing in the turn row ahead. They watched me for a moment before bolting into the trees. Then I saw a coyote loping across the field, far away to the south near where I'd shot Stickers.

A bit farther and I saw the glimmer of water through the trees to my right. I remembered Hoyt had called it Rhodes's brake. I slowed and shut off the ATV. With the noise of the engine stilled, the swamp was no longer just a mute blur of gray and green. It was suddenly alive with the cheeping of birds, the fussing of squirrels, and the swishing of the breeze through the canopy. Over all of this was the faint gurgling sound of falling water. Suddenly I heard a loud crack and a splash. I eased off the ATV and slipped ahead to investigate.

I hadn't gone far when I came to a ditch, nearly ten feet deep. It was cut into the field and ran a ruler line as far as I could see to the south. A land bridge crossed it, and the water trickled through a culvert pipe beneath it. The end of the ditch near the trees was dammed with a woven wall of sticks and mud. The water was still rocking from a disturbance, and I soon saw the heads of two beavers swimming out into the brake toward their home in a tight mound rising like an island between the cypress trees. In a moment they dipped beneath the surface and were gone.

I waited to see if the beavers would reappear, but the pond settled, and all was still again. Then I heard a vehicle and looked up just in time to see it pass slowly through a gap in the trees ahead. I saw a thin ribbon of asphalt and remembered the farmer's warning against paved roads.

I started back to the ATV. I'd only taken a few steps before I kicked what I assumed was just a flake of rock. But there was something unusual about it, and I bent down and picked it up. After turning it over a few times, I thought it looked a little like an arrowhead. I remembered Hoyt telling me there were a lot of them around here, but if it was one, it was only half of one. I tossed it into the weeds and moved on. I climbed onto the ATV, cranked it, and raced off to the south along the drainage ditch.

For three days all I did was explore the farm from sunup to sundown. Gert kept me supplied with ready-made bologna sandwiches in the refrigerator, and Hoyt made sure there was always a full can of gas waiting for me in the shed.

At night I lay in bed, my mind racing, remembering the places I'd been and planning where I wanted to go next. And only just before I drifted off to sleep did that nagging little reminder surface concerning Grandmother across the hall. It was a thing left undone I couldn't completely forget, no matter how much I tried. It hung over me like a school exam sometime in the future—something I should be studying for but didn't really have to yet.

34 BEULAH PLANTATION

Saturday morning, I was sitting on the edge of my bed pulling on my boots when I heard an unfamiliar ringing. I sat up and listened to the sound repeat itself and realized it was coming from below the floor. *The phone!*

I bounded out of my room and down the stairs to the small table where the telephone trembled with excitement it likely hadn't felt in years.

"Hello!" I gasped.

"Win?"

"Dad," I breathed.

"You OK?"

I nodded to the phone. "Yeah . . . I'm fine. This is the first phone call I've received here. I didn't even know if it worked."

"I've been calling for two days."

"I haven't been around much," I said. "How's Mom?"

"She's doing better. How are you doing?"

"OK, I guess. I don't have any money left."

"Well, you're supposed to be working on that. You made any progress toward what we talked about?"

"You mean with Grandmother?"

"Yes," he said, "of course that's what I mean."

"I tried on Christmas Eve. She threw a fit and almost killed me."

"Win, she's going to throw a fit. That's precisely my point. But you've got to keep trying. What's the worst thing that can happen?"

"I've never seen anyone that mad. I'm sort of scared of her."

"Win, listen. The most important thing you can do right now is get her out of bed. Don't you let her die on us before she changes her will."

"OK."

"What have you been *doing?*"

"Riding an ATV Hoyt fixed up for me."

"What?"

"It's like a motorcycle with four—"

"I know what it is. Jesus, Win. Come on now. You have to get focused."

I glanced up the stairs.

"OK?" he continued. "Are you hearing me?"

"Yeah."

"What are you going to do?"

"I'm going to get her out of bed."

"And?"

"And get her to change her will."

"Tell John to get hold of a lawyer. Tell him to draw it all up."

"OK," I said. "I'll keep trying."

"Fine. Good. We'll talk again soon."

"OK. Bye."

I hung up the phone, stared at the receiver, and took a deep breath. I reminded myself that what he was asking me to do was our only option. I had to try and talk to my grandmother again.

I went into the kitchen, got a honey bun, and sat at the table with it, procrastinating. In a moment Gert came in the back door, dressed in her white uniform.

"Good morning, Win."

"Hey, Gert."

"Going exploring again today?"

"Dad called," I said.

She got the serving tray for Grandmother's meals off a top shelf and set it on the counter.

"How is he?" she asked.

"He says he's fine."

She busied herself preparing Grandmother's oatmeal and coffee.

"He wants me to try and talk her out of bed again."

Gert dropped the stirring spoon for the coffee and bent to pick it up.

"I'm going to need your help," I said.

"I told you I don't want nothing to do with that."

"I know. I don't want to either. Maybe we should get Mr. Case over here."

She set the spoon on the tray again. "I don't know," she said.

"I'll go to the shop and see if Mr. Case is there. I also need to tell him about getting the lawyer ready."

Gert shook her head and kept working.

Outside everything was wet and cold and windblown under a gray sky. Typical Cottonlandia weather. When I arrived at the shop, the only person I found was Luther working on the hydraulics for one of the tractors.

"I don't know where he's at," he said. "You want me to call him?"

I was relieved to have an excuse to put off anything having to do with Grandmother.

"No, thanks," I said. "I'll come back."

I left the shop and drove to the edge of the woods at the north end of the property to see if the beavers were out working on their dam. The water in the brake was still and quiet, with no signs of life. I studied the old blacktop just ahead and thought again of the farmer's rule about not crossing any paved roads. But it seemed harmless. I doubted a car had passed in hours.

I drove up to the asphalt and saw I wouldn't need to cross it at all. Running in the grass beside it were the faint markings of an ATV trail. It appeared to me by taking the trail I could go around Rhodes's brake and get to whatever lay on the other side. I turned the ATV north and set out.

When I came around the other side of the brake, I was surprised at what I saw. In place of fields were giant, square lakes as far as I could see. Farther to the north, heavy, earthmoving equipment rumbled and coughed black smoke. *Must be catfish ponds*, I thought. *So this is what they look like.*

There were eight ponds, each of them nearly the size of a football field. I kept on around Rhodes's brake, keeping to a dirt road running between the ponds and the swamp. I made a slow curve out and around a peninsula of hardwoods and stopped the ATV when I saw what lay before me. About a half mile away was a towering, white house, four times the size of the one at Cottonlandia. It was surrounded by a neatly trimmed lawn of lush, green grass and water oaks. There were several outbuildings and a swimming pool. The scene was striking against the earth tones of the surrounding fields and swamp. Then I remembered Sikes Rhodes and reasoned I'd found her home.

I kept on toward the house with a mixture of curiosity and apprehension. As I drew closer, more of the estate came into detail. Then I heard a dog barking and saw a golden retriever standing on the lawn watching my approach. I slowed and considered turning back. Before I'd made up my mind another ATV came around the side of the house, racing toward me. On it was Sikes Rhodes.

35 CHARLIE RHODES

I wanted to turn and race away, but I was frozen in place, watching Sikes coming at me on her ATV, the golden retriever running behind her.

She pulled up beside me, dressed in jeans and a sweater. Her blonde hair fell from the edges of a pink knit cap.

"Hi, Win Canterbury," she smiled in an almost mocking way.

"Hey," I said.

The dog caught up and circled us and stopped and studied the trees. "I'm Sikes, remember?"

"I remember."

She looked at the dog. "That's King."

The dog came over to her, and she started to pet its neck. "Did you get lost?"

"No."

"You know it's hunting season?"

"Yeah."

"You could get shot riding near the woods without an orange cap."

I looked over at the brake as if I might see a hunter in the trees.

"There's nobody out this morning," she continued. "But you never know."

"I don't have an orange hat," I said stupidly.

"They don't wear those in New York City, do they?"

I shook my head.

"Dad thought you were a poacher. He wanted to call the game

warden, but I told him who you were."

"I was just riding. I'll turn around."

"You want to see the place?"

She still made me nervous, but I wasn't sure why. She was certainly pretty. And for the first time in my life I was around a person my age I felt I had nothing to offer.

"Is it all catfish ponds?" I asked.

She glanced at the heavy machinery moving in the distance. Her lip gloss glistened in the sun. "It's about to be," she said. "Dad's digging up the last of the fields out there."

"Are there fish in them yet?"

Her eyes widened, and she nodded proudly. "As soon as the pond's finished, a tank truck comes and dumps the fingerlings in. But they're still small right now." She held up her thumb and forefinger and showed me a gap of about six inches. "They're probably like that."

"I've heard you can make more money at it than growing cotton."

She shrugged. "That's what Dad thinks. But I miss the cotton."

I didn't respond.

"You want to go riding?"

"Sure," I said.

"Follow me back to the house. We'll get my truck."

"You have a truck?"

A glimmer of mischief came into her eyes. "Yeah."

"Like a real one?"

She started to turn around on the ATV. "Yeah," she said. "Come on!"

I'd grown wary of that phrase. Before I knew it, Sikes and King were racing away toward the house. I got the uncomfortable feeling I'd been talked into another Hoyt-like adventure.

I followed Sikes and King back to the Rhodes house. There were no field rows on their farm, so one could angle off in just about any direction that wasn't blocked by a catfish pond. I drove under the trees surrounding the home site and felt like I was being swallowed in luxury. Her ATV tracks made a trail of pressed grass across the lawn, and I was careful to keep my wheels in them. I passed several outbuildings, one of them with a sign above the door that read BEULAH PLANTATION OFFICE. Then I passed the pool and pool house, and finally arrived where Sikes was standing with King at the back door to the big house.

"Where's the truck?" I asked.

"It's in the shed. Dad wants to meet you first."

I shut off the ATV and gazed about. "This place is huge."

"He built it like one he saw in Natchez."

"Where's that?"

"A city south of here," she said. "It's where all the big plantation houses are."

I followed her up the back steps and into a small room full of boots and neoprene hunting waders.

"Check those feet, Miss Sikes," I heard a woman call out from inside.

Sikes turned to me and frowned. "Take off your boots," she said. "Roxy's always worried about tracking mud inside."

We took our boots off and left them on the floor. Then I followed her into the kitchen, where a Black woman in a uniform much like Gert's was at the counter making potato salad. The uniform was about the only thing they had in common. She was heavyset and probably half Gert's age. The kitchen itself looked like one you would find in a restaurant. All of the equipment was industrial-grade stainless steel and thick, black iron, with marble countertops; thick, wood chopping blocks; two oversize refrigerators, everything humming and smooth. Shiny copper pots and pans hung on a rack suspended from the ceiling.

"This is Win Canterbury," Sikes said.

Roxy turned and looked at me over her shoulder. "How you, Win?"

"Pretty good," I said.

She turned back to her task. "You two stay out of trouble," she said suspiciously.

"Daddy's in here," Sikes said, starting out of the kitchen.

We walked into a dining room that was even more impressive. It was nearly fifty feet long and twenty feet wide, with a twelve-foot ceiling. Filling up the center of the room was an antique mahogany table looking big enough to host the queen of England. Oil paintings of what I assumed were Sikes's relatives hung on every wall.

Although the setting and the style were different, it slowly occurred to me I was back among my type of people. This was the kind of lifestyle I'd been accustomed to, and a warm sense of relief slipped over me, some perception I was being naturally drawn back to where I belonged.

We passed through a set of giant pocket doors, partially opened to the living room beyond. Here we found Mr. Rhodes seated in his robe beside a tremendous fireplace, reading the morning paper. He was a short, heavyset man, instantly bringing to mind Teddy Roosevelt. He even wore the same rounded eyeglasses.

Sikes stopped in the middle of the room, and I stopped slightly behind her. Mr. Rhodes didn't look up.

"Here he is, Daddy," Sikes said.

He didn't lower his newspaper, but cocked his eyes up, peered over it, and studied me. I grew uncomfortable and jammed my hands in my pockets. Suddenly he shook the paper and folded it and set it on a lamp table next to him.

"So this is the Canterbury heir?" he boomed.

"It's Win," Sikes said.

"Poaching on my property," he said without a smile.

"He's just kidding," Sikes said to me.

"You're going to get yourself shot, boy."

"I didn't—"

"Come over here and shake my hand."

I swallowed and approached him, and he squeezed his warm, plump hand around my own. He squeezed just a touch too hard, a subtle warning against something.

"That's a fine place you have," he said.

"Thank you," I said.

Mr. Rhodes pushed himself up from the chair, turned, and looked out one of the tall windows. "Looks like we might get another nice day," he said. "Don't get many this time of year."

"I wasn't hunting," I said.

He turned back to me and nudged my shoulder, cracking a smile. "I'm just working on you, boy."

"You don't have to listen to him," Sikes said from behind me. "He likes to scare people."

"You hear that," he said. "That's exactly what you get when you live in a house full of women. No respect and an empty wallet."

"Daaaddy," Sikes groaned.

"So how is the old place?" he continued.

"It's OK," I said. "I mean, it still looks old, but it's OK."

He looked out the window like he could see it through the big brake. "Well, that's about to change," he said.

I studied him. I didn't know what he meant by that.

He took a few steps toward the exit into a grand hallway. "Good to meet you, Win Canterbury. I'm going to get dressed and get back in the fight."

I didn't respond to his strange metaphor.

"We're going riding in Red," Sikes said.

"Stay away from the ponds," he replied. "Your mother drove into town. She'll be back in a couple of hours."

"OK, Daddy."

36 SIKES'S TRUCK

I followed Sikes back through the kitchen and into the mudroom, where we put our boots back on. Then we went down the back steps, where King was waiting patiently. Sikes guided me toward a metal barn to our right, the dog falling in beside us.

"You must have done all right with cotton too," I said. "To build a place like this."

"I was born in Pittsburgh. Daddy did real estate before we came here."

"And then they built this place?"

Sikes flipped a latch to the heavy bay doors of the barn and leaned back, pulling on one. By the time it occurred to me to help, she was already walking it open.

"We moved here right after I was born," she said. "There wasn't a house or anything then. Just fields. Daddy said the real estate business wasn't as good anymore. He said money was in farming."

She turned to me, dusting her hands together. "So here we are. Farmers."

"Catfish farms don't seem like farming."

"It's always money first with Daddy. All he thinks about are his business deals. He still likes to buy land and houses too. He says it's good to invest in a lot of different things."

I looked into the barn. It was full of equipment; a riding lawn mower and various attachments, a workbench, power tools, woodworking equipment—most of it looked new and rarely used. In the center of it all was a red Ford pickup. It wasn't new, but it wasn't as beat-up and used as one would expect on a farm.

"Told you," she said.

She walked around the back of the truck and lowered the tailgate. King leaped up and into the bed, and she slammed it shut after him.

"Get in," she said to me.

I suddenly had flashes of my experience on the mattress with Hoyt. It occurred to me they might all be in this together. They might all be trying to run me off. But she was just a girl my age, I told myself. And she was pretty.

I sat in the passenger seat, my right hand gripping the armrest a little too tightly. She scooted to the edge of the seat, craned her neck to see over the steering wheel, and straightened her legs to reach the pedals. The keys were already in the ignition, and she cranked the truck with confidence and raced the engine. Then she turned to me and smiled mischievously. "Ready?"

"OK," I said, not sure about it at all.

She looked ahead, shifted into gear, and we lurched forward. Soon we were bouncing slowly across the lawn, making a wide swing toward the hardwoods on the perimeter. When we reached the trees, Sikes stepped on the brakes too hard and I was thrown against the dashboard. I heard King's toenails scratching against the metal of the truck bed as he tried to keep his balance.

"It's hard to reach the pedals." She laughed.

I scooted back in my seat and reached for the safety belt. "I'm OK," I said.

"You don't need the seat belt," she said. "I'll get better."

I looked over at her. "How often do you do this?"

"Not much. I just wanted to show you."

I clicked the safety buckle into place. "What's not much?"

"Like just a couple of times when I've had friends over."

She stepped on the pedal again, and we bounced through a small drainage furrow and up onto a dirt road circling the outside of the homesite. She laughed again. "Last time we ran Red into the ditch."

"I hope it wasn't one of those huge ditches," I said. "They've got some ten feet deep at Cottonlandia."

She nodded considerately. "It was pretty big," she finally said. "Daddy had to replace the whole front end."

I clutched the armrest tighter. "Great," I said.

"Hold on," she said as we sped up.

She stepped on the gas pedal so hard she had to lean into the steering wheel and come off the seat. I heard the engine race and the tires spin against the dirt like sanding wheels. King began scrabbling around in the back again, and I turned just in time to see him leap over the side of the truck bed and dash a few feet away onto the roadside.

"King jumped out!" I said.

But the tires were just starting to gain traction and she was focused on the road ahead.

"Yeah," she said. "He doesn't like this part."

I looked ahead again. "*What* part!"

Sikes didn't seem to notice I was about to pee my pants from fear of her driving. We were racing straight for a muddy field. We bounced off the road and plunged into the soft dirt. It was then I saw what must have been some of Red's older tracks, dim and rain-smoothed, going in all directions.

"It's perfect," she said. "They haven't dug this one out yet."

I stared ahead, feeling around with my left hand for something else to hold on to. It found nothing on the bench seat except for the buckle of the middle passenger safety restraint. I grabbed it and hung on like a bull rider. Sikes spun the steering wheel, and the truck leaned into a hard turn, churning against the mud and throwing an arc of the black muck twenty feet into the air. I leaned into the door as we made a complete circle. Then she spun the steering wheel again, and we straightened out and raced off in the direction of a faraway tree line.

Sikes looked over at me, electric with excitement. "Pretty fun, huh?"

I was still recovering, and we were still going too fast for me to be comfortable.

"Are you crazy!" I said. "Watch where you're going!"

She laughed and looked ahead again. "You can't run into anything out here."

"Except a ditch!"

"I know where the ditches are."

I didn't answer.

"Last time it was just one of the new ones the catfish people dug. I didn't know about those."

"Jesus! Slow down! There might be some more."

She sat back on the seat, and the truck slowed. In a moment we were ambling along toward the trees at a pace more comfortable to me. "Sorry," she said. "I thought you'd like mud riding."

I took a deep breath and loosened my grip on the door and seat buckle. Suddenly I felt like a wimp.

"I guess they don't do that in New York City," she said.

"It's just the last time I went fast through the mud, it sucked."

"That wasn't bad," she said.

"I know," I conceded. "At least I wasn't being pulled behind on a mattress."

"What?"

"Never mind. Let's just ride normal for now, if that's all right."

"That's OK," she said.

"It was fun," I apologized. "I'm just not used to everything around here yet."

She looked at me and smiled. "That's fine. We'll go slow."

Sikes drove us to the north end of the property, where we stopped about a hundred yards from the heavy equipment. The giant earthmovers groaned and crawled about the treeless plain like something on the moon.

"How'd you like to drive one of those?" Sikes said.

I looked at her. She was studying them intently. Too intently. "You're crazy," I said.

She turned to me and laughed. "Yeah," she said. "That would be crazy."

"People around here sure do like to ride things."

"I'll bet they leave the keys in them."

"Stop it," I said.

"What do they do in New York for fun?"

"I played hockey. Went to the park. Movies and stuff. Back when I had a life."

"I heard what happened," she said. "To your dad and all . . . I just didn't want you to wonder if I knew or not. You know?"

I frowned. "Seems like everybody's heard about it."

"Not really. Just around here. We don't get many new neighbors. Not much to talk about. Daddy says Mr. Denton at the store is like the talking newspaper of Walnut Bend."

"I don't like that guy."

"He's really pretty funny."

Raindrops began to appear on the windshield. "Can't you go two days without rain around here?"

Sikes seemed happy to change the subject. "You should see the place in summertime," she said. "Everything's so green it's like a jungle."

"It's already a jungle. Have you ever been out in that swamp?"

"Sure," she said. "I've been hunting with Daddy. It's mostly sticks and stickers and mud right now."

"And it gets better when it grows leaves?"

"You'll see," she said. "It's totally different."

I didn't respond. I suddenly felt like a drag.

"Most boys in school would give anything to have what you have, Win."

"A dad going to jail?"

"No, three thousand acres of swamp and farmland with your own four-wheeler. You realize how many people in this county have that?"

I shook my head.

"You'd better learn how to hunt and mud-ride and do it all because every boy in Greenwood's going to want to come to Cottonlandia."

The rain began tapping harder on the windshield. Sikes started Red and shifted into reverse.

"We better get back before the ground gets too wet," she said. "We'll get stuck for sure."

"I really don't want to have to walk back through this field," I said.

"Don't worry," she replied. "I know a shortcut. You may want to put your seat belt on for *this* one."

"Sikes!"

She turned and gave me that smile that should have made me nervous, but somehow it made things a lot better.

37 MRS. RHODES

We made it back to the barn without any new dents in Red, just before the rain started coming down in slanting sheets. Mr. Rhodes shouted from the back door he was going into town and that Mrs. Rhodes should be back shortly.

After Roxy made sure we left our boots in the mudroom, Sikes led me to the den, where we sat on the floor eating Goldfish crackers and watching an Adam Sandler movie. It had been so long since I'd seen a modern television it was like being in a theater. I drank in the experience while the wet cold slipped over the big house.

For lunch Roxy brought us each a tray with a pimento cheese sandwich, Doritos, and a Coke. We ate and started another movie, and she returned after a while and took the trays away. About two hours later we heard Mrs. Rhodes come through the front door.

"Packages, Roxy!" she called.

"Yes, ma'am, Mrs. Rhodes," came Roxy's reply.

In a moment we heard her coming down the hall. "Sikes?"

Sikes continued watching the television, chewing her Goldfish. "In here," she mumbled.

Mrs. Rhodes appeared behind us in the doorway. She looked like a larger version of Sikes: a bit too petite and pretty for what you'd imagine as farm matriarch. The way she was dressed she could have just stepped off Park Avenue in New York.

She seemed startled when she saw me. "Oh my!" she exclaimed. "Where did you come from?"

Sikes turned to her. "This is Win, Mom. He lives at Cottonlandia."

"Cottonlandia?"

"Yeees," Sikes said. "You know, the big farm next door?"

Mrs. Rhodes frowned with a snappy purse of her lips. "Of course I know *where* it is," she said defensively. "I just didn't know anyone lived there besides Mrs. Canterbury and the help." Suddenly Mrs. Rhodes's expression changed to concern. "Did . . . did . . . "

"No, Mom," Sikes groaned. "She didn't die. This is her grandson."

"Oh, good Lord," she said, putting a hand to her cheek. "I did hear something about that. You're the one— "

"Mom," Sikes interrupted. "Do you need some help with the packages?"

In a flash Mrs. Rhodes's expression changed from confusion to delight. "Oh, Sikes," she said. "You should see the dresses I got at Caroline's. They'll be perfect for Easter. I've got one for you and one for me."

"Easter's like four months away, Mom."

That didn't seem to quell her excitement about them. "Roxy's put them upstairs. Let's go try them on."

Sikes turned back to the television. "No, Mom," she said. "I'm not leaving my guest to try on a dress for something that's months away."

"Oh, it'll just take a moment."

"No," Sikes said. "We'll do it later."

Mrs. Rhodes frowned and shook her head and looked at me. "Teenagers," she said. "You teenagers."

"Nice to meet you," I said.

But I could tell even though she was looking at me, she was still thinking about those dresses. She turned and hurried away.

"Roxy!"

"Up here, Mrs. Rhodes."

I soon heard her feet going up the stairs. "All she does is shop," Sikes said. "I get so sick of trying on clothes."

I looked out the window and saw the rain had stopped. I thought I should start back and check in with Gert before she got worried and sent the farmer and Hoyt and the dogs after me.

"I better get going," I said. "Gert's probably wondering what happened to me."

"Why don't you call?"

I stood up and Sikes grabbed the bag of Goldfish and stood

before me.

"We don't really have a phone," I said.

"No phone?"

"Well, we do, but—you'd just have to see it."

"OK," she said. "I'll come over some time."

"There's not much to do."

"I'll bet we can find tons of old stuff around there."

"Probably," I said. "Thanks for showing me your place. I had fun."

"Sure. I'll see you later then."

"See you later, Sikes."

I drove the ATV back to Cottonlandia, the tires sliding on the slick mud of the turn rows. The sky was gray and evil-looking, and the temperature felt like it had dropped twenty degrees. Even though it was no longer raining, the air was like a cold mist slowly wicking into my clothes and chilling me to the bones. There was no way I was going all the way to the other side of the property to look for the farmer again. I just wanted to get back to Headquarters, get dry, and crawl into bed with the heater turned as high as it would go.

I finally made it back, with my teeth chattering and my hands red and numb. The place seemed more pathetic than ever after spending time at Beulah. It was like the playhouse version of Beulah. An abandoned playhouse, lost in the swamp, with nothing but a couple of ghosts in it. The weather and now the depressing contrast between the lives of me and my neighbors had left me in a foul mood. Just an hour earlier Sikes had seemed like the best thing that had happened to me since coming to Mississippi. Now I imagined her like all the others, using me for her own entertainment. All of them in their big, white house, among the luxuries I missed so much. Dangling before me the life I lost.

I parked the ATV in the shed and left my muddy boots before the back door. Inside the kitchen it was cold and empty. Gert hadn't turned on the heaters. I thought of Grandmother, lying up there, staring black-eyed at the water-stained ceiling, thin wisps of breath misting from the bright, red slit of her mouth. I made my way upstairs and into my room, where I got out of the wet clothes and shivered into dry ones again. After my teeth stopped chattering, I realized how much one could hear the house creaking without the gentle noise of the heaters to smother the sound away. The whole structure tightening and shrinking from the cold. I studied the gas heater against the wall. I'd never tried to light one, but I'd watched Gert do it. It didn't seem too complicated. Turn the gas knob and stick a match into the grill.

I went downstairs again and got some paper matches from the kitchen and went back up. I kneeled before the rusty old box and turned the knob until I heard the gas hissing from within. Then I tore lose one of the matches and began to scrape it against the abrasive strip. The matches seemed a little damp, and I went through four of them before I got one to light and held it out toward the grill. Before I was even a foot away the air woofed into a fireball before my face, blasting me backward. I lay on the floor, dazed, my heart pounding, the smell of singed hair drifting over me. After a moment I regained my senses and felt my face. Everything felt OK. I sat up and looked at the heater and saw it purring away with a harmless little lick of blue flame. Like I'd surely just imagined it had breathed fire at me like a dragon. Just as smug and evil as the rest of them.

The rain started to tap the windowpanes, and a gust of wind set the branches scraping against the house. The heater was already warming the room, and I thought again how nice it was going to be to crawl into bed and hide from it all and do nothing. Evil was still ticking and read three o'clock. I didn't know whether to believe him or not, but I cranked him like it hurt just to make sure. Then I crawled into bed and buried myself beneath the pile of blankets.

38 THE LIPSTICK SKELETON

I woke to Gert knocking on my door. "Win, you in there?"

"Yes," I groaned.

"Suppertime."

Darkness pressed around the one bedside lamp I'd left on. I looked at Evil suspiciously. Six o'clock.

"I'll be down in a minute," I said.

"I've got to take Mrs. Canterbury her supper. I'll be along."

"OK," I said, sitting up, groggy and confused.

The storm still howled and shook the trees outside. The rain had turned to sleet and blew against the windowpanes like a hail of pebbles. I thought of the same old venison hamburger waiting for me. It didn't seem possible I would ever be able to eat all of the deer meat. I was already tired of it.

I ate the hamburger like it was prison food, chewing and swallowing for fuel and routine, nothing more. Gert returned with Grandmother's tray just as I was finishing.

"I didn't see Mr. Case today," I said. "Did he come by?"

"Yes. Not more than an hour ago."

"I needed to talk to him!"

"You were asleep. I thought you already had."

I sighed. "No."

"Well, he won't be back with the weather like it is."

"Great," I said. "I'm going back upstairs."

"You OK?" she asked me. "You're not coming down with a cold, are you?"

"I'm fine," I said.

As I made my way back upstairs, I couldn't recall ever feeling quite like this. I wouldn't call my attitude foul, but darker and accepting of some impending doom. It was as if any optimism I'd had about improving my situation was completely washed away and replaced with a steadfast resolve to just exist in my misery and watch it passively like a stranger to my own self.

Back in my room the storm still howled and spit and scraped at the windows. I ignored it and climbed into bed with the old English literature book. I studied Dad's handwriting on the inside cover again. It occurred to me I might be all the things I disliked about him. *Maybe I was selfish and cold. Maybe I was dishonest. Maybe I would end up in jail too. Maybe this strange life was just the same person coming back on himself again.*

I turned a few pages and scanned the table of contents. "The Fall of the House of Usher." Never read it. Sounded perfect.

As I read Poe's macabre tale, it was obvious that divine intervention had put the story in my hands to confirm my suspicions that life as an individual was simply an illusion. This story of an old mansion, haunted by the living dead, could have been imagined in no other place but Cottonlandia. This *was* the disguised story of Cottonlandia.

I read on, the storm outside my window seeming to increase in parallel intensity with the storm raging outside the House of Usher. I couldn't put the story down. A tingling fear was spreading from my face, down my spine, and into my toes—settling into me like thousands of tickling ants exploring my body. And even had I wanted to put the story away, I dreaded the other story I would find when I left the world of Poe. The story playing out simultaneously on the other side of my head. Whatever I would see when I lowered the book and found myself face to face with my own Usher. I slowly turned the pages, dreading the last sentence, and finally seeing myself closing in on it. The narrator was fleeing the house. Then it was over.

But I was still here.

I set the book down. The heater breathed quietly against the wall, but I heard the house alive again. It sounded like a hurricane outside. Now nothing was an illusion. It was all real and tangible, and I was a live thing, lying there consumed with fear—helpless, breathing, hearing my own heartbeat, and waiting for whatever was to come for me. I stared across the foot of the bed at the knob of my closed door. I waited for it to move. I don't know how long I waited, but Evil ticked away the time. He was part of it, too, I thought. Evil and the heater and the phone. They were all part of it. They'd been waiting for me all these years. Waiting to get revenge for the sins of my father.

The only explanation I have for falling asleep is that my terror exhausted me. I must have passed out from fear. When I woke, I didn't know immediately what had brought me back to consciousness. Slowly the raging storm became apparent again and Evil ticked and the blue light of the heater danced on the walls of the dark room. Who had turned off my bedside light? My situation came rushing over me again, and fear constricted me like a straitjacket. Then came a flicker of intense, white light through the window behind me. An explosion of thunder followed that seemed to rock the old house to its foundation. But it wasn't the deafening noise that consumed my attention. Standing in my doorway, framed by the flash of lightning, was the lipstick skeleton.

I screamed. She didn't move. Her outline shimmered in the blue gaslight. I screamed again.

"I can't sleep," she said.

I couldn't speak.

"What's wrong with you?" she snapped impatiently. "It's just a thunderstorm."

"I'm sorry," I stammered.

"The storm's loud enough without you adding nonsense to it."

I realized whatever my reality was at that moment, screaming wasn't helping. Apparently, this was going to drag out longer than I expected.

"What do you want?" I said.

She came scuffling toward me. I backed against the headboard and braced my hands against the mattress.

"I just want some peace," she said. "That's a start."

"But . . . but how—"

"Turn some light on, will you? Before I fall down and shatter."

I slowly reached out my hand and turned the knob on the bedside lamp. Nothing happened. I turned it again.

"Power must be gone," she said. "At least we'll save some

money."

"Sit down," I said. "Chair's behind you."

"I know where the chair is," she snapped. "I bought that chair in England. You've probably never even been to England, have you?"

I shook my head no. She lowered herself into the chair and sighed. "Mr. High Society," she grumbled. "None of you know a *thing* about high society."

I didn't know if she was talking about me or Dad.

"See where it got the both of you," she continued.

Once I saw her firmly planted in the chair, I relaxed my hands on the bed and started trying to tame my racing thoughts and make sense of it all.

"You're feeling better now?" I stammered.

"I'm so mad at your father I could strangle him."

I didn't respond.

She sighed. "I suppose we've got some work to do."

I nodded.

"I guess your uppity sense of self-entitlement's been dead-on all along."

I didn't know what to say.

"Maybe at least you'll manage to hang on to the place for a few years more."

I felt guilt creeping over me. She knew. She knew everything. Her mind was crystal clear. It had always been crystal clear.

"You have anything to say?"

I shook my head. "No, ma'am."

She pushed herself out of the chair. "Very well," she said. "If you're just going to sit there being a bore, I'm going to try again to get some sleep. Sounds like I'll need it."

"Can't you all just let an old woman die in peace?" she said over her shoulder.

I watched her shuffle toward the door.

39 GRANDMOTHER LIVES

The storm passed just after four o'clock in the morning. I lay in bed, staring at the ceiling, listening to the house drip and creak until daylight slipped over the room.

"Gertrude!" I heard her yelling.

I jumped out of bed and rushed into the hallway, where I found her clutching the railing at the top of the stairs, peering into the darkness below. She was still in her nightgown, but the wig and lipstick were in place.

"Gertrude!" she yelled again.

"What do you need?" I asked her.

She turned to me. "You want me to kill myself on these stairs?"

"I don't think she's down there."

"Where is she?"

"She's probably in her house. She should be here soon to start breakfast."

Grandmother frowned. "I suppose you'll do. Might as well start making yourself useful."

I hesitated.

"Move!" she snapped. "Get over here."

I lifted her arm and put it over my shoulder and the sour milk smell of her consumed me like a fog. I stopped breathing through my nose and started downstairs with her. Other than the body fumes, there wasn't much to it. She couldn't have weighed more than eighty pounds. She had me place her at the head of the dining room table, then sent me after Gert.

I met Gert coming through the back door.

"She's up," I said.

Gert studied me for a second. "Where is—"

"Gertrude!" Grandmother snapped. "I hear you in there. Where's my bell?"

Gert hurried into the kitchen.

"I'm going back upstairs," I said.

"No, you're not," she said. "You started this."

I swallowed nervously and watched her open the cabinet above the stove. She began feeling around on the top shelf.

"Gertrude!"

"I'm coming, Mrs. Canterbury."

"Where's my bell?"

"We're getting it, Mrs. Canterbury. Hold on."

Before it occurred to me to help, her hand found what it was feeling for, and she brought down a dainty brass bell about the size of a shot glass. She passed it to me. "Take this to her," she said. "I'll get her coffee going."

"What does she need this for?"

Gert stopped and turned back to me. "You don't understand what you stirred up, but you're about to. You're about to appreciate when all you had was a quiet, creaky old house."

I could hear the ting-ting-ting sound of the bell out on the driveway where I stood waiting for the farmer. She rang it for everything and kept ringing it until her request was met, placing it in a small, matching dish on the dining room table between summons. Gert fluttered about the house like a curtain in the wind, trying to keep up; coffee, cream, sugar, too hot, where are my doilies, why aren't there fresh flowers, too cold, where's RD? Dead? Where's the paper? Reading glasses. The fine china from France? Roach on the floor, too hot.

"Come on, Mr. Case," I mumbled. "Where are you?"

He finally arrived and got out of the truck in his slow way and stood next to me, studying the house, listening to the ting-ting-ting of the bell.

"Well, I'll be darned," he chuckled. "I hear her."

"It's not funny," I said. "She's going crazy in there with that bell."

"What do you want me to do?"

156

"I don't know. Something."

"Let's go check on her. We'll give Gert a break."

The farmer took off his hat, and I followed him inside and into the dining room.

"Good morning, Mrs. Canterbury," he said.

She didn't seem surprised to see him. She replaced the bell on the tray and straightened her posture. "John Case, I know you're in on this. You've got your hand in my pocket like everybody else around here."

The farmer smiled. "It sure is good to see you up and about, Mrs. Canterbury. Is there anything I can do for you?"

Gert floated in and took the breakfast tray. She glanced at the farmer, then at the bell, finally still after all this time. She took a deep breath and hurried back into the kitchen.

"It's Sunday, isn't it?" Grandmother said.

"Yes, it is," the farmer replied.

"Then I'd like to attend service. Where's my Cadillac?"

"You gave it to Luther."

"I did not."

"About six years ago. You told him you didn't want it."

"I said no such thing."

The farmer started to reply, and Grandmother waited on the edge of her chair to retort. But he stopped himself and nodded politely. Grandmother sank back slightly. "Tell him I want it back," she said. "Immediately."

"I'm not certain he still has it, Mrs. Canterbury."

"He better still have it. That's stolen property as far as I'm concerned."

"I'll see what I can do."

"Very well," she said, satisfied. "You do that."

"In the meantime, Win and I can take you to church in my truck."

She frowned and reached for the bell and shook it vigorously. Gert appeared. "Get me back upstairs, Gertrude. I'd like to get dressed for Sunday service."

The farmer stepped toward her. "Let me help you, Mrs. Canterbury."

She raised her hand like she would slap him if he came closer. "Shoo!" she snapped. "I've managed a long time without a man in my life. I certainly don't need one now."

We watched the two women ascend the staircase, leaning into each other, taking one slow step at a time. Finally, they reached the top and disappeared. The farmer turned to me.

"Well," he said. "I suppose Deacon Leon is about as good as it gets for spreading the word about her health."

"Do I have to go?"

He chuckled. "Do you have to go? Son, this is all your show. I'm just here to lend a hand."

40 GRANDMOTHER GOES TO CHURCH

I tried not to think too much about the process, but somehow Gert managed to wash Grandmother so she didn't smell so bad. Then she helped her into a navy-blue dress. Both of them appeared exhausted by the time Gert delivered her to us downstairs. If Grandmother had any complaints, she didn't have the energy to express them.

On the way out to the church, I sat on an oil bucket in the back of the truck while the two women rode in the cab. The farmer drove slowly, but it was still damp and chilly with the remnants of the storm clouds hanging in the sky like pieces of dirty cotton. When we pulled into the parking lot, I saw the attendance was much less than it had been on Christmas Day. There were only six cars in addition to Deacon Leon's. The farmer got out and looked at me.

"Get the door for your grandmother and Gert," he said.

I climbed down and opened the passenger side door, letting Gert out first, then standing back while she helped Grandmother out.

The four of us approached the church, the farmer and Gert on each side of Grandmother. Grandmother studied the building and its surroundings. "What happened to this place?" she snapped.

"It's been a while since anybody paid it much attention," the farmer replied.

"Give somebody a free church and you'd think they'd at least put some paint on it every few years."

"Talk to Deacon Leon about it," Gert said.

"Deacon," Grandmother said. "Is that what he calls himself now?"

Once again Deacon Leon was greeting his small congregation at the door with his assistant lounging against the Cadillac behind him. When he saw us approaching, he seemed stunned.

Grandmother eyed the assistant with a look of disgust. "Who's the skank?" she said, a bit too loud.

"Uh-huh," Gert agreed.

"Come on now, ladies," the farmer said. "Be nice."

"Mrs. Canterbury," Deacon Leon exclaimed. "I've prayed for this day, and my prayers have been answered."

"I'll bet they have, Leon."

"I've got to say you look better than ever."

"Seems to me you're the one with the Cadillac now."

The smile never left the deacon's face, but it became a little more forced. "The Lord's been good to me, Mrs. Canterbury. He certainly has."

"My church has been good to you. When's the last time you took up a collection for repairs?"

"Now, Mrs. Canterbury—"

"Don't you 'Mrs. Canterbury' me. Answer my question."

The deacon hesitated. "Well," he eventually said, "the—"

Grandmother started inside. "That's what I thought," she said. "We start with today's collection. You turn the proceeds over to John, and he'll handle the rest."

Although she wouldn't admit it, Grandmother seemed exhausted by the time we got her back to Headquarters. Gert took her upstairs, and the farmer and I were left alone in the foyer.

"I'll call the lawyer tomorrow when his office opens," the farmer said. "I'll set up a meeting for the three of us."

"OK," I said.

He looked up the stairs. "She's going to kill herself going up and down to her room like that."

He turned and studied the living room. "I'll send Hoyt over to help you move her downstairs. Put her in there."

I immediately liked the idea. I didn't want the lipstick skeleton creeping around outside my room at night.

"We'll have to run that by *her*, of course," he said. "But I imagine once she takes those stairs a few more times it won't be hard to sell her on it."

"I'll be ready to help," I said.

He turned to me. "I've got to run home and check on Diane. I'll talk to you tomorrow."

"OK," I said. "Thanks."

He nodded and turned to go. I went to the phone and dialed Dad's new number. I was surprised when he answered.

"Hello," he said.

"Dad?"

"Yeah? Win?"

"Hey. I got her up."

"What? You did? How?"

"Well, she sort of did it herself. She came in my room in the middle of the night and said she was feeling better."

"Uh-huh," he said. "I knew it. She didn't have *me* fooled."

"It's not like she's doing jumping jacks or anything, but she went to church this morning. Mr. Case thinks Deacon Leon'll help spread the word."

"Good, good, good," Dad said, like his mind was racing ahead with plans. "You've talked to a lawyer?"

"Not yet. They're not open today."

"What? Oh, right. Sunday. Tomorrow then?"

"Mr. Case said he'd call tomorrow and set up a meeting."

I heard Dad take a deep breath. "Good," he said. "Now we're getting somewhere. Nice work, Win."

"Have they set your trial date?"

"Not yet."

"Where is this number?"

"I'm at my new apartment. Just moved in yesterday."

"How's Mom?"

"She's hanging in there."

"Have you seen her lately?"

"No, not lately. I may swing by this evening. How are you doing?"

"OK, I guess. School starts on Wednesday."

"Hang in there, son. We'll get out of this mess. You just got us past the first step."

"All right," I said. "I'll talk to you later."

"'Bye."

"'Bye."

After I hung up the phone, I stood there thinking about how our relationship had changed. It was always *him* wanting things from *me* now. I couldn't think of anything he had to offer me. It was like we were suddenly business partners instead of father and son. It was an unsettling feeling.

41 TRUCKSTOP

I stayed away from the house the rest of the afternoon, riding the turn rows on the ATV. The sky cleared toward evening, and the temperature began dropping quickly. As the sun slipped down through the branches of the swamp, a steady flow of wood ducks whistled overhead and splashed into the brake.

When I got back to the house, Hoyt's truck was in the driveway, headlights on, puffs of white exhaust coming from the muffler. I drove the ATV up to the driver's-side window and saw him sitting there, drumming his fingers on the steering wheel, the truck radio thumping out a country song. When he saw me, he quickly shut off the truck and got out.

"Look what I got," he said.

"What?"

He walked to the back of the truck and stood before the dog box. "Come check it out."

I got off the ATV and went to investigate. I saw two hound dogs huddled inside, whining and trembling with excitement.

"Those your dogs?" I asked.

"One is. Check out the other one."

"I can't really see."

"I got Warrior in there with Truckstop."

"Truckstop?"

"You dang right. Best coon dog in the county. We're talking blue ribbon, man."

I put my face closer, trying to get a better look, but it was too dark. "Which Warrior is in there?" I asked.

"The brown one! Brown Warrior! I'm trying to make coon hounds, not daisy sniffers."

I stood back. "Right," I said.

Hoyt continued to admire the dog box. "Got them in there falling in love," he said. "About two months and I'm gonna have my own blue-ribbon coon puppies. Big money. Biiig money."

"Then you can double-wide your house."

He tapped on the dog box, took a step back, and turned to me. "Getting ahead, man. That's what's it's all about."

"You hear about Grandmother?"

"I heard. Thought you might need to get rescued."

"I stayed outside all afternoon."

"Thought maybe you'd wanna go with me and watch these two lovebirds tree some coons."

"You want to go raccoon hunting?"

Hoyt threw his head back and studied me like I was crazy. "Man, I got Truckstop in there! How many times you get a chance to run a dog like Truckstop?"

"I don't know. I would guess not very often."

He started toward the driver's seat. "Dang right, not very often. Get in. We're gonna ease down the road and pick up your lady friend."

"Sikes?"

"Yeah," he said. "Come on!"

Before I had time to think about it, we were racing out the driveway, headed for Beulah.

"I don't know about this," I said. "Are you sure she'll like hunting raccoons?"

"It's 'coons, not raccoons. And everybody likes coon hunting."

"Do I need anything? A flashlight, maybe? I haven't even had supper."

"Naw, man, you're fine. I made us some sandwiches."

"How did you know Sikes and I hung out?"

"You can't get away with nothing around here, can you?"

"Seriously, how did you know?"

"Gert sent me looking for you when you didn't come back to the house yesterday. I saw your four-wheeler parked over there."

"Oh."

Hoyt glanced at me and grinned. "Man, you got more game than I thought."

"What?"

"I didn't wanna come knocking. Mess up whatever you had going on with Miss Sikes Rhodes."

I felt heat flushing my face. "We just went riding in the truck and watched television."

Hoyt looked ahead again and shrugged. "Hey, man, I'm just saying."

"I didn't even mean to go over there."

"Nothing wrong with a little kissy-kissy."

"There wasn't any kissy-kissy. I don't even think this is a good idea."

"Man, there's people that'd give a month's pay to run Truckstop for just one night!"

"No, I mean going to get Sikes."

"Listen, you know what they used to call me in high school?"

We turned on the blacktop, and I felt anxiety rise into my throat. I shook my head. "No," I said.

"The Bod."

"What's that got to do with anything?"

"I'm just saying I was pretty popular with the ladies."

"Just forget it," I said. "I don't want to go get her."

He looked at me again. This time he appeared concerned. "But I already called her house. I thought you'd like it."

"You called her!"

"Yeah. Her momma said she'd be ready. I thought you'd want me to."

I sighed. "OK," I said. "Fine."

42 COON HUNT

Hoyt waited in the truck while I rang the doorbell. The coon dogs were already barking behind me like they knew what was about to happen and couldn't contain themselves. It seemed like a lot of offensive racket for a sophisticated place like Beulah. I took a deep breath and rang the doorbell again.

In a moment I heard an ATV crank in the backyard. Then I saw its headlights falling over the lawn just before Sikes skidded to a stop in the driveway. I came down off the front porch and went to meet her.

She wore gum boots, jeans, a puffy, blue goose-down jacket, and a red knit cap with a fuzz ball on top. I would have thought she was going on a skiing trip to Aspen had I not known better.

"You ever done this?" she asked.

"No," I said.

"It's awesome."

"Hi, Sikes," Hoyt called out the window.

Sikes turned to him. "Hey, Hoyt. Thanks for taking us coon hunting."

"You're welcome, honey. Y'all ready?"

"Hop on," Sikes said to me.

Hoyt started to pull away. "I'll meet you around the west end of the brake."

"Should I have brought my four-wheeler?" I asked Sikes.

"No, just get on the back of mine," she said. "It's not far."

I rode behind her, leaning back with my arms braced on the game rack. We followed Hoyt's truck, the ATV engine noise and the howl of the crisp wind in our ears leaving me riding silently and nervous about several things at once. Hoyt eventually stopped about a mile down the turn row where the hardwoods of the swamp towered overhead. By the time we caught up to him, he already had the tailgate down, letting the dogs out. Sikes and I climbed off the ATV and stood on the dirt road, watching.

Truckstop came scraping and barreling out of the box like a bull looking for a fight. He was big and black with a tan nose. Warrior leaped out just behind him, and the two of them bounded off into the darkness of the trees.

"You ever seen anything like that dog?" Hoyt said.

"He's big," I said.

Hoyt returned to the cab and came back with a rifle and some equipment. He gave the rifle to me and dumped the equipment on the tailgate.

"Watch where you point that," Sikes said.

I looked at her. She reached over and took the rifle from me and held it with the barrel pointed at the ground. "You can't wave it around like that."

I nodded helplessly, feeling like the joke I imagined they thought I was.

"It might be loaded," she added.

Hoyt was digging through the equipment. "It's not loaded," he said over his shoulder.

"What kind is it?" I asked.

"Twenty-two automatic," he said.

Hoyt put on what looked like a miner's helmet, a hardhat with a light on the front, and a battery pack strapped around his waist. Then he turned to us and gave us each a flashlight. "Might be a little wet back there," he said. "If it gets too thick, just come on out."

I heard the dogs barking. It seemed they were already a half mile into the swamp.

"Think we'll get one?" Sikes asked.

Hoyt looked at her. "One?"

Sikes smiled.

Hoyt turned back to his truck and grabbed what looked like a big duffel bag, but I noticed it was on a frame as he put his arms into its straps and wore it like a backpack.

"Shoot," he said. "We're gonna fill this coon sack like Momma needs a winter coat."

"What do you do with them?" I asked.

"You can eat them and sell the hides," Sikes said.

"You stay close to Sikes tonight," Hoyt said. "You'll be just fine."

"I'm OK," I said.

Hoyt turned and pointed up at the sky. "You get turned around, follow that star right there."

There were stars everywhere. "No problem," I said.

Suddenly Hoyt stiffened and stared somewhere over our heads. I felt a chill race up my spine, and I turned and looked behind me.

"They got one treed," he said.

I turned back to him and realized he was only listening to the dogs. They were barking differently now: long, drawn-out howls instead of the short, choppy barking of before.

"Let's go," he said.

I looked at Sikes, but she already had her flashlight on, stepping into the trees.

43 THE GIRL CAN SHOOT

If he weren't considerate of us, I believe Hoyt could have sprinted through the woods like it was open highway. He rushed toward the dogs, stopping every now and then to let us catch up. I followed behind Sikes, wading through palmetto, ducking under vines, untangling myself from the black thorns, getting whipped in the face by whatever branches Sikes swept away. I didn't see how she was moving so fast carrying the rifle.

Eventually we came to the dogs leaping up at the base of a giant water oak. They bayed and raked at the bark and carried on like whatever was up there had insulted their families for generations. Hoyt stood a few yards back, circling the tree, using the hat light to search its uppermost branches. I heard a hissing sound and looked around until I realized it was coming from Hoyt.

"What's he doing?" I asked Sikes.

She was studying the treetop, watching Hoyt's light pass over it. "He's trying to get it to look at us," she said. "Then we can see its eyes reflecting."

"You have any idea where we are?" I asked.

"Sort of," she said, still watching Hoyt's light.

"I don't see how we can keep up with him," I said.

"He found him," Sikes said, pointing up. "You see it?"

I looked up, trying to see the coon. I saw nothing but a tangle of branches and leaves.

"See it?" she asked again.

"Not yet," I said.

"All right, you two," Hoyt said. "One of you knock it down."

"You want to shoot?" Sikes asked me.

"Go ahead," I said.

She didn't offer a second time. She worked the action on the rifle and brought it up to her shoulder like she'd done it a thousand times. I started to plug my ears, but she fired a shot before I was able to react. The noise was small and cap-like, nothing at all like the deer rifle.

"You hit him!" Hoyt shouted.

Overhead I heard branches popping and leaves swishing. Then I caught a glimpse of a large, furry blob plummeting down through the tangle. The blob finally hit with a thud, and the dogs rushed it, snarling and pinning it to the ground.

Hoyt waded into the fray. "Get off that!" he shouted.

The dogs instantly backed away, but they were still tense and worked up, rolling growls in their throats. The dead raccoon lay still on the ground, its upper lip lifted in a frozen snarl that showed sharp, tiny teeth. It must have weighed thirty pounds.

Hoyt picked it up and studied it.

"Dang, girl," he said. "You killed it deader'n a stone."

"That's a big one," Sikes said.

"Yeah," he said. "Big fat old buck." He lifted it over his shoulder and dropped it into the coon bag. "Need a couple more like him."

Once the coon was out of sight, the dogs instantly lost interest in it. They put their noses to the ground and trotted off into the darkness again.

"Let's get us another one," Hoyt said.

"You can shoot the next one," Sikes offered me.

"OK," I said, trying not to sound as reluctant as I felt.

Sikes passed me the rifle. "It's on safety," she said.

Hoyt started in the direction of the dogs, and Sikes fell in behind him. It seemed impossible I would be able to see a coon, much less hit it with the rifle. It appeared there was no end of ways for these people to make a fool of me. But for the time being I was trapped in this giant swamp. The darkness closed around me, and I clicked on my flashlight and hurried after them.

I was able to see the next raccoon after both Sikes and Hoyt got behind me and pointed over my shoulder at the tiny, glowing eyes.

Then I shot at it eight times before I finally brought it down. They congratulated me on my first kill, but I knew inside they were laughing.

Hoyt was tireless. Even as the hunt dragged into the later hours of the night, he ducked and charged his way behind the dogs like every tree was the first. After Sikes shot the next coon, we stopped trying to keep up with Hoyt, instead ambling along under the big trees, stopping every now and then to rest and listen.

"You hear about my grandmother?" I asked.

"Yes," she said. "Hoyt told my parents today."

"Have you ever met her?"

"She came to our house a long time ago, but I was too little to remember much. She was with your grandfather."

"Yeah. I never met my grandfather. I'm just now getting to know my grandmother."

For a moment we didn't say anything, listening to the dogs. I saw Hoyt's light passing through the treetops in the distance.

"I see him up there," I said.

"Yeah," she said. "Me too."

The dogs suddenly changed their barking and Hoyt began hooting and hissing.

"You ready?" I asked.

"Yeah," she said. "Let's go."

We watched Hoyt shoot the fifth raccoon. By the time Hoyt had it in the sack it sounded like the dogs were already a quarter mile away.

"How long will the dogs hunt?" I asked.

"Man," Hoyt said, "they want coons so bad they'll hunt until you make them stop. Especially Truckstop. He's like the Special Forces of coon dogs. He'll hunt all night and probably all the next day if you don't call him off."

"What time is it?" I asked.

"Ten o'clock," Sikes said. "I was thinking I'd better get back."

I was relieved to hear her make the suggestion. "Yeah," I said. "I better get back too."

"Hey, no problem," Hoyt said. "I've gotta go grab the dogs. Sounds like they ran off a ways. You know how to get out of here?"

Neither of us said anything.

Hoyt pointed to his left. "Head straight that way," he said. "It ain't far. You'll come to the field. You should see the truck."

I looked in the direction he was pointing.

"You can't get lost," he said. "You'll walk into water if you go wrong. Just don't walk through any water."

"I think we'll be OK," Sikes said. "Let's go, Win. I can ride you back to our house on the four-wheeler, and then Dad can take you home."

I followed Sikes as we found our way out of the swamp. I was so tired my legs ached. I no longer cared who was in front or who had the rifle or anything at all having to do with pride. I just wanted to get in bed.

After about fifteen minutes of walking, we broke from the trees and faced an open field. A giant, orange moon sat low on the horizon, illuminating everything in a strange, pale light. The heavy equipment was framed against the far trees, and the catfish ponds appeared as black, shimmering squares. It seemed like a vision one would comment on, but neither of us did. Without a word, Sikes started up the turn row. Almost a half mile ahead, I saw Hoyt's truck like a little white toy left in the moonlight. I settled into a rhythmic stride, focused on my heavy feet scuffling on the dirt road, the dogs barking somewhere behind us, deep in the swamp, far away like something in a hole. I imagined Hoyt out there alone and wondered if he was in the least bit scared. But I only wondered. I was too weary for sympathy. *Bed*, I thought. *Bed.*

At one point I suddenly came upon Sikes, waiting for me.

"It's not much further," she said.

"I see it," I said. "You don't have to wait for me."

She turned and moved on, and I watched her heels and picked up my pace so I wouldn't fall behind again.

We finally came to Hoyt's truck. Sikes opened the passenger-side door and left her flashlight on the seat. I came behind her and left mine next to it.

"Cool moon," she said.

"Yeah," I said.

I waited until she mounted the ATV and cranked it. Then I climbed on behind her and grabbed the game rack. Suddenly Sikes gassed the engine, forcing me to throw my arms around her waist to keep from falling backwards. Soon I was enveloped in the steady whine of the engine noise and the wind blowing past my ears. Sikes didn't seem to mind me holding closely to her and in that moment, it seemed I had known her for a long time. My hands were cold, and I slid them into the front pockets of her ski jacket and rested my face against her back and out of the wind.

"It was fun," she said.

"Yeah," I said. I would have said more, but I really didn't feel like saying anything at all. I breathed in the baby powder smell of her hair and closed my eyes.

44 STEPPING ON NECKS

By the time we got back to Sikes's house it was almost eleven o'clock. She went inside to get Mr. Rhodes while I waited in the driveway next to his Cadillac, kicking the mud off my boots.

In a moment Mr. Rhodes appeared at the front door in his night robe and slippers, keys in hand. Sikes stopped in the light of the doorway and gave me a little wave from behind him.

"See you later," I said.

"Wednesday," she said.

"Yeah," I said. "See you then."

The Cadillac was big and comfortable and smooth. In spite of being dressed for bed, Mr. Rhodes seemed alert. I could tell he had something on his mind.

We came to the highway, and he turned right and started back toward Cottonlandia.

"We got to make a stop up here," he said. "It won't take a minute."

"OK," I said. I didn't care. I was about to drift off to sleep.

About a mile up the road he slowed and swung off the highway into a small cluster of mobile homes. These homes made Hoyt's single-wide look like a palace. They were sunbaked, weather-streaked, and patched with tar and plywood. The yards were muddy ruts of bare dirt with an assortment of rusted-out cars laying about, some of them tireless on cinderblocks, others with doors missing and their hoods up. Mud-splattered children's toys lay scattered about.

Mr. Rhodes stopped and got out, leaving his car door open, the Cadillac dinging softly. He stood under the humming light of a utility pole, studying the mobile home closest to us. Some of its windows glowed with dingy, yellow light. After a moment he started toward it and went up three creaky, wood steps and rapped on the door.

I saw a silhouette dart across the window. Then another.

He knocked again. "Maisel!" he called.

Another light came on at the end of the trailer. Mr. Rhodes cocked his head at it and waited. In a moment the front door opened, and an elderly woman appeared with her robe clutched about her.

"Lot of cars out here, Maisel," Mr. Rhodes said.

She glanced over the yard.

"How many people you got in there with you?"

"Just my family," she said.

"You want me to come in?"

"You don't need to do that, Mr. Rhodes," she said.

"I don't like people making *their* problems *my* problems. This is starting to feel like my problem."

"Yes, sir," she said.

"You count four and send the rest out."

"Where they gonna go tonight?"

"That sounds like something else you're about to make my problem. And you already know the solution to it."

"We can't afford it."

"There you go again. Now it's late, and I'm not real happy about standing out here. I'm about to go sit in my car and wait while you decide who goes."

He turned and started back toward me. The lady watched him for a moment, then disappeared inside.

"Sorry about this," he said. "Sun goes down and the place fills up like a chicken house."

I didn't know what to say. I was fully awake again.

"They've got options," he added.

Another light came on inside, and I saw the shadows of people moving past the windows. Then a thin man about Hoyt's age stepped from the doorway. He led three little girls down the steps. They had blankets draped over their shoulders. The children looked at us curiously, but the man didn't even glance our way.

"There's more," Mr. Rhodes mumbled.

The man led the girls into the darkness. Mr. Rhodes shifted the car into gear. "But I'm not about to go into that rat hole."

"Where you think they'll go?" I asked.

He started forward and up onto the highway again. "They're already back inside."

I saw Denton's store up ahead.

"But you got to keep your foot on their neck," he added, "or they'll eat at your wallet like termites."

I didn't fully understand what I'd seen at the trailer park, but it left me with a dirty feeling. Mr. Rhodes dropped me off, and I placed my boots on the front porch and crept inside and upstairs to my room. I draped my jacket and jeans over the footboard and crawled into bed mostly dressed.

My body was tired, but my mind wouldn't sleep. I kept seeing the thin man and the girls walking off into the darkness. And the imagery soon led me to the reconstruction of my own predicament. In a moment I had a picture of myself in a damp, dark hole, swimming in a nauseating soup of problems.

I had no money.

I'd been abandoned by both of my parents.

I was trapped in a rotting, old house with two old women and a farmer who didn't seem to like me.

My life was over.

Finally, I saw Dad standing at the top of the hole, shoveling dirt loads of his expectation in on me.

My breathing became quick and my heart raced. My mind scrambled to find footholds and climb out of that dark place. I remembered we were selling the farm.

Then we'd have money.

Then I could move back to New York.

Stop. Don't think about it anymore.

I lay in the soft light of the gas heater, blocking any further thought of my problems. My heart settled, my breathing slowed, and my mind spun down. I closed my eyes again and remembered the strange way the moonlight fell across the fields. The way it cast the tall trees at the edge of the swamp in a silver-white light. Then I thought of Hoyt, still out there in the night, plunging ahead through the raspy palmetto. The dark, still water of the brake. I heard the haunting sounds of the coon dogs, echoing through the timber, like something from a dream.

45 NEW YEAR'S EVE

I woke the next morning to the mad ting-tinging of Grandmother's bell from downstairs. I looked at Evil and saw it was only seven o'clock. I put my head under my pillow and drifted off again.

The next time I woke it was to loud banging just across the hall. Evil said nine. The pillow was useless against such racket. I got up and opened my door and saw Hoyt in Grandmother's room, taking her bed apart. He saw me and straightened and holstered his hammer in his tool belt.

"Did I wake you up?"

I rubbed my eyes. "Yes."

"Sorry about that. Mr. Case said I had to get this done before she falls down those stairs."

I yawned. "It's OK. What time did you get back last night?"

"Shoot, I don't know. I figured I might not ever get to hunt with a dog like *that* again."

"Maybe when you get the puppies they'll be as good."

"That's what I'm hoping for. I got the two lovebirds penned up at the house right now, saying goodbye. It's New Year's Eve. That's got to be good luck, don't you think?"

"I guess."

Hoyt took a step toward the bed. "Well, I got to move all this down there and get back to the house. I'm supposed to have Truckstop at my buddy's by three, and Tammy wants me to take her out to the Catfish House tonight."

"What's Grandmother doing?"

Hoyt glanced at the stairs, and I thought I saw his eyes grow a little wider. "She's sitting down there at the dining room table."

I frowned. "I guess I better go talk to her."

"Yeah, well, Mr. Case says he's coming by about eleven o'clock to take you into town."

"Winchester Canterbury the third!" Grandmother screeched. "I hear you up there."

Hoyt yanked his hammer out of the tool belt and spun back to face the bed.

"I'll be there in a little bit," I called down the stairs. "I'm getting dressed."

I turned to Hoyt again. He was kneeling by the bed, tapping it with the hammer, watching me. "Jesus," I said. "Nothing wrong with her ears."

He shook his head.

"Never been anything wrong with my *ears!*" she shouted. "And watch your language!"

I took my time bathing and getting dressed, letting the clock run toward eleven as much as I could. All the while Hoyt was banging things apart and dragging them down the stairs. When I eventually started the descent to visit Grandmother, I met Hoyt coming up for another load. He glanced at me, pursed his lips, and made a silent whistle.

"What?" I said.

He showed me his hands like he was innocent and passed on.

The living room was strangely mixed with Grandmother's bedroom furniture, her big hospital bed looking very out of place in the middle of the floor. As I turned the corner into the dining room, her eyes drilled through me. She sat straight-backed at the head of the table, her lipstick gleaming and her wig in place.

"Wouldn't have hurt you to bring a load on your way down," she snapped.

"Yes, ma'am," I said. "I'll get something when I go back up."

"But I don't imagine you get much done anyway, sleeping in until nine o'clock in the morning like a princess."

"I was up late," I said.

"Me too. I've been thinking about the fact that I'm going to have to give my farm to a grandchild who couldn't care less about it. I suppose you'll sell it as soon as you're eighteen years old."

"Well, I haven't—"

"You have too. How else are you going to get back your fancy cars and airplanes and country club memberships?"

I looked down at my feet. "That's a long time off."

"That's right," she said. "And I'll be dead, so why should I care?"

I didn't respond.

"I can die knowing my son ruined our family name and lost everything of his *and* mine."

She was wearing me out. I just wanted to leave. I looked at her again. "We have the meeting with the lawyer today."

"I suppose you do."

"I think I should go wait outside for Mr. Case."

"When you two finish scheming behind my back, I'll be here waiting. I suppose I need my daily drag about town."

I nodded.

"And you tell John I want my Cadillac back."

"You think you can drive a car?"

"That doesn't have anything to do with it. It's mine and I want it back."

"Yes, ma'am."

"Go ahead," she said. "You're dismissed."

"Thank you."

I never thought I'd look forward to being with the farmer, but with Grandmother up and about, even his company would be a relief.

46 CLOSING THE DEAL

On the way into Greenwood the farmer spoke to me in his calm, deliberate manner, always keeping an eye on the passing fields and the sky as he talked.

"The lawyer's name is Tim Haney," he said. "He's the son of a friend of mine. Comes from a nice family. He ought to do a good job for you."

He took the cup from his dashboard, brought it to his lips, and put it back again.

"He didn't draw up the original will—that was done by a lawyer out of Jackson—but he's got a copy of it. I figured it'd be better to get somebody a little more local to handle this. He'll probably have to drive out and see your grandmother a few times. They charge by the hour, you know?"

I didn't know anything about how lawyers worked, so I stayed quiet. We passed Walmart and moved into the outskirts of the business district, full of drab, one-level buildings and two strip malls. It didn't appear anyone had built anything new in a long time. Then we crossed over the Yazoo River and into downtown, where several buildings were as high as five stories but still had that same feel of age and depression.

Tim Haney's office was on the second floor of the Planters Bank building. We parked on Howard Street and went through a side door up a flight of stairs. Mr. Haney's operation comprised a simple front office with a reception desk and his office behind it. He was out to greet us as soon as we stepped through the door. He looked to be in his early forties, with wire-frame eyeglasses and a neatly pressed suit topped with a bow tie.

"Hi, Mr. Case," he said, thrusting his hand out eagerly.

"Tim," the farmer replied, shaking with him. "Thank you for seeing us on a holiday. This is Win I've got with me."

"Hey, Win," he said. I shook hands with him too.

"Come in my office. My receptionist is out, so things are a bit of a mess."

It was a small office, but nothing about it appeared to be a mess. His desk was almost completely clean except for a stack of papers at the edge and a single folder opened before him. We sat in the two chairs before his desk while Tim settled into his own.

"Dad said to tell you hello," he said to the farmer.

"I need to get out that way and pay him a visit," the farmer replied. "How's your mother?"

"She's doing fine. Thanks for asking."

The lawyer turned to me. "So how do you like Mississippi, Win?"

"Still sort of getting used to things," I replied.

Tim nodded sympathetically. "I can imagine. Little different from New York City, isn't it?"

I nodded.

"OK," he continued, looking down at the folder. "Let me see . . . Couple of things. The easy part first. The will is fairly straightforward. She leaves everything to Winchester Jr., her only child."

He looked back at the farmer. "So we want to change this to divert the assets into a generation-skipping trust for Win here. I understand she's been sick for quite a while. And I understand we want to make certain the will is not contestable on the basis she is not of sound mind and body. So I'll go out there and visit with her a couple of times until I'm comfortable she knows what she's doing."

He glanced at me, then back at the farmer. "Does that all sound right to you?"

The farmer looked at me. "That's what we're doing, isn't it, Win?"

"That's right," I said.

The lawyer nodded. "OK. Now for the tricky part. Are either of you aware of the deal Winchester made with Charlie Rhodes?"

We both shook our heads.

The lawyer looked at me. "It seems your father got a limited power of attorney over her a few years back, claiming she wasn't fit to make reasonable decisions concerning her assets. He wrote a ten-year lease to Mr. Rhodes, starting next year, with an option to purchase the property at any time upon her death."

I looked at the farmer. He remained expressionless.

"He told me about the lease," I said. "But I didn't know about the rest."

The lawyer continued.

"If Charlie Rhodes gets nervous about any of these changes—thinks it might affect his deal with your dad—then he can stir up trouble."

"What do you suggest?" the farmer asked.

The lawyer nodded like he was waiting to tell us. "I think all we've got to do is have Win, as the new heir, sign a document stating his intentions to honor Charlie Rhodes's lease. A statement of intent, if you will. I think that will suffice."

"What kind of trouble can he stir up?" I asked.

"Here's the issue. Your father was supposed to make decisions for her benefit. I think it's arguable that the Rhodes lease was not for her benefit, but for his. As I understand it, this was not a transaction your grandmother would have approved of in any state of mind."

"So she could cancel it?"

"She could certainly contest it."

"And the deal would be off?"

"It's possible that she could fight it and win. Or lose. Regardless, it would cause a big mess financially and personally for everyone."

I stared at my shoes, taking it all in. When I looked up, the lawyer and farmer were waiting patiently for my decision.

"The lease starts next year?" I asked.

"That's right."

"They'll dig it all up?"

"They'll make ponds on the place, yes."

"What happens after ten years or if he doesn't buy it?"

"You'll get it back."

"And we can farm cotton again?"

The lawyer looked at Mr. Case. "I don't—"

"No, you'll never farm cotton again," the farmer said. "Once they dig up the topsoil, you'll never grow anything there again except catfish."

The lawyer turned back to me. "So yes," he said. "For all practical purposes, it will be a catfish farm from here on out whether he ends up buying it or not."

"And if I don't sign the statement of intent, then Grandmother could stop it all?"

"I think that is very possible. Mr. Rhodes would want to firm up his position in light of the new ownership. He would want new contracts reflecting the changes. And since we're trying to present your grandmother as being of sound mind, she would have to sign them."

"And then she'd know about everything."

"Correct. And she could contest every decision your father made."

I didn't want to look at the farmer. Suddenly I wished he weren't there. I took a deep breath and rehearsed what it was I was supposed to accomplish. *Sell it*, I remembered. *Sell it and get the money and get out of this place. Get my life back.*

The lawyer slid a document in front of me. "Here is the letter of intent," he said. "I just need you to sign it and have Mr. Case witness. I'll also sign as the trustee."

I had to look at him.

"It's up to you, Win," the farmer said. "I'm not part of this to get in the way. It's your family's property, and your father's certainly made his wishes clear."

"It was going to happen anyway," I said. But it came out more like a question than a statement.

The farmer didn't answer me.

"So are we all in agreement?" the lawyer asked.

It didn't feel right. I hadn't expected for it all to feel so wrong. I hadn't expected it all to be my decision. But I reminded myself again of why I was there. I remembered Dad's voice over the phone. *Sell it. Four million dollars.* And I thought of the sorry old house and the gray weather and the lipstick skeleton and the wet, muddy fields and the whole mess I was in and how much I just wanted my old life back.

"Give me a pen," I said.

The lawyer slid the pen to me. I signed on the line.

"Dad wants to sell it anyway," I said. "I guess it doesn't matter if it's catfish farms or cotton. It's what Dad wants."

The lawyer nodded and slid the document to the farmer. He took the pen and scratched his signature beneath mine. Finally, the lawyer signed it and closed the folder.

Part II

47 GREENWOOD HIGH

It wasn't until the holidays were over that I felt my new life really began. I'd gotten Grandmother out of bed, and everything was underway to secure the farm until I was able to sell it. Then I would have money again. Then I would leave Walnut Bend and try to remake my life in the city.

This isn't to say I *really* felt good about any of it. After all, I wouldn't have access to the money until Grandmother passed away. And she seemed to grow healthier and meaner every day. Living with her was like being trapped in a box with a yappy dog.

Then there was the heavier issue of my parents. So far, I'd done a good job of not thinking about it too much. Working on the Grandmother situation had been an effective distraction. Now I couldn't help but feel the slow creep of a horrible reality. My father faced a prison sentence, and my mother was sick and maybe crazy for reasons I didn't understand. And should I ever get a chance at another life, it would never be like my old one.

Maybe relief was in sight, but it could be years away. Meanwhile I had no choice but to figure out a way to survive Cottonlandia.

The farmer came to drive me on my first day of school. He waited in the foyer and observed the scene of Grandmother constantly ringing her bell and snapping at me about my table manners and Gert scurrying about to extinguish all her fires. Finally, I was able to get breakfast down, grab the bag lunch Gert made for me, and escape past him out the front door.

"Have a good day, ladies," I heard him say.

"I don't see my Cadillac out there, John!" she said.

"I'm working on it, ma'am," he said as he closed the door. I was already getting in the truck. I saw him smile to himself and start my way. What he had to smile about, I didn't know. The papers I'd signed made sure this was his last year of farming Cottonlandia. And it seemed he was more comfortable about it all than I was.

It was a clear morning as we pulled out of Headquarters and started toward the highway. The farmer scanned the fields and spit quietly in his cup. I sat up straight, feeling a surge of confidence. School was one place where these people wouldn't have anything over me.

"About time to start rowing up," he said to no one in particular. "Get the burn-down out."

I assumed those were farm terms, and I didn't want to talk about farming.

"Have you heard anything about my mom?"

He glanced at me. "I think she's doing better."

"You think I can call her soon?"

He hesitated. "I don't know," he said. "I hope so. She's not really herself yet."

"Is she crazy?"

"I wouldn't say that . . . I'd say she's sad. So sad she doesn't want to do anything."

"Not even talk to me?"

"When people get like she is, they can't make good decisions. That's why they need a doctor watching them."

"I don't see why it would hurt for me to talk to her."

"Sometimes people don't want you to see them until they're better."

"So she doesn't want to see me?"

"I didn't say that, and I don't know that. I'm just going by what the doctors say. They think it's best to leave her alone for a while."

I looked out the window just as we were passing a catfish farm. Giant, metal paddle wheels churned at the edges, oxygenating the water. On the calm sides hundreds of coots splashed and socialized.

I turned back to him. "Are you mad at me?"

"About what?" he said. But he knew exactly what I was talking about.

"About the farm?"

"I'm not mad at you," he said. "It's not my place to be mad about it."

"But you think I did the wrong thing?"

He didn't answer right away. "I think a boy your age is supposed to listen to their father. I think you ought to know it was his decision and not yours."

Greenwood High was a flat, red brick building with about as much character as a dog kennel. It was surrounded by a utility fence, bent and sagging. Kids poured out of cars and trucks and buses, and more of them were walking a dirt trail at the edge of the highway. I had never seen such a grubby collection of students.

We parked, and I followed the farmer as he navigated his way through the noisy mass of people toward the office. We waited in line until it was our turn at the front desk, and a woman gave him some paperwork. It was too loud in the room to hear anything they said. I watched him sign some things and give everything back to her but one page. In return she gave him a stack of books and an orientation sheet. Then he took me aside and put his hand on my shoulder. "You going to be OK?"

"I'll be fine," I said.

"They contacted your old school, and based on your records they decided to put you in the advanced classes."

"OK," I said.

"The office has my cell phone number if you need to call me. You want to write it down?"

I shook my head. "No, I'll be fine."

"All right," he said, handing me the books and sheet of paper. "You need to go to room 401. Then you follow this schedule."

"And I ride the bus home?"

"That's right. The number should be on that same sheet. It'll stop at the driveway. I'll have Hoyt or Luther leave the four-wheeler out there for you. Keys'll be on top of the tire."

"OK," I said. "See you later."

As I bumped my way through the hall to locate my locker, I found it hard to imagine all of these loud, grungy students quietly packed away into classrooms. I found it even harder to imagine a girl like Sikes Rhodes in such a place. I kept looking around for her but couldn't pick her out in the sea of bodies.

I eventually found my locker, put my lunch in it, and continued to room 401. The students there were nicer-looking and less rowdy, but I didn't see Sikes. I stood against the wall until a buzzer went off and the teacher told people to take their seats. I found an empty chair at the back and sat down with my books. A scrawny white boy in jeans and an undershirt and a Valvoline ball cap sat next to me, slumped down in his chair.

"Take your seats," the teacher repeated.

The kid turned to me. He looked at my shirt and my jeans and my shoes and then at my face again. After a moment he reached in his pocket and pulled out a can of Skoal and packed it against his leg, watching me the entire time. Then he opened it and took a pinch of the tobacco and stuffed it behind his bottom lip, making a demonstration of it to me. I turned away, but I felt him watching me.

"I swallow the juice," he said.

I didn't answer him.

The instructor had us open our math books to page twenty. I found the lesson and smiled to myself when I saw it was on algebra. I'd learned it two years before. I found my next two classes, English and history, to be even less of a challenge. Fortunately, we changed classrooms and I didn't have the distraction of the weird kid next to me. By noon I realized my biggest problem at Greenwood High was going to be boredom.

48 BUSTER

We broke for lunch at eleven thirty, and I followed the rest of the students to the cafeteria. I traveled through the food line, grabbed a tray, and accepted a plate of pork chops, mashed potatoes, and green beans. At the end of the line a woman gave me a small carton of an orange drink. Then I took my meal and found a seat near the wall at an empty table.

As I picked at my food I occasionally glanced up, looking for Sikes. I eventually saw her sitting with her friends at the far side of the room. I thought of going over to them, but didn't want to draw too much attention to myself, standing with my tray and crossing the floor.

After lunch we were let out into the schoolyard for a thirty-minute recess. I saw Sikes again, talking and laughing with two other girls at a cement picnic table. I started their way.

"Hey," I said.

She turned to me. "Hey, Win. How's your first day?"

"Fine," I said.

She turned back to her friends. "Y'all, this is Win. His grandmother owns Cottonlandia. Win, this is Julie and Sara."

Both of them were pretty and nicely dressed.

"Hey," I said.

Julie looked at Sikes and tucked her long, brunette hair behind her ear. "Is that the one next to you with the haunted house?" she asked.

Sikes laughed. "Yeah, but it's not really haunted."

"Did you make all that up!" Julie said. "All that stuff about the dead people in the attic?"

"It scared you, didn't it?" Sikes said.

Sara was a redhead with the smoothest skin I'd ever seen. She looked up at me and frowned. "Then she wrecked her dad's truck."

"It's *my* truck," Sikes said.

"Whatever," Sara replied. "She's got everything."

"I do not!" Sikes exclaimed, but she was smiling like she knew she did.

"Well, it *is* like a haunted house," I said. "I haven't searched the attic for dead bodies, but my grandmother's so close to dead she's almost a ghost."

"That's *so* mean!" Julie said.

"She's meaner," I said.

"Win is from New York," Sikes said.

"Having your own farm is cool," Julie said.

"You don't have to live there," I said. "You might change your mind if you did."

I saw Sikes look over my shoulder and frown. "What do you want, Buster?"

I turned and saw the scrawny kid from first period standing behind me, his lip still bulging with the tobacco. "Nothing," he said. He looked at me. "You know them?"

"Yes," I said.

He looked back at the girls. "Any y'all wanna go on a date?"

"Shut up, Buster!" Julie said. "Don't ever ask us that again. You're gross."

He adjusted his ball cap and looked at me and smiled with mischief. "Where did you come from?"

I still wasn't sure how to take the kid. "New York," I said. "I live at Cottonlandia now."

I thought I saw his eyes glimmer. "I know that place," he said. "You got some big deer. You shot any big deer?"

I nodded. "Yeah. I shot a nine-point a couple of weeks ago."

"I figured," he said. He looked at the ground and let a long line of brown spit fall from his mouth.

"Oh my God, Buster!" Sara said. "You are disgusting!"

"I can't believe they let you do that," Sikes said. "You can't chew tobacco in school."

Buster looked at her and twitched his chin. "Can and do," he said.

"They're going to send you to jail again."

Buster stiffened. "I didn't go to jail."

"That's not what we heard."

"You don't know nothing," he said.

"Why don't you leave us alone," Julie said.

He turned back to me. "You wanna go hunting some time?"

"Nobody wants to do anything with you," Sara said.

"I ain't talking to you," he said, still looking at me.

"I don't know," I said. "I don't know much about it. I've only been once."

"And you killed a nine-point?"

"Yes."

"Well, I figured they was running around like chickens over there."

"Ignore him, Win," Sara said.

Buster took a step back. "Man," he continued. "I can't even have a conversation with all the fussing going on in my ears. You wanna know how to knock down a big one, you come find me."

"All right," I said. "I'll keep that in mind."

He looked back at the girls. "Same goes for all three of you too."

"Shut up, Buster," Julie said.

"In your dreams," Sara said.

Buster looked back at me and smiled, touched the bill of his hat, and spat. Then he turned and walked off.

"Win, we've got to take you shopping," Sikes said. "I think Buster's attracted to the Hot Saddle."

I looked down at my pants. Then my feet. "What about these stupid tennis shoes with the lightning bolt?"

"All of it," Sikes said. "We need to save you while there's still time."

When I looked up, Julie was nodding in agreement. "The Hot Saddle has to go."

"I need a job," I said. "Any of you ever had a job?"

"I help my mother at her gift shop on the weekends," Sara said. "But I don't get paid."

"I need one where I get paid. Then I can buy some different clothes."

"He's out of money," Sikes told them.

"Won't your grandmother give you some?"

"All she spends money on is food and lipstick. She's so cheap she won't even plug in the phone."

"What?" Julie said. "Does she have help?"

"Yes, her name's Gert, and she wears pine straw in her ears. I don't know where the farm money goes, but it'll probably be a while before anybody sees any of it."

"You want to sit with us?"

"I guess so," I said.

"Stick with us and we'll keep Buster away from you," Sara said.

49 EXPERIENCE

After my last class I put all my books away in my locker. I wouldn't need any of them to study. Not for two years, it seemed. Then I looked at my orientation sheet, figured out my bus number, and headed to the busing area.

The ride home was like a third-world experience to me. The only thing missing was chickens on the roof. It was bouncy and loud and smelled of body odor and gas fumes. When I finally stepped out on the driveway to Cottonlandia, I savored a deep breath of the cool, fresh air coming over the fields.

I found my ATV parked behind the farm sign. I patted the top of the tire until I felt the key, climbed on, and raced for the shop, nearly a mile to the south.

I pulled up beside Hoyt's and the farmer's trucks. I heard them talking inside the metal building. When I walked through the bay doors, I saw the three of them standing over an old, rusty, beat-up Cadillac.

"That hers?" I asked.

The farmer nodded.

"It *was*," Luther said. "Six years ago."

"He like to not found it," Hoyt said. "Peepee had it out in the middle of his collard patch."

"Does it work?" I asked.

"There's not even an engine in it," Hoyt said.

"Are you going to take it to her like that?"

"We're thinking about it," Hoyt said.

"Yeah," Luther said. "Thinking about it."

"Let's call it, boys," the farmer said. "Luther, you got lockup."

The farmer started past me, asking as he went, "How'd it go today?"

"Good. I learned everything they were teaching in eighth grade back in New York. It's going to be easy."

Hoyt came up beside me, and we followed the farmer out into the cool dusk. "What you doing over here?" he asked.

"I wanted to see if I could get a job."

"Shoot, yeah, man! We got tons—"

The farmer stopped and turned to me. "What kind of experience do you have?"

"Like what?"

"That's what I'm *asking* you."

I felt myself falling into one of his traps. "I've never had a job," I said.

He continued to his truck. "Last time we talked about this you weren't interested in learning. So if you don't have any experience, I don't have a job for you."

I looked at Hoyt. He turned up his palms with an "I don't know" look.

I felt anger rushing to my face. "I want to learn now," I said. "I need the money."

The farmer climbed in his truck and shut the door. He hung his elbow out the window and looked at me. "Lots of people need money. Why should I give you mine?"

"Because this is my farm! And I want a job!"

"What do you know about a job? Tell me what you think a job is."

"That's stupid. It's where I work and you pay me."

"It's when I pay you for something I want."

"Fine."

"So when you figure out what it is you can do for me that I want, come back and maybe I'll pay you for it."

"How do I know what you want?"

He started the truck and put it in gear. "Experience," he said.

I was left standing on the dirt road with Hoyt. I turned to him. "Why does he have to act like such an asshole?"

"Maybe he's just got a lot on his mind. Man, you never can tell what a person's got on his mind."

"How am I supposed to get experience when he won't give me a job? I thought he'd *want* me to ask for a job."

"He just said to think of something he wanted, didn't he? Let's find something he wants."

I frowned and shook my head. Hoyt started looking around. "Come on, let's go see what we can find. There's tons of stuff that needs doing around here. Tons!"

I followed Hoyt around the side of the shop, where he stopped, looking over a dirt-and-grass lot of miscellaneous farm implements—chemical tanks and disks and cotton wagons and all sorts of things one would pull behind a vehicle. Some were new-looking, and some were rusty and overgrown with weeds like they hadn't been used in years, but everything was ordered in neat rows, regardless of its condition.

Hoyt pointed to the trees at the back of the lot. "I'll tell you what. There's all kinds of trash blown up into those trees. He hates that stuff, and doesn't seem like we ever get around to it. Man, I bet he'd *really* like you to pick it all up."

"OK," I said.

He turned to me. "That's *something*."

I frowned. "I don't see why I have to beg him for a job."

"Man, *forget* about that. You ain't begging; you're trading, see? He gives you money for something he wants—like that garbage picked up. After you start to learn about things around here, you'll just *know* what he wants and he'll pay you all the time. Like me. See? That's what he's *saying*. That's *experience*."

Suddenly it all made sense, but I was still annoyed.

"He could have just told me that," I said.

Hoyt started past me, and I followed him back toward my ATV. "He wanted you to figure it out. Things stay with you when you have to figure them out for yourself."

I didn't answer. Hoyt stopped at the ATV and waited for me. "I been working for him for nearly fifteen years," he said. "He wants it done right, but he's real fair. And he'll do just about anything for you."

"OK," I said. "I'll come back tomorrow and ask him about the trash."

"Yeah, man. Don't worry about it."

I climbed on the ATV and cranked it.

"How's it running?"

"Good," I said.

Hoyt slapped his hands against his thighs, and dust puffed out and hung in the air. "All right, then," he said. "I got some coon hunting to do tonight. I'd take you with me if it wasn't a school night."

"Do you have Truckstop again?"

"Naw, but I got Warrior. She's good. The brown one."

"Maybe next time," I said.

Hoyt started toward his truck. "Before long I'll have a bunch of *baby* Truckstops."

"I'll see you tomorrow," I said.

The next morning it was storming. I didn't know what was worse, staying inside with Grandmother yapping at me or going out into the cold, windblown rain. I had nearly a mile to travel on the ATV and then no telling how long waiting for the school bus. Despite my frustration with the farmer, I kept glancing out the window, hoping he'd come for me.

The farmer didn't show, but just as I was pulling on my rain jacket, I saw Mrs. Rhodes's Land Rover pull up to the house. By the time she beeped the horn, I was already out the door.

I climbed onto the back seat and slammed the door behind me. The inside of the car was filled with the big-hair perfume smell of Mrs. Rhodes, but it was clean and warm and dry. And Sikes was turned, smiling at me from the front seat, looking pretty and free of worries.

"Mr. Case called and said you might want a ride," Sikes said.

I pulled off my jacket and put it on the floor. "Thanks," I said.

"I don't know how anybody can be expected to stand out in weather like this," Mrs. Rhodes said. "Lord."

On the way to school they asked me more about my old life in New York. I told them about the private planes and the trips to Aspen and the Hamptons and hockey and Broadway plays—my life only a few weeks before. Now it all felt like I'd been on a fancy trip and was back to my real life, talking about it. But what mattered to them was that I'd been there. I'd been that person once, and it meant something to them.

"We can pick you up some other days," Sikes said. "We can drop you off, too, if I don't have after-school stuff."

"Like what?"

"Violin lessons. Volleyball. There's all kinds of stuff to do. You should sign up for something."

"Maybe," I said. "I'll see how it goes."

Once we got to school Sikes and I went our separate ways. Buster didn't sit next to me in first period, but I caught him looking at me a couple of times across the room. He had a curious way of staring at a person, like he'd asked them a question and was waiting for an answer.

I ate lunch with Sikes and her friends, rain pelting the cafeteria windows. I saw Buster sitting by himself across the room, eating slowly and staring at his tray. Occasionally I caught him glancing at me.

It had stopped raining by the time the Rhodeses dropped me off after school. I didn't want to go inside and get tangled up with Grandmother, so I left my shoes on the front porch, pulled on my gum boots, and went straight for the ATV. It was time for another job interview.

50 FIRST JOB

"Pick up trash?" he said.

"That's right."

He looked across the back lot and studied the trees. I glanced at Hoyt. He was standing not far from us, wiping his hand with a rag and pretending not to listen.

"All right," the farmer finally said. "I'll pay for that."

Hoyt looked at me and gave a small pump of his fist.

"Can I do it now?" I asked.

The farmer turned and started for the shop. "Go ahead," he said over his shoulder. "Six dollars an hour. Pay you when you're done."

"Do you have a trash bag?" I asked.

"Show him where everything is, Hoyt. Get him started."

Hoyt showed me where the trash bags were kept in the shop and then said he'd show me how to clean the tank on Saturday since it might get my school clothes dirty.

"You work on Saturday?" I asked.

"Man, we start to work every day but Sunday this time of year. Gotta get rowed up and burned out and planted."

"What does that mean?"

"Make the rows. Kill the weeds. Put the seeds in the ground. You'll figure it all out."

"Yeah," I said.

I went out to the back lot and started stuffing the bag with bottles, aluminum cans, oil cartons, and windblown plastic. I filled one and went back for another. By then the farmer and Luther had gone and only Hoyt was left, closing up the shop.

"You OK over here by yourself?" he asked.

"I'm fine."

"You wanna get a few more trash bags before I lock up?"

In a moment I was standing in the road, holding a box of garbage bags, watching Hoyt drive away. The sun glowed cool orange through the far treetops, and a soft breeze punctuated the sudden loneliness of the place. But for some reason I didn't feel lonely. I felt part of something for the first time since I'd come to Cottonlandia.

Friday morning Grandmother told me Tim Haney had been out to see her the day before.

"You people don't waste any time, do you?" she asked. "Now you've got lawyers swarming me like bees."

"It's just one," I said. "He needs to make sure you're well."

"I'll bet he does. Where's my Cadillac?"

"They're getting it ready for you."

"What'd they do to it? It was fine the last time I saw it."

"I think they're just cleaning it up."

"How long does that take?"

"I don't know."

"You tell them I want it out there in the driveway where it used to be."

"Yes, ma'am."

She acted like she wanted to say something else but couldn't think of anything at the moment. Then she frowned and pinched the little bell and started ringing it. Gert appeared out of the kitchen.

"Yes, ma'am?"

"More tea," she said.

"Yes, ma'am."

Saturday I woke before daylight, dressed in front of the heater, and crept downstairs and past Grandmother's new room. Gert wasn't up yet, so I poured a bowl of cereal for myself, ate it quickly, and slipped out the back door.

The ride to the shop was bone cold, and I had to draw the hood of my jacket so tightly that only a small hole was left to see through. When I arrived Luther was already there, opening the doors.

"Morning, Win," he said.

"Good morning."

I followed him inside. "Grandmother's asking about the Cadillac again," I said.

Luther shook his head. He walked over to a floor heater and flipped it on. I moved in front of it and felt myself begin to thaw.

"What was she like before she got sick?" I asked.

Luther approached the car and studied it. "Mrs. Canterbury's always been good to everybody. Now, she wants to know where every penny of her money goes, but I tell you, not a year's gone by that I didn't get a Christmas bonus. And I never heard of nobody she wouldn't help out."

"That's hard to believe."

Luther chuckled. "I'm not saying you didn't get a lecture with that help, but if you could stand her mouth, she'd help you out."

Hoyt skidded to a stop outside, jumped from his truck, and sprinted toward us like he needed a fire extinguisher.

"What's wrong!" I said.

He stopped beside me and began rubbing his hands together before the heater. "Nothing," he said. "What are you talking about?"

There was no emergency. It was just Hoyt coming to work.

They told me the farmer was in town buying seed that morning. I grabbed my garbage bags and got back to picking up trash while the other two went to work on the big John Deere picker. It wasn't long before Hoyt trotted up.

"I thought of something," he said.

"What?"

"Once you get done with that, you can clean the spindles on the picker."

"OK," I said. "Whatever that means."

"It's not fun, but you'll learn something about the machinery. And I *know* he'll pay you for it."

"Fine," I said. "But it might take me the rest of the day to get this trash picked up. It's everywhere back here."

"That's fine. No hurry. But ask Mr. Case about cleaning the spindles when you see him."

"OK, I will. Thanks, Hoyt."

"Hey, man. No problem."

51 THE PEASANT NEXT DOOR

The farmer came over the following morning to drop off groceries and take us all to church. The prospect of Sunday service seemed to calm Grandmother, although the ride out wasn't completely free of accusations concerning the lawyer and her Cadillac. Once we approached the church and saw someone had already started scraping off the old paint and replacing the rotten wood, she seemed even more at ease, feeling that her world was straightening up.

I made it through Deacon Leon's sermon, thinking mostly about spending the afternoon with Sikes. Thinking about why I wasn't excited about it. Something was wrong, I just didn't know what.

Before the farmer left I asked him about cleaning the spindles. I could tell he was impressed by the way he studied me for a moment with his eyebrows raised.

"What do you know about spindles?" he asked.

"Not much. I plan to know a lot more by the time I'm done."

He watched me a moment longer. "OK," he finally said. "I'll pay for that."

Just after noon I drove the ATV through the back fields and around the brake to Beulah. I parked in the gravel driveway beside Mr. Rhodes's black Cadillac and Mrs. Rhodes's Land Rover.

Roxy answered the doorbell and invited me inside.

"You got a visitor, Sikes," she called to the second floor.

When there was no answer, she shook her head and started upstairs. "Wearing Roxy out," she mumbled to herself.

"Good afternoon, Win," I heard someone say.

I turned to my left and saw Mr. Rhodes sitting on a large, leather sofa in the library. In front of him was a coffee table. He had a double-barrel shotgun disassembled on the table, and he was busy wiping the components with an oil cloth.

"Hi, Mr. Rhodes," I said.

He glanced at me but kept at his work. "You duck hunt?"

"I never have."

"I'll bet half the ducks in this county fly into my brake."

"Don't we own some of the brake too?"

He didn't even stop wiping. "For now, you do."

I swallowed.

"You know what duck-hunting leases are worth these days?" he continued.

"No, sir."

He put the barrel down and looked at me. "Per acre, more than catfish and cotton."

I didn't respond.

"I spoke with your lawyer last week. Looks like it's all going to work out."

"OK."

"He says Mrs. Canterbury seems to be clear as a bell about everything."

"She's not clear about turning her land into a catfish farm," I said.

"I suppose you can put that one on your father."

"Win!" I heard Sikes call. "Come upstairs."

Mr. Rhodes twisted in his chair and directed his voice in her direction. "No boys upstairs, young lady!" he boomed.

"Does Sikes know about our lease to you?" I asked.

He looked back at me and frowned. "I don't talk about my business with the females. Involve them and they think they know how much money you have. Then they spend more than they should. That's some more advice for you. Remember that."

"Win!" she called again.

"Christ, will you just go tell her to come down here?"

"OK," I said. "See you later."

I walked into the hallway and saw Sikes standing above me. She motioned for me to come up. I pointed my chin in the direction of her father. She waved her hand dismissively.

"Just come on," she said.

Sikes met me at the top of the stairs, bright and pretty and free of worries as always. "I'm packing," she said. "Come see what I've got."

The second floor of their home was laid out in similar fashion to Cottonlandia, except there were more rooms and they were bigger, and the ceilings were higher. Instead of a narrow hall was a spacious sitting area with oil paintings on the walls. The floor wasn't cold hardwood but thick, cream-colored carpet. Instead of the spotty warmth of gas space heaters, warm air breathed quietly out of ceiling vents.

I followed Sikes to her room down on the left. It struck me that I'd never been in a teenage girl's room before, and suddenly the sick feeling I'd carried up the stairs was replaced by a tickling sensation.

The room had yellow walls and more of the plush carpet. It smelled like her hair and her clothes, of fragrant bath soap and flowers. It was full of large, curving antique furniture, the most impressive being a canopy bed, plush with pillows and a downy bedspread, something fit for a princess.

Scattered on her floor were stacks of winter clothes and beside them an open suitcase. Leaning against her bed was a pair of skis and beside them some white ski boots. She walked to her bed and turned to me. "We're going snow skiing," she said. "Look at my new skis."

I looked at them, but I wasn't really seeing them.

"Where?" I said.

"Crested Butte. Been there?"

"No, but it's not far from Aspen, so I know where it is."

She admired the skis again. "I can't wait. You'll have to ride the bus to school, but we'll just be gone for a week."

Crested Butte wasn't Aspen, but it was close enough. It seemed they were taking over my life piece by piece.

"Win?" she said.

I looked at her. "What?"

"Don't you like my skis?"

Suddenly I couldn't stand being there. Everything was wrong. "I need to go," I said.

"But you just got here."

I searched for an excuse. "I know," I said. "I forgot I told Gert I'd help her this afternoon."

"OK," she said, a bit hurt.

"Have fun on your trip," I said.

I couldn't leave fast enough. I went back down the stairs and out the front door without saying goodbye to Mr. Rhodes. He already had everything a person could want. Now he had his foot on my neck too.

52 THE PRESSURE IS ON

After I left Beulah I drove to the shop and found Luther vacuuming the Cadillac. He glanced at me, lifted his chin in greeting, and kept working. I pulled a stool away from the workbench and sat on it, watching him. After a moment he straightened and shut off the vacuum cleaner.

"You know it's Sunday?" he said.

"I know. I just came to see if anyone was over here."

"You like picking up trash *that* much?"

"Not really. You got anything else you need me to do?"

"You better ask Mr. Case about that."

"No, I mean for free. Like with the car."

"You must be bored," he said.

I spent the next hour helping Luther clean the car. He didn't say much to me except for occasional bits of advice concerning my work. I sensed he wasn't completely comfortable with me being there, and I didn't understand that. But I wasn't looking to understand anything that afternoon and I wasn't looking for conversation. I just wanted to take my mind off things for a while. And I didn't want to do it alone.

After we'd done all we could, Luther stood back and looked at it and shook his head. "I guess we ought to just haul it over there. It'll never work."

"She's usually in a better mood on Sundays. Besides, it's not like she can drive it."

Luther frowned doubtfully. "Get the tow rope out of the truck bed. Let's hook it up."

We tied one end of the rope to the trailer ball of the farm truck and the other to the front axle of the Cadillac. Then Luther had me get in the car and steer while he pulled the two tons of rusted, creaking metal out of the shop and toward Headquarters. The flat tires clopped over the road, and it was all I could do to lean on the steering wheel and keep it straight. We hadn't gone far when I heard a slap and a bang and turned to see all the rubber off the back left tire laying behind us. We continued on with the rim grinding and squeaking on the gravel.

Eventually Luther swung into the front yard and made a wide circle and pulled me to a slow stop in front of the house. There was just enough room for another car to squeeze past if they drove part of the way onto the lawn.

Luther got out and came to my window.

"Right here?" I said.

He looked at the house windows. Back at me.

"You know she's watching us," I said.

"I know. And I don't hear her complaining."

"I guess people can drive around it."

He shrugged. "Let's get her unhooked."

When I went back into the house later, Grandmother didn't say a word about the Cadillac. Which was fine with me. I was glad I didn't have to hear about it anymore.

The telephone started ringing about seven o'clock, and you would think someone had shot Grandmother in the ass.

"Who's calling here this time of night!" she shouted.

I bounded down the stairs.

"I want to know who that is!"

"It's probably Dad," I said, reaching for the phone. "Geez."

"You know how much that call's going to cost me?"

"He's calling *us*," I said. "It won't cost anything."

"Costs electricity!"

I lifted the phone to my ear. "Hello," I said.

"Win, it's Dad."

"Hey, Dad."

"I'm not sending bail money!" she said.

"Is that Mother?" he asked.

"Yes. She's living downstairs now. She's basically right behind me."

"That's right," she said. "And I'm listening to every word."

"Jesus," Dad said. "There's still just one phone in the whole house?"

"Yes."

"OK, well, catch me up on things."

"Why did it take you so long to call me?" I asked.

"Son, I've been so tied up in this legal mess I hardly have time to breathe."

"How's Mom?"

"She's fine. She's doing better. Has the lawyer gotten your grandmother to sign everything?"

I glanced over my shoulder. I saw her sitting up in bed, staring holes into me. "I don't think so."

"Why not?"

"He said it might take a while."

"A while for what?" Grandmother snapped.

I leaned close to the phone and lowered my voice. "Dad, there were some things you didn't tell me about."

"Like what?"

I glanced at Grandmother. She was staring at me, but I didn't think she could hear. I turned away from her again. "Like that thing with Mr. Rhodes," I said.

"Oh, that. Yeah. Well, that's what lawyers are for."

"I wish I didn't have to decide."

"Win, I told you I can't get close to this. The feds are watching me like hawks. I'm counting on you."

"I know."

"You need to be a man about this."

"I did everything you said."

"Is she still listening?"

"Yes."

Dad sighed. "I'm going to need some money, Win. I'm not going to be able to pay all these legal bills with my assets frozen."

I didn't know what to say, but I knew what was coming.

"Can you talk to her?" he asked.

"About that?"

"Yes," he said.

"Why can't *you* ask her?"

"Ask me what?" she snapped from the bed.

"Look," Dad continued, "it doesn't have to be this week, but I'll need you to ask her about it soon."

"I don't know, Dad."

"Listen, Win," he said. His voice carried a hint of desperation. "The future of this family is up to you. Don't lie down on us."

"I'm not," I said.

"Don't let us down."

I shook my head. I felt like crying. "I won't," I said. "I'll try."

I heard him sigh with relief. "Good."

Both of us were quiet for a moment. I felt Grandmother staring at me from her bedroom. "Tell Mom I said hello," I finally said.

"I will," he said. "I'll call again soon."

53 MONEY THE HARD WAY

Monday, I caught the bus at the end of the driveway and rode to school with the rest of the country kids. During lunch I sat by myself, away from Sikes's friends. It wasn't long before Buster strolled up to me, his lip bulging with tobacco.

"What's up?" he said.

"Hey, Buster."

"Figured you'd be over there with the queen bees."

"No. Sikes is out of town. I don't need to be hanging out with girls all the time anyway."

"Sara likes me," he said. "She just don't know it."

"You think so?"

"I know so. Them girls don't know what they want. All you got to do is *tell* them what they want about five times and they start to believe it themselves."

"You think?"

"Yep."

"So you think if you ask Sara enough she'll go on a date with you?"

"Yep."

"What are you going to do with her?"

"Shoot, I don't know. Movies or something."

"I can't see it happening."

"You will."

"Are you a farm kid?" I asked him.

"I'm whatever," he said. "I been running tractors since I was six. I can fix most anything."

He watched me like he was waiting for me to say something.

"So what you gonna do?" he finally said.

"About what?"

"About everything. You don't know nothing neither."

I couldn't tell if he was being aggressive or just lacked tact, but he was making me nervous. "I know plenty," I said. "I probably know more than everybody in this grade."

"About what? You ain't in New York anymore."

"What's that got to do with it?"

"You ever fixed a tractor?"

"No."

"You ever blowed up a mess of beavers?"

I didn't know what to say.

"That New York stuff ain't gonna do you any good around here," he said. "I can teach you some stuff."

"I appreciate it," I said, "but I'm working every day except Sunday. I don't have time for anything else."

"Sunday's fine."

"I have church on Sunday."

He nodded resolutely. He knew I was putting him off. "All right, then. You change your mind, I'll be around."

"OK. Thanks."

I watched him turn and walk off. Somehow, I felt like he'd gotten something out of me, but I couldn't quite figure out what it was.

The picker had four rows of sixteen spindle bars. Each bar had twenty spindle sleeves. I had to knock each spindle from its sleeve, replace it with a new one, then screw the sleeve back into the bar. It was tedious work, but most of the time Hoyt and Luther were close by, tinkering with some other part of the machine. Usually they pulled me aside and showed me what they were doing, explaining the importance of the many maintenance tasks.

The farmer was spending a lot of time in town negotiating prices on seed and fertilizer, chemicals, and fuel. Sometimes we'd see his truck far across the fields, driving slowly down the turn rows, examining the dirt and the weeds. When he was at the shop, he sat at a small, dusty, metal desk in the corner studying the calendar, the weather forecasts, and the economy to decide when would be best to plant and when to harvest and whether to presell the cotton or hold back for better prices. Sometimes he walked out and looked over what we were doing, occasionally grabbing a wrench or a grease gun and leaning in to adjust something himself. Hoyt and Luther seemed to know what needed to be done and the pace of it all, and if he asked anything of them, it was phrased more as a question than an order.

"Luther, you think we should replace that left rear tire?"

"It's looking pretty slick, Mr. Case."

"What about the hydraulic line on the lift, Hoyt? Didn't we have to put some J-B Weld on the collar last year?"

"Yeah, I'll make sure it's still holding."

I worked every day after school replacing the spindles. Sometimes I even stayed after they locked up, long enough to hear the faraway rifle shots of deer hunters in the late evening, until after the sky had gone purple dark and the wood ducks whistled overhead, making their nightly journey to the still, black waters of the swamp. Occasionally I heard gunfire popping from the other side of the brake and wondered if it was Mr. Rhodes with his fancy shotgun.

On Monday I didn't wait for the Rhodeses to pick me up. I boarded the school bus. During lunch I saw Sikes sitting with her friends, but I didn't approach them. I ate alone, trying not to draw attention to myself. She glanced at me a few times, then came over to me.

"We came by this morning," she said.

"I'm sorry," I said. "I should have called. I've been so busy I needed the extra time on the bus to do my homework."

She knew I was putting her off.

"Do you not want us to drive you?"

I hesitated. "I'll let you know," I said. "Thanks."

She studied me for a moment. "OK," she said. "Just let me know."

Sikes walked back to her friends, and Buster slipped up beside me.

"You know where Booga Den is?" he asked, dripping tobacco from his mouth.

"No," I said.

"It's about two miles behind your place."

I watched him, waiting to hear the point of his statement. But he just looked at me.

"OK," I finally said.

"I live there," he said.

I waited.

"Maybe I'll come by some time," he said.

"Fine," I said. "But I'm usually working."

"Yeah, me too. But I might anyway."

"OK," I said.

That weekend Hoyt showed me how to use the steamer to clean all the components of the picker head. I didn't ask the farmer about this, and when he saw me working, he didn't comment. That afternoon he gave all of us an envelope with a check in it. I made $175 for my first full week.

"How do I cash this?" I asked Hoyt.

"Mr. Denton'll take it."

And he did. After charging me 5 percent. But I didn't see I had any options and neither did he.

The way I'd left things with Sikes wasn't sitting right with me. I drove over, and we threw sticks in the backyard and watched King fetch them. Neither of us said much. I could tell she was unsure how to act around me. When I told her goodbye that evening, I left her without any promises.

"I guess I'll see you later," I said.

"OK," she said. "I'll see you at school."

The following week I helped Luther grease the bearings on the Orthman, a giant, plow-like device pulled behind the tractors to form the rows. The weather was mostly overcast and wet and cold, and there seemed to be a sense of unspoken urgency developing as January slipped into its final days. We all began to work later into the evenings, the big utility lights humming in the mist overhead. The farmer brought us fried chicken or hamburgers from town, or we'd make quick peanut butter and jelly sandwiches from lunch supplies kept in a small refrigerator on the workbench. Sometimes I didn't get back to Headquarters until almost eight o'clock, relieved to find Grandmother asleep and the house quiet.

The last Saturday of the month I stood outside the shop with the three of them and watched a crop duster swoop over the far trees and pass low across the fields, a fine mist coming from its wings.

"2,4-D," Luther said. "Mean stuff."

"What does it do?" I asked.

The farmer looked at me.

"Kills the weeds," Hoyt said.

The farmer looked out at the plane again. "Hopefully," he said. "Hoyt, why don't you get Win rigged up with one of the sprayers? I saw some henbit and some poa annua down around the northeast corner."

"Yeah," Hoyt said. "Plane can't get everything. Come on."

Tim Haney stopped by the shop one afternoon. The farmer approached his car window and leaned on the doorframe and listened to him for a few minutes. Then the lawyer drove away, and the farmer came back toward me. He stopped at the workbench behind me and began putting some drill bits back in their case.

"Will's done," he said. "Tim says it all looks pretty solid."

I felt that queasy feeling again. "So there's nothing left to do?"

"Nope. He said Charlie might even start clearing the west end of the brake a few months early so he can move equipment through."

"I think he plans to buy it," I said.

"I imagine he does. He's a man that likes to control things."

For some reason I thought the farmer might say something to make me feel better about it all. But he didn't. He closed the drill case and walked off.

That moment was the first time I felt the true weight of the changes I'd set into motion. I wondered what Hoyt and Luther would do after the season was over. There would be no jobs at Cottonlandia for cotton farmers. In spite of it all, everyone seemed to be quietly going about their business. For some reason, that made it even worse.

54 DYNAMITING BEAVERS

Every Sunday the farmer took his wife to an early service at the Presbyterian church in nearby Cleveland. Afterward he shopped for our groceries, delivered them, and took me and Grandmother and Gert to hear Deacon Leon. Grandmother still hadn't mentioned her car sitting out in the yard like some dead, metal elephant everybody had to drive around. She never even glanced at it.

The church looked better every time I saw it. It had a new roof and a fresh, white paint job. The missing and cracked windowpanes had all been replaced, and the potholes in the parking lot were filled with gravel. Grandmother was at her best on Sunday afternoons after Deacon Leon's service had calmed her. It was the only day of the week Gert and I got any peace around Headquarters. We ate lunch together, and afterward she napped and then took short walks across the lawn in the late afternoon. I read some of Dad's old books or drove the ATV to the shop where Luther had a collard patch. Sometimes locals or friends of Luther or both would be there picking collards, and the occasion doubled as a way to socialize.

I spent a week walking the turn rows with a backpack sprayer, killing weeds, feeling punished, wishing I were back at the shop with the rest of them. But I didn't complain. And at the end of each week I got my paycheck, cashed it at Denton's store, and put the money away in my dresser drawer.

In February I no longer heard gunshots in the early morning and late evening. A stillness came over the land. I continued spraying weeds manually while Hoyt crawled the tractor sprayer across the fields, followed by Luther pulling the Orthman.

One Sunday afternoon I was finishing lunch when I saw an unfamiliar ATV pull up in the front yard. It was bigger than any I'd seen and had a metal toolbox mounted on the back and a large, metal basket on the front.

"Who's that?" Grandmother snapped.

I set down my fork and studied the person as they came to a stop. "It's Buster Tillman," I said.

Despite Sikes's warning against the likes of Buster, it felt good to see another boy my age. He was still sitting on the ATV when I came outside.

"Hey," I said. "What's up?"

He leaned over and spit a long stream of tobacco juice. "Nothing yet," he said. "But I got some dynamite."

"Dynamite?" I said.

Buster nodded.

"Where did you get that?"

"I got lots of it."

"What are you going to do with it?"

"Blow something up. Wanna come?"

"Like what?"

"Beaver dam."

"Why?"

"You watch and you'll know why."

"Yeah," I said. "Hell yeah. Hold on while I get my four-wheeler."

"No problem," he replied, smug with victory. "Come on."

I followed Buster as he drove toward the north end of the fields. His ATV moved about as fast as he did, ambling up the turn rows, taking its time. It wasn't long before I realized he was headed toward the beaver damn I knew of at the edge of the brake.

Eventually we pulled to a stop at the culvert. "You're going to blow up our beaver dam?"

Buster was already digging in the storage box mounted on the back of his ATV. "This ain't the only one you got," he said. "You got lots of them."

"How do you know?"

"Because I been over here blowing them up."

"You have?"

He pulled out several sticks of dynamite and some wire. He turned to me. "There's big money in it. Fifty bucks a beaver."

"But . . . but they're our beavers. Are we going to get in trouble?"

Buster set the dynamite supplies down, reached back into the storage box, and brought out some hip waders. He leaned against the ATV and began pulling them on.

"Man," he said, "you got to kill the beavers. They mess up the drainage."

"You think we ought to ask the farmer first?"

Buster pulled his second boot on and looked at me again. "Ask him?" he said. "He's the one that pays us to do it. My dad's the beaver man."

Buster waded out into the dark water carrying six sticks of dynamite and the detonation fuse.

"How far back should I get?" I called out.

"Well, I ain't gonna blow it while I'm out here," he replied over his shoulder. "You stay where you are until I get finished."

"Are they in there?"

"They're in there. Napping."

"How many, you think?"

"Hard to say. Could be two. Could be ten."

He spent about fifteen minutes at the beaver lodge shoving dynamite into it. Then he connected one end of the detonation fuse and started back my way, spooling it out behind him. In a moment he was attaching the spool to a homemade contraption on the back of his ATV that looked like a toilet paper roll holder.

"Let's go," he said.

We took the ATVs about a hundred yards up the turn row, the fuse spooling out behind Buster. Then we dismounted again, and he began attaching the fuse to two screws on the detonation switch.

"Where do you buy dynamite?" I asked. "I mean, can you buy it at the store? I've never seen it for sale anywhere."

Buster spit. "You can get it at the hardware store . . . But you got to have a license."

"Have you got a license?"

He tightened the last screw and held the switch out to me. "Man, they don't give a fifteen-year-old a license for this kind of stuff."

I looked at the switch. "You want me to do it?"

He shook the switch at me. "Just press the green button."

I took it carefully, making sure my finger was nowhere near the green button. "Are we going to get in trouble for this?"

"Naw, man. I told you Mr. Case asked us to do it."

"But you don't have a license?"

"My daddy does. Now turn around and watch. It's wake-up time."

I don't remember pressing the green button. All I recall is what sounded like a cannon going off and feeling the cannonball hit me in the chest. But then it wasn't exactly like a cannonball because it was a full-body blow pressing my eyes back into their sockets. That was immediately followed by mud and sticks pelting me like I'd been shot in the face with a shotgun. It was the most violent sensation I'd ever felt in my life. Even after I was able to crouch to the ground and ball up with my hands over my head, mud and sticks continued to rain down on me.

When it all stopped, I uncurled and looked myself over, making sure I still had my arms and legs. I was covered with globs of mud and twigs and wet leaves, but I didn't see any missing parts. I looked for Buster, my heart racing and in shock, afraid that something had gone terribly wrong. The ATVs were coated with the same sticky debris.

"Buster!" I yelled.

"What?" he replied.

I saw him sitting down, leaning back against the other side of his ATV, calmly loading his mouth with another pinch of snuff.

I dropped the detonation switch. My hands trembled uncontrollably. "Jeeeesus Christ," I said.

Buster shoved the tobacco tin back into his pocket and turned to me. He had one small speck of mud on his shoulder. "How you like that for an alarm clock?" he said.

If the explosion was disturbing, ground zero of the beaver kill was something I'll never get out of my head. When we arrived on the scene, I saw the beaver den had disappeared completely, scattered over the water and bits of it hanging in the trees. Eight beavers lay either stone dead, flailing in the water, or crawling about the underbrush like the wounded on a battlefield. They were all bloody and torn and missing arms and legs.

"Jeeesus Christ," I said again.

"Wakey, wakey," Buster said, admiring the carnage.

While I stared on in horror, he took his time digging in the storage box until he pulled out a revolver. He opened the cylinder, spun it, slapped it closed again, and started out into the water. For about fifteen minutes he waded through the swamp, calmly executing all the wounded beavers with a shot to the head. When he was done, he came ashore and searched the underbrush for those crawling away. Three more shots were fired. When he came back to the ATV, he was dragging a beaver that looked like it could weigh sixty pounds. He dropped it beside me.

"Check out that fat sucker," he said.

I stared at the dead animal but could make no response. Buster began making trips out into the swamp, dragging them back by the tail and stacking them beside me, announcing the profit tally each time.

"Two hundred. Two fifty. Three hundred." When he'd counted out $400, he stopped and admired his pile.

He spat. Looked at me. "You got mud on your face," he said.

I wiped my face.

"Four hundred dollars," he said. "Two for you, two for me."

I nodded absently.

"And we'll get some more when I sell the meat."

55 BUSTER'S BOOGA DEN

We loaded all the beavers into the big, metal basket on the front of Buster's ATV and started back. When we got to the turnoff into Headquarters, Buster stopped and waited for me.

"I better run these back to the house," he said. "Daddy'll bring the tails over to Mr. Case tomorrow, and we'll get paid."

I was partially over the shock of it all, but not entirely. "Is that how everybody kills beavers?" I asked.

"Most. It's the best way. You can trap them, but that takes a while and you don't get as many."

"Maybe we should stand farther back next time."

Buster spit. "Yeah," he said. "I'll bring some longer cord."

"OK. Then I'll see you at school."

"You ever ride over there to Sikes Rhodes's house?"

"Yeah, sometimes."

"They got the setup, don't they?"

I nodded.

He thought for a moment. I sensed he didn't want to leave. "Hey," he said, "next deer season we need to kill us a buck over here."

I suddenly felt guilty for not inviting him to hunt. "Yeah," I said. "I guess I was just a little tired of deer hunting."

"I don't never get tired of deer hunting."

"I think I ate too much deer meat. I'm still eating it."

"Shoot, we'll sell it. Don't you worry about that. You get it on the ground, and I'll handle the rest."

"OK," I said. "I better go get cleaned up. I'll see you tomorrow, Buster."

That evening I found Hoyt in the shed, up to his shoulders under the hood of a tractor.

"Hey, Hoyt?"

"What?"

"You ever seen them kill the beavers?"

"Yeah, man. They blew up a bunch of them today. You didn't hear that?"

"I was there! With Buster Tillman."

Hoyt withdrew and looked at me and smiled. "What'd you think?"

"I just can't believe that's how you do it. I mean, it was like a massacre. I think Buster used too much dynamite."

He chuckled and leaned into the tractor again. "Man, you can't never have too much dynamite. Not for nothing."

"It's a weird way to make money. I'd have never thought of that."

"There ain't no weird way to make money. And that's why me and you ain't driving Cadillacs, because we don't think about it."

The following week Buster thumbed $250 into my palm on the schoolyard. It was for my share of the beaver kill, which included the money he'd made for selling the meat. I eyed the cash, thinking mostly of how happy I was not to have to give Mr. Denton his cut.

That night I put the money into my dresser drawer with the rest of my savings. I didn't know how much I had, but it had to be getting close to a thousand dollars. And as much as I'd thought I needed it before, I really couldn't think of anything to spend it on.

Hoyt and Luther finished forming the rows just before the rains came again. This time the storms were heavy and hard. The fields became as sticky and slick as grease, and it was impossible to get any of the equipment into them. For the rest of February, they continued performing maintenance on the tractors while I wandered the turn rows spraying weeds. In March the crop duster came again, dropping potash over the fields in a fine mist. The ground was finally dry enough to get the tractors out again, and this time they hooked up two Orthman plows and set off to row up again.

Luther had me inspecting last year's poly pipe, giant flexible plastic hoses that came in mile-long rolls. He wanted to see how much of it we'd be able to reuse when they started irrigating. It was heavy, tedious work, unfolding the muddy plastic and inspecting it all for leaks. Sometimes I'd have a hundred yards of the stuff stretched down the turn row.

One day Buster invited me to his farm. We drove through a strip of woods at the back end of Cottonlandia and onto the blacktop. After a while we came to a dirt road and traveled it until we arrived at Booga Den. The community wasn't much more than a couple of abandoned buildings between fields. Other than the Tillmans' farm, there was an old schoolhouse and caved-in service station with broken windows.

We stopped at Buster's mailbox, and he leaned over and got the mail.

"Does the school bus pick you up here?" I asked.

"Naw, Daddy takes me out to the highway or I walk or something. It ain't far."

Even though it was only a few miles to the west of Walnut Bend, Buster apparently caught a different bus to and from school.

The Tillmans' three-bedroom frame house sat under white oaks at the edge of the two hundred acres they leased. Two steel buildings behind the house made up the center of their operation.

Mr. Tillman sat on the front porch in a wheelchair. Had he been standing he would have looked like a weathered, sorrowful stork. Buster introduced me and told him we were going out back to see the shop. Mr. Tillman shook my hand and nodded to me. Then he watched us go with a blank look on his face.

"What happened to him?" I asked.

"He and my older brother got in a car wreck about two years ago," Buster told me. "Daddy can't feel nothing from the waist down."

"Where's your brother?"

Buster hesitated. "He died."

"Man," I said.

Buster nodded thoughtfully. "I miss him a lot. We did everything together."

"So who helps you with the farming?"

"Nobody. I can handle two hundred acres."

"So you have to do everything?"

"Yeah. I pretty much do it all. Run the equipment. Set the

dynamite. Daddy can drive me around, but that's about it."

"How does he do that?"

"He's got our truck rigged up on the column. Government paid for it. He can pull himself up in there and everything."

Buster showed me his shop, full of tools and projects and a single red tractor in the middle of the floor.

"You want something to eat?" he asked me.

"Sure," I said.

We crossed the yard again and went into the house through the back door. Mrs. Tillman was sitting on the sofa, watching television. Buster introduced me to her. She didn't get up, but she nodded politely with the same suspicious look I'd seen on Mr. Tillman.

"We're gonna get some dinner, Momma," he said.

Buster cooked hot dogs for us in the microwave, and we ate them in silence at their kitchen table. As I ate I felt a heavy sadness hanging about the place. It seemed to weigh on everyone but Buster.

I was eager to get outside again after we finished our hot dogs. Night had fallen, and for the first time I noticed the sound of crickets.

"You wanna hang out in the shop some more?" he asked me.

"I better get back," I said.

Buster looked at his feet. "I hate Sunday nights," he said.

We both stood there for a moment.

"Why did the girls think you went to jail?" I asked.

Buster looked at me. "Don't listen to them," he said.

"Did you get kicked out of school?"

I couldn't see his face well in the darkness, but he shifted his feet like he was nervous. I felt him staring at me. He didn't answer.

"I was just wondering," I said. "I guess it's none of my business."

"You're my friend," he said. "It's your business."

"OK."

"Yeah, I got kicked out for a while. But I didn't go to no jail. Not like they think, anyway."

"Where did you go?"

"Some other place."

"OK. Well, why did they kick you out?"

He didn't answer me. I was growing uncomfortable with how he looked at me.

"Forget it," I said. "It doesn't matter."

"Yeah, it does. But I wish people wouldn't talk about things they don't know nothing about."

"It was just the one time," I said. "That's the only thing I ever heard."

"I hate Sunday nights," he said again.

"You don't need to tell me the story," I said. "I need to get back anyway."

Buster nodded.

I hesitated. "So I'll see you around," I finally said.

"OK," he said.

56 THE WRONG WARRIOR

Buster wasn't the only one with problems. One afternoon in late March I got to the shop and found Hoyt and Luther unloading buckets of oil from the back of Mr. Case's truck. I parked my ATV and went to help.

"What's up?" I said.

Hoyt grabbed a bucket, looked at me, and lifted his chin. Then he walked off with it into the shop. It wasn't like him not to say anything. I looked at Luther.

"He's in *baaad* shape," Luther said.

"What happened?"

Luther glanced at the shop. "His dog had the puppies."

"Well, that's good, right?"

"They got spots."

"So what?"

"Like Warrior," he said.

I studied him. I still wasn't getting it. "But Warrior doesn't have spots."

"One of them does."

I got it. I looked over at Hoyt. He was walking toward us again, hanging his head, dragging his feet. "He fell in love with the wrong one?" I asked.

Hoyt nodded to himself and passed by.

"How'd that happen?"

He grabbed another bucket. "I don't want to talk about it," he said.

I searched for words. "Can you get Truckstop back again? Can't you try again?"

He looked at me. "One shot at the big time. I had it. I blew it. Truckstop's got bad taste in women."

"Get him back?"

Hoyt shook his head and passed me by. Luther grabbed two buckets. "I told him all that stuff. You can't talk to him about it right now."

Just then the farmer pulled up in his truck. "Win, come take a ride with me."

I looked over at Hoyt once more. "We'll figure something out," I said.

I left Hoyt hanging his head about his dog problems and walked around the farmer's truck and climbed in. He pulled away and started for the blacktop at the back end of the property. "Hoyt sure is upset about those dogs," I said.

"Yeah, I was worried about that," the farmer said. "He gets something dreamed up, and you can't beat it out of him."

"He's been thinking about those dogs ever since I met him."

The farmer shook his head. "I know . . . He'll be OK."

We turned onto the highway and set out around the back side of Rhodes's brake. "Where are we going?" I asked.

"I need to run by the house. Need you to help me move a dishwasher."

It suddenly occurred to me I'd never been to his house before. I'd never met his wife, Diane. I really didn't know anything about him outside of Cottonlandia.

"Having a little trouble with my knees," he continued.

"What's wrong?"

"Oh, nothing but old age. Football injuries catching up with me."

"You played football?"

He brought the spit cup to his lips, replaced it, and nodded.

"In college?" I said.

"Yeah. University of Alabama."

"I've heard of them. They're good, aren't they?"

"They've been known to win a few."

We passed the west end of the brake, and I saw Beulah far off in the distance, standing massive and white like something on a postcard. The heavy equipment was gone, and the new ponds were shimmering with water, the giant aerators churning at the edges.

"Looks like he's got fish in the new ones," I said.

"Yep," the farmer replied. "He's all in."

I suddenly wished I hadn't said anything. I was relieved when the farmer changed the subject. "You heard from your father lately?"

"No," I said. "He doesn't call much. He's real busy with the trial."

"How are things at school?"

"Pretty good," I said.

"Seems like you've made some friends."

"Well, Sikes and Buster."

"Buster teaching you a thing or two?"

"He knows a lot about farming and beavers."

"Yes, he does. It's been tough around there since his dad got hurt."

"He told me his brother was killed."

The farmer nodded. "Yeah, it's a sad situation. I know they struggle."

We came to an intersection and turned toward the setting sun, a giant, orange orb hanging over the flatland.

"Was your dad a farmer?" I asked.

"All my life," he replied.

"Is he still alive?"

"No. He passed about ten years ago."

"What about your kids?"

The farmer spit into his cup again. "I've got one son. He sells insurance up in Little Rock."

"He didn't want to be a farmer?"

"His wife's from up there. It's her family's business. I suppose he does pretty well."

We continued in silence for another couple of miles before he turned into a driveway. Before us was a brick, ranch-style house set under a grove of pecan trees with a neatly mown lawn. Off to the side was a metal building. Everything was as modest and tidy as I expected.

The inside of the house was neat and clean and worn. It smelled of potpourri and Pine-Sol. Mrs. Case came out of the kitchen wearing an apron. She was small and held a cheerfulness behind her eyes.

"Hey, Diane," the farmer said. "I don't think you've met Win Canterbury."

227

"Nice to meet you, Win. I've heard so much about you."

She wiped her hands on her apron and held one out and I took it.

"He's not working you too hard, is he?"

"No, ma'am."

I followed them into the kitchen where an old dishwasher sat in the middle of the floor. The farmer studied the new one installed beneath the counter.

"Looks like Jimmy got it to fit," he said.

Mrs. Case turned to me. "We had our old one so long we didn't know if they made them that size anymore."

I helped the farmer drag the dead appliance outside and load it into his truck.

"Thank you, boys," Mrs. Case said from the doorway.

"I'll be back after a while," the farmer said.

"So nice to finally meet you, Win. Please come by more often."

"OK," I said. "Nice to meet you too."

As we drove away, I found myself strangely envious of the farmer's uncomplicated life. While the rest of us were worried about wrecked families and friends and coon dogs and money, it seemed his biggest problem was replacing his dishwasher.

57 BUSTER'S PLAN

Hoyt was closing up the shop when the farmer dropped me off. I stood outside under the humming utility light waiting for him. He knew I was out there, but he took his time, putting little things away, scuffling across the floor, sadness weighing him down.

"It's just some dogs," I said.

He glanced at me, then picked a Pepsi can off the workbench and dropped it into the trash. He looked around, searching for something else to do. Finally, he shook his head and walked over to the wall and flipped off the lights.

"I don't see why you can't get Truckstop back and try again."

He passed me and started for his truck, and I fell in behind him. "It was a one-shot deal, man. I blew it."

"You didn't know he'd like the wrong one?"

Hoyt stopped and turned to me. "It don't matter whose fault it is. That don't change the fact I ain't never gonna get ahead."

"You can save money."

"Man, I barely got enough every month to pay my power bill. I'm just an old farmhand. Ain't making *rockets* or nothing."

"You're not old."

"I feel old." He kicked the dirt and stared at his boots. "Man, I just wanted to get her a double-wide. You know? That's all I wanted. That ain't asking much."

"You'll think of something."

"A man just wants to be a man, you know?"

I nodded.

"And all I got to show is a squirming pile of Oreo-looking, toe-sniffing puppies."

I didn't respond.

"Gonna have to put them in a box and sit out in front of Walmart with them."

"You can sell them for something, right?"

He looked up at me. "Man, I'll be lucky to give them away."

I didn't answer. He turned and continued to his truck. I stayed where I was, feeling useless against his melancholy.

"I never had the stomach to kill no puppies," he said over his shoulder.

Saturday afternoon I was at the workbench sorting the socket set for Luther when Mr. Tillman's pickup truck pulled up before the shop and stopped. I saw Buster sitting in the passenger seat. He raised his chin at me.

The farmer approached the driver's side and started talking to Mr. Tillman. I stopped what I was doing and walked outside.

"What's up?" I asked Buster.

"Checking on your beavers."

"You want to come over this weekend?"

He nodded. "Yeah. I'll come around Saturday afternoon."

"You want to spend the night?"

"Yeah. I'll bring something you'll like."

"What?"

"You'll see."

"Don't blow up my house or anything."

"Naw, man. Just wait."

Buster arrived on his ATV just before sunset. He parked beside the Cadillac and was eying it curiously when I came out of the house to meet him.

"Where'd the car come from?" he asked.

"It's Grandmother's."

"No way in hell that thing runs."

"It doesn't. But she wants it there."

Buster got off his ATV and walked around the car, inspecting it. "Man, you know how much fun it would be to drag this thing out in a field and shove some dynamite under the seats?"

I started to object, but then realized it would be fun. But I didn't want to encourage him. "Come on," I said. "What are we doing? What's the big surprise?"

Buster came away from the car and approached me. He stopped and dug in his pocket and pulled out a small, wooden tube about the size of a cigar. He held it in front of me. I tried to figure out how it would explode.

"I don't know," I eventually said. "What is this thing?"

"Coyote caller," he said.

"For what?"

"For calling coyotes."

"It barks?"

"Naw, it makes a sound like a rabbit getting killed. Listen."

Buster put the caller to his lips, puffed his cheeks, and blew. It emitted the most spine-chilling sound I'd ever heard. Like the shrill scream of a baby getting tortured. I felt goose bumps run up my arms.

He lowered the caller and watched me.

I heard the front door open and turned to see Grandmother on red alert, scanning the lawn.

"What was that!" she snapped.

"Buster's coyote caller," I said.

"Get it out of here!"

"Yes, ma'am," I said.

She went back inside, and I looked at Buster again. "Jesus," I said. "Coyotes like that?"

"They love it. But we ain't gonna use it on coyotes."

I waited for him to go on.

"What are we going to use it on?" I asked.

"Girls."

"Girls?"

"That's right. I hear Julie and Sara are staying over at Sikes's house tonight. We're gonna scare them."

"That's a terrible idea."

"Girls love getting scared."

"No, they don't."

"You just wait. Let's go."

"No," I said. "Mr. Rhodes'll probably shoot us."

"I already drove by there. Both cars are gone. It's just the girls and the maid."

"You've been thinking about this all day, haven't you?"

"Since Wednesday when I heard them talking about a sleepover."

I frowned. "I don't know."

"I wanna ask Sara to go on a date with me."

"With a coyote caller?"

"No, that's just the first part. Just to get her attention. I ain't to the asking yet."

"I think it's a bad idea," I said. But I said it in a way where both of us knew I'd committed.

Buster got a twinkle in his eyes that showed about as much excitement as he was capable of.

"It's gonna be fine," he assured me. "Come on. I don't know them people real well. I need you with me."

58 SHOTS FIRED

It didn't matter how much Buster told me our prank was OK. I knew it was a bad idea. I didn't see how anything good could come of it. And I couldn't explain to him my feelings about mixing with the Rhodeses. But deep down I really did want to see Sikes. Now I was going to see her when it really hadn't been my idea at all. Which somehow made it OK.

It was dark and windy when we parked alongside the brake and set out the rest of the way on foot. The home stood lit up behind the oaks like a presidential mansion.

"We got to figure out what room they're in," Buster said.

"They watch TV in a den downstairs."

"Bet they'll be in there. Or in her room doing their hair or something."

"Her room's fifteen feet off the ground," I said.

"They got trees."

I shook my head. "Jesus."

When we came to the lawn, Buster slowed and I got behind him.

"Where's the den?" he whispered.

"Go to the left."

I followed as he slipped around the house and crept up to the den window. When I peered over his shoulder, I saw the girls lying about on the floor in their nightgowns, eating popcorn and staring at the television.

Buster reached in his pocket and pulled out a spool of fishing line. He began unwinding it in the light of the window.

"What's that for?" I asked.

"This is your part," he said.

"I don't want a part."

He found the end of the line and held it before his face. There was a small fishhook on it. "It's the deal closer," he mumbled.

"What are you going to do, tie her up?"

He spat. "Naw, just hold on."

He took the fishhook and hooked it into the window screen and began backing away, spooling the line as he went. I hurried after him.

Buster stopped beside a big oak tree about fifty feet from the house. From there we could see the window clearly, but not the girls. He held the line out to me, and I took it reluctantly.

"When I tell you to, pinch the string and start rubbing it back and forth."

"What's that going to do?"

Buster looked at me. "Man, you don't learn nothing in New York, do you?"

"Not about fishing line on window screens. No."

Buster reached in his pocket and pulled out the coyote caller. "Here we go," he said.

"Wait! What if they see us standing here?"

"They can't see us."

Before I had time to say another word Buster put the caller to his lips, took a deep breath, and let out that awful, nightmarish squeal of something in the throes of an agonizing death. When he lowered the caller, all night sounds had stopped. Everything had ducked away and gone into hiding. I felt my heart drumming in my chest and clear up to my ears.

Inside the house, nothing moved.

Buster hit it again.

I saw Sikes's head poke up a little ways back from the window. She stared at the blackness with a blank expression. Then Julie and Sara appeared behind her, looking over her shoulder. Someone shoved Sikes, and she staggered a couple of steps toward the window and quickly backed up again.

"I think they heard," I whispered.

But Buster wasn't finished. "Not yet," he said.

He hit it again.

This time the girls jumped to action, their screams frantic and mute through the glass. We watched them tripping over each other, fleeing the room. Then all was still again, and the window was empty. I felt the string in my hand, wondering why he'd never told me to rub it.

"OK," I said. "I think we scared them."

Buster watched the house and didn't answer.

"Buster?"

"Get ready," he said.

I looked back at the house and saw Roxy creeping into the den, the girls huddled behind her. The girls stopped halfway across the floor while Roxy crept closer to the window.

"Hold it," Buster said.

"I *am*."

Roxy crept closer, bringing her hand up to shield her eyes and peer over the lawn. When her nose was nearly touching the glass, Buster said, "Go."

"What?"

"Rub it!"

Before I even gave thought to what I was doing, I pinched and slid my fingers up the string. The vibration traveled through the fishing line and transferred to the window screen, rattling the wire mesh like fingernails were scraping it. Roxy leaped backward, startled. Once she fell out of the picture, I saw the girls, boiling in hysteria. Suddenly Sara doubled over and puked.

I dropped the line.

"Buster," I said. "Let's get out of here!"

He looked at me. "Did Sara just throw up?"

"Yes!"

He shoved the caller back into his pocket and took a few steps toward the house. "Hey!" he yelled. "It's just us!"

"Holy crap, Buster! I'm leaving!"

I took off running across the lawn. Suddenly the back door slammed open and Roxy appeared with Mr. Rhodes's shotgun. She pointed it at the sky, and I saw an orange flame leap from the barrel just before I heard the explosion. I dove to the ground.

"It's Win!" I yelled. "Don't shoot!"

Roxy stood there gripping the shotgun tightly, her chest rising and falling in the house light.

"Win, you better get your butt home before I fill it with

buckshot!"

"We just wanted to surprise the girls," came Buster's voice from somewhere out in the trees. "Tell Sara it's Buster Tillman."

Roxy fired the shotgun in the air again, and I flattened myself until my cheek was pressed into the wet grass.

"I don't care if it's Jesus Christ himself!" she yelled into the darkness. "You boys better git!"

I scrambled up and made a dash for the brake.

I waited at the ATVs for ten minutes before Buster came strolling up the turn row.

"What took you so long?"

"I had to get my fishing line."

"Do you just want to die?"

"She only had two shots in that thing."

I shook my head in amazement. "So is that how you wanted it to go?"

"Not really."

"Yeah, me neither. I'm sure Sara's head over heels in love with you now," I said sarcastically.

Buster climbed on his ATV. "I thought we'd at least get to talk to them," he said.

59 UNEXPECTED VISITOR

I spent most of Sunday afternoon anxiously expecting Mr. Rhodes's Cadillac to pull into the front yard. Sikes showed up on her ATV instead. I took a deep breath.

"Who's that?!"

"It's Sikes Rhodes, Grandmother."

"Since when did they decide to grace us with their presence?"

I ignored her and walked outside. Sikes parked beside the old Cadillac and waited for me.

"It wasn't my idea," I said.

By the blank way she looked at me, I couldn't tell what she was thinking.

"Buster just wanted to talk to Sara," I continued.

She pulled off her knit cap, and a big smile spread across her face. "That was a pretty good one, Win."

"It was just Buster's coyote caller. I didn't think it would go like that. Is your dad pissed?"

"I told Roxy not to tell my parents. But she's pretty mad about it."

I frowned and looked at the ground. Sikes got off the ATV. "But Roxy's scared of everything," she said. "She hides if she sees a black cat."

"Every time I go over there now, I'm going to have to worry about getting shot."

Sikes laughed. "She wouldn't have shot you."

"I don't know about that. Is Sara OK?"

"She's fine."

"You just gonna let her stand out in the yard?!" Grandmother snapped from inside.

I rolled my eyes. Sikes looked at me curiously. "Grandmother," I said. "I think she wants to see you."

"Sure," she said. "You owe me a tour, anyway."

I presented Sikes to Grandmother, and she eyed her from head to toe. "Nice to see you again, Sikes," she finally said. "Please teach my grandson some manners."

"Yes, ma'am. Nice to see you again too."

"I'll show you upstairs," I said.

"You certainly will not," Grandmother snapped. "You'll stay out on the porch where I can see you."

"What? Why?"

"Because I'm not convinced you're a gentleman."

"What if we stay in the front yard?"

"Fine. As long as I can see you."

I sighed. "Come on, Sikes."

We walked out onto the lawn where Grandmother could see us, but far enough away so I didn't think she could hear.

"You see what I have to deal with?" I told her.

"She's just old-fashioned."

"She's a pain in the ass."

"You're a pain in the ass!" Grandmother shouted.

"Jesus, come on. Let's walk out to the fence."

"Watch your language!"

Sikes smiled discreetly, and we started walking. "So you're hanging out with Buster now?" she said.

"I'm not really hanging out with anybody. He just started coming over. He says he's got things to teach me."

"You know he got kicked out of school last year?"

"I know. He doesn't like to talk about it."

"I think they took him to jail."

"He said they didn't."

"What did he do?" Sikes asked.

"I don't know. I asked him once, and he wouldn't tell me."

"He was out of school for almost a whole year."

"Well, he's been teaching me ways to earn money around here."

"You won't make any friends hanging out with Buster."

"The last thing I'm worried about right now is making friends."

"You should join something at school. Like play a sport or get in a club."

"I don't have time. I have to work."

"You *have* too?"

She wouldn't understand, and I didn't want her too. I wondered what she would think about her dad buying Cottonlandia and turning it into a catfish farm. The secret I was keeping from her seemed to create even more distance between us. It wasn't anything that was her fault, but it was hard to see her without being reminded of everything that had been taken from me and everything I was about to lose.

"No, don't guess I *have* to work," I said. "But I want to."

Sikes took a step toward her four-wheeler. "I guess there's no tour today."

"Guess not," I replied.

"Come over again when you can. I'll make sure nobody shoots at you."

I smiled half-heartedly. "OK. See you around."

60 UNWANTED VISITOR

The farmer said the planting was to start on April 15. The first two weeks of the month we put out liquid nitrogen to give the cotton oxygen. Then Luther started over the fields with something called a "do-all" to knock off the tops of the rows and get them ready to receive the seed. On exactly the fifteenth of April they loaded the planter with the cotton seed, and Hoyt crawled up into the cab and followed behind the do-all.

I asked them questions about everything, and I couldn't wait to get home from school in the afternoons to help. I constantly felt like I was missing out. Hoyt wasn't completely over the disappointment of his puppies, but he wasn't dragging his feet, and I could detect his irrepressible optimism welling up from within. Luther never had a lot to say, but he was steady and quick to smile. After working next to him for a while, I couldn't help but sense he was a lot smarter than he let on.

One day I was called to the office after school. I found Dad waiting for me.

"Hello, Win," he said.

He was thinner than I remembered. The lines on his face stood out more, and his eyes were sunken and twitchy. I shook his hand, and the handshake was weak and uncertain. I felt a little sick at seeing him.

"Hey, Dad," I said, confused. "What are you doing here?"

"Thought I'd pick you up from school today," he said, like it was something he did all the time.

"OK," I said.

I followed him out front and got into a small rental car that smelled like cigarette smoke. I saw a pack of Marlboro Lights on the console.

"Do you smoke now?" I asked.

He leaned over me and put the cigarettes away in the glove box. "Every now and then," he said. "Helps me relax."

We pulled away from the school and started toward Walnut Bend. "So how have you been?" he asked.

"OK," I said. I didn't even know where to start with him. He wasn't part of any of it. Telling him anything was giving him a piece of something I'd earned.

"Your mother said to tell you hello."

"Why doesn't she tell me herself?"

"She's a lot better now."

"Then why won't she call me?"

"She will," he said. "Soon."

"Why didn't you tell me you were coming?"

He glanced at the glove box. "Well, it just sort of happened that I got some time off. Sort of a last-minute thing."

"But you've got to go back?"

He took a deep breath. "Oh yeah," he said. "I've got to keep fighting this thing. I've got quite a battle on my hands."

I looked out the window and didn't respond.

"Got our apartment sold," he continued. "That was about the only thing they let me cash in. It helps some with the legal bills. Let me pay back a couple of friends I had to borrow from."

I looked at him. "What about all of our things? What about my hockey equipment and my skis and all my clothes? Where is it all?"

"We've got a lot of stuff in storage."

I tried to make a mental list of everything in my old room. Strangely, I thought of nothing I really missed. Nothing I needed.

"You still living in your new apartment?"

"Sort of."

I looked at him.

"That's one reason I came down here," he continued. "I wanted to talk to you about that."

"What do you mean?"

He glanced at the glove box again. "Hand me those cigarettes, will you?"

I got him the pack, and he shook one out with trembling hands. He put it to his lips, cracked the window, and dug a lighter out of his pocket. He lit it and sucked on it hard and blew the smoke out the window. I felt like I was staring at a stranger.

"You're going to talk to your mother soon," he said. "She'll be upset about some things."

"About losing the apartment?"

"There's a little more to it than that."

I watched him take another pull on the cigarette.

"You remember Amy?"

"Yes. Your secretary."

"I'm living with her," he said.

"Did you lose your apartment?"

He stared at the road ahead. "No," he said. "I've been living in her apartment."

Suddenly the realization of what he was saying hit me.

"You've been cheating on Mom?" I said.

"Yes," he said like he no longer cared about hiding anything.

"And Mom knows?"

"Yes."

I studied his face. He didn't seem sorry at all.

"How long?"

"Since before all this. A while."

"A while?"

He looked at me. "I wanted to tell you myself. I wanted you to hear it from me."

"Pull over," I said.

"Look, son, sometimes these things happen to grownups."

"You came all the way down here to tell me that? What am I supposed to do, Dad? I can't even talk to her."

"Well, it's not just that. I need help. I can't do this alone."

I didn't know what he wanted. I didn't know what to say. I just wished he'd stop the car and let me out. I couldn't stand the sight of him.

"If I don't get some more help for my legal bills, then I don't stand a chance of getting out of this."

"So you really came down here to get money from Grandmother?"

"Well, and to talk to you about, you know, the situation with Amy."

"Just stop the car."

"We're almost there."

"Let me out!"

He pulled off the road and stopped. I got out, slammed the door, and started walking across the field. I heard the car window going down behind me.

"Come on, Win."

I turned back. "I've got money in the top drawer of your old dresser. You can have it all. Just get it and leave."

61 MOM

It was almost dark when the farmer found me. I was walking alongside a dirt road at the south end of the property. He slowed the truck and drove beside me.

"He's gone," he said. "You need a ride?"

I didn't answer right away, then nodded. He stopped, and I walked around the front of the truck and got in.

"I hope he never comes back," I said.

"Try not to let it all get to you, Win. I know it's hard."

"He screwed everything up. Everybody's life. And he acts like it was just something that happens sometimes. He *made* it happen."

The farmer didn't answer.

"He acts like I'm supposed to help him. What am I supposed to do?"

"You need to keep doing exactly what you're doing."

"How am I supposed to do all this?"

He put his hand on my shoulder. "You'll figure it out," he said. "It'll all be fine."

I didn't respond.

"Win?"

"What."

I felt him looking at me. "You're doing a good job. I'm proud of you."

I don't know if it was the farmer's words or the load Dad had dumped on me, but suddenly it felt like too much and I wanted to cry. But I clenched my teeth and held it back.

The money was still in the drawer. On top of it was a piece of paper with a phone number on it and "Your Mother" written next to it. I shoved the paper in my pocket, went back downstairs, and started out the front door.

"Where are you going this time of night?" Grandmother snapped.

I faced her. "I'm going to Sikes's house."

"Why?"

"None of your business. And I hope you didn't give him any money."

She studied me with her trembling face. For the first time I could remember, she didn't argue. I turned and walked out.

Sikes answered their front door, dressed in a man's undershirt and sweats and her hair pulled into a ponytail. She was barefoot, and I suddenly imagined her doing nothing for the last hour but sitting cross-legged on the edge of her bed, painting her perfect toenails. She had a look of anticipation, like someone was coming to rescue her from a life of boredom.

"Where did you come from?" she asked.

"You mind if I use your phone?"

"Of course not. What's wrong with yours?"

"I just want some privacy," I said.

She studied me. "Sure," she said. "You can use the one in the library. I'll close the door."

"Thanks."

She closed the giant pocket doors and left me in the silent, dark mahogany room where Mr. Rhodes read his newspapers and made his business deals. I sank into one of his oversize leather club chairs and grabbed the phone on the table next to me.

"Hello?" she answered.

"Hey, Mom. It's me."

"Win? Oh Lord, Win," she exclaimed desperately.

"Where are you?"

I heard her sniffling.

"Mom?"

"Yes, sweetheart?"

"Where are you, Mom?"

"I'm in sort of an apartment where I have help. But how are you,

Win?"

"I'm OK."

"Are you really OK? Please tell me the truth."

"Yes, I'm fine."

"I didn't know," she said. "Your dad said you don't have a phone."

"Well, I got it working, but it's not reliable. There's no answering machine or anything."

"I'm so sorry I haven't called."

"I saw Dad today. He told me everything. He told me about Amy."

I heard her sniffle again.

"Mom?"

"Yes?"

"I hate him. He did all this. It wasn't anything you did."

"Oh, Win. It's just so messed up. I'm so sorry."

"You don't need to be sorry about anything. It's him that needs to be sorry. I never want to see him again."

She didn't answer.

"When are you coming down here?"

"Down there?"

"To Cottonlandia."

She seemed surprised I would ask. "Well, I don't know," she said. "I don't know if I'm welcome there."

"It's where I live, Mom. Why wouldn't you be welcome?"

She didn't answer me right away. "Win," she said, "you can't imagine how hard it is for me to say this, but I'm not fit to be your mother right now."

"What do you mean?"

"I can't even take care of myself. I'd just be a burden."

"Are you going to stay up there?" I asked.

"For a while. Until I'm better. As long as you're OK."

"It's different down here, but I'm fine."

"Maybe in a few months you'll come visit me," she said.

"I've got money for a plane ticket. But I'll try and call soon."

"OK, sweetheart. It's so good to hear your voice. I love you."

"You, too, Mom. 'Bye."

I hung up the phone, sank back into the chair, and tried to sort through my thoughts. I felt sorry for her, but in a distant, helpless way. It wasn't a sorrow that hurt me, and I was ashamed it didn't. It was still hard to believe she felt it was OK to abandon me. How could someone tell you they loved and missed you, yet they didn't want to see you? But if she needed taking care of, I certainly wasn't prepared to do it. I'd had enough dumped on me already. Maybe it was better for all of us if she stayed in New York for a while. But at least now I knew all the pieces I had to work with while navigating my new, strange life.

62 DUKE

Saturday morning, I followed Hoyt to his truck and peered over the tailgate at a cardboard box. Inside were eight puppies stumbling about on a moving blanket. They were mostly white with splotches of black. Like Oreo ice cream.

"They *are* kind of cute," Hoyt said.

"Where are you taking them?"

"Figure I'll run up to Walmart during lunch and see if I can give them away. You know, they'll be good friends to somebody. They just ain't gonna be mad at coons."

I noticed one of the puppies had a collar draped over it. I pointed to it. "You already give that one away?"

"Check him out," Hoyt said.

I reached in and untangled the puppy from his siblings. I cradled him to my chest and read the name tag. It said:

Win Canterbury
Cottonlandia Plantation
Walnut Bend, MS

I looked at Hoyt. "This mine?"

He smiled, deeply proud of himself. "Yeah, man. I didn't name him. Figured I'd let you do that."

I looked back at the puppy. I'd never considered such a thing.

"What do I do with it? I mean, what does it eat?"

"It ain't a *it*. That's a full-bred buck of a coon hound. Son of

Truckstop. Lady killer. You just give it dog food, man. You can buy it anywhere. Heck, best dogs I ever raised was on deer guts. They eat just about anything."

I looked back at Hoyt. "Thanks," I said. But I wasn't sure about it at all.

"He'll be a good friend. Start thinking of a name."

"All right," I said. "I will."

"I got you some starter food on the front seat. Go get it and take him in the shop and put him in that big paper towel box that's there before an owl carries him off."

When I brought the puppy home that evening Grandmother declared it a "thing of filth." She made it clear she didn't want any dogs living in her house.

"But Hoyt says the owls will get it."

She waved her hand in the air dismissively. "I don't want to hear what that fool says."

Gert frowned at her and motioned for me to bring the box into the kitchen. We set it near the back door, and she prepared a bowl of drinking water and another for me to put the dog food in. She set both of these in the box, and the puppy began lapping at the water.

"Miss Canterbury ain't gonna set a foot back here," Gert said to the puppy. "Don't you worry about a thing, little fella."

We stood back, watching it drink.

"I need to name him," I said.

"He sure is pretty," Gert said. "Is that a coon dog?"

"Well, sort of. It's a coon dog that doesn't like coons."

Gert shook her head and started toward the sink. "You never know," she said. "You never know."

"I guess I'll just feed it and watch it grow," I said.

She glanced at me. "You ain't never had a dog?"

"No."

She chuckled. "Well, you certainly got another chore on your hands."

Buster came over after church, and I showed him the puppy in the kitchen.

"You can't tell," he said. "Just because its momma wasn't a good coon dog don't mean it can't get it from its daddy or its grandaddy."

"I don't really care," I said.

"What are you gonna name it?"

"I don't know."

"Duke. You got to name it Duke."

"Why?"

"Because it sounds strong and it's easy to call."

"OK," I said.

"I brought the .22. You wanna ride over to the brake and shoot turtles?"

"I don't want to blow anything up."

"It's just a .22," he said, innocently.

"What else have you got in that toolbox?"

"Well, I got some other stuff too."

"Yeah," I said. "That's what I thought."

We spent all afternoon near the ruins of the old beaver dam, shooting turtles. We had to sit quietly until they poked their heads up, and then Buster would fire and wade out to retrieve them. He put them all into a crocus sack.

"What are you going to do with them?" I asked him.

"Eat them."

"What do they taste like?"

"Like snake."

"You seriously think I've eaten a snake?"

"Like frog legs."

"Try again."

"Fine. Like chicken."

As the swamp grew dark, mosquitoes drifted up from the leaves and whined about our faces.

"When did these things get here?" I asked.

"That time of year," Buster said. "Come May they'll just about tote you off."

I slapped at the mosquitoes and wondered how long Buster wanted to stay. When it was too dark to shoot, he got up and loaded the sack of sixteen turtles into his metal box.

"You wanna see something else real cool?"

The mosquitoes were about to make me dance. "Yes," I said. "Let's see something else."

He pulled a small flashlight out of his pocket and started past me.

"This way," he said.

Whatever he had in mind, it looked like we weren't going far. I started after him. "I wish we had some insect repellant," I said.

"It's worth it. You'll see."

There was a faint footpath at the edge of the brake. For several minutes I followed Buster through the darkness, slapping at insects and swiping vines and branches from my face. Finally, he stopped, and his light was moving up and down a large rise in the ground.

"Check it out," he said.

I stopped and tried to see whatever it was I was supposed to be impressed with.

"A hill?"

"Yeah. What you think it's doing in the middle of a swamp?"

He was right. It suddenly occurred to me there was no natural reason for it.

"I don't know."

"Indian mound. There's Indians buried under there."

I felt the hairs stand up on the back of my neck. Suddenly the night sounds were louder. I didn't feel the mosquitoes.

"How do you know?" I asked.

"Dig your hand around in there."

"Hell no."

"I pulled bones out of there before."

"Like big ones?"

"Naw, just pieces. Pottery too."

"How'd you find it?"

"Just wandering around."

"Are we still on our property?"

"Yeah, man. All them dead Indians are yours."

"Great. Let's get out of here."

Buster came to me with the light. "Pretty cool, huh?"

"Yeah. Let's go."

"Ain't no end to cool stuff around here."

"I guess not," I said.

63 EARLY COTTON

The cotton appeared as little, green leafy shoots about ten days after we planted it. In the following weeks we put out more nitrogen and roamed the fields in the sprayer truck, looking for a flea-like bug called a thrip. Luther usually drove, with Hoyt riding shotgun, ready to jump out and inspect the plant leaves or adjust something about the truck. There wasn't much for me to do but ride between them and listen and learn. Sometimes the conversations were about the work at hand, but most of the time they weren't. Luther usually talked about church and family cookouts while Hoyt schemed about money-making ventures. Nothing frustrated Hoyt more than Luther's resolve that he'd never be more than a farmhand.

"I'm just a poor old country boy," Luther said. "Same as my daddy, same as his daddy."

"Well, me too. So what?"

"Got no education."

"Me neither! Don't mean you can't win sweepstakes or something."

"Ain't wasting my money on that stuff. White man got it all rigged up, anyway."

"It ain't rigged! How is it rigged?"

Luther frowned. "Advertise like you gonna win a million dollars when you ain't got no chance in hell."

"People win all the time! All it costs is a dollar."

"You spend *your* dollar on it, then."

Luther stopped, and Hoyt hopped out, took a few steps into the field, and studied the cotton leaves. In a moment he was satisfied they were bug-free and climbed back up and slammed the door.

"I tell you where the money is," he continued. "The money's in selling all this farm equipment. Who's got the biggest house in town?"

Luther shrugged.

"Dang John Deere dealership fellah, that's who. Probably sitting out by his pool right now."

"He don't get money unless we get it first."

Hoyt thought about that for a moment. "Well, we all give it to him."

Luther shook his head. We were all confused.

Sometimes we saw the farmer off in the distance, riding slowly up and down the turn rows with his elbow out the window, studying the tiny plants, watching the sky.

"What's he looking at the sky for?" I asked.

"He's worried about hailstorms," Hoyt said.

"Hailstorms? Now?"

"Shoot yeah," Hoyt said. "You get a blue norther this time of year, everything dry like it is, it'll sand-blast the little cotton plants."

"Then what do you do?"

"You got to start all over."

"Well, when is there nothing to worry about?"

Luther chuckled. "November," he said. "When you get the money in your hand."

"Until then," Hoyt continued. "There's *always* something to worry about. Hurricanes, boll weevil, economy."

"Tractor breaking down," Luther said.

"Drought," Hoyt said.

Luther nodded to himself. "All kinds of stuff."

Despite the perils they described, Luther and Hoyt seemed to leave all the worrying to the farmer, like it was his job. We bounced along in the sprayer, "taking care of the babies," as Hoyt put it.

"I tell you what else you can do," Hoyt said. "You can just look at who's driving the nice cars. They usually got something figured out."

"Deacon Leon's got a nice car."

"There you go! It can't take much to be a dang deacon. I'll bet that sucker's raking it in."

Luther nodded. "Yep. He better. That girl that rubs on his leg like a housecat, she's got claws."

By May the fields were a carpet of green. Even the swamp itself seemed to turn green overnight. The edges swelled with blackberry bushes and ivy. Insects thrummed from within like something warmed in a stove, revived. Gusts of warm, dry, dusty air came at us through the truck windows.

"Warming up to be a hot one this summer," Hoyt said.

Luther wiped his forehead like he already felt it. "It's always a hot one," he said.

Hoyt reached across me and turned the knob for the AC. The vents coughed out dust, a few leaves, and dead insects. He held his hand in front of the stream of air until it grew cool. Then he shut it off again.

"Works," he said. "Gonna need it."

Luther took one hand off the wheel and looked down at me. "You gonna really know what's it's like to work a farm when you start irrigating."

"Is that what I got all the poly pipe ready for?" I asked.

Luther nodded. "Tote that stuff around in the heat, and it'll make a man out of you quick."

There was a general buzz of inattention at school as the final day of classes approached.

"What are you doing this summer?" I asked Buster in the cafeteria.

"Working," he said. "We got two hundred acres of beans to irrigate. Dad says it's gonna be dry."

"How can you tell?"

"You just get a feeling about it," he said.

"You still kill beavers in the summer?"

"Year-round. But we've got time to make a crop of beans."

"Hoyt says we'll start putting out irrigation pipe next week," I said.

"You'll probably run the poly pipe to some pumps. I don't think you have any pivots on your place."

"What's that?"

"Those huge sprinklers. Got tires on them."

"Right. No, we don't have one of those."

"How's Duke?"

"He's good. He runs around in the yard some now."

"I'll come by," he said. "Maybe we can go over to the Rhodeses' pool."

"After Roxy shot at us?"

"Just tell Sikes we're coming over this time. Them girls don't know nothing."

I frowned doubtfully. "We'll see. I'll let you know."

On the last day of school, Sikes caught up with me at my locker as I was cleaning out my old PE clothes and books and stuffing them into a backpack.

"You working this afternoon?" she asked.

"Yeah. What are you doing?"

She seemed hesitant to tell me but realized it was too late. "Some of us are going to the country club for a little while. It's no big deal."

"End-of-the-year party?"

"I doubt many people will be there," she said.

I pulled another book out and dropped it in my pack. "We've got a lot of irrigation to get out," I said. "The best time to do it is early in the morning and late in the afternoon when it's cool."

"You working all summer?"

I nodded. "Every day but Sunday. Then we have church."

"Come over Sunday afternoon, then. We can swim in the pool."

I looked at her. "Yeah, Buster asked about that."

She frowned. "You've got to get out more, Win. You don't have to hang out with Buster all the time."

"I like Buster. We're on the same level in a weird way."

"You are *not* on the same level as Buster."

I closed my locker for the last time and zipped my pack. "Looks that way to me," I said.

"I'm not even going to argue with you about that," she said. "I'm just saying you should come out with us sometime and stop feeling sorry for yourself."

"I'm not feeling sorry for myself."

"Whatever," she said.

I hefted my pack onto my shoulder and started toward the buses. "I didn't get an invitation, Sikes," I said over my shoulder.

"You would if you acted interested in something besides Buster Tillman and farming."

I didn't answer.

"You're not a *farmer*, Win."

I turned to her and smiled. "I'll see you on Sunday."

She shook her head, frustrated. "Don't bring Buster."

That night I lay in bed reading a Sherlock Holmes mystery. The house was quiet except for the thrum-thrum of the ceiling fan overhead. I thought I heard something tap on my window but dismissed it as a moth. Then I heard it again, louder this time. I got up and peered out into the yard and saw Sikes looking up at me. She waved for me to come down.

I pulled on my clothes and crept downstairs and out through the kitchen door.

"What are you doing?" I asked.

"You want to go riding?"

"Now?"

"Sure."

"They're going to hear me crank the four-wheeler."

"I've got my truck," she said mischievously.

"What?" I said, looking around.

"I left it out by the gate so your grandmother and Gert wouldn't hear."

"Jesus! You drove it here on the highway?"

"Just from my house. It's only like two miles."

"If your dad finds out he's going to kill you!"

She grabbed my hand and pulled me along. "Nobody will find out," she said. "Come on!"

There was that phrase again. And still I followed.

64 PERFECT DISASTER

We raced across the moonlit lawn to Sikes's truck.

"You know I have to work tomorrow?"

"Oh, hush."

"Where are we going? It's late."

"Just come on!"

Despite my complaints, I could think of nothing I'd rather be doing. I was filled with jittery excitement. I was defenseless against anything she wanted to do.

We reached the truck, and she stopped and turned to me. "You want to drive?"

"No," I said.

"It's easy."

The thought of Sikes's father catching us was bad enough. Wrecking her truck was even worse.

"No," I said again, starting for the passenger side.

In a moment we were off, Sikes making a U-turn by the front gate, flipping on the headlights, and starting back out the driveway. To my relief she didn't drive too fast and seemed genuinely interested in being careful.

"Just stay on the dirt road," I told her.

"I am. I want to show you something."

We emerged from the grove, and the fields stretched away on either side clear to the dark line of trees. I looked up and saw the moon full and white and cool. Then far ahead I saw the lights of a car passing slowly on the blacktop.

"Did you pass anybody on the highway?" I asked.

"Just two people."

"Were you scared?"

She laughed, still excited from the experience. "Yes! I pulled off in the ditch for the first one."

"Jesus, Sikes."

"The second one was easy."

In the distance the church stood quietly under the big utility light. Suddenly a doe leaped across the road in front of us, and Sikes mashed on the brakes, slamming me against the dashboard. I fell back against my seat in time to see a yearling scramble across the gravel after its mother.

"That was close!" Sikes said.

I fumbled for my seat belt, a surge of panic flashing through me. "Let's at least get wherever we're going before you wreck us."

Sikes laughed and pressed the gas again.

She drove us out to the church, where she turned into the parking lot, stopped, and shut off the truck. "Come on," she said. "We have to walk from here."

"Walk where?"

"You'll see."

I followed her around the back of the church, where a thin strip of field separated us from the edge of the swamp rising tall and lush and silver in the moonlight. The air was cool and wet, and the utility light hummed softly in the stillness. All about us was the smell of the damp, freshly turned earth. She stopped and waited for me and grabbed my hand when I came close. I opened my fingers, and she slid hers between them and squeezed softly, and I felt a warm feeling pass through me. She looked around.

"You see," she said. "It's not so bad here. It's not always gray and rainy and cold."

I was still thinking about her hand. Thinking I never wanted to let go. If I could just stand there and hold her hand all night, I wouldn't need anything else.

She pulled me toward the field. "This way," she said.

We started long-stepping across the tops of the rows. I thought briefly about the tiny cotton plants we were crushing, but then I felt the softness of her hand, and as long as I was holding it, I didn't care if we were mowing the whole place over. As we approached the trees, the sound of cicadas rose like something electric pulsing from the thick greenery. The heavy smell of fat, wet vines and leaves and honeysuckle fell over us. Then she stopped under the dark overhang of tree limbs.

"Back here," she said.

She pulled me into the trees, and it seemed we were on a dim footpath. She pulled me along through moon shadow under the tall white oaks and gum trees. When she stopped, I pressed close to her and assumed she'd lost her way.

"Look," she said quietly.

I studied the dark outline of trees around us. At first, I saw nothing unusual. Then gradually I began to pick out strange shapes low to the ground.

"Buried Indians?"

"No," she said. "It's a cemetery. An old cemetery."

Any other time it would have been the creepiest place I'd ever seen in my life.

"Cottonlandia people are buried here," she said.

"Like my relatives?"

"No, Black people. From a long time ago."

She pulled me off the trail, and we stepped slowly around the headstones.

"Be careful," she said. "There's sinkholes."

In a moment we came to a fallen tree where she sat down, and I sat beside her. She squeezed my hand again.

"How did you know about this place?" I asked.

She swung one leg over the tree, faced me, and began drumming her fingers on my hand. "Roxy's daughter got married at your church. After the service some kids showed it to me."

"I never realized we had so many dead people everywhere," I said.

"What do you mean?"

"Never mind."

Sikes didn't say anything for a moment.

"I don't get you sometimes, Win. Like, why do you work so much?"

I thought about it. "At first I wanted the money. Then I didn't really have anything to do with the money. I mean, it's not enough to live in New York with or anything. But I realized it keeps my mind off things. I can't imagine sitting around thinking about my problems all the time."

"Is your dad in jail?"

"No. He's working with lawyers to try and fix it all."

"You think he'll go?"

"I don't know."

"Is your mom better?"

"Yeah, but she doesn't want to come down here. She's in some sort of nursing home."

"Why don't you go see her?"

"She could come see *me*."

Sikes didn't answer.

"I guess she just needs some time by herself. I don't know. There's nothing I can do about it."

Her fingers were still, but I felt her watching me. I wanted to change the subject. "Why'd you leave the party?" I asked.

"It was over."

"Didn't you have some friends to spend the night with or something?"

She shook her head. "No."

I stared at our hands.

"I wanted to come see you," she said. "I didn't want you to be alone."

I took a deep breath.

"You know, you can kiss me if you want."

I slowly looked up at her and saw her face, smooth and perfect in the dim light. I'd never kissed a girl. I leaned toward her, and she must have come toward me at the same time because suddenly our lips were pressed together, soft and wet. Then she pulled away and I was left there, not knowing what to do or say but feeling more excited and optimistic than I'd ever felt before. Then she squeezed my hand, which I'd forgotten about.

"You ready to go?" she said.

"OK," I said.

When I stood, my legs were shaking. She sounded so calm. She pulled me along, neither of us saying anything.

Once we were back in the truck, Sikes sat up straight behind the wheel and turned the key. Nothing happened. She turned it again. Still nothing.

"What's wrong?" I asked, dread creeping over me.

She leaned toward the steering column and looked at the key. "I don't know," she said. She turned it again. Nothing.

"Sikes," I warned. "You better get this truck started."

She turned it again. "I'm trying," she replied, a hint of desperation in her voice. "Nothing's happening."

"I can see that."

She turned to me, her hand still on the key. "I don't know what else to do."

I held out my hands. "I know even less than you about this thing."

She sat back in her seat and started sobbing.

"We need to go call for help," I said.

"But we'll be in trouble."

"We're already in trouble, Sikes."

She shook her head. "I can't believe this."

"We can't just sit here until the sun comes up. Come on, let's walk back to the house. I'd go by myself, but I don't want to leave you out here."

She hesitated, then opened her door. I met her near the tailgate, and we started the long walk to Headquarters, neither of us speaking, the night silent except for our feet crunching on the damp gravel. All I could think about was how something so perfect had turned into such a disaster.

65 BUSTED

It took us a half hour to walk to Headquarters. We went around back, where I told Sikes to wait for me outside the kitchen while I called the farmer. I went inside and heard Duke whining and scraping in his box.

"Shh," I said. "Go back to sleep."

He whimpered and settled, and I crept into the foyer.

"Who's that!" Grandmother snapped.

"It's just me," I sighed.

"What are you doing up so late?"

"It's nothing, Grandmother. Go back to sleep."

I continued to the phone and dialed the farmer's number written on a piece of paper nearby. After several rings he answered, more alert than I'd expected.

"It's Win," I said.

"Is someone in trouble?"

"Yes. Me. I was with Sikes, and we got the truck stuck out by the church."

There was a pause. "OK," he said. "Is she with you?"

"Well, she walked back with me. She's outside right now."

"Good. Does Charlie Rhodes know?"

"No, sir."

"I'll need to call him."

"Are you sure?"

"Yes. It's his daughter; he needs to know."

"OK."

"I'll be over shortly."

I hung up the phone and took a deep breath.

"Nothing good ever happens after ten o'clock," Grandmother snapped.

I ignored her and went back to stand with Sikes and wait for whatever was about to come down on us.

The farmer's headlights swung into the driveway ten minutes after the phone call. He motioned for us to get in. Sikes scooted to the middle, and I got into the passenger seat and closed the door. As we started to the church, he seemed more tired than upset.

"What happened?"

"It just wouldn't start," I said.

"I thought you said it got stuck."

"Well, not in the mud. It just won't start."

The farmer frowned. He picked up his handheld and clicked the mic button. "Hey, Hoyt?"

"Yes, sir?"

"Turn around. They got engine problems. I don't think we'll need the tractor."

"I'm almost there. I'll come see what I can do."

"OK," the farmer said. "See you in a minute."

As we neared the church, we saw Mr. Rhodes's black Cadillac swing off the highway and start toward us. I heard Sikes sigh and sink in her seat. I thought about grabbing her hand but didn't want the farmer see me do it. *It's ruined,* I thought. *The kiss and everything is ruined.*

The farmer stopped next to Sikes's truck, and Mr. Rhodes pulled up behind us. I got out and waited for Sikes. We heard the door of the Cadillac open, and in a moment Mr. Rhodes's big frame was outlined in the car's headlights.

"Get in the car, Sikes," he said firmly.

She left without a word and went around to the passenger side of the car and got in. Mr. Rhodes walked past without acknowledging me.

"Thanks, John," he said.

"No problem, Charlie."

Hoyt's little truck suddenly scooted up beside me and skidded to a stop. He got out and looked around. At me, at Sikes's truck, at the

263

Cadillac. Then he looked at me again and grinned. He gave me the thumbs-up, held discreetly against his chest. I frowned and looked at the ground.

"Hoyt, you wanna look at this thing?" the farmer said.

He trotted over to Sikes's truck and climbed in. After a second, I heard the truck start and Hoyt racing the engine. He left it running and got out again.

"Had it in drive," he said. "It's OK."

Mr. Rhodes shook his head. "I'm sorry about all this, fellows."

"Hey, you know kids," Hoyt said.

"We need a little excitement around here every now and then," the farmer said. "Hoyt, why don't you drive it back to Beulah and I'll meet you over there."

"Got it," Hoyt said. "See you in a minute."

Hoyt pulled away in Sikes's truck. Mr. Rhodes finally turned to me. "Did she drive it over here by herself?"

I tried to think of the best way to answer the question. "I rode out to the church with her," I said.

Mr. Rhodes nodded thoughtfully. "OK," he said. He turned back to the farmer and breathed out through his nose. "All right, John. I'll see you at the house."

The farmer drove me back to Headquarters.

"It seems like you might have done something wrong," he said. "But I really can't think of what."

I didn't respond.

"Certainly can't blame you for getting in the truck with her."

"I just feel bad for her."

"She could have killed herself on that highway."

"I know," I said.

"But nobody got hurt," he said. "She'll get in a little trouble, and it'll do her some good, and then you two can get back to being kids again."

I looked at him. "Sorry about waking you up. Everybody's going to be tired tomorrow."

"Well, I suppose you'll feel *some* consequence from all this. I expect you at the shop at six."

"I'll be there."

"I know you will."

66 LAY-BY

A week after I fell in love with Sikes Rhodes, I drove the ATV to Beulah to apologize. For what, I wasn't sure. But I wanted to see her.

Roxy met me at the front door. "She's grounded, Win. Up in her room. Can't do nothing but go to church camp and read her summer reading books."

"For how long?"

"You'll have to ask Mr. Rhodes."

"Come in here, Win," I heard Mr. Rhodes say.

Roxy stepped aside and let me into the house. I found Mr. Rhodes in his big leather armchair. He lowered a magazine, took off his reading glasses, and studied me like he was waiting for me to say something. I thought again about apologizing, but then didn't see the use.

"She's getting out of hand," he said. "Got to throw the fence back up for a while."

"Yes, sir."

"How's the cotton growing?"

"Fine," I said. "Still pretty small."

"John's not working you too hard, is he?"

I shook my head.

"I don't see how he does it. Especially when this heat really sets in."

I didn't respond. I knew he was getting at something; I just wished he'd go ahead and get there so I could leave.

"I've tried to get in touch with your father a couple of times, but I

265

can't seem to reach him. Does he have a new number?"

I wanted to leave so bad my knees were trembling. "I don't know," I said. "I don't know what he's doing."

"I suppose it really doesn't matter. I've been dealing with Tim Haney. I just felt your father should sort of know a little about the progress of things."

I shook my head. "I don't know."

"Very well, Win." He put his reading glasses back on and peered at me over their rim. "Next time my daughter tries a stunt like that, you see if you can talk her out of it."

"I'll try," I said.

The farmer called it lay-by. We'd done all we could do in the fields. The rest of the summer would be spent controlling the weeds by hand and watering.

"In a month those plants should be high enough to hide a rabbit," he told me. "That's what you want."

Work made it easy to keep my mind off Sikes. Each day we started at sunrise, toting loads of poly pipe in one of the farm trucks and pulling it out in lengths that were sometimes a half mile long. At the end of each pipe was a water pump nearly as big as Hoyt's truck, mounted on a skid next to a tank of propane. This machine pulled the water up from the aquifer deep underground and filled the poly pipe like a giant garden hose.

Rarely was there a cloud in the sky. By ten o'clock the sun seemed to hum with heat, baking everything till it was hard and dusty. We got in and out of the trucks so much it was useless to run the air conditioner. We rode with the windows down, the vinyl seats slick and sticky and gritty. The dust was everywhere, in your eyes, your nose, your ears. By lunchtime no one was talking. Our faces were red, our cheeks hot to the touch, our heads throbbing. We drank ice water and ate peanut butter and jelly sandwiches in the shade at the edges of the fields, chewing slowly, dreading going back out there.

Every day after work I went upstairs and peeled off my wet clothes, black with sweat and grime. I walked naked to the washroom and drew a cold bath. Then I slipped into it, savoring the water as it cooled my body and eased my throbbing head. The dirt and sweat fell off and settled. I heard Gert outside, tidying up behind me. When I got back to my room, my dirty clothes were gone, and in their place was a fresh towel and clean laundry. I made sure the air conditioner was roaring on full and stood in front of it and let it blow-dry my face and hair.

As miserable as the work was, physically I felt better than I'd ever felt in my life. It wasn't just my muscles getting lean and hard or my skin getting bronzed and tough, it was in my mind too. I was part of something, and people were counting on me; it was a type of health I'd never experienced before. I was earning money and respect for the first time. Even Grandmother seemed to quietly approve of me, even though she wouldn't admit it. When I came dragging in the front door hot and sweaty and smelly, she didn't say a word. If the farm was working, everyone was happy.

When I lay in bed at the end of the day, feeling the soreness in my muscles and the sunburn on my face, I could almost forget it was all coming to an end soon. Almost. A sickening sense of regret never failed to crawl over me in the darkest hours of the night. And when I allowed myself to look into the future, there was nothing but catfish ponds as far as the eye could see.

67 GRANDMOTHER'S TALK

I sat across from Buster on the front lawn as the afternoon cooled and the cicadas rose and the squirrels twitched and fussed in the trees. Duke lay in my lap, squirming for attention.

"I kissed her," I said.

Buster spat and looked at me. "Dang it," he said.

"What?"

"She's just so good-looking."

I peered down at Duke. He rolled over, and I began scratching his stomach.

"Where?" Buster asked.

"In an old graveyard behind the church."

"Dang it," he said again, shaking his head. "I can't even think about it."

"It's hard to believe."

"Is she your girlfriend?"

"I don't know. I haven't seen her since. She's grounded."

"For kissing?"

"No, for driving on the highway."

"She's the one that needs to go to jail," he said.

Duke rolled over, leaped across my legs, and ambled the short distance to Buster. He pulled him into his lap and scratched him behind the shoulders. "That's right, Duke," he said. "I ain't giving up on you. I can tell you got some coon dog in you."

"What do you want—" I started to say.

"Man," Buster suddenly said, looking up again, "I just can't stop thinking about it."

"I know. Me neither."

"I got to call Sara. She's ready to go on a date. I know she is."

"Have you talked to her since you made her puke?"

"No."

"That might have set you back some."

Buster frowned.

"What do you want to be when you grow up, Buster?"

"Farmer. Beaver man. What else?"

"But you could do anything. You're smart."

"I can't help that," he said.

"But you could make a lot more money doing something else."

"Yeah, but then I'd be doing something else."

"So you don't even think about it?"

Buster jostled the puppy around and shook his head. "One day I'm gonna get about five hundred acres," he said. "That's all I need."

Duke ran back to me and jumped into my lap again.

"I'll have to start off leasing a place," Buster said. "Until I save up enough money . . . Maybe I could lease some from you?"

I felt the weight of my secret again.

Buster sensed my hesitation. "Or we could work it together," he said. "Do like a profit share. Lots of people do that."

I thought about Mr. Rhodes's bulldozers tearing the road around the brake. I imagined them coming like German tanks to destroy the place.

"But if I were you," Buster continued, "and I had all this coming to me, I'd keep it pretty close. Wouldn't get mixed up with too many people."

"There's just so much I don't know," I said.

"Hey, Mr. Case is about as good as they get. You'll know a bunch after this summer."

"You ever thought about catfish farming?" I said.

"Man, who wants to be a catfish farmer? This is the best farmland in the world. You can go anywhere and be a catfish farmer."

Duke whined. I scratched him on the stomach, thinking of some way to change the subject.

"You want to ride up to Denton's and get some Cokes?" I said.

"I guess. Then you can show me the graveyard. I wanna see where it all happened."

I found a hammock in the garden shed and hung it on the front porch beneath an old, iron ceiling fan. The metal hooks were already on the wall, like it had been there once before. On the days when I didn't get with Buster after work, I lay in the hammock and read and napped with the fan humming overhead and cicadas buzzing in the breezeless, heavy relief of late afternoon. Gert would bring me a pitcher of iced tea and a glass and set them on a wicker table within reach. Sometimes I spent hours just lying there, feeling the satisfaction of a hard day's work in my muscles and bones, drifting in and out of a guiltless, drugged sleep, interspersed with visions of Gert quietly refreshing my pitcher of tea, the fan humming, the cicadas buzzing.

It was mostly during those times on the porch that my thoughts drifted to Sikes. I imagined her imprisoned at Beulah like a princess in a castle tower. So close, but so far away. I wondered what she was thinking. For now, I was the heir next door. Maybe her boyfriend. And as long as she was grounded, things would stay that way.

I just wanted time to stop. Right then and there. I knew life had never been more perfect and would never be so again.

One day I woke to find Grandmother sitting in a garden chair on the other side of the wicker table. She stared over the lawn, her head trembling like it was all she could do to hold it up, but her dark eyes pulling in everything. I didn't move. I didn't make a sound.

"Winchester?" she said.

I jumped a little.

She looked at me.

"Ma'am?" I said.

"You know what you have now, don't you?"

I wasn't sure what she was talking about, but I nodded that I did.

She looked away again. She stared across the lawn like she could see through the trees and out over the fields. "That's all I can ask . . . that you know."

"Yes, ma'am."

"I don't want to hear about what you or your father plan to do with the place. As long as you know. I've done all I can do, and now you've got to live with the rest."

I knew exactly what she was talking about, and I swallowed

against it. But I had questions and I finally had an opening to ask them.

"Why didn't Dad want to be a farmer?"

She looked at me, then back at the lawn again.

"Sometimes," she began, "when you grow up with things, you take them for granted. I suppose he thought he could find something better. At one time, I did too. I lived in France for two years, thinking I wanted to be a painter. Then I moved to Chicago."

"Why'd you come back?"

"My father died, and I came home to be with my mother. I meant to go back to Chicago, but I didn't. I met your grandfather while I was home. He was a banker in Greenwood."

"And you decided to stay?"

"He wanted nothing more than to marry a farm girl. He loved the delta. He was never much of a farmer, but he was smart enough to know it. He leased out the land."

"Did he profit-share?"

She glanced at me suspiciously. "Yes," she said. "On occasion he did."

"But you didn't really want to stay at first, then he talked you into it?"

"You might say that. And it was the best thing that ever happened to me. It's a mean world out there. But no matter what happens in it, the land will always provide. For the table and the soul."

"But you won't get rich."

"That's the part your father doesn't get. You're already rich."

"In a different way."

"In a better way."

I looked over at the pitcher of iced tea. The ice was melted. Gert had been gone for a while.

"And you're mad at him because he doesn't understand?" I asked.

"Mostly because I'm a selfish old lady that's used to getting what she wants. And he's just like me. The only difference between me and your father is he screwed up and I didn't."

"Did you give him money the last time he was here?"

"Of course I did. He's my son."

"You know, you could have come up to New York at least once. I could have had a chance here. I didn't know."

Her eyes started to brim with tears, but I wasn't sad. She hadn't earned my pity. She'd screwed up as much as Dad. She realized it, too, but she was too stubborn to admit it.

"I didn't say I don't have regrets," she said. "I suppose we all do."

I certainly did, but I wasn't about to tell her any of it. Even had she asked. I didn't even care enough about her to hurt her. She was still a stranger to me, and that was her fault and something *she'd* have to live with. That was one thing I wasn't going to put on myself.

Gert appeared through the front door and seemed surprised at the scene.

"Can I get you something, Mrs. Canterbury?" she said.

Grandmother didn't respond.

"A glass of iced tea?" Gert suggested.

"Just help me to my bed," Grandmother said. "I'm done."

And she was. Grandmother was ready to die.

68 DEATH

Gert met me coming down the stairs early the next morning, her eyes wide and white with terror. "I think you need to check on Mrs. Canterbury," she said.

"What's wrong with her?"

She shook her head and stepped aside so I could pass. I walked into Grandmother's room and saw her lying on her back in bed. She had her wig on, and her hands were straight down at her sides, her eyes and mouth open like she'd seen something on the ceiling and screamed at it and been frozen that way. At first, I thought I saw blood running across her cheek, then I realized it was a heavy streak of lipstick. I looked down again and saw it still clutched tightly in her right hand.

"Go touch her," Gert whispered from behind me.

I didn't answer her. I turned and walked out and went to the phone.

"She's dead," I told the farmer.

"OK," he said calmly, like he'd been expecting it. "I'll make some calls. I'll be there shortly."

The farmer arrived about the same time as the ambulance out of Greenwood. I stood on the front lawn with Gert, happy to let him handle everything. Eventually they rolled her out covered on a stretcher, put her into the van, and took her away. Then the farmer returned to us.

"Gert, why don't you clean things up inside. Win, you get in the truck with me and let's ride to the shop."

Even with all that had happened that morning, the farmer still drove with his elbow out the window, inspecting the fields.

"What now?" I asked.

"Your father's flying in tomorrow. They'll probably have the funeral on Thursday."

"What about Mom?"

"I don't know. He said he'd talk to her."

"Where am I going to live?"

He glanced at me. "Where do you want to live?"

"Here."

"I don't imagine Gert wants to go anywhere. I think it'll be fine as long as there's an adult at the place."

Hoyt and Luther were already out spraying and setting up the irrigation. We found them at the north end of the property and told them what had happened. Then the farmer said he had to go into town and make funeral arrangements.

"Everybody get back to work," he said. "It's business as usual."

He left me with them and pulled away.

"Did you touch her?" Hoyt asked me.

"No," I said.

"Why you go and ask him a thing like that?" Luther said. "It's his grandmother."

I looked at Hoyt, and he shrugged apologetically.

"Would you have touched her?" I asked.

"Heck no!"

"All right then."

Luther frowned. "Grab this pipe, you two. Seriously! We got work to do."

That afternoon the farmer drove me back to Headquarters and checked on Gert. She already had the living room back like it had been except for the bed. The farmer said he'd send Hoyt over to disassemble it later. Then he looked down at me.

"You going to be OK by yourself tonight?"

I wasn't sure, but I didn't know my options. "I guess," I said.

"You're welcome to come sleep at my house," he said. "Or I'm sure Hoyt'll be glad to have you."

"I'll see how it goes," I said. "I'll call if I need you."

I lay in bed, waiting to see or feel something sinister related to Grandmother's death, but nothing came. If I felt anything at all, it was that she was gone—not just her body, but her spirit and the heavy, unpredictable mood she brought to the place. Now the house was nothing more than an empty, old house, full of the creaks and noises typical of any such place. When I closed my eyes for the night, I dropped into a sound sleep and didn't wake until Evil went off the next morning.

When I came downstairs Gert had breakfast ready for me as usual. Bacon, toast, two fried eggs, and orange juice. She also had yesterday's paper, in which I'd started reading the agricultural section. The only things missing from the scene were Grandmother and her little brass bell.

"Sleep well, Win?"

I sat down, put my napkin in my lap, and pulled the newspaper toward me. "Real good," I said.

"I slept pretty good myself," she said.

I spread the paper out and took a swig of orange juice while scanning the cotton futures. Gert remained across the table from me, standing with her hands clasped before her.

"Guess it's just me and you now, Gert," I said.

"Yes, sir," she said.

I took a bite of toast and drained the last of the orange juice.

"Can I get you more juice?"

"Yes, please. And another piece of toast."

She disappeared into the kitchen and returned with the juice pitcher and toast. She placed the toast on my plate and refilled my glass. "Should I get one of the rooms ready for your dad?" she asked.

The thought of Dad arriving sickened me. I was hoping not to think about it, but now I had to. "I guess so," I said. "Let him sleep in the living room. I'll tell Hoyt to leave the bed in there for now. At least until he leaves."

"Yes, sir."

"And tell him not to wait up for me. I'll probably be back late."

She looked at the floor and nodded. Once again, I sensed that split loyalty she felt between Dad and the rest of his family.

I drove to Buster's house in Booga Den. I found him in their shop welding steel bars together into a frame about the size of a refrigerator box. A giant floor fan circulated the air behind him, but it was still hot as oven breath inside. He shut off the torch and flipped up the face shield. Sweat ran in beads down his face.

"Hey, man," he said. "I was about come see you."

"Did you hear?"

Buster set the torch down and stood up and pulled off the mask. "Yeah," he said. "What'd she look like?"

"Her mouth and eyes were open. I think she died trying to put on her lipstick."

"That's weird."

"Yeah. What are you making?"

He turned and looked at the metal frame. "Gonna wrap that with canvas and make a deer stand out of it. You can sell one for about three hundred bucks."

"You put it in a tree?"

"Yeah. You use a forklift or something. Lift it, chain it to the tree, then build you a wood ladder to get up to it."

"That's pretty cool," I said, admiring it.

"Yeah."

"You don't mind if I stick around for a while, do you? Dad's coming, and I don't want to see him until I have to."

"I don't mind."

The rest of the afternoon I helped Buster cut and install wood planks in the floor of two deer stands he'd already completed. His father called us in to supper about six o'clock.

It was the first time I'd ever seen his mother off the sofa, much less cooking. The house was suddenly more cheerful, with her clanking about in the kitchen and the smell of roasted meat and boiled vegetables hanging in the air.

We all sat at their table while she served us pot roast and mashed potatoes and green beans. I would have enjoyed it more if she hadn't kept looking across the table at me and smiling and watching me eat.

"Good stuff," Mr. Tillman said.

"Yeah, Momma," Buster said.

"I'm just so happy to have company," she said. "Win, you're such a nice boy."

I didn't know what to say, so I just nodded and smiled.

"Momma, really," Buster said.

She looked at him, beaming. "Buster's been so happy since you moved to town."

"Honey, you're embarrassing Win," Mr. Tillman said.

After supper I followed Buster back out to the shop.

"Sorry about that," he said. "She acts like I ain't never had friends."

I assumed he hadn't ever since his brother was killed.

"Listen," he said. "I figured out a way to catch a lot of fish that don't involve dynamite or electrocution. Legal too."

"How?"

"I'll show you. Come on."

69 THE FUNERAL

Buster got what he called a "bug zapper" off their workbench. It was an electric lantern with purple bulbs and a wire screen around it. We loaded it into the toolbox of his ATV, along with a car battery, scoop net, tent pole, and a homemade contraption about the size of a shoe box with a household electrical outlet on one end and wires hanging out the other.

"Inverter," he said.

"What does it invert?"

"DC power to AC power. Follow me. We're gonna head back toward your place."

I followed Buster on my ATV along the deserted blacktop, lightning bugs hanging and glowing in the air around us. We passed Cottonlandia and kept on toward Beulah, my thoughts suddenly turning to Sikes, wishing she were with us. When Buster cut around the brake and onto the Rhodes property, my thoughts switched to Mr. Rhodes and his dislike of trespassers.

We didn't go far before Buster swung into the trees and the dark brake was in his headlights. I parked beside him and climbed off the ATV. Frogs and cicadas cheeped and rattled in the night air.

"I don't suppose you asked permission for this."

"I come here all the time. They can't see us up in this little cutout. Good fishing."

I slapped a mosquito on my neck. "You didn't answer my question."

Buster held the inverter out to me. "You didn't ask one. Hold this."

I grabbed it and turned and looked behind me while Buster continued to rig his contraption.

To my left I could see the glimmer of the catfish ponds, lying like black mirrors in the sky glow. When I turned back, he had the tent pole dangling the bug zapper out over the water. Then he took the inverter from me and plugged the light cord into the outlet. Finally, he attached the loose wires on the other end of the inverter to the car battery. The bug zapper flickered and glowed and hummed. In a few seconds bugs attracted to the strange, purple light sparked against the screen and fell into the water below.

"You just had to electrocute something, didn't you?" I said.

"Hey, but it ain't the fish," he said. "Watch."

In a moment the water was boiling with fish snapping at the precooked feast. Buster got the net, and with one swipe, he backed away with what must have been thirty bream flipping gold and silver in the night.

"You can sell these, too," he said.

"You've got all kinds of ways to make money."

Buster took the fish to his toolbox, got out a crocus sack, and dumped them into it.

"I got to," he said. "Things are gonna be tight until Momma goes back to work."

I slapped another mosquito on my cheek. "Why doesn't she work now?"

"She got laid off at the power plant last year. It's hard to find jobs these days. Her and Daddy both get government checks, but it don't nearly cover it all."

"So you just find ways to make money?"

"Yeah. Two hundred acres of beans don't get you very far. Especially after paying for fuel and seed and things to fix the equipment."

"Don't you get tired of having to do everything yourself?"

"I'd rather it be that than be in a wheelchair. Daddy's about bored out of his mind most of the time. On a big farm there's things he could do like oversee the work and run the numbers, but on a farm our size you got to be in the field."

"Maybe he can get an overseer job?"

"Somebody's got to drive me around."

"And buy your dynamite."

"Yeah. That too."

I got back to Headquarters a little after nine o'clock and saw Dad's rental car in the driveway. I put up the ATV and went in through the kitchen. When I walked into the dining room, I saw him standing in the foyer waiting for me. He looked even worse than I remembered, his cheeks sunken and hair thin and wispy and grayed.

"Hello, Win," he said.

I didn't stop. "Hey," I said. I passed in front of him and started up the stairs. I felt him watching me from behind.

The next morning, I slept in. At eight o'clock I bathed, dressed in my New York clothes, and went downstairs. I saw Dad already in his suit, reading the newspaper at the dining room table with the remnants of breakfast before him. He put the paper down and smiled at me. "Good morning," he said.

I walked to the phone and dialed the farmer's number. Mrs. Case answered. I announced myself and got straight to the point. "Will you tell Mr. Case to come get me?"

She didn't hesitate and said she would, like maybe she knew what was going on. I hung up and walked past Dad into the kitchen.

"Let's talk, Win," he said.

I kept on and didn't answer. Duke whimpered at me from his box.

"Hold on, Duke," I said. Gert had left my breakfast on the counter, and I took the plate in one hand and scooped Duke up with the other. Then I went out the back door.

I was sitting in the yard petting Duke when Gert came out of her house wearing a black mourning dress.

"You ready, Win?"

"Go ahead," I told her. "I'm riding with Mr. Case."

She gave me a disapproving look and continued around the house. In a moment I heard Dad's rental car pull away out front. Not long after that I heard the farmer arrive, with Mrs. Case following in her car. I put Duke back in the kitchen and went to meet him.

As usual, the farmer didn't have much to say. We drove most of the way in silence, broken only when we pulled into Greenwood and stopped at a four-way. "I don't like being in the middle of this," he said.

I looked out the window and didn't answer him.

"What did he say to you?" he asked.

"He didn't say anything. I didn't give him a chance."

The farmer turned right and headed toward downtown. He glanced in his mirror to make sure Mrs. Case was still there.

"If you keep this up, it's going to get mighty hard to undo things," he said.

I didn't respond.

"I want you to talk to him before he leaves. I don't care what you think about him now or what you think about him later; keeping this stuff inside will rot you."

I didn't answer.

"You hear me?"

"Yes, sir," I said. "I hear you."

The service was held at Greenwood Episcopal. Mostly old people attended, but Buster and his family were there, too, along with Hoyt and his family, Luther, Mr. Denton, and the Rhodeses. It was the first time I'd seen Sikes since the night her truck wouldn't start. She gave me a little sorrowful wave, and I lifted my chin at her.

An usher directed me to the front row, where Dad and Gert were already sitting. The farmer nudged me forward, and I grabbed his sleeve and tugged him along. He turned to Mrs. Case, and she nodded for him to go ahead. He followed reluctantly as I walked up to the end of the pew opposite my father.

The priest gave a thirty-minute service, talking about Grandmother and her life and her civic contributions to the area and about the meaning of death as it relates to the church. Finally, he discussed the necessity of grief and the meaning of the pain one felt over losing a loved one. But I didn't need consolation. I still felt like I never knew her and I felt no sorrow for her. I was more concerned with trying not to look at Dad than I was about listening to the sermon.

After the service was over, the farmer stood. I looked at him and his eyes were red. "You need to help carry the casket," he said.

I looked back at the casket. Dad, Hoyt, Luther, and Mr. Rhodes were all starting toward it. I looked at the farmer again and shook my head.

"Get up," he said. "We can talk about it later."

I frowned and followed him to the front, where we positioned ourselves along the casket opposite the others. Hoyt and the farmer and I grabbed our side and started out of the church with it. I expected it to be heavy, but it felt like an empty wooden box.

After we loaded the casket into the hearse, I went with the farmer to his truck. We pulled into the funeral procession and started the short drive to the cemetery.

"Why'd you make me do that?"

"I'll put up with you being mad, but I won't stand by and watch you do things you'll regret."

"You already watched me do *one*," I said.

He didn't reply, but he knew exactly what I was talking about. He reached across me into the glove box to get his tobacco. He bit off a piece and put it back.

"Why didn't you stop me?" I said. "You could have stopped me."

He stared ahead and worked the tobacco in his cheek.

"You just sat there and agreed with everything," I said.

He took the cup off the dash and spit into it and put it back. Then he looked at me, and I saw his jaw tighten. "Let me tell you something," he said. "I've been dealing with my own problems for fifty years. I don't need yours too."

The way he said it made me nervous. I looked away and swallowed.

"So don't you give it to me, you hear? Don't you put that on me."

I remained quiet.

He looked ahead again. "That place means more to me than it does to all three of you put together," he muttered.

The procession pulled into the cemetery and broke up as people found parking places. Not far from us I saw the small tent set up for the graveside service. The farmer spit the plug of tobacco into the cup.

"We're gonna go stand under the tent and do this right," he said. "She had her flaws just like everybody else, but she also did a lot of good for a lot of people. She deserves your respect."

"OK," I said.

We stood under the tent with the rest of Grandmother's friends and a few distant relatives while the priest gave another short sermon. People sniffled and wiped their eyes with handkerchiefs. The farmer put his big hand on my shoulder, and it was good to know he wasn't mad at me. Then Gert began to moan and sway like she was about to pass out. Luther had to step up from behind and support her.

Eventually they lowered the casket into the ground, and it was over. People stood and wiped their faces one last time and started for their cars.

On the drive back I watched giant cloud shadows slide over the flat delta, filtering the direct heat of the sun. I thought it would be a good day to be in the fields, and there was nothing I wanted more than to get back out there with Hoyt and Luther and lose myself in the work. Still, even though I wasn't going to let it rot my insides thinking about it, I knew I had to settle things with Dad first.

The farmer pulled up before Headquarters and shut off the truck.

"Is anybody working today?" I asked him.

"I think we'll piddle around for a couple of hours," he said. "Don't feel like you need to come out there."

"I'll be out there," I said.

Dad's car pulled up behind us and stopped. I took a deep breath. "I'll see you in a little bit."

"Take your time," he said. "I'll be at the shop."

The farmer pulled away, leaving me and Dad standing in the gravel drive, facing each other like gunfighters. Gert had already disappeared around the side of the house.

"I'm sorry," he said.

"I want you to get off my property."

"Listen, Win—"

"You're trespassing," I said.

"Just hear me out, will you?"

I didn't answer. I wished the farmer would have stayed. I wished Hoyt and Luther were with me. They'd take my side.

"I came all the way down here," Dad continued. "I'd like to talk to my son."

"You made me sell Cottonlandia," I said. "You set me up."

Dad squinted his eyes in confusion. "Is *that* what this is all about?"

"Now I'm the one that's messed up everybody's lives."

Dad shook his head in amazement. "This farm is all we've got left, Win. Don't you understand that?"

"Yes, I do," I said. "But you sure don't."

"You're upset because you don't want to sell it now? You told me you hated this place."

He was right. I had. And maybe I wouldn't have felt so bad if it really were all his fault.

"How come I've got to be the one to tell everybody? What are they going to do?"

"You want me to talk to Hoyt and Luther?"

"No! I don't want them to know yet . . . I just want you to leave."

He studied me for a moment, then nodded his head. "OK," he said. "I'm going inside to get my things."

I waited until he started for the front door. Then I went around the side of the house to get my ATV. As much as I dreaded having to do it, I realized I couldn't live with my secret any longer. I was going to have to come clean with everyone. It was coming to an end for all of us, and there was nothing I could do about it.

70 REGRET

After Dad left, I found the farmer at the shop. He was sitting at the workbench scratching figures on a small notepad he always carried in his top pocket. Hoyt and Luther had already gone home and changed and were back out working on the poly pipe.

"It's not your fault," I said. "I'm sorry I said all that."

The farmer set his pencil down and looked at me. "We're gonna be fine, Win."

"But what about Hoyt and Luther? I need to go ahead and tell them. They have to find jobs."

"They already know."

"You told them?"

The farmer nodded. "They've known for a while. Since before you even got here."

"What will they do?"

"I've talked to a few people. I think Luther can get on with Frank Miller a few miles up the road. Hoyt's handy enough to pick up most anywhere. They'll be OK."

"They haven't even mentioned it to me."

"You might think of them as your friends, Win, but they think of you as their boss. It's not something they'd feel comfortable talking to you about."

"But I don't want them to think of me like that."

"That's the way it is."

"What about you?"

He glanced at his notepad. "Weather's held out so far. Cotton's looking good. I'll get the last crop in and probably have a little money to hold me over while I find some other place to lease."

It seemed like a big thing to not be sure about. "If I had the chance to do it over again, I wouldn't have signed those papers," I said.

"I know."

"I could have fought it. Maybe had the contract canceled."

The farmer didn't answer me.

"What do I do now?"

"Right now, you finish what you started. If you want to help Hoyt and Luther, get out there with them and let's make the most out this crop. If we have a good year, then their bonus will get them off to a good start next year."

I nodded. The farmer studied me. "You know," he said, "this really affects *you* more than them. At least they know all the pieces. Have you talked to your mother yet?"

"Not in a couple of weeks."

"You need to call her."

"I know."

"You need to keep her involved. She can use your help. You might think you're just a kid, but from what I've seen, you've got a pretty good head on your shoulders."

It felt good to hear him say it, but it brought back memories I was ashamed of. I looked at my feet. "I don't like how I was before," I said. "I don't want to be like Dad."

"You're the same person you always were. It just took a bucket of ice water to find you."

I looked up at him. "So you don't think I'll end up like him? You don't think it's something that's in me that I can't do anything about?"

"From what I've seen, you're going to be a good man, Win."

There was relief in those words that washed over me.

"Now go on out there," he said. "They need you."

The fields were solid, ruler-straight lines of green. The poly pipe was stretched down all the turn rows, laying deflated and flat, waiting to swell with water. The big aquifer pumps were positioned and primed. Hoyt and Luther talked about the Fourth of July as the day we'd start watering. In the meantime, we continued spraying for weeds and patching the soft plastic of the pipe material. Sometimes the coyotes chewed holes in it, and deer often used the flat surface as convenient walking paths, punching tears with the tips of their hooves.

I didn't talk to Hoyt and Luther about it being their last season, and they never brought it up. It felt good to know they'd accepted me in spite of the decisions Dad and I made. Like the farmer said, the most I could do for them was help finish the season. I realized it was the most I could do for myself too.

"Hello, Mom."

"Win, honey. How are you?"

"I'm good. How are you doing?"

"I'm feeling much better. I hope the funeral wasn't too hard on you."

"How did you know?"

"Your father told me," she said.

"Did you talk to him?"

"Yes, we talk some. I would have come to be with you if I could have. The doctor doesn't want me traveling."

"I know."

"I hear you're learning to help out at the farm."

I didn't know what all she knew about Dad's scheme and my involvement in it, but I didn't want to go into it with her. Not yet.

"I might have some money soon," I said. "I might be able to get an apartment for you."

"We'll see. You just tend to yourself for now, Win."

"Then I can come back up there and be with you. It won't be like it used to be, but we should have enough to be fine."

"I miss you so much, son."

"It's OK, Mom. You just get better. I don't care what happens to Dad."

"Win, I'm going to leave you to make your own decisions about your relationship with your father. I can't be a part of that. That's going to have to be between the two of you. But I'll support whatever you do."

"I don't even want you thinking about him," I said.

"I don't have much of a choice. We have a lot to work out."

"Are you getting a divorce?"

She hesitated. "I don't know. Like I said, we have a lot to work out."

"Can I come visit?"

"I don't think I'm quite ready for that, Win. But soon."

"Or I can fly you down. Dad's not here. And I've got Gert to help us."

"I'll let you know. You take care, OK?"

"OK, Mom."

"I love you," she said.

"Love you too."

Tim Haney came by the shop one afternoon at the end of June. He had me get into the passenger seat of his air-conditioned car so we could talk about my situation out of the heat.

"Looks like everything's working out, Win. The first lease payment you'll see from Charlie Rhodes will be in December."

"How much is it?" I asked.

"Approximately two hundred thousand dollars per year."

It sounded like a lot of money, but I had no idea how much apartments in New York cost.

"He says he plans to execute the purchase option next year."

"I figured he did," I said. "What about Gert? How does she get paid?"

"In the past she got a check for eight hundred dollars a month. I assume she works for room and maybe board outside of that."

"What does that mean?"

"As long as she is given a place to live and her expenses are handled to some extent, then she works for very little."

"Who is paying the bills?"

"My secretary is handling that. We're continuing to pay Gert as well."

"So I don't need to do anything?"

"Not at this time. But there is one more thing we need to talk about. In addition to the trust, your grandmother's left her entire estate to you. It amounts to roughly six hundred thousand dollars in cash and securities."

"She didn't leave Dad any?"

"Well, she wrote his law firm a large check just before her death. I assume to cover his legal expenses."

"I guess now I've got enough to get Mom a place to live."

"I think we should hold off on entrusting your mother with large assets at this time. She's heavily medicated for serious depression issues. And she doesn't need to be living on her own."

"She sounded fine when I talked to her."

"I spoke with her doctor. She's making progress, but she still has episodes and needs to be monitored."

"So we just sort of put it all in a savings account?"

"That's right. I think covering her expenses at the assisted living facility is the best way to help her right now."

"OK," I said again. "Let's do it."

Telling Sikes goodbye was going to be hard, but I knew she'd be OK. It was Buster I was worried about. I knew he wasn't going to take it well at all, and I dreaded having the talk with him. I put off seeing him as long as I could, but eventually I had to face him and get the guilt off my chest.

71 MISSISSIPPI SUNSET

Buster stopped on his ATV before my hammock and stared at me like he was wont to do.

"What's up," I said.

"I guess this whole place is yours?"

"I suppose."

Gert appeared with perfect timing and replaced my pitcher of tea with another cold one full of ice. Then she refilled my glass for me and took a step back. "Anything else I can get for you, Win?"

"No, thank, you, Gert. That'll be fine."

She turned to Buster. "Good afternoon, Buster."

"Hey, Gert."

She turned and slipped inside again.

"Dang it," he said. "You're out here like Caesar."

"I'm out here because I'm tired. Have you been laying poly pipe?"

"Naw, we dry-farm. But I wish we *did* have some irrigation. You got to have a pivot sprinkler or level the land. Both of those are expensive."

"Sorry I haven't been by," I said. "I've just been busy."

"I figured with your grandmother dying and all you might be upset or something."

"I'm OK."

He stared at me blankly.

"I've got something to talk to you about, Buster."

"Yeah, I've got something to talk to you about too." He climbed off his ATV and opened the toolbox. He hefted out a five-gallon propane tank and set it on the ground.

"This," he said.

I studied Buster's latest trick to impress me.

He reached back into the box and pulled out a deer rifle and held it toward me. "And this . . . go together like chocolate and peanut butter."

I got out of the hammock and approached him, inspecting the propane bottle. "I don't get it," I said.

"Come on," he said. "It'll make you feel better."

"I feel fine."

"No, you don't. Come on."

I followed him on my ATV out of the grove and down a turn row to an area we called the dump. It was a place where Hoyt and Luther deposited torn poly pipe and empty oil containers and other trash until they hauled it off in the winter. Buster got off his ATV and dragged a wood pallet out of the pile and put it on top of his toolbox.

"You don't have to do this, Buster," I said. "Whatever you're doing."

He didn't answer me. We turned around and started back the way we came, stopping halfway, with the fields on all sides of us. He got off the ATV again and flopped the pallet into the middle of the dirt road.

"Come help me," he said.

Pulling a newspaper out of the box, he gave me half and told me to ball up the pages and shove them into the gaps between the pallet slats. In a moment we had the pallet stuffed like a newspaper sandwich. Then he got the propane tank, clanked it down on top, and looked at me.

"What now?" I asked.

"Nothing."

"Nothing?"

"Not until it gets dark."

"And I guess I just have to wait and see what that means?"

"That's right."

I didn't have the heart to ruin Buster's surprise, so I held off on having the talk with him. We went back to Headquarters and had Gert fix venison burgers for us. We ate them at the dining room table like a couple of young kings, and I could tell Buster enjoyed being pampered. After supper he wanted to go check for beavers in the brake, so we took off again, racing toward the sun setting big and orange over a sea of green.

The swamp was so lush and thick it was hard to even see the black water from the turn row. Buster walked up and down the edge of the trees and stopped and peered into them and studied the ground and listened. Finally, he looked back and stared at me. This time I decided to see how long it would take him to say something.

I waited. He stared. I looked away at the sky glow where the sun had disappeared behind the trees. Three deer browsed in the cotton at the edge of the far trees. When I looked back, he was still watching me.

"What!" I finally said.

"Nothing. There's no beavers."

"It's almost dark," I said.

"Yep. Come on."

Back at Buster's surprise he dug a cigarette lighter out of his pocket and kneeled next to the pallet. He lit the paper and backed off. I jumped on my ATV and started it.

"Man, are you crazy! Let's get out of here!"

He watched it, making sure the paper caught.

"Buster!" I said. "That things going to blow up like a grenade."

He turned to me and spit. "Grenade, my ass. That's kids' stuff."

I shook my head. "I'm out of here!" I gassed the ATV and raced toward the island. When I reached the main driveway, I stopped and looked back for Buster. Nearly a hundred yards behind, he was just starting to get on his ATV, the pallet leaping in flames with the white propane tank right in the middle of it.

"You crazy idiot!" I mumbled. "Get out of there!"

I watched him ease away, the firelight dancing behind him, casting long shadows up the turn row. In a moment he pulled up next to me and stopped.

"You've lost your mind," I said to him. "That thing could have blown you to bits."

He got off the ATV and opened the toolbox and pulled out the deer rifle. "Naw," he said. "Get down behind your four-wheeler."

"Jesus," I said. I got behind the ATV and peered over the seat. Buster was already crouched behind his, aiming the deer rifle.

"Should have saved this for the Fourth of July," he said.

"Are we about to die?"

"But I figured you needed it early."

"I really don't need it, Buster. I'm fine."

I heard the rifle click off safety. "This," he said, "is what you call a Mississippi sunset."

BOOM!

It was the rifle shot I heard first. Then I saw the propane tank explode into a blinding fireball mushrooming into the air like a mini atomic bomb. The fields were cast in yellow light clear to the edges, and I heard leaves swishing on the pecan trees to my left. It was over in seconds, but the image of it was burned into my brain forever. Both of us were left mesmerized, staring at the glowing embers of the pallet scattered up and down the turn row.

After a while Buster said, "How you feel now?"

"Good," I said.

72 TELLING BUSTER

Buster and I rocked on the porch, thinking about the Mississippi sunset. I imagined Mr. Denton or the farmer or somebody, at least Gert, was going to come by any minute to ask if we knew anything about the explosion. But the night had closed over us all like nothing happened.

Buster looked at me. "What'd you wanna talk to me about?"

"Charlie Rhodes is going to turn this place into a catfish farm," I said.

He didn't react.

"That was it," I said.

"I knew something was wrong."

"After this harvest he's going to start clearing the west end of the brake to connect his property."

Buster looked away. "What else?"

"He going to buy the place too. He's got an option to buy it."

He nodded his head slowly, thinking about it all.

"And I'll be going back to New York."

"You don't belong in New York City."

"Maybe not, but I've lived there most of my life and I can make it work. Maybe one day I'll come back here."

"No, you won't."

He was right, but I didn't respond.

He looked at me again. "When you think you're leaving?"

"I don't know. Soon."

"I thought we'd run a farm together."

"I know."

"Kill some beavers."

"I'd like that," I said. "But I've got to go back to New York."

"You act like it's what you want," he said.

"Funny thing is," I said, "I did want it. But now I don't and it's too late."

Buster stood and faced me. "I'll think about it," he said.

"Think about what?"

"About how to fix things so you can stay."

"You can't fix *anything*. It's already done. The papers are signed."

Buster stared at me.

"Look," I said. "I don't like it any more than you. Let's try and have fun while I'm still here. Hoyt's having a Fourth of July party on Friday night since we've got to start watering on Saturday. He said I could invite anyone I wanted. You want to come?"

"Yeah," he said like it was obvious.

"Then I'll pick you up that afternoon."

"Good," he said, turning to go. "Meanwhile I'll get us a plan."

"Plan for what?"

Buster got on his ATV and drove away.

Friday afternoon we knocked off from work at two o'clock to go home and get rested and ready for Hoyt's party. About five o'clock the farmer came back for me, and I told him we had to pick up Buster. We drove out to Booga Den and found Buster waiting in his driveway with a large, canvas duffel bag.

"What you got, Buster?" the farmer asked suspiciously.

"Fireworks," he said. "It's legal."

"I'll bet. Go put it up."

Buster looked at his bag and frowned. He went and set it on the porch and came back and slid in next to me.

"I'm sure Hoyt will have enough entertainment as it is," the farmer said.

"Have you ever seen a Mississippi sunset explosion?" I asked.

Buster elbowed me.

The farmer put the truck in gear and shook his head. "No, but I don't imagine I need to hear about it."

Hoyt's yard was packed full of cars and trucks. An American flag waved from the top of his trailer, and we heard music blaring out back. The farmer let us out and said Hoyt would arrange for us to get home that night.

"You're not going to stay?"

"Little old for this, boys. Y'all have a good time."

We walked around to the backyard, where we saw Luther and his family and Hoyt and Tammy and all the rest of the kids and grandkids and a few others I didn't recognize. A jacked-up, black four-by-four pickup was parked with its doors open, screeching rock and roll music. Just behind it was a picnic table covered with food. And behind that was Hoyt's ATV, hooked to a mattress and covered in mud like they'd already taken some turns on it. I pointed to it.

"I wouldn't do that if I were you," I said.

Buster studied it.

"Hey!" Hoyt called out to us. "Come join the party!"

We said hello to everyone and started filling our plates with fried chicken and potato logs. Meanwhile Hoyt dashed off into the trailer.

"I got Plan A figured out," Buster said.

"What are you talking about?"

"About how you're gonna stay here."

Hoyt suddenly appeared again, dragging a cardboard box out the back door. "Hey, everybody," he called out. "I had to cross the state line to get *this* stuff."

"Lord," Tammy said.

He dragged the box into the crowd and opened it and we peered inside. It was full of giant fireworks.

"Why don't you wait until it gets dark, honey," Tammy said.

"I am!" he said. "I just wanted to let everybody know we gonna light this place up like Disney World tonight."

Buster looked at me, and I knew what he was thinking.

"This isn't our party, Buster," I said.

"Anybody wanna ride the dirt sled?!" Hoyt called out. He looked around the yard, cocked and loaded. Nobody said anything. "I'll go," one of the kids finally said. "Me too," another one said.

"Easy, Dad," Bubba said.

"Let's go!"

Hoyt took off on the ATV with the squealing kids trailing on the mattress.

"Come on," Buster said to me. "I'll tell you about Plan A."

We sat down in the grass with our food and a couple of Cokes, and Buster began.

"So I was thinking about all this," he said. "Why does Mr. Rhodes want to lease Cottonlandia?"

"So he can grow catfish and make money."

"Right. If he didn't think he could make money in the catfish business, then he wouldn't want to do it."

"Probably not," I said.

"So I just need to kill all his catfish."

I stopped chewing and looked at Buster. "That's your Plan A?"

He nodded, satisfied. "Yep. Just a stick of dynamite per pond kills every fish in there deader'n rocks. They won't know *what* happened to those things."

I looked away and shook my head. "I thought you were smart."

"I can do it so there's not a trace."

I looked at him again. I couldn't believe he was serious. "Buster. You don't think they might hear it?"

"I'll just wait until they're gone. One stick ain't that loud."

"It's loud enough for somebody to hear. And they'll know it was you. How many fifteen-year-olds you know ride around here with dynamite? And how are you going to know when they're gone?"

"Because I know things," he said.

I shook my head. Buster frowned and took a bite of his chicken. He chewed. "I could *do* it," he said, like I was missing my chance.

"No. What's Plan B?"

"Pour about fifty gallons of diesel fuel in there."

I set my chicken down on my plate. "Buster, you *really* want to go to jail?"

"It's not as good as Plan A. They'd test the water and know what it was. But he'd lose a bunch of money cleaning it up. Maybe so much he'd just want out of the business."

"You're not doing any of that," I said.

"If I trailered a welding machine over there one night, fired it up, and dropped a line in the water, I'd give every one of these things their own little electric chair."

"Is that Plan C?"

"No, I just thought of it."

"Will you shut up about killing his fish?"

He looked at me. "I'd do it for you. Keep you from having to leave."

"It's just the way it is, Buster. Neither of us can do anything about it."

Just then Hoyt came circling back with the kids, no longer squealing, but holding on patiently, bearing the chaos.

Buster shook his head. "I ain't giving up yet."

"Don't do anything stupid."

Buster didn't answer.

73 SIKES'S WEDDING

The actual day of July Fourth wasn't a holiday for us. We got into the fields early and fired up the irrigation pumps. Hooked to the pumps and lying perpendicular to the field rows were the quarter-mile runs of poly pipe. We watched them swell full of water, then walked down the lengths of them with a long-handled hammer called a poly puncher, tapping holes in the soft plastic, one for each row. Out of the holes the water drained into the troughs and began its long journey clear to the other end of the field. When the water had made it all the way down, we turned a valve to start a run on another quarter-mile section. The pumps ran all day and night, and it took about a week to water the entire farm.

During this time Buster didn't come by, and I almost felt his frustrated thinking from two miles away. I was thinking too. It was getting hard to work on a farm I knew I was going to lose.

One day I drove to the brake during our lunch hour. The heat had us all in a bad mood, and I wanted some time alone. I parked the ATV near where the old beaver den used to be and got off, expecting to have the place to myself. Right away I heard the groaning and clanking of heavy machinery along the swamp.

I got back on the ATV and drove out to the highway and down the roadside toward Beulah. I hadn't gone far when I saw Mr. Rhodes standing in his golf attire at the edge of the trees, talking to a man in a hard hat. I pulled up next to them and stopped. Mr. Rhodes glanced at me and went back to talking. I waited patiently, listening to them and hearing the machinery tearing at the swamp just beyond the trees. They were discussing something about a survey. Eventually they came to an agreement, and Mr. Rhodes watched the man in the hard hat walk away.

"What's going on?" I asked.

He turned to me. I sensed his impatience. "I got some fellows cutting a road through that stuff," he said.

"Already?"

He frowned. "I'm about to put in a big operation over there, son. As soon as I write your family that check, my equipment's rolling in."

"Looks like it's already rolling in."

He studied me. "What do you need, Win? I'm late for a golf match."

His tone with me had changed.

"I just didn't think you'd start so soon."

"Yeah, well, I did."

"But we haven't even gotten the cotton in."

Mr. Rhodes turned to go. "Talk to your dad about it."

"It's my property," I said.

"Then talk your lawyer," he said over his shoulder.

I saw myself standing as helpless as the thin man in the mobile home.

On Sunday I told the farmer I wanted to take a few days off to go see Mom. "I'm going to help her find an apartment," I said. "Someplace we can live when I move back up there."

The farmer thought for a moment. "Have you talked to your dad about it?"

I shook my head. "I don't want to see him or his girlfriend. So don't tell him I'm coming."

The farmer frowned. "I don't know what shape your mother will be in to go house hunting."

"I just feel like I should see her."

"I understand. I'll arrange your flight and a hotel. And I'm going to get Hoyt to go with you."

"What about the irrigation?"

"Me and Luther can handle that. You don't need to be going up there by yourself."

I wanted to be mad at Sikes. I wanted to hate her and all the

Rhodeses. I didn't want to think about the fact that I was the only one to blame for ruining everything between us. I wrote a letter to her that night, which I drove over to Beulah and left in their mailbox.

Meet me at the church tomorrow night at 8:00 p.m. Come on your FOUR-WHEELER!

—Win

The next night I was sitting on the steps to the church when I saw the lights of her ATV passing on the roadside out by Denton's store. The mosquitoes weren't as bad as they could be, with the soft breeze sweeping across the fields. The cicadas rattled in the air, and in the distance I heard the giant swamp throbbing and pulsing with frogs and insects. I didn't know if she was still grounded or not, but the excitement of our secret meeting fluttered in my stomach.

I stood as she pulled up before me and shut off the ATV, smiling mischievously. She was wearing jeans and a T-shirt and a ball cap with her hair pulled out the back in a ponytail. She was even prettier than I remembered. I thought, *Right now I have it all. In a few minutes I won't have anything. How did I ever screw this up?*

"Hey," she said, like she was proud of whatever she'd just pulled off.

"You still grounded?"

She swung her leg over the ATV and got off. "Not really. Sort of. Sometimes they forget."

"What'd you say?"

"Nothing. Mom's asleep. Dad's out of town. Roxy's gone home."

I wanted to grab her hand. I wanted to take her back to the cemetery and kiss her again. My head raced with excuses to put off what I planned to tell her.

"So what do you wanna do?" she asked.

"I don't know," I said. "I just wanted to see you."

She moved past me and looked over the field toward the cemetery. "You want to go to the cemetery again?"

I swallowed. "I don't think we can get through the cotton now. It's pretty high."

She turned back to me. "Think we can get inside the church?"

"Like break in?"

"No, just climb in a window or something."

"Maybe."

She watched me. "Well, come on," she said. "Let's try."

I walked around the outside of the building, trying each window. I eventually found one that slid up, and I was suddenly looking over the faint outline of folding chairs in the dark room. I helped her up, and she scrambled over the ledge and touched down inside.

"Come on," she urged. "It's kind of scary in here."

I pulled myself up and over and found myself beside her in the flat heat of the hollow room.

"Have you ever been to the podium?" she asked.

"No," I said.

She was already feeling her way up the aisle, the old wood floor creaking beneath her tennis shoes. I followed behind her. In a moment she was standing behind the podium where I'd seen Deacon Leon deliver so many of his passionate speeches. To my left I could just make out the chair where his assistant sat with her collection basket.

"Praise the Lord!" Sikes said, loud enough to make me nervous. "I'm free!"

"For now you are," I said. "You better quiet down."

"Have a seat, Mr. Farmer Man."

"I can't even see you."

"Hold on," she said. "I've got a candle up here."

I heard her digging in the podium. "And . . . some matches."

"Somebody might see it, Sikes."

She struck the match, and it flared against the grainy darkness. She lowered it to the candle, and a tiny flame flickered and cast a weak, yellow light over the room. I took a few steps back and sat in the first chair behind me.

"We could get married in here," she said.

"What are you talking about?"

"If we got married. We could do it right here at Cottonlandia."

I swallowed dry. "I guess we could."

"Think how big our farm would be. It would be huge!"

"I haven't thought about that."

"Come over here," she said. "We'll stand in the aisle like we're getting married."

"I don't know about that, Sikes. I mean—"

She stepped from behind the podium and moved to the head of

the aisle. "Come on, Mr. Farmer. It's your wedding day. You can take time off to get married. Then you can go back to work."

I stood weakly and moved to her. She took my hand and pulled me close, then grabbed the other hand so we faced each other.

"I now pronounce you man and wife," she said.

"Are you supposed to be Deacon Leon?"

"Yes. Now kiss me."

I moved my face close to hers and felt the bill of her ball cap press into my forehead. She giggled and tilted her head.

"Can't wear that at the wedding," she said.

Then our lips were pressed together, and I thought, *There's no way. No way I can tell her.*

She pulled away and squeezed my hands. "It's hot in here," she said.

I nodded weakly.

"Let's go."

"OK," I said.

She pulled me back toward the open window, pausing for a moment to blow out the candle. In a moment we were outside again, and the breeze cooled the sweat on my face. We sat on the front steps, and she leaned on my shoulder, holding my hand tightly in her lap. A car moved slowly on the highway beyond.

"We really could get married," she said.

"We're just fifteen, Sikes."

She sat up and looked at me. "You don't want to?"

"Well, yes. I can't think of anything I'd like better. That's just such a long way off. Things could happen."

"Like what?"

"Like—I don't even know why you like me."

She laughed. "I don't either."

"You don't even know me very well. I might not turn out to be like you want."

"Why would you worry about that?"

"Because I worry about it."

She leaned into me again and squeezed my hand. "Well, don't. I have to go in a minute."

I took a deep breath.

"Let's just sit here," she said.

"I want to kiss you again."

She laughed and sat up and looked at me. "You don't have to ask, you know?"

74 RETURN TO NEW YORK

My talk with Sikes certainly hadn't gone as planned. And for three more nights in a row I met her behind the barn at Beulah, where we held hands and walked along the brake and kissed. We didn't talk about anything important. As far as she knew, there was nothing in the world to worry about. And the longer I was with her, the more my secret lodged in my throat.

Thursday was just another hot mirage of irrigation. At the end of the day we leaned against the truck, drinking water from the cooler that was so cold it made me gasp.

"New York City," Hoyt said. "Dang."

I crushed my cup in my hand and tossed it into the bed of the truck. "I told him you didn't have to go."

He didn't seem to hear me. He stared over the fields, absorbed in giant thoughts. "Tammy's gonna do a flip."

"We don't have to stay long," I said. "I just need to see Mom. And I've got to make plans to move back up there."

The farmer's truck disappeared around a point of trees backlit with the setting sun. Hoyt slammed his tailgate and turned to me. His face was suddenly drawn with concern. "I got to get some clothes. Man, I ain't outfitted for this."

"Just wear what you have. It's not a big deal."

Hoyt thought about it for a moment more. "I'll be ready," he said.

"OK," I said. "Then I'll see you tomorrow morning."

That night I packed my suitcase. When I was done, I took it

downstairs and set it by the door. I looked out on the porch for Buster, thinking he might be sitting in the chair by the hammock, waiting for me, but the porch was as deserted and still as the rest of the place.

I got the ATV and left to meet Sikes behind the barn at our usual time.

"I'm going to New York tomorrow," I told her.

"You didn't tell me that. For how long?"

"A few days. I need to visit Mom."

"Is she better?"

"I don't know. I'll find out."

"I hope she is. Then she can come down here too."

"Yeah," I said. "We'll see."

"Let me know when you get back. You can call me, too, you know?"

"OK," I said. "I'll see you soon."

The next morning, I crossed the tarmac to board the twin prop for my long-overdue return trip to New York. Hoyt followed in a Kubota ball cap, T-shirt, jeans, and work boots. He carried a beat-up, canvas duffel bag that looked like it had been used to store greasy wrenches. He sat across from me and stared at the headrest in front of him and clutched the armrest like we were about to blast off in a rocket.

"Have you ever flown before?" I asked him.

He didn't look at me. "Yeah," he said. "But not like this."

"How else is there?"

"I went up in a crop duster with a fellow one time."

"That's got to be a lot scarier than this."

He looked at me. "At least I could talk to him right there in front of me. I don't like the pilot so far away."

"It'll be fine."

Hoyt frowned. "I like to know the man on the pedal."

After takeoff he stared out the window as the flat, alluvial plain of the delta fell away beneath us. His hands relaxed on the armrest, and he sank in his seat a little. After a couple of minutes, he looked at me again and adjusted his ball cap. He was smiling like a six-year-old. "New York City," he said.

A little of Hoyt's anxiety returned once we landed in Jackson.

When we exited the plane, he followed me to the display and stood gazing around behind me while I looked up our next gate.

"You got your boarding pass?" I asked him.

He dug in his pocket and pulled out a wad of papers. "I don't know, man. I got a bunch of stuff."

"I don't know why Mr. Case sent *you*," I said. "You don't know anything about this."

He was too busy sorting through the crumpled papers to hear humor in anything.

"Let me see it," I said.

He frowned and gave it all to me. I sorted out what he needed, smoothed the rest, and gave it back to him.

Once we lifted off for Atlanta he seemed more at ease. It wasn't until we landed and entered the swarms of people in the giant terminal that he started acting nervous and fidgety again. He trailed me through the crowd like people were after us, and I navigated our way down escalators and onto the train and down the long terminal that hosted our final flight to New York. Arriving at our gate with an hour's wait ahead of us, we found some chairs near a back wall. Hoyt sat in one and caught his breath and faced the crowd like he'd fight to the death for his space.

"Man, you could be a millionaire with a couple of hot dog stands around here," he said. "Dang circus."

"You hungry?"

"Yeah, but I ain't going back out there to do anything about it."

"Everything's expensive anyway. If you found a hot dog, it'd be about five dollars."

He looked at me with disbelief. "Five-dollar hot dog!"

"Probably."

He shook his head. "I told you. Millionaire."

Just after noon we touched down at JFK. I heard and smelled New York before we even exited the terminal, the heat over disinfectant and fuel and traffic. This was something I hadn't noticed before, and now it fell over me like a nauseating fog.

Outside I hailed a taxi, and we climbed in the back seat with our bags. I pulled a scrap of paper out of my wallet and read the address of the Walsh Nursing Home to the driver. He nodded and peered into his side mirror, preparing to dive out into the traffic. I heard Hoyt take a deep breath. I looked at him. "It'll be easier from here," I said.

"Feel like flies have been swarming me all day," he said.

"That part won't change."

"Anywhere we can get a hot dog for less than five dollars? I'm starving."

"Me too. We'll eat when we get to Mom's place. I think they have a cafeteria."

Suddenly the taxi driver mashed the gas, and we plunged into the stream of traffic.

"Whoa, buddy!" Hoyt shouted.

"It's all right," I said. "That's how they drive around here."

He pressed his palms flat against the seat and braced himself as the driver accelerated and wove his way toward Manhattan.

"Take a dang crop duster over this any day," Hoyt mumbled.

75 A HURRIED REUNION

The Walsh Home was on the Upper East Side on York Avenue, not far from our old apartment. As we drove through Manhattan, Hoyt peered out the window and up at the tall buildings.

"I ain't never been to the Grand Canyon," he said. "I bet this is what it's like being at the bottom of it."

When we arrived at Walsh, I left him at the second-floor cafeteria while I took the elevator to see Mom. I found the door to her room open and walked in to see her sitting in a reclining chair, watching television. Like Dad, she looked much older than when I'd last seen her. But while Dad still appeared to have some energy, she looked tired and sad.

"Win, sweetheart," she said.

The room didn't look much like the hospital room I expected, but more like a little apartment. I walked over, and she stood and hugged me. I thought I'd feel some closure in that moment—some sense my life was back on track, that I was gathering up the scattered pieces and putting them together again—but her hug was frail and weak and I suddenly realized why the farmer had been uncertain about my visit. If this was all I had to cling to in New York, I didn't see how we were going to make it.

I leaned against the edge of Mom's bed while she sat back in her chair and waited for me to tell her about my life since I'd been gone. My mind raced with what I was going to talk about. It seemed useless and cruel to say anything about how I'd grown to love Cottonlandia. And she already knew how I felt about Dad. I had to focus on our future. So I told her about the new lease and that Cottonlandia was being turned into a catfish farm and would likely be sold to the neighbors. I told her about Grandmother changing her will and leaving everything to me. We wouldn't have as much money as what she'd been accustomed to, but we'd have plenty for a good life. And I didn't plan on Dad getting any of it. She listened and nodded in a strange, detached way, like hearing my voice was more important than anything I said.

"But we have to have a place to live, Mom. I don't know how to do that. How do we do that?"

"Oh, sweetheart, it will all work out," she said.

"But we have to *make* it work out, Mom. I could be here in three or four months."

"We'll find a nice place to live. It will all be fine."

"Who's going to do that? Who do I have to talk to?"

"We've got plenty of time, Win."

"But I don't like not knowing."

"Tell me about your new friends," she said. "Have you made some new friends?"

"Yes, but I don't want to talk about that."

"You seem so grown up."

"Mom, come on. I'm just trying to figure everything out. I don't want to live with Dad. I want us to get our own place. I need you to help me do that."

"You're just a boy, Win. You shouldn't worry yourself with those things. I want you to tell me about your new friends and what it's like in Mississippi."

I felt myself growing frustrated with her. But then looking at her, I realized she was all I had left. Being angry with her wouldn't help either of us. She simply wasn't her old self yet. She wasn't ready to talk about the future. So I told her about the farmer and Hoyt and Sikes and Buster. I didn't tell her everything, but enough to convince her it hadn't been nearly as bad as I'd thought. That I'd been OK. That she shouldn't worry about me. And then I told her I was going to be in Manhattan for a couple of days with Hoyt and that I'd be back in the morning to see her. I gave her another hug and left.

I found Hoyt still in the cafeteria, sitting before two empty plates of food. He appeared too full to get up.

"All good?" he asked me.

"Yeah, all good. Let's go."

"They got a smothered pork chop special up at the buffet. You haven't eaten anything."

"I'm not hungry," I said. "Let's find the hotel."

Hoyt got up. "Hey, man," he said. "Whatever you want. I'm just here to help."

I hailed a taxi, and we climbed in and I gave the driver the address for the Holiday Inn. It was supposed to be one of the least expensive hotels in Manhattan, but it was still almost $300 a night. I would have found something cheaper had it not been near the nursing home and just a few blocks east of our old apartment on Fifth Avenue.

Hoyt drummed his fingers on his thighs, obviously waiting for me to talk to him. Finally, he couldn't contain himself.

"Well, I guess it didn't go too good up there?"

"She's given up," I said.

"Maybe she's just not feeling good. She's been sick, you know?"

"She's sick in her head. Sort of like Grandmother was."

"Hey, you know how to fix that, don't you?"

I wasn't in the mood for Hoyt's attempt to cheer me up. I didn't answer him, and he went to drumming his fingers again while the taxi driver braked and accelerated and weaved through the traffic.

"Why didn't you ever say anything to me about the catfish?" I asked him.

"Didn't seem like any of my business," he said.

"Yeah, it is. What are you going to do?"

"I don't know. I've been talking to some people. I know the parts manager up at the John Deere dealership. I might be able to get on over there and work my way up."

The thought of Hoyt working inside didn't sit right with me. "You can't work at the tractor dealership," I said.

"Why not?"

"Because you like to be outside. You wouldn't like it."

"Hey, man, I'll be OK."

I looked out the window at the traffic and the buildings and the people. "I wish I could undo it all," I said. "I just want you to know that."

"You can't carry all that around with you. We're OK."

"No, you're not."

"Hey, man."

"What?"

"Look at me."

I did.

"Do I look like I'm upset about anything? I'll tell you when I'm upset."

I nodded, unconvinced.

"We're gonna get it all figured out for you. That's why we're up here. Getting started."

It was nearly five o'clock when we checked into the hotel. We took our bags up to the room and tossed them on the beds. It was the plainest hotel room I'd ever stayed in, but Hoyt looked about, beaming.

"Man, this is high-end stuff," he said.

"It's not bad."

"Got a microwave. Check out that remote control to the television. I bet it makes the window shades go up and stuff."

"No, it won't. Are you ready to get something to eat?"

"You get robes here?"

"No."

Hoyt looked disappointed for a second, but the look didn't last long. "Yeah," he said. "I'm always ready to eat."

We went downstairs again and out onto the busy sidewalk. I started up Third Avenue with Hoyt following. He kept looking up and around with amazement, falling behind, hurrying to catch up, and falling behind again. We walked several blocks to Sixtieth Street and turned right. Only then did Hoyt fall in beside me.

"Dang, you're picky," he huffed. "There's places to eat everywhere."

"It's my old neighborhood," I said. "I thought I'd just see it again."

He looked up. "You lived up in one of those?"

A lonesome feeling settled over me that I didn't expect. I felt like I no longer belonged in this place. Part of me suddenly wanted to turn and start back. "Yes, not far from here," I said.

"Where'd you park?"

I told myself I was being unreasonable. I had grown up on these streets. I had memories and friendships in this place. There was no reason for me to feel like a stranger.

"There's garages underneath," I said. "But a lot of people don't even keep cars in the city."

"That's crazy," he said. "Y'all have a car?"

I wished Hoyt would stop talking. I wished I was alone.

"Yeah," I said. "There's a deli up ahead. They have good sandwiches."

"Man, you don't never get your money's worth at anything called a deli."

"What about a sub shop?"

"Now you're talking. Nobody putting on airs in a sub shop."

A few more blocks ahead I saw the twin lions marking the entrance to the Aston Club. We passed it and turned the corner onto Fifth Avenue. Suddenly there I was, stopped face to face before Jules Brevard.

76 EMERGENCY

Jules was leading two boys I didn't recognize. All my loneliness and apprehension suddenly dissolved. In that moment it seemed like the comforts of my old life were simply something I could stroll back into. I felt like I was home again, hanging out with my best friend.

I smiled. "Hey, Jules."

He stared at me like he didn't believe what he was seeing. His eyes looked me over, taking in the Hot Saddle jeans and the Gentlemen's Club shirt and the Super Foot tennis shoes. "Win?" he said.

"Yeah," I grinned. "It's me."

He looked at Hoyt, then back at me. "What are you doing here?"

"Visiting right now. I'm moving back in a few months."

"Back where?"

"I don't know. Somewhere nearby, hopefully."

I glanced at Jules's friends, expecting him to introduce me. But he kept staring at me.

"You look different," he said.

"Yeah, I work outside a lot. I'm sorry I haven't called. Things have been crazy."

"I thought you were staying in Mississippi."

I shook my head. "No. I just sort of got stuck down there for a while."

"OK," he finally said. Then he looked back at his friends. "Come on, guys."

Jules brushed past me, and I felt a rush of panic. "Hey," I said. "You want to eat with us at Henry's?"

314

Jules stopped and turned back to me. "We're going to the Aston Club."

I forced a smile. "You sneaking in through the kitchen like we used to do?"

He gave me a condescending smirk. "No. That's lame."

"Oh. Well . . . I'll be here for a couple of days. I'll come by tomorrow."

He studied me like he couldn't believe what I was suggesting.

"You better not," he said.

I couldn't respond.

"I'll see you later," he said, turning to go. I watched them round the corner, feeling like I was going to get sick.

"Hey," Hoyt said to me.

"That's how it's going to be," I said, suddenly seeing my new life in the city as it really was. As I'd known it was going to be all along. Everything I'd been dreading was really going to happen. It had already happened.

"Come on," Hoyt said. "Who needs friends like that?"

I looked down at my feet. "They don't even want me in their houses," I said to myself.

"Win?"

I looked up at him, but his face was blurry and distant. He put his hand on my shoulder. "Forget them."

"He was my best friend."

"Well, you got more friends now, don't you? You got me and Luther and Buster and Sikes."

"I feel sick."

He tugged me along. "Of course you do. You haven't eaten anything since this morning. Show me where that sub shop is."

I nodded weakly and moved past him.

Eventually Hoyt stopped trying to make me feel better. I was in a dark funk, and nothing he said could pull me out of it. We finished our sandwiches and started back for the hotel. I walked slower this time, and Hoyt walked beside me.

"You gonna show me your old house?"

"Apartment."

"Whatever. Where is it?"

"Don't worry about it."

"You don't wanna see it?"

"No. And I don't want to talk about it anymore."

Hoyt started to say something else, but was interrupted by his cell phone ringing. He stopped and pulled it out and looked at it.

"Who in the heck?" he said. "I didn't know this thing reached that far."

He answered it. "Yeah?"

I watched while he listened and nodded slowly without saying anything. After he hung up he looked at me with a blank expression, and I knew immediately something was wrong.

"That was Luther. He says Mr. Case is sick."

"With what?"

"I don't know. Says he passed out at the shop and they had to take him to the hospital."

"We've got to get back there," I said. "We need to change our flight to leave in the morning."

Hoyt nodded. "Yeah. We better. How do we do that?"

77 RETURN

Dad was the last person I wanted to talk to, but I didn't know what else to do. I used Hoyt's cell phone and called him from the hotel room.

"Hi, Win. How are you?"

"I'm fine. Is Amy there?"

He hesitated. "Yes. She's here. What's going on?"

"I'm in Manhattan. I need her to help me change my flights."

"In Manhattan? Where?"

"At a Holiday Inn on the Upper East Side. Can you get her to help me?"

"I'd like to come by and see you."

"I don't want you to come by. I just need Amy to help me. Mr. Case is sick, and I need to get back to Mississippi."

"What's wrong with him?"

"I don't know. Can you just get her to help me?"

He hesitated again. "Sure," he said. "I'll put her on."

I called Mom early the next morning and told her I had to return to Walnut Bend for an emergency. We flew out standby and were in the air by nine o'clock. When we touched down at the Greenwood airport that afternoon Luther was waiting in one of the farm trucks. We threw our bags in the back and crowded into the front seat.

"How's he doing?" Hoyt asked.

Luther shook his head. "He's still at the hospital."

"What'd they say it was?"

"Maybe heat stroke."

"Man, he don't never get heat stroke."

"I say he's just too old to be out there like that. I told him to stay in the shade, but you know how he is."

Hoyt shook his head. "I should have known better."

"Think we ought to go see him?" I asked.

"I been by there already this morning. Said he wants us to run the water. We already behind. And you know it being Saturday he won't let nobody work tomorrow even if the place is on fire."

We left straight from the airport for Cottonlandia. As we drew near the farm, I saw the fields falling away in all directions, thick with leafy cotton plants as tall as my thighs, somehow so much taller in just two days. We turned off the highway onto the main drive, and I realized how much I'd missed the sound and feel of the gravel popping under the tires. We pulled up to the shop, and the dust drifted over us along with the smell of diesel and the greenhouse health of the young cotton. Hoyt got out, filled the water cooler, and dropped a sack of ice in it from the shop freezer. Then he strapped it in the truck bed, and we set out again toward the south end of the property.

In a couple of hours we had four of the nine pumps going and water running down the rows to irrigate nearly three hundred acres. Buster and his dad showed up in their truck and asked what they could do to help. Hoyt pointed to his left and said we could use them to get the water running at the west end of the property. Buster lifted his chin at me. "I've got another plan," he said.

I frowned. "I don't want to talk about it."

They pulled away, and we got back to work, making sure the water was making its way down the rows. We didn't stop until sunset. Then we met back at the shop, where far away we heard the pumps continuing their work like little factories in the night. Hoyt and Luther thanked Mr. Tillman for their help, and he drove off, leaving Buster standing on the dirt road.

"You mind if I stay over?" he said.

It seemed complicated, but I saw Buster was already committed. "No," I said.

Hoyt got into the passenger seat of Luther's truck, and I climbed into the back with Buster. Luther started toward Headquarters, the truck slowly moving up the dirt road like it was as tired as we felt.

"You got some clean clothes?" Buster asked.

"Yes," I said. "You can borrow some, and you can sleep on Grandmother's bed."

"She die in it?"

"Yes."

"I ain't sleeping on that."

"You can sleep with me then."

"Fine," he said.

Luther dropped us off and left to take Hoyt home. I lugged my suitcase through the front door, Buster following. Duke came bounding out of the kitchen and leaped up at me. He looked and felt ten pounds heavier.

"How you, Duke?" I said, trying to keep my balance.

"Gert's been feeding him good," Buster said.

"Yeah," I said. I dropped the suitcase at the foot of the stairs, kneeled, and scratched my dog behind the ears.

"You don't get spooked staying here by yourself?" he asked.

"I try not to think about it," I said.

"What was New York like?"

"I wish I never had to go back," I said. "Let's get some iced tea and go on the porch with Duke."

Gert had left a full pitcher of tea in the refrigerator, and I got it and two glasses of ice and headed out the front door. When I came outside, Buster was sitting in the rocking chair. I poured the tea and got into the hammock and hefted Duke up beside me. Buster took a drink and sighed. "The way I see it," he said, "your biggest problem is getting your mom to move down here."

"I don't want to talk about it, Buster."

"But I've got it figured out."

"I'm not blowing up his ponds or poisoning the fish. I'm not doing anything illegal."

"Don't have to."

"And you're not either."

"Nope," Buster said.

"Good. I'm moving to New York. That's all there is to it."

He stopped rocking and leaned back in his chair. "We're gonna talk him into leasing another place."

"Of course," I said sarcastically. "You want some more tea?"

Buster sat up and jammed his hand down in his pocket, pulled something out, and gave it to me. It looked like a small stick.

"What's this?"

"A piece of bone."

"What kind of bone?"

"You remember the Indian mound I showed you?"

"Yeah," I said.

"I dug it out of it. I think it's part of some Indian's leg."

78 BUSTER'S BONES

I studied the small, brown chip of bone Buster had given me.

"How does this help anything?" I said.

"You just mention the words 'Indian burial site' to the state, and they won't so much as let you spit on this dirt. They'll shut this place down and wrap it so full of yellow tape you'd think it was Christmas."

I held the bone shard out to him.

"No," he said. "You keep it. Show it to Mr. Rhodes."

I frowned. "Why?"

"I remembered Dad telling me to keep my mouth shut about that stuff, and I never knew why. Figured he just didn't want anybody else to have it. Couple of days ago I heard of a fellow over in Swan Lake that got shut down this year because of Indian artifacts in his fields. Then I remembered about all this stuff. And I got Dad to take me to the library so I could research it on the internet."

"But the bones aren't in the fields."

"Maybe. Maybe not. Mr. Rhodes don't know that. You tell him to cancel the paperwork or we'll go to the state on him."

"Come on, Buster. He's a big-time businessman. You think he's just going to go for that?"

Buster looked at the ground and didn't say anything. I thought about the little Indian bone up against Mr. Rhodes. I imagined him laughing uncontrollably at it.

"You got to let this go," I said.

"Well, we always got Plan A," Buster said.

"Shut up about Plan A."

"And Plan B."

I was tired of him going on about it. "Shut up about all your plans, Buster. It's just stupid."

He looked at the ground, defeated.

"I've got to focus on my future," I said. "And it's not here. I've got that through my head, and you need to get it through yours."

"You know you're gonna have to give that dog to me?" he said quietly. "Duke ain't no New York City dog."

"Now you want to make me feel guilty."

Buster shook his head. "No," he said.

"Then stop talking about that."

He kept his eyes on the ground and began snapping a twig between his fingers. After a moment he looked up at me. "You're my best friend, you know? Since my brother died, I never thought I'd have a friend like that again."

"I haven't even known you that long," I said. It was a sorry reply, but it was all I could think of.

"But you were my friend," Buster continued. "I ain't stupid. I know them girls don't like me. Nobody likes me."

"I'm still your friend. And that other stuff's not true."

Buster dropped the twig pieces and looked up at me. "You wanna know why I got kicked out of school?"

"If you want to tell me."

"After Daddy got hurt, it was a while before he could drive. We had a big beaver job to do, and we needed the money. I figured I'd take some dynamite to school in my backpack. Then I'd just get off the bus at the place with the beavers and take care of it myself. I showed it to some kid—"

"Jesus, Buster. Why do you always have to show off the stuff?"

"What else do I got to show off? You like it, don't you? I made best friends with you over it."

"Yeah, but not at school. No wonder they kicked you out."

Buster looked at the ground again. "Well, I didn't go to no jail."

"I'm surprised you didn't."

"Sent me to the juvenile detention center. Had to nearly fight my way out of that place."

"Why don't you just tell people what happened?"

"Would you?"

"I don't know," I said.

"I ain't normal. I know that. But I don't wanna remind nobody about it. Maybe I'd like to go to those country club parties someday. Kiss people like Sikes Rhodes. Maybe in a couple of years Sara *will* go on a date with me. Maybe everybody'll just forget."

"It's not that bad," I said.

"You leave and I got nothing."

"What do you want me to do, Buster?"

"I just want you to stop giving up."

I sighed. "Let's go to sleep, Buster."

He stood up. "I'm going home," he said.

"Why?"

"Because I don't wanna be here."

"Come on."

He started out into the yard.

"Buster, seriously."

He didn't stop.

"You at least want a ride?"

"No," he said.

I lay in bed that night with loneliness pressing on me like a lead blanket. I felt terrible about how things had gone with Buster. Then I thought about Sikes, snug in her bed, just a couple of miles across the big swamp, oblivious to everything, waiting for me to call her. It was all so tangled and confusing that my thoughts locked up against it.

79 HOSPITAL

I woke to sunbeams falling across the floor, feeling empty inside. I dressed and went downstairs to find Gert in the kitchen, still wearing her black mourning dress.

"Where's Buster?" she asked.

"He didn't spend the night," I said. "He went home. Do you want to go to church?"

"I do. You should too."

"I didn't say whether I did or didn't. I just asked you."

"When you already knew the answer. Now sit down and eat some of this."

I sat down at the kitchen table and watched her scoop a ham and cheese omelet out of the skillet onto a plate.

"If we're going, you'll have to ride behind me on the four-wheeler," I said.

"Fine with me," she said.

Gert brought the steaming plate to me and set it before me with a cold glass of orange juice.

"What will you do after I leave?" I asked her.

"I got cousins in Tchula. I guess I'll go down there."

"What about Mr. Case? You think he'll be OK?"

Gert sat down across from me. It was the first time she'd ever been at a table with me. "You know why he's sick, don't you?"

"They think maybe a heat stroke," I said. "They still have to do some tests."

Gert shook her head. "Call it what you want," she said. "When you take away a man's work, he's got no more reason to live."

"He told me he was going to find another place to lease. He told me that just after Grandmother died."

"He's seventy-six years old. He ain't got time to find another place and get it like he wants. He's been getting Cottonlandia right for forty years."

"That doesn't make sense, Gert. To get sick because you lose your job."

Gert touched her hand to her heart. "Your heart thinks, too," she said. "And you can be heartbroken over more than just a loved one."

On the way to church, Gert rode on the back of the ATV, clinging to me like I was being attacked by a giant, starving crow. It was embarrassing pulling up into the churchyard, but no one seemed to pay us much attention.

It was hard to tolerate an hour of Deacon Leon, whose sermon didn't offer any solutions to my problems, but I got through it on Gert's behalf and hauled her back to Headquarters. There, Hoyt was pacing in the yard in front of his parked truck.

"You ready to go see him?" he asked me.

"Yeah," I said.

I got into the little truck with him, and we left to visit the farmer.

"You wanna drag away that old car next week?" he asked me.

"I don't care," I said. "I guess we can let Mr. Rhodes bulldoze it like everything else."

Hoyt glanced at me. I looked out the window, studying the far trees.

"Gert says he's sick because he's heartbroken," I said.

"Over what?"

"Losing the farm."

Hoyt shook his head. "Don't listen to that voodoo. He's sick because he's too old to get out in the heat like he does."

"I've heard of it before," I said. "That old people don't live long after they retire."

"You think he'd want to quit on us before we got this cotton in?"

"No."

"Dang right he wouldn't. I bet he can't hardly stand lying in that hospital bed thinking about us out there by ourselves."

What Hoyt said was encouraging. "You're right," I said. "It's not time for him to quit. He'd never quit on anybody."

"I think people just want to feel like they're needed. He's got a lot of people counting on him right now. Two of them sitting in this truck. A wife back home."

"We need to let him know we need him," I said.

"Don't worry about it, man. They might let us load him up and bring him home today."

We found Mrs. Case sitting in the room beside the farmer's hospital bed. She was calm and tired-looking.

"Hello, boys," she said.

The farmer lay propped up with an IV tube feeding clear liquid into his arm. The television was off, the windows shades were up, and an empty food tray was on his bedside table. It appeared he'd lost weight, and he had the same colorless look to his skin I'd seen with Dad. He looked like a weak, old man instead of the lumbering bear I'd always known him to be.

The farmer smiled at us. For the first time his expression carried no trace of sternness. "Good to see you boys," he said.

Mrs. Case excused herself to go for coffee downstairs and left us alone with her husband.

"Looks like you ate something," Hoyt said, pointing at the tray.

"Hard to make a meal on what they send through that tube," he said. He looked at me. "How was New York City, Win?"

"It was awful."

"Yeah, well, sorry I cut it short for you."

"I'm glad you did," I said.

"You ain't never seen anything like all those tall buildings," Hoyt added. "Man, you got to work to find the sun around that place."

The farmer chuckled. "It's good to see the two of you survived."

"You ready to quit your nap and get out of here?" Hoyt asked.

"I feel pretty good, Hoyt. But this doc's tough on me."

"When they gonna turn you lose?"

"They said maybe tomorrow. Still got some test results to get back. I'll tell you what, though, just lying here doing nothing's gonna kill me before anything else."

"Look, I'm just joking with you," Hoyt said. "We got everything handled. Got a full water rotation in last week. Tillmans came over and helped us catch up. Everything's looking good. You just do what the doc says."

"And I took Gert to church this morning on the four-wheeler," I said.

The farmer chuckled again. "I'd liked to have seen that."

For a moment it seemed like we'd all run out of things to say. There were a lot of things I wanted to tell him but didn't know how. Especially with Hoyt standing there.

"Well," Hoyt finally said. "You want us to get you anything?"

"You boys go enjoy your Sunday. You got a big week in front of you. You'll need the rest."

"You're getting enough rest for all of us," Hoyt joked.

"Believe me," the farmer said. "They can't let me out of here fast enough."

Hoyt tapped him on the leg. "We'll come get you tomorrow," he said.

The farmer nodded and smiled weakly. The look he gave us said everything I didn't want to hear. He wasn't sure about anything.

80 BUSTER'S GONE

After Hoyt dropped me off at Headquarters, I changed clothes and drove the ATV to Booga Den, where I found Buster's dad sitting on their front porch.

"Hey, Mr. Tillman."

"How you doing, Win?"

"OK. Have you seen Buster?"

"I thought he was with you."

"No," I said. "He told me he was going home last night. He was upset about me leaving."

A concerned look came across his face. He turned his wheelchair toward the front door. "Give me a minute and we'll go look for him. Meet me around back."

I found his truck next to the barn and waited until he wheeled out the back door and down the plywood ramp next to the steps. In a moment he was next to me.

"You need me to do anything?"

"Open the door if you don't mind," he said.

I opened the driver's-side door and watched him grab a loop handle on the frame and pull himself up into the seat.

"Hop in," he said.

Like Buster had told me, all the controls were on the steering column. He cranked the engine, pulled a lever to shift into gear, and worked a set of smaller levers to accelerate and brake. We pulled out of the yard as smooth as any truck I'd ever been in.

"I guess he told you about me moving back to New York," I said.

"Yeah, he told me. And he has been a little upset about it."

"I don't know what else to tell him. I wish I didn't have to go too."

"His mother and me haven't seen him so happy in a long time. It's been good for all of us."

"I don't want him to go off and do anything crazy. He's been talking about some crazy things."

Mr. Tillman pulled onto the blacktop.

"He got like this after his brother died," he said. "He ran off for a couple of days."

"He's been talking about killing Mr. Rhodes's catfish."

Mr. Tillman frowned. "Lord, I hope he doesn't do anything stupid."

"We better get over there."

"That's where I'm headed."

We drove around to the back side of Beulah, where the bulldozers had been tearing the road into Cottonlandia. Mr. Tillman pulled off, and both of us studied the catfish ponds.

"I don't see anything unusual," he said.

"You know where he likes to park?"

"That little cutout on the brake?"

I nodded.

Mr. Tillman crossed the ditch and started up the edge of the brake. Before long we were at Buster's cut. I got out and walked a short distance into the woods until I saw his ATV parked at the water's edge with the toolbox open. I stopped and looked around. There was nothing but the still, black water and the thrumming of insects and mosquitoes floating before my face.

I returned to Mr. Tillman. "His four-wheeler's back there."

"That ain't good," he said.

"Let's go out to the ponds."

We spent an hour driving the checkerboard of access roads among the ponds. There was no sign of Buster.

"You think he's hiding from us?"

"I don't know. I guess all we can do is pray he don't get into any trouble. We ain't gonna find him until he wants us to."

"You think he spent the night out there?"

"He's so hardheaded I reckon he did. I'll take you back to the house. Maybe you can head over there again this evening."

"You think we should call Mr. Rhodes?"

Mr. Tillman glanced at me. "If Buster gets arrested, we're in a heap of trouble. I'd hate to stir things up before we have to."

After I left the Tillmans I decided not to wait until later to continue looking for Buster, and took the ATV back to Buster's cut. This time I found the toolbox closed.

"Buster!" I called out.

A group of wood ducks flushed and whistled away through the trees. Then there was nothing but silence. I walked back out to the field and scanned the ponds. All I saw was flat land and dark squares of water. There was nothing more to do but go home and wait for him to show up and hope he didn't get himself into trouble.

That night I lay in bed thinking about Buster, out there in the swamp with the mosquitoes swarming him. It was hard to accept that he was doing it for me. And even harder to accept that whatever he was doing was worthless.

"Stupid Buster," I said to the darkness. But I didn't believe the words. I knew it was just noise to ease my guilt. And the worst part of it all was that I knew, wherever I was going, I'd never have a friend like him again.

81 THE DAD I NEVER HAD

I woke early and drove back to Buster's house. I found Mr. Tillman on the porch again. As soon as he saw me, he shook his head.

"He came back to his four-wheeler at least once yesterday," I said. "The toolbox was open the first time and closed the second time. He's sleeping somewhere."

"You checked all around your place?"

"The only place he could be is the garden shed, and I got this four-wheeler out of it this morning."

Mr. Tillman took a deep breath. "All right. I'm gonna ride the roads again today. At least we know he ain't hurt."

"I'll come back over here and let you know if I see him."

Back at Cottonlandia I made the rounds with Hoyt and Luther, checking the pumps, patching the pipes, and running the irrigation. Close to noon Hoyt stopped the farm truck and left it running while he jumped out to turn the valve on one of the wellheads. Luther and I waited as the dust off the turn row caught up to us, drifted through the windows, and stuck to our sweat. I studied a set of pliers laying on the dashboard and felt myself starting to slip into what Luther called the "stares," when the slow heat has cooked away almost all your energy and you find yourself just sitting and staring and not thinking about much at all.

"What's he doing?" I heard Luther say.

I rolled my eyes up a bit to see Hoyt standing by the pump, his cell phone to his ear, looking back at the highway. In a moment he turned, shoved the phone in his pocket, and started back toward us.

When he was close enough for us to hear, he called out.

"Dang heart attack. Mr. Case had a heart attack."

I snapped out of my trance.

"Today?" Luther asked.

Hoyt got into the truck, put it in gear, and started turning it around.

"No, Friday. They got the tests back, and he's got something wrong with his heart. They're gonna operate on him tomorrow."

Luther shook his head.

"Is he OK?" I asked.

"They gotta do some kind of bypass on him. Luther, we need some help. That was Mrs. Case on the phone, and she's over there now. She wants us to come sit with him while she goes home and gets some things."

"I can get some of my cousins to come over," Luther said.

"All right," Hoyt said. "Let's get back to the shop so I can get my truck."

"I'm going," I said.

"All right. Come on, then."

Hoyt left me at Headquarters to clean up while he went to his house and did the same. He was back for me in forty-five minutes. I got in his truck with him, and we left for Greenwood. He wasn't saying much, which told me he was worried. Which got *me* worried.

"What's a bypass?" I asked.

"The pipes going in and out of your heart get clogged. You got to unclog them."

"Is it dangerous?"

"Man, any time you go messing with somebody's heart like that it's dangerous. Especially for an old man."

Once we were in the lobby of the hospital, Hoyt stopped. He looked around. "I need to find out who the doctor is and figure all this out."

"Go to the information desk," I said.

Hoyt looked where I was pointing. "Yeah, OK. Why don't you go up and hang out with him."

"All right," I said.

Hoyt started for the information desk. "Hate these dang places," I heard him say.

The farmer was awake when I entered the room, lying in silence like he'd been the day before. Only this time he had an oxygen tube connected to his nose.

"Hey," I said.

"Afternoon, Win," he croaked.

I pulled a chair up to the edge of the bed and sat down.

"Looks like I might be here a little longer than we thought," he said.

"Hoyt's downstairs talking to the doctor. Luther said he'd get some help at Cottonlandia."

The farmer smiled weakly. "Looks like I might not get this last crop in after all."

"Don't talk like that," I said.

"Hoyt knows what to do."

"You're not going to die," I said.

"Who said anything about dying?"

I felt my throat growing tight. "You still have a lot of work to do. They can't do this without you . . . I can't do this without you."

"Hey," he said. "Nobody's dying. I'll get this little issue handled, and you all can take me home."

"Everything's going wrong," I said. "This is all wrong."

"Win, it's life. If you think of it like a math problem, you're gonna be miserable."

But I wasn't hearing him. "No matter what happens," I said, "no matter where I go, I need you. You're the only person I've got left who makes any sense. Everything you say is right."

He lifted his hand from the bed and put it on my shoulder. I felt tears running down my face. I couldn't look at him.

"I wish you were my dad," I said.

"Win," he said.

I wiped my face with the back of my hand. I didn't answer.

"Look at me," he said.

I did.

"That means a lot to me," he said.

I looked away and wiped my face again. It was too much for me. I suddenly didn't want to be there. I got up and started for the door.

"Win," he said.

I shook my head. "I could have had it all," I said. "I had it all."

"Hang in there," he said.

Hoyt suddenly came through the door and stopped at the sight of me with tears streaming down my face. He looked quickly from me to the farmer. Then back at me again. "He dead?"

I shook my head again and left the room. I walked down the long hall to the elevator, my eyes blurred and the noises around me like something far away. I went down to the lobby and out the big double doors into the sunlight.

I stood there for a moment, staring at the pavement. I don't remember deciding what I was going to do, but I started walking toward the old business district of downtown.

Buster was right. I had given up. I hadn't really tried hard enough. Not as hard as what I owed all of them. I couldn't live with that.

Later on, I discovered I had walked sixteen blocks, but that day the grainy cement of the sidewalks and the street crossings all passed beneath my eyes like a treadmill. All the way to Howard Street and the stairs leading up the side of the old bank building to the lawyer's office.

When I entered Tim Haney's anteroom, I saw his secretary sitting at the desk. She was young and plump with a kind face. His door was shut, but I heard him on his phone.

"May I help you?" she asked.

"I need to see Mr. Haney," I said.

"And you are?"

"Win Canterbury."

Her eyes softened. "Oh, yes, Win. Let me tell him you're here."

She stood and knocked on the door and peered behind it. "Win Canterbury," I heard her whisper.

She shut the door again and came back to her desk. "You can have a seat, Win. He'll be with you in just a moment."

I sat in a chair against the wall until I heard him end his phone conversation. A moment later he stepped out to greet me.

"Win," he said, looking about the room like there might be someone else with me. "This is a surprise. What can I do for you?"

I stood. "I need to talk to you," I said.

"Sure," he said. "Come in my office. I'm sorry to hear about Mr. Case. How is he?"

"He's having an operation," I said.

The lawyer went around his desk and motioned for me to have a seat.

"Well, our prayers are with him," the lawyer said.

In a moment I was seated across from him, in the same chair where I'd signed the paperwork that had started this all. He leaned forward in his desk chair, waiting to hear what I had to say.

"You can't talk about anything I tell you, right?"

"That's right," he said curiously. "It's called attorney-client privilege."

"You can't tell anybody? Not even the government?"

He shook his head. "No. I can't discuss anything you tell me with anyone."

"Good," I said. "I want to blackmail Mr. Rhodes."

82 BLACKMAIL

I waited by Hoyt's truck until I saw him come through the sliding doors of the hospital lobby, walking fast and huffing. When he saw me, he held up his palms and rolled his eyes.

"Dang, man," he said. "Where you been?"

"Tim Haney's office."

"What? I been all over this place looking for you."

"Sorry," I said. "I just didn't like seeing Mr. Case like that."

Hoyt frowned and got into the truck. He leaned over and unlocked my door, and I climbed in the passenger seat.

"It's gonna be all right," he said. "Hospitals just give you the creeps."

"I need to go back by Tim Haney's and pick up some contracts," I said.

"Sure," he said. "No problem."

I picked up the contracts from the lawyer, two crisp documents in a manila folder. There was a cover sheet with instructions on what to do. On the way back to Walnut Bend, Hoyt kept glancing at the papers as I looked them over, but he didn't ask me about them. When we turned into the driveway, I told him to drop me off at Headquarters.

"Sure you're all right?" he asked.

"Yeah. I've just got some business I need to take care of."

I drove the ATV out into the fields and crossed over toward the old beaver den. The sun was sitting low in the sky, watery and orange through the treetops.

"Where are you, Buster?" I said.

But the fields were empty, and the edges of the swamp were dark. Just before I pulled around the back side of the brake, I glimpsed something red hanging back in the trees. After surveying the scene for a moment, I got off the ATV and walked a short way into the woods, where I found the clearing Mr. Rhodes had bulldozed. Hanging on a branch was Buster's red Massey Ferguson T-shirt.

"Buster!" I called.

Nothing. Mosquitoes began settling on my skin, and I backstepped and brushed them away. I sensed he was close. Maybe even watching me.

"I'm not giving up!" I shouted.

Wherever he was, he wasn't answering.

I parked in the driveway beside Mr. Rhodes's Cadillac. The smell of oleanders drifted over me as the cicadas thrummed and pulsed in the cooling air. I released the handle grips and saw my hands trembling without something to steady them. I grabbed the folder from behind my back, where it was tucked into my jeans, and started for the front door.

"How you, Win?" Roxy greeted me.

"Hey, Roxy. I'd like to speak with Mr. Rhodes."

"Come in, Win," I heard him boom from his study.

I took a deep breath and started past Roxy as she stepped aside. When I entered the library, I found Mr. Rhodes in his chair with a whiskey tumbler in one hand and the remote control to the television in the other. A golf tournament was airing, and he watched it intently.

I stopped a few feet from his chair.

"What do you think about this Tiger Woods fellah?" he said, keeping his eyes on the television.

"I don't know anything about him."

"I think he might just be the man to beat these days."

"I want you to cancel the lease on my farm," I said.

He slowly looked up at me and kept his eyes on me for a moment. Then I saw his hand rise and point the remote control, and the volume went mute.

"I want to keep Cottonlandia like it is," I said.

He glanced at the folder in my hand. "Well, Win, we're pretty far into this deal for people to start having second thoughts."

"I didn't know better."

"Sit down."

"I don't want to sit down."

He set the remote control on the table and took a sip of his drink. "I'll tell you a valuable lesson my father taught me. When I was eighteen years old, I inherited a building in Chicago from my grandfather. I'd never seen it. Never even been to Chicago. That building didn't mean anything to me except money I couldn't get to. I wanted to sell it as quickly as possible. So I called a real estate guy in the area and he told me he could sell it for five hundred thousand dollars. That was a lot of money for a teenager. You know what my father told me?"

I shook my head.

"He told me to go look at it first. He said to always make sure you put your own feet on the ground of any real estate you own before you make a decision to get rid of it. I thought it was going to be a waste of time, but I needed him to help me sell it. So I went to Chicago to appease him. You know what I found?"

"No, sir."

"The city was starting a renovation project in that part of town. They were giving low-interest improvement loans to local business owners and clearing out the slums. Anybody could see real estate values were about to go up. I waited a year and sold my building for three million dollars."

I understood his lesson. "I didn't get a chance," I said. "I didn't know better."

"Well, let this be a lesson to you. The painful ones are the hardest to forget."

"You can go other places. There's plenty of places to have a catfish farm."

He took another sip of his drink. "Cottonlandia is the most convenient for me. The most cost-effective. It's just business, Win, nothing personal."

I took another deep breath. I reached in my pocket and pulled out the Indian bone. I approached him and set it on the lamp table. He studied it curiously.

"What is that?"

"An Indian bone," I said.

He removed a pair of reading glasses from his top pocket, slipped them on, and studied it more closely.

"There's Indian bones and artifacts on Cottonlandia," I said. "If the state archaeologist finds out about it, he'll shut it down. He'll never let you dig."

Mr. Rhodes pulled off the glasses, replaced them in his pocket, and looked at me. "Are you blackmailing me?"

"Yes, sir. I am."

"You're feeling a little big for your britches, don't you think?"

"I don't know any other way."

He glanced at the folder. "And I suppose that's going to contain a cancellation agreement I'm going to sign."

"It does."

He chuckled and took another sip of his drink. "Son, you're in over your head."

"I know."

I thought I detected a slight twitch at the edge of his mouth. He set his drink down and faced me. "I've never heard of Indian artifacts around here. I think you're making this up."

"You haven't heard about it because nobody wants to get shut down. But I know people who know where they are. One of them gave me that bone."

"And they're in the fields?"

"Yes," I lied.

"So what if I blackmail *you*? Did you think about that?"

"There's another contract in this folder. It's called a nondisclosure agreement. It says you won't talk about anything of archaeological significance on our property. Not to anybody. You have to sign that too if you want me to let you out of the lease."

"*Let* me out of it?"

"That's right."

He stared at me without speaking for what seemed like a full minute. I imagined he was about to jump out of his chair and grab me by the throat. If he was trying to intimidate me, it was working. I felt my hands trembling, and my stomach grew queasy. Eventually he held out his hand, and I gave him the folder. He put his reading glasses back on and opened it. I waited while he scanned the documents.

"You really did your homework on this, didn't you?" he muttered while he was reading.

"I had some help."

"I see. That little pissant Tim Haney's already countersigned."

I didn't respond.

After a minute he looked up at me again, leaving the folder open in his lap. "This doesn't do much for neighborly relations, does it?"

"It's just business," I said. "Nothing personal."

"Don't be a smart-ass. It's always personal."

I swallowed and didn't answer.

He stood and pulled up his belt. "Fine. Let's go see some bones. Like I told you, it's always a good idea to put your eyes on your real estate."

83 BUSTER IN THE NIGHT

I followed Mr. Rhodes outside to his Cadillac. I thought about running and getting on the ATV and just leaving. Let him stand in the driveway and chuckle as I fled.

"Win?" I heard her say.

I turned and saw Sikes standing in the door.

"Where y'all going?"

"Business, sugar," Mr. Rhodes said over his shoulder.

She looked at me. I nodded to her weakly and got into the big car. It was dark now, and he turned on the headlights and eased out of the driveway. When we reached the highway, he turned right and sighed like he was starting to feel his time was being wasted.

"I don't know if I can find them at night," I said.

"Oh, that's not a problem," he said. "I've got a flashlight in the trunk."

I sank lower in my seat. He glanced at me.

"I'd just as soon get this over with," he toyed. "Nobody needs any loose ends."

We passed Denton's store and turned into the driveway to Cottonlandia. The cotton stood like a thick wall of green on both sides of the headlights. He stopped the car and turned to me.

"Where to?" he asked cheerfully.

"We might have to walk. I don't know if you can drive this car into the fields."

"Looks pretty dry out there to me. I'll take my chances."

"Keep going. Take the last turn row on your right."

He nodded, and the gravel began to crunch under the tires again. *I'll at least show him the mound,* I thought. *At least then I can claim I'm not a liar. At least I can tell Buster and Sikes and the rest of them I tried.*

We turned off the main drive onto the turn row and headed north across the field toward the tall wall of swamp. Then we came up against the trees, and I pointed him left. He swung the big car into what felt like a narrow tunnel between the cotton and the briars and brush reaching out. They scraped against the car, but he didn't seem to mind.

We were almost to the beaver den when we both saw the figure standing in the headlights like a ghost. Mr. Rhodes stopped the car and squinted.

"What the hell?" he muttered.

The figure was shirtless and covered from head to toe in mud.

"Who the hell is that?" Mr. Rhodes said.

"It's Buster Tillman," I said.

He looked crazy the way he just stood there, white eyes staring into the headlights. I got out, closed my door, and approached him. "Buster?"

"What."

"What are you doing?"

"Standing here," he said.

Mr. Rhodes came up beside me holding a flashlight. He'd left his trunk open and the headlights on, and the Cadillac dinged steadily behind us. "What's wrong with him?"

"You need to go home, Buster," I said. "Your parents are worried about you."

Then we all heard the puttering of an ATV coming around the west end of the brake. In a moment, headlights swung onto the turn row and approached us. Sikes stopped beside Buster and shut off her four-wheeler.

"What's going on, Daddy?"

"What is this? A party?"

She looked at Buster, then back at us. "Why is everybody out here?" she said.

"Go back to the house, Sikes," Mr. Rhodes said. "Aren't you still grounded?"

"I've been grounded long enough."

Mr. Rhodes shook his head and turned to me. "I don't imagine you want me to tell them your big secret, do you?"

"Buster already knows," I said.

"What big secret?" Sikes said.

"Bones," I said. "There's Indian bones on Cottonlandia."

Mr. Rhodes spread his arms with an exaggerated motion. "All in the fields," he said facetiously. "Like a big cemetery. Gonna shut us down."

"Shut who down?" Sikes said.

I frowned and looked at Buster. He hadn't moved. He was still standing in the headlights watching Mr. Rhodes now. The dinging of the Cadillac ticked away the seconds.

"Win says he's going to show me some of these bones," Mr. Rhodes continued.

Buster still hadn't moved out of the headlights. "They're everywhere," he said.

Mr. Rhodes looked all around. "Well, show me some. Let's see them."

"What you want?" Buster said. "Leg bone? Arm bone? Skull?"

"A skull? Why not? Sure, let's see a skull. That should be interesting."

Buster nodded. "Come on," he said.

Suddenly I knew where Buster had been for the last two days. It was all I could do to contain the thrill racing up my spine.

Buster walked into the cotton. Mr. Rhodes flipped on his flashlight and checked his polished leather shoes and frowned and stepped carefully behind him. Sikes came up beside me.

"Tell me what's happening, Win."

I laughed quietly. "I can't believe it," I said. "He's crazy."

"Who?"

I saw Mr. Rhodes stop about fifteen feet into the field. And then I saw Buster stand with a dull, yellow object that appeared to be a stone from where we stood. But I knew exactly what it was.

"Where did you get that?" Mr. Rhodes said.

"Right here. I just dug it up."

Mr. Rhodes took it from him and examined it. "Is that part of a skull?"

"Yeah. That's what you wanted, right?"

"Did you put this out here?"

"They're all over the place," Buster said. "I've known about them for years."

"*Who* are you?"

"Son of the beaver man."

Mr. Rhodes turned and looked at me. "What's going on here?" he said. "Are you planting bones in the fields?"

"I don't know anything about that," I said.

"Don't mess with me, boy," he said. The tone of his voice was mean and threatening.

Sikes stomped her foot. "Daddy! What is going on?"

Mr. Rhodes dropped the skull fragment and stared at me while he answered his daughter. "I'm buying Cottonlandia," he said. "Turning it into catfish farms."

"You ain't now," Buster said.

"Shut up, kid," Mr. Rhodes snapped.

"Bones everywhere," Buster said.

"You can't turn Cottonlandia into a catfish farm!" Sikes said.

"We'll shut you down," Buster continued.

Mr. Rhodes turned to Buster. "I don't know who you are or what you have to do with any of this," he said, "but I can have you sent to jail for tampering with archeological artifacts."

"Maybe," Buster said. "That don't help *you* none."

"Daddy, what did you do?"

"Look, sugar. I leased this place long before Win even got here. Hell, his dad signed the papers. Now Win's got second thoughts about that deal. Thinks he can blackmail me out of it."

"Why won't you stop then?" Sikes said.

He looked at me. "Now you got the women involved. I could have told you that'd be a lot more effective than blackmail."

"If you turn Cottonlandia into catfish farms, I'll never speak to you again. That's just mean. Why can't you buy something else?"

Mr. Rhodes stared at her.

"Stupid catfish," she said.

"I've already sunk a nice chunk of money into this operation," he said. "It's got nothing to do with being mean."

"He'll pay you for it," Buster said.

Mr. Rhodes glanced at Buster like he wanted him to be quiet, but didn't say anything.

I didn't know where I'd get the money, but I decided to go with Buster's momentum. "That's right," I said. "I'll pay you for it. For the road and whatever else."

He continued to stare at Sikes. Then he began to chuckle. "Christ," he said. "You kids. . . "

"Right now, Daddy," Sikes said. "You stop this."

He began to laugh and step back toward us through the high cotton.

"Daddy!" Sikes demanded.

He held up his hands. "Look, kids, it's late. I'm not talking about it tonight."

"How about tomorrow," I said.

He went to his car and opened the door. He looked back at me. "I'll think about it."

I looked at Buster, still standing in the field. It was dark, but I saw the whites of his teeth.

84 A GLIMMER OF HOPE

Mr. Rhodes pulled away in his Cadillac, leaving the three of us standing in the turn row.

I turned to Buster. "I told you I'd fix this," he said.

I took a breath, my blood racing with the thrill. "It's not fixed yet," I said.

"He won't do it," Sikes said. "I'll make sure he doesn't."

"Where have you been sleeping, Buster? A hole in the ground?"

"That old church out there. Window's open."

"Did you dig up the whole Indian mound or something?"

"A lot of it."

"Jesus. You better get your four-wheeler and get home. I told you your parents are worried."

"And take a bath," Sikes said.

He grinned smugly. "I'll see you tomorrow then."

"Yeah," I said. "Tomorrow . . . Thanks, Buster."

He turned and started away from us. "No problem," he said over his shoulder.

Sikes and I watched him step into the swamp and disappear down some trail he'd worn to the Indian mound.

"Why didn't you just tell me?" Sikes said.

"I don't know. I guess I wasn't ready to change the way you thought about me."

She grabbed my hand and squeezed it. "I'm your girlfriend," she said. "You can tell me anything."

But I wasn't hearing her. "You really think he'll cancel the leases?"

"Yes," she said. "I'll make him. And so will Mom."

"All this isn't over yet, Sikes. Mr. Case is still sick, and we don't *really* know what your father's going to do."

She let go of my hand and backed toward her ATV. "I'm going to talk him right now," she said. "Stop worrying so much. I'm sure Cottonlandia and Mr. Case will be fine."

I took a deep breath. "I hope you're right."

"Come on, it's late. You want a ride back to Beulah?"

"I feel like walking."

"Fine. Weirdo. I'll see you tomorrow."

"OK."

She climbed on the ATV and started it.

"Hey," I said. "Did you say you were my girlfriend?"

She looked back at me. "Yes. What'd you think?"

"Well, I—I don't know. But it's good. I'm glad."

She smiled. "You don't know anything about girls."

I watched her pull away, and suddenly I was there alone with Cottonlandia falling away in all directions and the big sky overhead.

"No," I said to myself. "I sure don't."

I started the journey back to Headquarters, my feet falling softly on the dirt of the turn row. An owl called from deep in the swamp, and birds stirred in the brush. Everything seemed suspended in time. Like I was leaning over the edge of a cliff with someone holding on to my shirttail.

"Just keep pulling," I said.

When I got back to the house I went inside and called Hoyt, telling him the whole story.

"Well, man," Hoyt said.

"You have to let Mr. Case know tomorrow," I said. "Before the surgery."

"But he hasn't canceled the leases yet?"

"No, but just tell him anyway. Tell him he's working on it."

"OK," he said. "You want to come with me?"

"No," I said. "I'll be with Luther. But you tell Mr. Case there's no catfish leases. There's no change. I'm staying. Everybody's waiting for him to get better."

Just before dawn I dressed in my work clothes and drove to the shop. Luther was already there, sliding open the rolling door in the muggy stillness of the dawn hours. I parked and followed him inside to fill the water cooler. Luther never said much, but I could tell by his sly grin that Hoyt had told him about my conversation with Mr. Rhodes. But that morning it didn't feel right to have our minds on anything but the farmer.

Just before noon I sat in the truck, waiting for Luther to walk over and start one of the pumps. I saw him stop halfway and straighten and pull his cell phone from his pocket. He turned and looked at me as he answered it, then looked at his feet. It was hard to see his face, angled under the bill of his cap, but I studied it the best I could. It seemed like an eternity passed while I watched him listen to the phone framed against the wide expanse of field. Then he lowered it, snapped it shut, and looked up at me. He grinned and nodded.

85 NEW BEGINNING

As Sikes predicted, Mr. Rhodes signed the lease cancellations the following week. He drove them over to the shop in his Cadillac. He got out and approached me under the hot sun, holding out the contracts.

"Here's your farm, kid," he said. There was something about the way he said it that told me he knew he'd done the right thing and felt good about it. I sensed some vague murmur of long-buried compassion in his money-hardened heart.

I took the folder from him.

"It's all straight," he said. "No funny business. Clean cancellation and a nondisclosure on whatever it was you boys planted on me out there."

"Thanks," I said.

"And don't worry about paying me for the road. I figure it's good for neighborly relations."

"Thanks," I said.

"But you keep my daughter out of trouble."

"How am I supposed to do that?"

He shook his head. "Yeah, I know. I suppose when you raise a teenage girl way out here in the country like this, she's bound to jump the fence on you a time or two."

I didn't know what to say to that, so I just nodded in agreement. Mr. Rhodes looked out over the horizon to the north.

"Get yourself a shotgun," he said, "and I'll show you how to take some ducks out of the brake this winter."

"OK," I said. "I'd like that."

He held out his hand, and I shook it.

A few days after the leases were canceled, Mrs. Case brought the farmer home. He seemed to be recovering fine, but he needed a wheelchair and it was going to be a while before he could get around without help. Hoyt went over to mow his lawn that evening and took me along to visit. The farmer and I sat on the front porch with the distant noise of the lawnmower in the backyard and the smell of cut grass and dust hanging in the fading light. It seemed to me time had suddenly slowed.

"Supposed to rain tomorrow," I said. "It'll get that west end wet for us."

"I hear you're gonna have to deal with some pretty rocky soil over there on the north line."

"Maybe," I said.

"Maybe you and Buster need to clean it up."

"OK," I said. "I don't how much he put out there."

"I don't either. And I don't want to. I figure it all needs to go back where it came from."

"Yes, sir," I said.

"Good. And that'll be the end of that craziness."

I nodded. "When do you think you'll be ready to come back to work?"

"I don't know. Seems you guys got it all covered. I figure it's about right I spent a little time with Diane. You know how long it's been since I've taken a vacation with her?"

"I wouldn't call this much of a vacation."

He chuckled again. "Yeah, well, as soon as I get on my feet again, I think I'll take her to the Florida Keys. She's always wanted to go down there."

"Sure," I said. "Mr. Tillman's going to supervise until you're ready to come back."

"He's a good man. He knows what to do."

"It's just temporary," I said.

"Sounds like a plan," he said. "So you ready for school to start back up?"

He didn't want to talk about farming. In his head he was already on vacation.

"Yes, sir."

"Maybe you'll get a little more involved this year."

"I was thinking so. Maybe basketball. If I have time after school."

"Look," he said. "I'm all about tending to your responsibilities, but you've got plenty of money now and plenty of help around here. I expect you to be a kid while you can. You'll have plenty of time to get old and stare at the weather all day."

"Yes, sir."

"Maybe your friend Buster can teach you how to shoot the right way."

"I guess I've still got a lot to learn."

"I think you've got a pretty good start."

I nodded.

"You call me if you want to talk about anything. I'll be right here."

"I will," I said.

A flock of blackbirds passed overhead, squawking and dipping synchronously into the tops of his pecan trees. Hoyt's mower shut off, and we heard him drop the tailgate of the truck.

"I'm glad you're better," I said.

He reached over and patted me on the shoulder. "Me too," he said.

As I felt health gradually returning to Cottonlandia, the uncertainty of my real family began to stand out like an old sore that just wouldn't heal. There was still one important man in my life I hadn't resolved issues with. And I wasn't looking forward to making the call.

86 HARVEST

"Dad?"

"Hi, son."

"How's it going?"

"You know," he said. "They can't kill me."

It was the first time I'd ever heard a hint of defeat in his voice.

"How are you doing?" he asked.

And it was the first time I remembered him asking about *me* and sounding like he meant it.

"I'm OK."

"How's your mother?"

"She's better," I said. "I talked to her a few days ago."

"You know I've got a new place now," he said.

"You're not living with Amy?"

"That situation's been over for a while. I've got my own apartment. Well, it's supposed to be anyway, but you wouldn't know it if you walked in here. Got papers and file boxes all over the place. Kind of a mess."

"You should call Mom," I said. "She wants to hear from you."

"Did she say that?"

"No, but she's all by herself, Dad."

"I don't know," he said. "I messed things up pretty good."

"Just call her," I said. "It's not like things can get any worse."

He chuckled. "No, I suppose they can't."

Both of us hung in silence for a moment. I realized it didn't matter if he knew about Cottonlandia or not. None of it mattered to him now. And it was strange talking to this man who no longer felt like my father at all, but just like some person I knew. A person I no longer owed any personal information. Simply business.

"I'm going to bring Mom down soon. Gert can take care of her."

"That's good."

I felt sorry for him and I was ashamed to feel that way.

"I better go, Dad."

"OK," he said. "We'll talk soon."

"Sure," I said.

School started again in late August. Sikes was more open to Buster hanging out with us once she learned his part in saving Cottonlandia. She also realized me and the Tillmans were going to be spending a lot more time together, working on the farm. If she wanted me, she was going to get Buster too.

Buster made his own adjustments. He stopped chewing tobacco on the schoolyard and showed more outward respect around Sikes and her friends. He admitted to me that he'd probably been using the wrong approach in trying to get Sara to go on a date with him.

"Maybe she's just not the right one for you, Buster."

"She's the right one," he said, confidently. "I just ain't got them hopping all over me like you. I got to work at it. But I got a new plan."

He stared at me.

"What's your plan?" I asked.

"Trap her."

I frowned. "That sounds like a good one, Buster. You let me know how it goes."

"You're gonna be there with me."

I didn't get into it with him. I'd learned it was pointless to try and get anything out of Buster's head. I'd find out soon enough. And I did.

Some of our classmates arranged a Memorial Day party at the country club and Sikes asked me to come. Even though I had to work the next day, I knew it would mean a lot to Sikes if I went. I didn't tell Buster about it. I couldn't imagine he would want to go, but I didn't want to hurt his feelings either.

Friday afternoon I stood on the porch at Headquarters waiting for the Rhodeses to pick me up. I felt a small pang of panic when Buster pulled up on his ATV. He was dressed in khakis, a button-down shirt, and new lace-up leather shoes. His hair was trimmed and combed. It was almost hard to recognize him.

"I'm going too," he said.

There wasn't anything I could do. Everybody was invited. And when Sikes and her mother arrived, he climbed onto the back seat of their Range Rover like they were expecting him.

Sikes looked at me.

I rolled my eyes.

Sure enough, by the end of the night I saw Buster and Sara sitting on a pool chair, holding hands.

"I'm not believing this, Sikes," I said. "He did it."

"She said she hated him."

"Well, she doesn't seem to now."

After the Rhodeses dropped us off that night Buster stood in the driveway, beaming at me.

"Told you," he said.

"That was your trap?"

"Yep. You see, I figured something out when I was planting them bones. Girls are a lot like that."

"Like bones?"

"It ain't always about the things themselves, but about the appearance of the things."

"There's nothing wrong with you, Buster."

"Maybe not," he said. "But sometimes you got to dress things up a little to get their attention."

I smiled and shook my head. "I'll have to think about that," I said.

"Something else you need to think about. We got hunting season coming up. I could come over here and help you plant some green patches for the deer."

"Whatever you think. I don't know anything about that."

"Lots of stuff around here you don't know anything about yet."

I smiled. "Whatever you say, Buster. I'll see you tomorrow."

He grinned. "Yeah," he said. "See you tomorrow."

It took me and Buster nearly a week of evenings to find most of the bones he'd planted in the fields. We put them in his crocus sacks and hauled them back to the Indian mound and reburied them. He thought it was all pointless and I wasn't so sure about it myself, but I sensed it was the right thing to do. The farmer hadn't been wrong about anything yet.

We didn't talk about it, but all of us knew Mr. Case wasn't coming back full-time. Mr. Tillman treated his new job like it was going to be his for a long time. Hoyt and Luther respected him as their new boss right away. It helped that his soft-spoken demeanor was much like Mr. Case's, but they also knew that with two thousand acres of cotton to get out, we needed his experience.

Deciding the exact time to harvest was crucial, and there were a lot of variables that went into the decision. Either Buster or I (and sometimes both of us) rode with Mr. Tillman every day after school and helped him check the maturity of the plants. He counted the bolls, both open and unopen, and kept his figures in a ledger, noting the percentage. Then he peeled back the leaves on those bolls closest to the stalk, called the money bolls, and checked for hull stains. But even with the hard facts, a lot about the decision was instinctual. Only someone who had judged cotton plants for years could fully gauge their condition.

With September came cool breezes rattling the browning pecan leaves and chilling the sweat on our cheeks. Tall white clouds moved into the clear skies and cloud shadow slipped over the fields and foretold of something bigger coming from the north. Along with the change in weather came the mourning doves, lighting in the pecan trees, echoing their lonely coo, anticipating the harvest along with the rest of us.

On a Thursday in the middle of September Mr. Tillman decided enough of the cotton bolls were open and told Hoyt and Luther to stop the irrigation. It had been a long, hot summer of monotonous work and they took off their gloves and threw them into the back of the truck like they meant it.

The next day the crop duster flew in like long awaited air support over a battlefield and we all felt a surge of renewed energy and optimism. For two days the plane dove over the trees and leveled out across the fields, dropping a fine mist of defoliation chemicals. Meanwhile Mr. Tillman negotiated with the local gins, factoring in proximity and the rebates they offered for keeping the seed they'd sell for oil to another mill in Greenwood. Hoyt and Luther made sure the harvesting equipment was in top condition for the long days ahead, checking the hydraulic hoses and the tires on the picker, getting the module builder in working order.

Once Mr. Tillman decided enough leaves had fallen off the unopened bolls and their moisture content was right, he gave Hoyt the go-ahead to start up the picker. They all worked from sunup until late into the night, depending on when the dew settled over the plants and brought the moisture content back up. Once the thirty-foot-long modules of cotton were formed and dropped into the fields, Buster and I spent the evenings covering them with tarps to keep them dry. At least once a day Mr. Tillman drove up next to one of the modules, reached out, and plucked a bit of the cotton and inspected it for stains and staple length and hull trash.

"It's good stuff," he said. "High grade."

The gin trucks ran all night long. As tired as I was, I lay awake for a while listening to them groaning into the fields like a distant army of tanks, sweeping their giant search lights over the modules and loading them up for transport to the gin. I don't remember much about what happened at school during those two weeks. My mind was always on the fields and the men and the machines. I didn't want to sleep. I wanted to be there for every minute of it.

By the middle of October, we had it all out. Over the next week the last of the modules were hauled away and Luther mowed the stalks so the fields looked just like I'd seen them in December the year before. The wispy white clouds of autumn drifted south and behind them came the grey wool of early winter. In the mornings and evenings I heard the rifle shots of hunters in the still air. I smelled the richness of the dirt again, bare and fertile and breathing. At the end of the month Luther closed the shop and padlocked the door. It was time to rest. It was time for everyone to go home.

87 HOME AGAIN

Mrs. Rhodes took Buster, Sara, Sikes, and me into Greenwood for a class Halloween party at the VFW. By this time Buster had presented Sara with so many of his tricks you'd think he was the quarterback on the football team. She was smitten with him.

Hoyt and Tammy took a short vacation to the casinos in Tunica. When he returned, he helped me hire a contractor to make repairs and improvements to the property. On both the big house and Gert's house we had the rotten wood replaced, put on new roofs, and painted them inside and out. I was strangely hesitant to make too many big changes, but Sikes had her own opinion about that.

"You're certainly going to make a good farmer," she said. "You're already acting like you don't have any money."

"What are you talking about? I just spent more on these houses than I've ever seen in my life."

"Well, you're not done. You need to update the kitchen and bathroom for your mom. And you need another bathroom downstairs. And some of this old furniture has to go."

"I want to keep the old phone," I said.

"Fine. It can be a decorative antique. But you need new ones too. And satellite internet and at least two televisions."

"I don't even watch television anymore."

Sikes put her hands on her hips. "Well, maybe your company does."

"Whatever."

She smiled, satisfied. "Good," she said. "You and Buster go blow up beavers and shoot deer and all that while Mom and I do the rest."

I started to object but stopped myself. I realized she was right. And I didn't know the first thing about getting a house ready for a lady.

"Fine," I said.

Sikes brought her mother over the next day and they met with the contractor and took over. While the women spent my money, I focused on deer hunting with Buster. In the end, it did turn out nice. And the old bones of the house were still standing as solid as ever.

I went back to New York once more at the end of November to bring Mom down. She was still on medication but seemed to be doing much better. The house was close enough to ready for her, and Gert was restless to have someone else to look after.

Mom had always been a city girl, and I knew she had no idea what to expect. But when Hoyt and I turned into the driveway with her riding between us on the truck seat, I knew what she felt.

"It's beautiful," she said.

"You should see it when the cotton's in," I said.

She breathed in the place like she'd found home.

Just before Christmas, Dad was sentenced to five years in prison for tax evasion. He'd known about the canceled leases for months, but he'd never brought it up to me. I called him the evening before he turned himself in to the federal prison.

"I'll be nearly fifty years old when I get out of this, Win. You'll be in college."

I didn't know what to say. It did seem like an awfully long time.

"The thing is," he continued, "you're probably better off down there than you would be in the city."

"I want to be a farmer, Dad."

I heard him chuckle a defeated, amazed laugh to himself.

"I'm serious," I said. "I want to run Cottonlandia one day."

"Sounds like you're doing it now."

"No, I'm still just a helper."

He grew silent. "I'm proud of you," he said. "Proud of what you've done in spite of me."

"I'm part of something down here, Dad. It feels like I should have been here a long time ago. Like none of that up there in New York was real."

"Guess it helps to finally have some money again."

"It helps to have people that care about you. It seems like the rest works itself out."

He didn't have an answer to that. He didn't understand.

"You'll see, Dad. One day you'll come back here and see what I mean."

"I hope so," he said.

"Well, I better go. Hoyt's taking me to see his new coon dogs he got with his bonus money."

"All right, son. Merry Christmas."

"Yeah," I said. "You too."

I hung up the phone and stared at the floor. After a moment I heard the sound of coon dogs yapping in the distance. I pulled away from thoughts of Dad and dashed upstairs to get my hunting jacket.

The racket of the dogs drew closer and stationed itself before the house. I threw on the jacket, grabbed my orange cap, and rushed into the hall again just as someone started rapping on the front door.

I paused before Mom's room and saw her in bed with a book. "I'm going coon hunting with Hoyt," I said to her.

She looked up at me and lowered her reading glasses. "OK, sweetheart," she said. "Be careful."

The rapping came again, and I started down the stairs. "I'm coming!" I called out.

I opened the door to Hoyt, his eyes wide and his chest rising and falling like he'd just run a marathon. The headlights of his truck fell across the driveway behind him.

"Where you been?" he asked.

"You just got here," I said. "Jesus."

He turned on his heels and started for the truck. "Come on!" he said. "Wait'll you see them."

"I'm coming! I'm right behind you."

I adjusted the cap lower over my ears against the bite of the cold and followed Hoyt into the yard toward the barking. Duke came up next to me and trembled with excitement. As my eyes adjusted to the darkness, I saw the metal dog boxes in the truck bed. Then I saw Sikes and Buster standing near the tailgate, their breath misting before their faces.

"Hey," I said. "Where did you two come from?"

"Hoyt called us," Sikes said.

"He's got two new Warriors," Buster added.

It felt good to see both of them, and the lingering heaviness of my phone call with Dad fell away.

Hoyt was already jumping into the driver's seat. "Somebody's gotta climb in back," he said as he shut his door.

Buster turned and sat on the tailgate, grinning like he'd solved a problem. "Come on, Duke," he said. "Now's your chance."

Duke hurried to him, and Buster lifted him up.

"Get in front, Buster," I said. "I'll ride back here."

"You don't want to sit next to me?" Sikes said.

"I've never ridden on the tailgate. I want to."

Sikes gave me her pouty lip, but Buster jumped down and I took his place.

"Clock's ticking," Hoyt called out. "Coons are swarming the swamp like termites."

"We've got all night, Hoyt," I said. "It's our Christmas break."

"Well, come on then!"

Sikes and Buster went around and slid onto the passenger seat. I held on to one of the dog boxes as he put the little truck into gear and scratched out in the gravel. With my other hand, I pulled Duke close and rubbed his neck. I watched the rocks pass beneath my feet for a moment, then looked up at the lights of Headquarters, filtered through the magnolia leaves and pecan limbs. We pulled through the gates and out of the trees. Hoyt turned up a country song on his radio, and I heard Sikes and Buster singing along. The dogs yapped their anticipation at the still night as the comforting smell of the fertile delta soil came across the endless fields and hung over me thick as soup.

ABOUT THE AUTHOR

Watt Key is an award-winning novelist, screenwriter, and speaker. His debut novel, ALABAMA MOON, was released to national acclaim in 2006, won the prestigious E.B. White Read-Aloud Award, and has been published in eight languages. In 2009 ALABAMA MOON was made into a feature film starring John Goodman. In 2015 ALABAMA MOON was listed by TIME Magazine as one of the top 100 young-adult books of all time. Key's subsequent novels have received starred reviews from publications such as *Kirkus*, *Publishers Weekly*, and *School Library Journal*. In addition to his novels and screenplays, Watt writes fiction and nonfiction articles for both local and nationally distributed publications and publishes horror as Albert Key.

Learn more about Watt at wattkey.com and albertkey.com

Made in the USA
Middletown, DE
13 October 2023

40726652R00205